THE CHEMICAL MARRIAGE

The Crow's Head

Adrian Stumpp

Pale Muse Publishing Co.

PALE MUSE

D1738892

ISBN-13: 9798441727686
ISBN-10: 8441727686

Cover design & author photo by: Britta Stumpp
Library of Congress Control Number: 2018675309
Printed in the United States of America

For Britta

"The putrefaction of the Philosophers is the head of the Crow a blackness transparent and shining."

GEORGIUS AURACH DE ARGENTINA, PRETIOSISSIMUM
DONUM DEI, 1475.

PRIMA MATERIA

"For the Masters of this Art, who have invented or found out the Prima Materia, and the whole Mystery they have, I say, plainly demonstrated, and as it were, indigitated the direct way of working, and made all things naked and plain to us, when they say: Nature contains Nature: Nature exceeds nature, and Nature overcoming Nature does rejoice, and is transmuted or changed into another Nature."

—ROGER BACON, RADIX MUNDI, 1292.

Then compression of dreams, heat, fear, and love into an egg of all mass and nonexistent dimensions breathes consciousness, gravity, space, photons, time, quarks, muons, neutrinos, electromagnetic current, and all of it exponentially expanding. There is a pulse and there is a fierce contraction and the birth of neutrons, protons, electrons. How something nonexistent becomes infinite. The universe filling a void which did not exist before there was a universe to fill it. The miracle of hydrogen, helium, and lithium congeals and collapses. An unflinching atheist god vomiting carbon, nitrogen, oxygen.

Æons spin. Pinwealing gases, cosmic rays, microwaves, quasars, nebulae, supernovas, the far-flung thermonuclear cataclysm burning and cooling, seeping and seething, excoriating matter and antimatter and bending light. Chaos swallowed in the vacuum. Galaxies drift like ashy snowflakes in the cosmic storm. Silence and spume of subatomic reactions bleeding clouds across the niflheim and these dividing and multiplying, separating and distilling the ever-foaming slag.

Time before time: a thought there is no method of saying. If time is measured in the revolutions of the earth on its axis and the moon around the earth and both of them together around the sun, how to measure the impossible expanse that passed and passed again before there existed earth or sun? Except to speak of atomic decay. The breaking of vessels. A woman falling out of the sky. Logos made flesh. Except to speak of a beautiful youth, the hue of lightning, buoyed in a dream upon the back of a serpent.

Auroras in the eerie depths. Throbbing heart. Violence and shock of chemical weeping when the universe was already ancient and the earth no more than swirling dust in the shadow of a solar uterus. Prenatal spasms of a ripening sphere. Its rudderless drifting and blind collisions, slow-motion embraces of proto-worlds glowing golden hot like yolks smashed together, atmospheres spilling across burnt space, alembic molten and charred ejecting jets of liquid and gas. Womb engorged with sanguine vapors, vast embryonic waves, invaginated tectonic plates, molten iron oceans scorched brilliant white beneath sulfuric clouds. Only to freeze. Tightening cold. Shiver that hardens. Silence and numb epochs of turning and turning around and around a mother whose only lullabies are hydrogen and fire. The dormant orb of ice gliding deep in sleep. Only to melt.

Slowly, with time, the sun warms the crucible. Amniotic water incubates the quickening earth. It is a brooding and an elongated meditation on thaw. Blue skies reflecting blue oceans. Deep in the sky dreams the sun and deep in the ocean the earth dreams of a sea-tortoise dreaming a wooden bench, painted white, dreaming of the dreamer. No longer a child but not yet a man. The sea is nearby and a salt breeze strokes Damian's face. Beneath him the damp grass. He sees the distant wharf and street-traffic. The sun is high and dazzling and where Damian lies in bed, dreaming, he feels it fall through slatted blinds hot and white across his eyelids. He is aware of his sleeping body and he knows he is dreaming a familiar dream from his childhood. He approaches the white bench. The woman is sitting on it. As Damian knew she would be.

In bed he twists among the sheets and rolls over. He sees the dreamscape and feels the bed-linens and contracts into a fetal ball. The woman is older than him—more than ten years, less than twenty—but in the years Damian has had this dream her age and appearance have never changed. It is only he who has aged in the last four years. As a child, he sat on her lap and she seemed large, kind, knowing. But now he is an adult and she is small and dark and freckled with dimpled cheeks, kinky hair, and a white dress. Damian sits beside her on the bench and puts his arm around her. She leans against him. Together they quietly watch the sea. He would like to speak to her but has never been able to speak in this dream. When he tries, nothing comes out and panic rises up his throat. It has not occurred to him what he would want to say to her if he could, so many years have passed since last he tried.

The sky is flattened by a single shade of pastel blue. Midday. Summertime. But the stars are visible and enormous, the stylized seven-pointed stars of cartoons and religious iconography. Their color reminds him of reflective chrome, like shapes wrapped in foil paper. They swing from side to side as if suspended on invisible strings, and then they are in motion, flying in trajectories of some complicated geometry. Stars orbit one another and whirl across the horizon, closer and closer to one another, but they never collide. Stars poise motionless before zipping around, only to rearrange in a new pattern on the sky. Damian watches with detached curiosity the stars scatter and assemble again and again. The woman holds his hand in her lap. From time to time she squeezes it.

He lies in bed a long time afterward with his eyes closed, feeling the acidic trails of tears on his face, the thudding of his heart, the melancholy and hopeless fear this dream has always inspired.

After a while he opened his eyes.

December twenty-ninth. He showered and dressed and ate and what he could remember of the dream brewed black tannins in his heart. The sea-breeze, the stars at midday, the way their patterns and movements seemed both arbitrary and choreographed, the woman and her black hair and white dress and caramel skin.

Four years since the last time he'd dreamt of this woman only days before being orphaned for the third time. He'd known it promised something then, too, for all his life this dream dragged calamity close behind. Damian was unnerved with what it could do to him now he had no one left for it to kill, and then the phone rang and he had his answer. The caller neither introduced himself nor asked to whom he spoke, but only dictated in a thick Korean accent the address where the exchange would take place. "Upstairs," the caller said. There'd be two men. "Ask for Hyeon-gi." Damian would bring fifty-thousand dollars and leave with twenty-thousand dollars. "New Year's Eve," the caller said. "Ten o'clock," and hung up.

He brushed his teeth and rubbed deodorant on his armpits. Thought about shaving but decided against it. The moment of truth lay forty-eight hours away and the interim stretched out menacingly before him. The money was locked in a safe in the warehouse, all five-hundred bills, plus extra, in case of flaws. He still had a lot of work to do. Perhaps the slowest hours of his life and the most important. For four years he'd thought of little better than money, but the dream shifted something in him. Embarking the bus, he found it difficult to care whether or not he would soon be rich.

He'd been five or six the first time he dreamed of the dark-haired woman but he was ten when he realized her recurrence. It must've been a weekend because he'd spent the day riding his bike around the neighborhood, which was how the dream began: riding bikes with the favorite stuffed animal of his childhood, a bicycle for each of them, him and his albino pig with glass eyes and a bow tie. The boardwalk and the sea and the velocity of cartoon stars. The white bench and the dusky woman in a white summer dress. He'd sat in her lap and stroked her kinky black hair and she'd grinned down at him with enormous eyes and apple cheeks and squeezed his hand to her neck. Woke the next morning to morbid fever and a sensation like burning and freezing at the same time. His eyes scalded if he closed them and his hair swabbed the blankets in sweat so thick his shadow stained the mattress. Gooseflesh puckered his body and his teeth could not stop chattering.

Week of night-sweats and hallucinatory dreams and lost time. His mother took him twice to the doctor but in the end it was only a severe flu. The fever broke, but not before Damian learned a pain to make him wish he were dead, a pain from which he could not recoil. The dark-haired woman taught him how his body could betray him. The whole world could shrink to the scope and breadth and quality of pure hurt.

His mother was dead and his stepfather was dead and he moved to San Francisco with everything he owned packed into a twelve-year-old Toyota Camry with a bloody head-gasket and fucked up struts he sold upon arrival. Worked three part-time jobs and saved and saved for the warehouse and the tools he filled it with.

In the beginning, just getting off the ground, he'd done any job he could get: petty drug dealers and small-time gamblers, coyotes and car thieves. He budgeted every cent and allowed himself two meals a day. Boxed macaroni and cheese, ramen noodles, tacos from a vendor in the next street. He lived in a studio apartment on the edge of the Mission until the city made it illegal to be poor. When the rent hiked higher than he could hustle he washed down to Bayview with the rest of the dregs who refused to leave the city. Took a studio on the fourth floor of a converted hotel with a payday loan service and a convenience store on the ground. He made no friends. His only thoughts were for poverty and the money that could cure it.

A couple years of this and he traded in the petty crooks for fancier ones. Corporate accountants putting band-aids on broken books. Shorthanded paymasters buying civil servants with discounted kickbacks. Immigrants laundering capital through infrastructure contracts to ship expensive pharmaceuticals to third-world homelands. A fence in Tennessee converting hot electronics into bounty on the heads of white slavers. He set up an offshore bank account under a stolen identity and dealt strictly through a short list of agents. He didn't want his clients to know who he was or how to find him. He worked for the agent and the agent worked for the client. His dad taught him that. To keep distance. Remain a self-employed contractor.

Damian had been working with Gangjeon Jae-kyeon, the Korean agent, the caller on the phone, for over a year but only met him twice. Every drop took place at a different location and Gangjeon sent two new men every time, usually young Koreans. This would be the second time Damian allowed him to pay in cash at the exchange. It was a pain in the ass but he was willing to put up with it. Gangjeon was a regular customer and a good business partner, well connected, who consistently brought Damian high-end jobs.

The bus spit him into rainfall. Overhead, pink foam glittered, predawn, receding fog ghost-lit by streetlamps. The rain pushed off to the east and he could see down the wide trough of Market Street to the end of the world, or so it seemed. Heaven a blue pane blemished by contrails in a frame of skyscrapers. Sirens spiraled over and under the drone of cars but the blocks south were almost deserted. His nostrils twitched at sour kimchi, spilt liquor, vomit, turmeric, coffee. In the gutter a blood-spotted piece of cotton gauze. Across the street from the gated block of warehouses, a green-haired punk lit a cigarette and leaked smoke from his mouth the same color as the fog. When he noticed Damian staring, he flipped up the collar of his leather jacket and turned his back.

Hunched over a table in the warehouse, neck cocked at an angle that felt like lightning, a jeweler's lens screwed to his eye, latex gloves and needle-point tweezers. Damian threaded security strips until early afternoon. Until his temples pounded and his neck cursed when he moved it. He fought the headache with a handful of ibuprofen chased by generic cola, took a fifteen minute sack-lunch break, walked the cramps out of his knees, and sat back down to affix the holograms. He fucked up two-dozen before he got the first one right. Closing time came after sunset. Better to stop before the quality tanked. Still more than a day's work ahead, but he was burnt out and up against the law of diminishing returns.

2.

There was a bar across the street from his apartment building, but every time he went in there he ended up getting punched, so he started frequenting a gay biker joint around the corner. Denim and leather. Stools repurposed from stray construction equipment. Flimsy steel and brass rivets. Polished chestnut tables inlaid with delicate chrome arabesques. Damian squeezed between the dress blues of a naval officer and a lanky man with facial tattoos a half shade blacker than his skin. Ordered whiskey, neat, and pointed to his coat crumpled on a table. When the tumbler came clear he sniffed it. Gin. "Get this shit away from me," he said. The bartender winked and thrust his chin in the direction of a tall blonde already coming to join him.

"There must've been some confusion. You have my drink." The blonde man placed a whiskey in front of Damian and slid the gin to the other side of the table.

"My mistake," the matchmaker said and smiled and left them alone to get better acquainted.

"How long you been waiting?"

"Couple days. Gangjeon was in here earlier." The Czech sucked gin over his front teeth. "Maybe he was looking for you?"

"I talked to him."

Somebody hit the jackpot on the pinball machine. Dancing lights and the peal of electronic trumpets.

The Czech, Pavel, had been a good contact once before. He was a local heavy, like Gangjeon, a customer with a broad network, international clients, deep pockets. The two men had been circling the last six months, sniffing each other to see how the pieces might fit. They did the one job together, no hassle, but Damian wanted forty cents on the dollar. Pavel thought the price too steep. Damian had said if Pavel ever wanted to find him, this place was as good as any.

"I showed yours to a couple people. There might be interest, if the price is right."

"You should see my new ones." Damian shrugged. "You know the price."

Pavel slumped until his head was on the table, sat up, and laughed. "Your problem is you can't decide if you want to be an artist or a merchant."

"I'm a merchant."

"Then think like a merchant. You'll move more merchandise with a thinner profit margin."

"My profit margin's thin enough," Damian said, and sipped his whiskey. "Quality product is expensive."

"Scale back the quality. It doesn't have to be perfect, just good enough." There was the sharp clack of pool balls colliding and Damian turned his head. He made eye contact with a woman at the next table. Dirty blonde hair, pink blouse, short denim skirt and long wool legwarmers. Eyes painted on and blank like they were meant to be seen but could not see. Pavel raised his finger for the matchmaker to bring another round. "I know a place next time we meet. It's better."

"Next time?"

The woman at the next table was still looking at him. Eyes that stared and didn't see. Irises of cornflower blue. She was a little older than him, maybe thirty, and she was alone. He stared her down, waiting for her to blink, flinch, anything, and for all he knew she could be blind.

"Certainly," Pavel said. "For negotiations. My client isn't willing to pay forty cents on the dollar. Think about it and we'll talk again."

Damian picked up his glass and a curious silence descended, as though a hundred simultaneous but unrelated processes converged on the same pause. The pool game ended and the pinball machine was abandoned. The drink orders were all filled and every conversation in the artificial dusk trailed off. Damian thought if he walked outside the same peace would permeate the entire city. He held his breath and waited but nothing polluted the hush.

"I saw your girlfriend last night," Pavel said, and stroked the table with a napkin where he'd spilt gin.

"Ain't got a girlfriend," Damian said, and drank.

"No? Hispanic girl, curly hair? Long legs, round bottom? I swear I saw you send her off so we could talk that day in South Beach."

Damian squinted into the green glass shade of a hanging lamp. He hadn't been laid in six months and she'd been a waif, as glow in the dark as himself. No one had been with him the day he met Pavel in South Beach to arrange delivery for the job.

"Too bad. I thought you looked happy with a girlfriend. You had a sense of humor. You smiled more. But maybe it's the artist in you doesn't like being happy."

"Careful or you'll break my heart."

Pavel got the matchmaker's attention and drew a checkmark in the air with a finger. "I'm prepared to pay thirty cents. That's the market."

"Now you're trying to hurt my feelings," Damian said. Pavel finished his drink and paid and threaded through the crowd of courting lovers to the front door and back into the breach. Damian nursed his drink and practiced getting used to a thirty-cent market. The woman at the next table was looking at him again. A quarter dropped in the jukebox and Johnny Cash spoke of a pale horse and the man who sat upon him was death and hell followed with him. When Damian rose to leave, the woman stood up.

"You look familiar," she said, and there it was, the minuscule squeeze of her pupils trapping the light needed to focus his image on her optic nerve. Not blind but drunk. "Where do I know you from?" But Damian wasn't helpful. He'd never seen her before in his life.

That night he dreamed a magpie made a nest in his sheets and laid eggs and he didn't notice until they hatched. The tiny pink bodies bobbed on his mattress, mouths bigger than their heads, and Damian opened the studio window so she could bring them food, but all she could find were cigarette butts, bottle-caps, band-aids. One by one the bobbing heads slowed down like windup gears and stopped.

The next day he finished the holograms and left the paper out to air dry while he started cleaning up. When they were ready for inspection, he set up the electric magnifying glass on the table and investigated each feature of each bill at three different powers of magnification and divided them into piles of good and defective. He bundled what he needed and stowed the briefcase, finished cleaning the warehouse, and wiped the computer. It was after midnight and he was exhausted. In the parking-lot he piled the defectives with the overstock into a steel fire pit, added the zinc plates and photographs, doused it all in lighter fluid, and struck a blaze.

He dreamed of dogs barking. He couldn't tell how many. Bent, razor-spined beasts with black gums and eyes swollen shut with mucus. He ran and ran but they cornered him on a moving bus and it hurt when they ate him. He woke gasping, back arched and legs tangled in the sweaty sheet. But he was glad to be eaten in this dream. Relieved. Because there was no bench, no stars, and no white dress.

The fog-weave wasn't as thick as Damian expected. Still confusing, but thin and penetrable, like looking through scratched glass. The address was in Forest Hill, the next-to-last house on the block, three stories, double garage, and a veranda on the second floor. Cars covered the curb to the end of the street.

A suburb in the middle of a metropolis. It reminded Damian of his childhood neighborhood. There'd been a sandbox in the backyard and a labrador retriever the same shade of blonde as his mother. Violin lessons and daytrips to the library and little league summers. Damian was an only child though he had a twin sister who would've been twenty minutes older than him if she hadn't been born dead. Twice more his parents conceived and miscarried. The babies didn't take. Sometimes they do and sometimes they don't was the explanation his mother had given. It all happened on a street a lot like this one.

A guy in a Stanford sweater answered the door, burly and dopey-eyed, beer bottle dangling against his thigh and pop music crashing at his shoulders. New Year's Eve party. In the living-room a clutch of shiny girls fumbled with the thick palms of the long-limbed lugs they wanted to dance with. Girls stepped into the middle of the room and swerved on half-exposed hips as though the boys only needed to see how it was done before they could dance. In the kitchen a bottle was put in Damian's hand and he was escorted to the third floor and pointed to an open door at the end of the hall. A study with a bookshelf and a desk and a make-shift wet-bar. In the middle of the room was a coffee-table and around it three chairs and two of them filled with Koreans. Small and flat and dark like gingerbread dolls, one older and pockmarked, the other little more than a teenager with angry eyes and a permanent grimace.

"You're early," the younger one said in an accent that couldn't make consonants behave in his mouth and made up for it by biting hard on the vowels.

Damian sat down and placed the briefcase on the table next to the unopened beer he'd brought from downstairs. The younger Korean fingered the lock and tried to say, "Combination."

"I think our arrangement was supposed to involve an exchange."

The younger one slid his eyes like sharp threats all over Damian. He tried to stay calm but his voice was volatile. "Please. Combination."

Sweat seeped from Damian's neck and his chest tightened. These exchanges always made him nervous, but now he was getting scared. Etiquette required everything to play according to a prearranged script in order to keep all parties as relaxed as possible. His agreement with Gangjeon was being breached. The three men exchanged tense glances. Damian considered the situation. He couldn't decide how best to proceed. Downstairs the music stopped and there was a few seconds of chatter among the New Year's Eve crowd. The next song started. The older man spoke to his partner and they traded a few lines of Korean. The younger one stared fangs at Damian's throat and pulled a gym bag from under his chair and flung it on the ground. Damian relaxed a little. Not until he exhaled did he notice he'd been holding his breath.

He stacked bundles of cash on the coffee table and counted it back into the gym bag and the Koreans did the same with the briefcase. They checked the middle of the bundles, making sure he hadn't padded them with blank paper. They deliberated over several bills and spoke to each other in low voices. Damian thought they weren't counting the money—they were reading serial numbers, looking for duplicates, confirming the quality of his work.

"When you guys are done, I'd like to keep the briefcase," he said. "I normally wouldn't care, but that's a two-hundred dollar briefcase and this is a fifteen dollar gym bag."

The Koreans stopped talking and looked at him as if they didn't understand why he was still there. The younger one grinned and said something a little too loud to be meant for his friend, and Damian heard a door open down the hall and approaching footsteps. "Oh, fuck," he whispered, but he didn't stand up. Not even when they entered the room. He just sat with his elbows on his knees and the gym bag between his shoes. Even when he felt small, soft hands on his shoulders, he just sat there thinking he should've listened better to his dad's advice.

They bound his wrists and ankles and fixed him with a ball-gag and taped a white pillowcase over his head. There were four of them now, speaking in leisurely voices as they tied him to a chair. They took their time collecting the briefcase and the gym bag and closed the door behind them when they left. The hood let in light but he couldn't see through it. He could breathe through his nose, though it was dank and claustrophobic and tight on his throat.

His dad had told him about the extensive research required before accepting a new client, finding out who they were and who they worked for and for how long, what they intended for the counterfeit and where the real money came from to buy it. Damian hadn't done any of that. He'd been greedy, he was in a hurry, and it made him sloppy. You might get away with it once or twice, his dad had said, but sooner or later you'll pay for it and you probably won't get a chance to learn from your mistake.

He thought they were deciding how long to hold him before they let him go. He told himself they would probably drive him off to the middle of nowhere and untie him. He wondered how much longer before the cops showed up. He thought how he was only thinking these things to keep from crying. It wouldn't do any good to think about what was really going to happen.

The door opened and something pointy was held to his throat. He was made to lie on the floor and a tourniquet was rigged to bind his wrists to his ankles. If he struggled with his legs it would jerk his shoulders out of socket. If he yanked too hard with his arms he could dislocate a hip. They carried him downstairs and through a doorway and down again into the dark and the cold. The party sounds had stopped. A car trunk popped and he was dumped into a tight space and the door slammed overhead.

Before long they were moving. Damian cursed his arrogance and stupidity, but he couldn't think much more, because breathing took all his concentration. His jaw burned from being extended so long and his body bore down on the ball-gag, narrowing his airway, nostrils pressed flat against the trunk floor. His arm muscles threw tantrums and his legs sobbed. Pain made him breathe in frantic bursts. Deep inhale, he thought, hold it in, let all the oxygen seep into your bloodstream, exhale slowly, calm down, focus on this one breath. Molten lead in his lungs dissolved slow breath by breath, but he was nauseous—a combination of disorientation, car motion, dried out mouth, the obstruction of the gag. A charlie-horse snapped his thigh and concentration scattered. He tried to breathe slowly and deliberately but the pain in his thigh and mouth and chest were outrageous and he kept realizing he was holding his breath.

When his mind resurfaced the car was still and a beat later the trunk popped and he was dragged out by the tourniquet and dropped hard on the ground. He bit down on the gag and braced his whole body against vomiting but what he tasted was bile. Then came the first blow to his ribcage. A fact so certain and absolute he didn't feel the next few blows to his head and back. His stomach gusted like a fierce wind from his nostrils and painted the inside of the pillowcase. He didn't feel emptied out but rather filled with a substance heavy and hot and hardening.

There was a startled gasp and the ground near his head bounced as a body smashed into it and scurried away. Silent seconds before labored breathing and commotion in every direction. The awkward staccato thuds of a fistfight, and he dared hope the Koreans had been attacked. Another tense silence and a nearby clatter hit the ground and the rhythm of people running away. Korean voices arguing or negotiating or pleading, he couldn't tell, and the vibration and keen of the car raging off. Damian squelched panic and stiffened his body for the blows to resume.

Instead, he was pushed onto his side and nimble fingers unsheathed his head. The gag was removed and the tourniquet untied. Through vomit film he could make out in the dark a full-lipped boy in an orange jacket, hood pulled tight on round cheeks and moist black eyes. The boy wiped filth from Damian's face and smeared it on his own pants. He grunted and lifted Damian onto the thin fulcrum of his shoulder. He was short and Damian's head swung dangerously close to the ground, but the boy shored himself under the weight and took the first heavy step into fog.

Wait, Damian wanted to say, put me down, I can walk. But already he could feel his eyes flutter and tunnel-vision.

Cool skin against his forehead and in stages Damian managed to open his eyes and focus his vision. Around him soft golden light and a small but expensively furnished room, all dark woods and muted fabrics. The boy unzipped his orange jacket and undid the hood. Out spilled long raven curls, the swell of breasts, jeans that hugged the smooth curve of round hips and fleshy thighs.

3.

He woke up in bed. The room was dimly lit by soft bedside lamps and everything beyond the mattress sunk in shadows. He shifted onto his side and felt cool sheets against his skin and realized he'd been undressed to the waist and gauzes applied to his wounds. The door was open and he could see light down the hall and his clothes in a sodden pile next to the bed. There was distant piano music and woody incense. His mind was overwhelmed and his body hurt everywhere. For a while he lay in the gentle light and looked at the ceiling because it was all he could stand to concentrate on.

"Thank god," his rescuer said when she found him awake. She stood out of sight. He hadn't heard her coming and he startled upright. She sat beside him on the bed and flashed a penlight in his eyes. "I bet you have a concussion. I was going to call an ambulance if you didn't wake up soon."

Her voice was gentle but the sound made his head throb. He let silence gather until the pain backed down his neck. "Why didn't you?" His head felt thick and heavy and his voice sounded detached from his mouth.

"I thought you might not want the attention. Considering."

"I was mugged."

She sighed and nodded. "Then why were you tied up? Why didn't they take the four-hundred dollars in your wallet? And why don't you have any I.D.?"

"Look," he said, and closed his eyes. The thick feeling in his head started to pound. "Where am I?"

"My condo."

"And where's that?"

"Portside. I was coming home from a party, and lucky you, I decided to cut through that parking-lot to walk along the bay."

"How did you fight off four of them by yourself?"

"It was foggy." She shrugged. "It wasn't much of a fight. When they saw I had a phone and I wasn't afraid to use it, they got more interested in getting away than in getting me."

Damian scoffed and pressed his hand against his forehead to stop the shaking. "You're real fucking lucky."

"So are you," she whispered. "You're welcome."

He tried to rub his eyes but the cartilage stung so bad he didn't dare touch his face again. He apologized and said this was the worst headache of his life, could he get some aspirin? She brought two pills and a glass of water. She wanted to check the swelling on the back of his head but she'd need more light. He buried his eyes in the pillow and let her probe his scalp. When she was done he squinted into the glaring overhead light and for the first time had a clear look at her.

"It's you," he said.

"It's me."

"I dreamed about you."

"I dreamed about you, too," she said.

Her name was Nathalie Jevali, and she was a student at Berkeley, born in Brazil and raised all her remembered life in Marin County. She was three years younger than Damian but shared his birthday, April ninth, and she'd dreamt of him off and on nearly all her life. Her dream was never the same except for the ending. She could remember it starting with horseback riding or a day at school or playing soccer, dancing, even flying, she never knew if or when Damian would show up until she opened a door and entered a place with low blue light and loud music. A café or a bar. There he'd be, sitting on a stool, staring at the counter between his hands. Nathalie would sit next to him and only then would he look at her.

When she was small she had to climb the stool to sit beside him and she thought he was a ghost. As a teenager she thought he was a pervert and woke feeling defiled for looking at him. Only in the last few years had she decided he was drunk and desperate, and she pitied him.

Usually the dream ended with him looking up, but occasionally it lasted long enough for them to look at each other before she woke, and only once did it seem to go on forever, her looking at him and his frozen stare, and she realized once he looked up he turned into a mannequin. Whatever had animated him fled, and looks of dread and tenderness mixed on his gaunt face.

The dream also meant something very different to her. Where Damian took her for an omen of inevitable catastrophe, she thought of him as a warning. One time, when she was seventeen, she saw him and the next day was invited to lunch with her dad. Because of the dream she said no, and her dad spent a week in bed with food-poisoning. Another time she went with friends to Tahoe for spring break and dreamed of Damian and came home early. She ended up going with another friend to a dance performance in Oakland and spoke to the director afterward. "It was just dumb luck," Nathalie said. "I really loved what she was doing and she was accepting students and it worked with my schedule. It was perfect. But it never would've happened if I hadn't come home early."

And those were just the most dramatic examples—the warnings usually saved her in much smaller, less nameable ways—usually nothing happened, she believed, because she listened to the warnings. God knows how many misfortunes she avoided by heeding him. "You help me all the time. In little ways."

"But how do you know what the warnings mean? Whether

to do things or not do things?"

"I just listen," she told him and pushed a graceful finger against her heart. "Something inside knows."

The night before last she dreamed of Damian and decided against a party she'd been planning to attend in Palo Alto. "If it hadn't been for that dream I wouldn't have been around to save you."

"I dreamed about you the night before last, too," Damian admitted. "And last night I got shoved in the trunk of a car and beaten up in a parking-lot."

Nathalie didn't have anywhere to be and they spent New Year's Day lounging around her condo. They watched TV and he helped her prepare their meals—clean dishes made delicious by nothing but the natural flavors of raw ingredients: onion, bell-pepper, avocado. She was big on sticky rice and warm flour tortillas, which she ate with everything, even soup. Every few hours she checked the dilation of his eyes and the swelling on his head. He was certain he had bruised ribs. It still hurt to expand his lungs. The blow to the back of his head had been bad enough to blacken both his eyes, but he wasn't disoriented anymore. If he had a concussion—and Nathalie couldn't believe he didn't—it seemed pretty minor, but he'd need to see a doctor to know for sure. "Your brain could be bleeding and we'd never know. You could go to sleep and never wake up."

"Thanks for pointing that out," Damian said. "Really. It means a lot to me."

"Let me ask you a question. Have you ever fantasized about setting your house on fire?"

"No."

"Not even a little? I won't judge you."

"Not yet."

"Would you rather be invisible or have x-ray vision?"

"I guess it depends."

Nathalie nodded, considering his answer. "What's your favorite color?"

"Magenta."

"Oh my god," she said excitedly and put her hand on his. "Good answer."

Imperious and provocative, her attitude grated on him, the way she promised to keep in touch and made him promise the same. The entitled air of her, like he existed for her convenience. The way she put on expensive clothes just to lounge around the house, the self-conscious way she presented herself and not a stitch out of place, as if the whole world was paying attention. She was a rich girl, obviously, raised to be a pain in the ass. Granted, she was beautiful, but beautiful like a porcelain doll. Looking at her was better than touching her could ever hope to be. In Damian's experience her kind of beauty added up to more trouble than it was worth. But she was a vigilant nurse and he was a guest in her house. And she saved his life.

"Do you ever smell colors? I have a sister who smells colors. Synesthesia, it's called. She says orange doesn't smell like oranges. I don't know why that bothers me, but it does."

Damian's head started pounding again and Nathalie stopped talking long enough to fuss over his bandages. She asked if he wanted a drink. She might have a couple beers and there was white wine, but he was fine with coffee and aspirin. "What would you do if you fell in love with someone and you found out she could smell colors?"

"I don't know," Damian said, holding an icepack against shut eyelids. "Probably nothing. What should I do?"

"It wouldn't bother you?"

"I'd stop showering and dress in all white. But it wouldn't bother me."

"What if she could hear shapes?"

"Hear shapes," Damian said, and frowned.

"Yes," Nathalie said. She looked quite serious. "Hear. The sounds made by shapes."

"I think I could live with that."

"Even though your children might inherit it?"

"I don't want children."

"You don't like kids?"

"I adore kids," Damian said. "I hate parents. Parents are bad for kids."

"Do you think you could ever be happy with someone who couldn't smell colors or hear shapes?"

"It hasn't worked out so far."

"I wonder," she said. "Do you think I talk too much?"

"Whatever gave you that idea?"

Mostly they talked about their dreams. When she first saw him Nathalie hadn't thought he was the man from her dream, only they looked similar, as the man in her dream was older than Damian. The way she described him, the sweat-soaked hair and greasy skin, the rabid look bleeding desperation from his eyes, it sounded to Damian like she'd been dreaming not of him but his father. Although his father hadn't become a drunk until well into his forties. She, too, was younger than the dark-haired woman in his dream. A decade if not a little more. The resemblance was still striking. Anyway, it was just a dream.

"I'm certain," she said over coffee, "something connects us besides the dreams. If we figure out what it is, maybe we can figure out what the dreams mean." She told him about her family and friends, her studies and passion for music and especially dance. Dance above all else was her reason for breathing, she said, she could dance all night and never get tired, it was the only thing that made her feel truly alive, truly free and connected to the earth, like she was heavy and light at the same time. Sometimes she started dancing and fell into a kind of trance, she was so immersed in the music and the sensation of her body in motion, and she'd come back to herself feeling no time had passed, and in reality it was hours later. "I don't know," she said. "I don't think I can tell you why it means so much to me. If I could explain it, I wouldn't have to dance it."

That made sense to Damian. He thought he understood. For sure he believed there were things that couldn't be said, so maybe they could be danced. "I'd be a liar if I claimed to have tried it," he said. She thanked him with a radiant smile and the simple beauty of it embarrassed him. Like holding a door for a stranger and being rewarded with a hundred dollars. She understood his blushing and saved him from it by asking if the coffee was good. He hadn't thought of it but the coffee was wonderful.

"It's my favorite," she said. "I'm glad you like it, too."

Damian was dizzy again and he laid back against the couch with a damp washcloth covering the top of his face.

"Have you ever pretended to be something you're not?" she asked.

"Every day."

"Me, too."

Otherwise they didn't have a whole lot in common. She was a dancer and he preferred reading. She was German and Brazilian but grew up on Belvedere Island. His ancestors came from Romania and Wales but really he was from Cincinnati. Damian owned his own business and Nathalie worked part time at a coffee-shop. Her family was affluent, obvious without her mentioning it, and his was dead. Nathalie had five younger sisters. Damian was an only child. In a delicate tone she asked what happened to his parents. He didn't want to talk about it. She nodded. Uncomfortable silence and Damian didn't attempt to bridge it. Nathalie laughed but her earlier enthusiasm was exhausted. She looked disappointed and Damian felt responsible.

And then a discovery: Nathalie mentioned she'd been to Cincinnati once, it must've been a decade ago, with her father. On a business trip. Damian asked what she thought of it. She shrugged. She was only there for three days and spent all her time in a hotel room watching pay-per-view movies. "But I like traveling," she said. Damian liked traveling, too. So that was something. "Where have you been?" she asked, and that's how they figured out they both spent last New Year's Eve on the Las Vegas strip. At the same hotel. Eating breakfast every morning at the same buffet.

After his parents split up his mother got a job in Seattle. Eventually, they moved in with the man who later became his stepfather, on Puget Sound. Nathalie spent her childhood summers less than a quarter mile away at her family's cottage. They were in Rome at the same time as well—Damian had been thirteen and Nathalie ten—probably flew there on the same airplane, which Nathalie remembered laid over in Baltimore and arrived at Da Vinci International in the early morning, shortly before sunrise, the same as Damian. His flight left the day after school let out at the end of May. Possibly May thirtieth, the day after Nathalie's parents' anniversary, when her father had taken her to Italy for three weeks.

"Not definitive proof," Nathalie decided, "but possible."

Damian had to agree. What struck him as amazing and totally beyond doubt, though, was the fact Nathalie's ex-boyfriend lived in the same building in the Mission Damian used to live in. Two or three times a week, for almost a year, they'd walked the same sidewalk, entered and exited the same building, rode on the same elevator.

"Crazy," Nathalie said. "How many times we almost met but didn't."

They looked at each other for a while. Not staring, but looking, and gradually the mood changed between them. They grew husky, comfortable with one another, warmer to each other. Damian felt the intimacy that waxes up between two people who turn silent and attentive in shared company. She wanted to hear more about his family. He smiled and shook his head. "I don't want to talk about them." So she asked about his work, what was it exactly he did for a living? He changed the subject. She insisted. "Sorry," he said. "That's private too."

"I told you about my job. And my family."

But Damian only shrugged.

"Keeping secrets just makes you look guilty. Someone who didn't know you might think you're a criminal or a pervert or something. You're not a pervert, are you?"

"Maybe," he said. "I haven't thought about it."

"What if you were a sex maniac?" she said, and grabbed his wrist. "Wouldn't that be terrible for me?"

"I see how it could ruin things."

Nathalie's nose crinkled at a thought. "How are we going to figure out what the dreams mean if we don't talk to each other?"

But he would not be moved. Frustrated, she threw her hands up and skulked off to refill their coffee cups.

He followed her to the kitchen and said, "We have the same birthday. If there needs to be something to it, why can't it be that?" He told her he didn't believe in prophetic dreams, which was a lie, and how he thought the whole thing—the shared birthday and the dreams, the near meetings and her rescuing him—was all a coincidence, which was not a lie. "Or maybe not a coincidence, but the other thing. What's it called?" He sighed and shook his head. "The thing where you don't know what you're looking for until you find it and realize you need it. Serendipity, maybe?"

She looked sullen but didn't interrupt him. She just listened. Now he'd spent time with it, he didn't think she was actually the woman from his dreams. She was too young and only vaguely, superficially, resembled the woman on the white bench. And that's how dreams are. Even she said earlier she didn't at first think he was the man from her dreams, only they looked a little bit alike.

"Still," he said. "You saved me. I owe you my whole life, which isn't much. But I'll always be grateful to you for every breath I take. You're the only reason I'll get to take those breaths. I'm in your debt. If you ever need me for anything. And I mean it: anything, big or small, once or a million times. I want you to tell me. I'll do whatever you need me to do."

"I didn't do it for a reward."

"Look," he said, "I gotta go. But maybe I could see you again?"

"Sure," she said, and "Yes," she said, and Damian's heart did things it had no idea how to say. For an instant. Then his heart remembered he was a pauper and an orphan. It told Damian he clung to the edge of existence by his fingernails and if he blew away no one would notice he was gone, and his heart shriveled in his chest and festered like an infection, like if he cut into it with a scalpel, a river of pus would bleed out.

The Great Work begins the same as it ends.

4.

Nathalie had plans for the afternoon and offered a ride. By the time she dropped Damian off in Bayview she could tell he was happy to be rid of her. She insisted they exchange phone numbers and balked when all he offered was a landline. She made him give a list of reasons why he didn't own a cell before she would believe he wasn't holding out on her. He couldn't afford one, he said, he worked mostly from home and the landline was sufficient. A cell-phone was a leash meant more for the convenience of other people than the owner, even though other people weren't expected to pay the bill. It made her feel like a spoiled brat and she hated it. To his credit, he didn't say anything rude—he got quiet and polite and she could feel him drawing away from her, but he promised to call and she believed him. She'd been dreaming of him almost all her life and he'd been dreaming of her, too, and whatever it meant would keep them in touch.

He was twenty-four but still only a boy. Strange, but kind too, and no one had ever looked at her the way he did. It wasn't calculated or hungry or judgmental. It wasn't lewd but neither was it reverent. The way he looked at her was just seeing her plain. It did not seek to reduce her or categorize her or quantify her. She might possess dangerous powers he could not survive. She might shatter if he touched her.

Later, she went to the movies with friends and all she could think about was the way Damian looked at her. Like he didn't know what she was, like she was as likely to bite him as help him, like she might know secrets. That's as close as she could get to it: he looked at her like he'd found something he had no idea how to see. Yes. He looked at her the way she thought of herself and he haunted her because of it. If he found her as unknowable as she did meant he might be able to know her as she was. If that made sense. She wasn't so sure it even made sense to her.

She didn't see him again for over a month. Her days filled with commuting and classes and rehearsals. Plus she worked a few hours a week as a barista at a coffeehouse close to campus. For the real world experience. Because her dad said it was important and because she enjoyed it. Taking the orders and mixing drinks, the machines humming under her fingertips, the peculiar preferences of regular customers and keeping the complicated details straight in her mind. Economizing her motions and the sequence of tasks for greater efficiency. The frenzied rush of a packed house when her brain went to sleep and her body took over, muscle memory kicked in, hands and legs so much faster and more accurate than her mind.

Muscle memory was the point of dance drills, the repetition of movement so ingrained in the very structure of the body it could be performed without thinking. The legs knew, hips, arms, back, knew the movements without thinking about them. And wasn't work—wasn't all movement—a form of dance? And then she read an article by a neurosurgeon that said there was no such thing as muscle memory. It was actually the brain wiring itself to perform the task without interference from the conscious mind. What she'd been taught to call muscle memory was actually accomplished in the brain, not the muscles. Synapses formed connections and made tasks automatic. Independent of thought. Like breathing. Like digesting. Like ovulating. You didn't think about them and yet you were doing them, performing them all, the repetitions of the body, the rituals of a living organism. Say the universe exists, and you invent matter. Say matter responds to stimuli, and you invent motion. Say the motion is repetitive, and you invent a pattern.

Say the pattern is meaningful, and you invent dance.

And what, she wondered, does it mean when the pattern breaks? January was cold, among the coldest on record, with nightly lows near freezing. The idyllic procession of the seasons she'd known all her youth now ragged and hoarse with real winter. The eternal springtime abruptly finite. Mortal. It made her conscious of the earth right beneath her feet, so close and yet absolutely foreign to her. But it was down there, underneath the halo of multinational satellites and the ping of networking computer servers, invisible crisscrossing radio signals, down, beneath the warm glow of omnipresent city light and the steady pulse of electrical current, covered in the steel and glass and concrete ecosystem of an orphaned species. Underneath, just a few feet from the vulnerable skin of her toes, was the earth—the actual earth—the only planet known to invent life. She thought of megalithic astrologer-priests recording with mathematical certainty the progress of gods across the night sky. Cycles of fixed stars and spans of cosmic time deeper than the geology of an infant planet.

Once a month she met her dad for lunch, this time at an Indian restaurant not far from his offices in the financial district. White rice, coconut shrimp, and spicy chicken tikka masala served in plain chrome tureens, naan baked in an authentic Tandoori oven. A small place, even by neighborhood standards, with a partial view of Lotta's Fountain. The street was overcast and secreting mucus, the ornate Victorian pillar lamp-headed and glowing bronze in the pale teal of early afternoon smog.

"Kronocell," her dad said. "I'm meeting with them next week."

Nathalie smiled and tried to look happy. When these lunches went well, she treasured them—but too often they decimated her for weeks in a black glaze of hatred for her father, hatred of herself for hating him. They could implode without warning and averting disaster came down to small things. Big smiles. Feigned interest. Compassion for the devil.

"Fascinating, don't you think?" Kronocell. Cryogenic preservation. Fascinating. And Nathalie zoned out the white noise of his baritone, half hearing him talk about the limited liability company of his wet-dreams. She'd heard it all before. Her dad, like all narcissists, tended to repeat himself. Cryonics, as an immortality method, struck her as absurd science fiction. But the technology existed and her father, a budding futurist, was on the lookout for ways to monetize what had always been god-given. Water. Oxygen. Free will. His fortune sprang from the steel industry but he was a forward thinker and the wealth potential of coal and carbon was on the wane. Innovative technologies were his new thing and he saw a chance to sell people their own vanity: the conceit of living forever. "They say if it weren't for disease and the effects of aging, the average human lifespan would be something like five-thousand years."

She already knew this. He'd told her before. She also knew at the current growth rate, global human population would reach nine-billion souls by mid-century. Running at maximum resource capacity, estimated sustainable global population was roughly four-billion people. She'd said this last time and thought about repeating it but decided not to. It would only ruin his mood.

Kronocell took its name from Kronos, the Greek titan, father of the gods. Time itself. The battle for immortality was really a battle against the destructive powers of time. The toll time takes on the body. The fact immutable of time running out. On a long enough time line everyone's life expectancy finally falls to zero. More than two-hundred people had already undergone the procedure, postmortem, and five times as many were on the waiting list, monthly payments automatically deducted from checking accounts for services they wouldn't receive until after death. Her father supported a congressional lobby to get cryopreservation covered by insurance providers. Nathalie had seen photographs of the preservation chambers, like seven-foot chrome water-heaters, the faceless, nameless cylinders warehoused in single-file rows and stamped with the Kronocell logo, their contents maintained at a consistent internal temperature of -180º Celsius, awaiting the theoretical morning when the technology would be perfected to reanimate raw meat, consumers secure now in the cure for whatever killed them in the dark old days of the twenty-first century. Whether that day came or not, a fortune was going to get made and Sebastião Jevali intended to make it.

"I'd wish you good luck, but I know luck has nothing to do with it."

"At any rate there's always an element of chance."

"It'll be fine. You're prepared. They aren't idiots. No one commands a board room the way you do." She was not above kissing his ass to get what she wanted but she wasn't doing that. It was a fact. He had an intuition for manipulating people. He knew when to flatter and when to bluster. Within five minutes of meeting someone he could tell how to bend them, whether they'd respond best to threats or compliments, appeals to duty or greed, reminders of rugged individualism or the common good. Some people he told they were doing the right thing whether he believed it or not. Others he promised would make a shit ton of money even if he knew they wouldn't. He said what he needed to say to get what he wanted. Nathalie was repulsed by his willingness to say it and awed by his ability to know what to say.

"Your faith in me is humbling. And appreciated. As always."

And he always got what he wanted. In the end. He was a force of nature and she believed in him the same way she believed in gravity, the heliocentric solar system, photosynthesis. She was never one of those children who, confronted by the suffering and injustice of the world, wondered why the adults couldn't get together and agree to change things. She knew the world was never going to change and she knew the reason why. She called him Dad. He wasn't a genius or a goblin but his will power was unrelenting. He would not accept no as the answer to any request, no matter how trivial or fleeting, he simply persisted. Moment by moment, day after day, he slowly wore the world down.

Now he would wear Kronocell's board of directors down. "It's a fantastic deal for them," he said. For a decade he and his money lurked around the periphery of the company but only in the last several months had he become obsessed with it. There were currently thousands of tech start-up companies in the Bay Area and he speculated in hundreds of them. He owned a company that specialized in putting together venture capital to turn research and development into application prototypes. He'd invested heavily in Kronocell and brokered deals on the company's behalf, partnering with interests in medical research, technology, and equipment. He was on the board of directors and had been buying up stock in the company through various entities under the umbrella of the Jevali Holdings Company. He'd positioned himself for total corporate takeover, but to make the whole thing legal, he needed consent of the governed.

"It's the best thing for everyone involved," she agreed. "They'll see." Nathalie couldn't be less interested in any of this but he couldn't see that. Of course not. He refused to see it. Until he mentioned the work she'd be doing this summer at the Gilman foundry in Berkeley.

"Great preparation for a company like this. Long term, Kronocell would be the perfect opportunity to make your mark, wouldn't you agree?"

Nathalie flinched. Not much, but he noticed. Fuck. It was the kind of involuntary reaction she could've controlled if she'd seen it coming, but it caught her off guard. She'd spent the last few summers in that god-forsaken foundry and the thought of going back this year was like being slapped with a reed. Her face felt split open. Hot blood and brilliant pain. Something dark and secret inside her suddenly ripped out, exposed and molested by air and light.

He frowned but held her gaze. "You'd be perfect for it. You're young, creative, empathetic, a woman. Perfect branding. It's an emerging market. There are no rules yet. It'll be people like you who take advantage of it. So why not you?"

She tried the big smile again but it was no good. Her face wouldn't do it. The mask she'd shown him flayed and sloughed. Mayday. She could feel her expression, the numb muscles of her face faking the motions but composing something closer to agony. Game over. She rallied, tried again, but despair was too overwhelming. The conversation stalled. Silence spread out and suffocated the table like the steeping fog beyond the windowpane.

After a minute, her dad offered a reconciling grin and started over. He asked about work, which was going fine, she supposed, and school, also fine. He asked about the condo and she said there might be something wrong with the thermostat. Sometimes it stuck and the heat wouldn't turn off. It would say sixty-eight degrees when it was actually eighty. This was a lie but she told it to comfort him. If she told him everything was fine he'd assume she wasn't taking care of the condo. He was convinced something had to be wrong at all times and if she was unaware of this it was because she wasn't paying attention.

He promised to send someone to fix the thermostat and mentioned he'd seen her mother a few days ago. "On the spiral staircase," he said. "She was wearing a blue dress. Very pretty." Then he reported the most recent adventures of her younger sisters: Rosalie lived in the dorms at Stanford. Her official major this quarter was Psychology, but her true studies, as ever, were party drugs and boys. He hadn't heard from her in months, which meant her life was either fine or rather bad indeed. Eugenie, spending the year at boarding school on the east coast, was lonely and homesick but enjoying her independence. Carolina stayed in her room all the time. She dyed her hair absurd colors and wrote bad poetry on her arms and legs in black marker, which stained her clothes. She wore too much eye makeup. When he complained, she declared her hatred of him. The two youngest, Angela and Bianca, still loved him.

"Although," he said into his linen napkin, and seemed to be regretting already what he was about to say, "Bianca. I took her to the children's museum and she asked me to remind her again how we were related."

Nathalie shrugged. "She's nine."

"That's the sort of thing nine-year-olds say?"

"Nine-year-olds are still trying to master sarcasm. They haven't graduated to silent hostility."

To illustrate the point, she turned away from him and found Lotta's Fountain out the window. It wasn't just another fountain in a city cluttered with public trinkets. A hundred years ago the fountain was a meeting place for survivors searching for loved ones in the aftermath of the great earthquake. As a teenager she used to wait at the fountain and imagine who might be coming to meet her. Just pretending. No one but her dad ever came but it was fun to make believe. She didn't want to spend another summer in the stuffy offices of the Gilman foundry—she never hated anything so passionately in her life—and she wished for an earthquake terrible enough to damn the Richter scale. Let it swallow the whole fucking state of California if it would keep her from that hellhole. Selfish and melodramatic and she didn't really want it to happen, but she wished for it anyway.

"I've upset you."

"I upset myself."

"Perhaps," he said. "I might've encouraged it."

"I don't want to go back to the foundry." There. She said it. All this time she thought she'd been working up the nerve to get it out, but she'd been wrong. Her energy had gone into resisting what she wanted to say, but her dad finally wore her down. She was too exhausted not to say it. Nathalie slumped against her chair and realized how tight she'd been sitting. Leaning forward, shoulders collapsing towards her knees, wadded up like that. She changed her posture and her posture changed her view. She relaxed. Well-being strummed her nerves like harp strings.

"What would you rather do?"

"Dance."

"Couldn't you do both?"

Nathalie shrugged. She wanted to dance all the time, not a few hours a week in the evenings.

"At any rate, I'm sure something else could be found for you if you're ready for a new challenge. You're applying to grad school?"

"Yes," and it was half true. She wanted graduate school like she wanted the steel foundry. She'd filled out half a dozen applications for MBA programs because he wanted her to, but she didn't plan on sending them.

"It's hard sometimes. Knowing what to do."

"I know what I want to do."

He nodded. "What you want and what you need aren't always the same thing. A task can seem pointless at the time, but later, when you look back on it, you see how important it was." Everything would work out, he promised, and the foundry was part of it. School was part of it. Experience and education. Truth be told, the corporate world belonged to fools and followers. With her talent and intelligence she'd be able to do whatever she wanted if she made it easy for people to talk themselves into letting her. That was the point of credentials. Most people, especially business people, were blind to talent and allergic to intelligence, but they knew how to read a resume. "Maybe you won't end up working with me. Hard to hear, but if it's what you decide, I'll accept it. You're my daughter. Loving you is the easiest thing I've ever done. I may not be blood of your blood, but you are my living heart."

And just like that, she knew she'd end up sweltering another summer at the foundry. Sly bastard. The fact she was not his natural daughter made her feel more—not less—attached to him. Like the fact he chose to be her father even though he owed her nothing made him more her father than the father of the five girls conceived through his body. Knowing she was chosen gave her the best feeling in the world. It made her important—and indebted.

"You don't have to make a final decision right now. But will you at least agree to think about it?"

"Okay."

"And whatever you decide, I'll support."

"I'll think about it," she said, and sighed, and didn't bother faking a smile. Her dad paid and they parted on the corner of Geary and Kearney. Fog smoked beneath a leaden sky, bruised except a small column of light atop Lotta's Fountain.

5.

At home, she reviewed notes made on index cards for a business analytics class, plowed a tome of data analysis, first in a black heat, and a second time slower with a pen and a fresh stack of index cards. She opened her laptop to compare her reading notes to the lecture notes, flipped to the chapter review and compared the questions to her study guide, naming the shit she understood and the shit she still needed to figure out. She made a list of things to do in the morning before class, dropped a bag of white rice in a slow-cooker, set the timer, slung her gym bag over her coat shoulder, and stalked to the Embarcadero rail station. Two hours of dance class, a cold shower, a highlighter taken to a text of corporate law on the BART from Oakland, and another hour of drills on the living-room floor before eating rice with a wooden mixing spoon straight from the pot. Her feet were blunt clubs and fire popped knots in her thighs. Fuck you, lactic acid. On the news, worldwide aid poured into a dozen Asian countries devastated by a massive tsunami the day after Christmas, but Nathalie didn't really pay attention.

Her feet hurt and she couldn't quit thinking about her dad. His interest in immortality seemed a stupid ambition when she considered the earth, the sun, the galaxy, all had cycles of birth, development, maturity, decline, and death. The moon went around the earth and the earth went around the sun and the sun spun at the edge of the spiral arm, slowly dragged into the black hole deep in the heart of the Milky Way, the Milky Way on a slow motion collision course with the Andromeda Galaxy. But not to worry—the sun would exhaust its hydrogen and go supernova long before that happened, the arithmetic of galaxy clusters would add up to entropy, and what good was everlasting life in a doomed universe?

Nathalie lay in bed, her mind a cold torch, light without warmth, shining bright on things she would rather not know. Her dad did not love her for who she was—he only loved what he could remake in his own image. She'd said she would think about working at the foundry, but she already knew it was going to happen. Her hesitation was a pretense—she would never give her life to the dance, not truly, not heart and soul, because she was too scared of her dad's disappointment. She wasn't his natural daughter, not his responsibility—he *chose* her and she wanted to be worthy of being chosen. And yet in order to be chosen she had to be someone she was not. She wanted her dad to love her, to be proud of her, the real her, the girl in Nathalie's heart. Not the girl he could turn her into. This is what made her curl like scar tissue over a festering burn. This sorrow. This seared nerve throbbing. This blistered love.

She dreamed of her mother, dead but awake, tongue wrenched out at the root, hands clipped off like foliage, pounding bloody wrists on the inside of her cryopreservation chamber.

South of Market Damian got off the bus and found once again the cold's monotonous clench. In the sky the sun glowed small and white and on earth Damian's mouth smoked. His hands stabbed the pockets of his coat and he shivered another block southwest to the chain-link gate, which secured a complex of industrial warehouses. Damian's printing hole. Thirty-foot rectangles stacked a dozen abreast and a half-dozen deep with alleyways in between and a string of parking spaces along one side. The porous cement painted powder blue had faded gray.

Smog stained pale green patches of the peeling paint.

The warehouse was climate controlled and divided by a drywall partition into a makeshift darkroom and a lab. The lab was in the front with an arc-light burner on one wall opposite an intaglio printing-press homemade from recycled parts. There was also a process camera, two industrial sheaves of acid-free cotton-linen blend paper with red and blue fibers in the weave, a desktop computer, diazotype printer, digital scanner, and hydraulic paper-cutter, as well as several cans of green-to-black color-shifting paint, boxes of gray, green, red, blue and black inks in various shades, a six-foot folding table, and an arsenal of cleaning supplies for sterilizing the lab. He put on a hairnet and latex gloves and a yellow polyurethane jumpsuit over his clothes.

After setting up he mounted an authentic one-hundred dollar bill before the process camera's accordion and focused it on the viewfinder. Aside from meeting Nathalie his last job was a total loss. He was running out of ink and plates and barely had enough cash saved to pay rent. After what happened on New Year's Eve he'd been scared shitless but desperate for work. He'd phoned Gangjeon a couple times but the calls went straight to voicemail without ringing. Not disconnected, then, but turned off. Or dead and never recharged. The second time he left a message without giving his name: call me. But Gangjeon never called.

He'd gone to see the Czech, Pavel, who'd been a decent connection once before. He slipped a new hundred-dollar bill under Pavel's nose, explained how his last job went down, the shitty spot it put him in, and asked for work. Damian wanted fifty cents on the dollar because his stuff was worth it. Pavel refused to pay more than thirty-five cents no matter how good it was. Stolen counterfeit was probably all over the Bay Area and by now the feds would be wise to it. Brings the value down. Damian said thirty-five would be fine but it took Pavel another week to get back with an order. One-hundred-thousand dollars due in two weeks. Damian never worked so fast. His father had warned him never to counterfeit under pressure. It made you sloppy and the smallest imperfection could ruin the entire run. You'd end up with a lab full of money that wouldn't fool a kindergartner. The process was slow and painstaking, but if you got greedy and hurried, you could end up in prison for a long time.

Damian took several pictures of the front and reversed the bill to photograph the back. Verisimilitude lay in the details, the textures and shades of things, the complexity. It required patience. Discipline. Critical self-assessment. People would believe in a lie if it showed them what they expected to see and it was Damian's job to make lies ring true.

The process was a modified version of the one his father taught him when Damian was twelve. Several changes had been made to the features of money since then which made high quality counterfeit difficult to find. Damian was forced to develop newer techniques, but the base layers were the same ones he'd learned from his father. The results were excellent but made it nearly impossible to produce large quantities in a short time.

He felt guilty for not telling Nathalie about his parents. She was so eager to hear about them and so willing to know him —her own life opened up, flaws and all, and she wasn't afraid to let him see. He didn't deserve her generosity. The concussion had tossed his sense. Made him temporarily forget who he wasn't, too slow sorting his thoughts from gunk in the dull haze, and he'd accidentally given her his real name. It made her the only living person who knew him as Damian Lancaster. The first thing he told anyone he met was a lie: his name. It felt good to know someone he had not yet lied to. He made up his mind not to lie to Nathalie, no matter what, and what could he tell her about his parents that wasn't a lie?

Damian spent most of his childhood ignorant of his importance in the life of his father, who was so often absent, but he'd been as mythic to his father's imagination as his father was to his. Damian was the reason for everything his father did. He knew it and knowing it bit his heart because it was useless now. It only meant knowledge couldn't keep a lifetime or the heart it fills from being wasted. The most important thing is working for yourself, his father often told him. You don't want to make money for someone else while they throw you a wage, even a decent one. It's not worth it. Living on someone else's schedule by someone else's rules and everything you do belongs to them. They'll keep you just happy enough you won't be able to get out from under them, and not one iota better off.

Damian's mother hadn't seen it the same way. His father used to tell him his mother's greatest talent was for worrying. The woman was a genius at panic. She could find things to worry about no matter how perfect the situation. Feed her chicken and she'll taste salmonella. Buy her diamonds and she'll fear burglary. Promise her the stars and she will want a warranty. She could portend the end of the world in a rainbow and find a way to turn lemonade into lemons. Rotten ones. Everything she possessed was only good to her if it was something she could lose. For her, a dependable income and an insurance policy went a long way and anything else meant more trouble than joy.

But she only thought that way because she loved her son and wanted to protect him. He'd been the center of her existence, he understood that now, the sun of her domestic solarsystem. Sure. Damian was the sun and his mother the earth and his father the shadowy moon, darker, more mysterious and less tangible, but constant all the same in orbit around his little family. Every once in a great while Damian saw the dumb hunger of his father's eyes upon his mother and in them heard the rumor of a world that existed before Damian filled it up. His father's gaze was often sharp or casual or humorous or tender. Only fixed on his mother did it engorge and turn wonderstruck. If his peripheral vision caught Damian watching, he transformed as a man awakened, embarrassed by the trance, or surprised by it, or ashamed.

Sometimes, long before he comprehended the mechanics

of their groans and percussion, Damian could hear his parents at night or on late weekend mornings. As he grew he understood his father's perception of his mother was nothing like his own. To his father she wasn't the resourceful mender of broken toys or the dispenser of sage advice. Not the intelligent problem-solver or healer of skinned knees or sorceress of wild adventures incanted from the etched-black page. To him, she was a thing. Exactly the sum of her duties as mother and wife and housekeeper. An object to be pacified and negotiated and acted upon. And she thought of his father the same way. To her, his father was worth the work he did and the money he made, and their marriage as much an economic exchange as anything else. They didn't treat each other like people. His father was provider and his mother was caretaker, and to Damian they were the sun and the moon, but they were not people.

He couldn't imagine telling Nathalie any of that. He couldn't tell her his dad had been a rare books dealer with a small used-bookstore near the university and an overstock warehouse near the river. He couldn't tell her the summer Damian turned twelve his father asked if instead of playing baseball he'd like to spend a few hours each weekend working for him at the warehouse. He could make a little money and learn how to operate a printing-press. And what his father taught him wasn't about books, but exactly what he said: how to make a little money and operate a printing-press. He couldn't tell Nathalie that. She saved his life. He promised not to lie to her. If he couldn't say the truth he would say nothing at all.

After a couple dozen photographs of both sides of the bill he ejected the negatives and took them to the darkroom, little more than a sink hidden behind thick curtains at the far end of the warehouse. He switched to red lights and developed the photographs and set them aside to dry while he set up industrial-sized fans to vent the chemicals. He started the computer and installed graphics software. He did this every time and when finished he always reset the hard-drive, so unless he was actually using it, the computer was always empty.

When the prints were ready he scanned them into the computer and opened them in the software. He went through the pictures and amalgamated the best features into a composite and started sharpening the details. Blending images, matching colors, airbrushing blemishes, darkening hazy lines and fading them again until they were correct. For Damian this was the drudgery, the real agonizing part of the whole process. When he was a teenager, his dad taught him a trick for how to do it: immerse yourself in the details until you obsess over them. Reach a point where they're all that matter to you, until you've forgotten hours in them. As long as you resist the monotony, you'll make mistakes. The job isn't done until you've been absorbed in it. Like so much else his father taught him it required imposing the task upon himself until he forgot how much he hated it.

And he supposed that was the biggest difference between him and Nathalie, why now his heart felt sick at the thought of her. She was rich and he was poor: she did something she loved for nothing and he did something he hated for money.

6.

The house in Forest Hill, prosaic in the dark and fog, disturbed Damian in daylight, haunted by what had happened there. Returning to the crime scene was dangerous but with Gangjeon out of communication it was the only way to find out who attacked him, why they did it, and where they were now. For a few days he kept surveillance on the house but there was no sign of the Koreans or the college kids. It was vacant. A FOR SALE sign in the yard. He called the real estate agent, pretended to be an interested buyer, and learned the house was held in trust by Golden Age Property Management. At the Bayview library he logged onto the internet and found out the trust was a partnership with an investment firm called Chariot Financial, the North American branch of Vrana-Hesperian Financial Services which had offices in Los Angeles, São Paulo, Sidney, and Berlin. Vrana-Hesperian was a subsidiary of Hesperian Investment Capital, a division of Hesperian Corporation, headquartered in Prague. They had a website but it was pretty barebones for such a large corporation, and not very helpful.

Pavel had a friend who owned a restaurant in Little Russia a few blocks south of Geary Boulevard. They met in the office next to the kitchen, a square more like a holding cell with small sooty windows placed just beneath the low ceiling. There was a desktop computer against one wall and an outdated promotional poster for a boxing match on the door. The two men huddled around a side-table on armless chairs drinking coffee and eating pastries. Pavel licked his fingers and pulled his smile into a mute arc. "Have you got it?"

"See yourself," Damian said and handed Pavel a one-hundred dollar bill.

Pavel investigated both sides of the bill and ran his fingers over the paper surface. "Amazing," he muttered and held it up to the light. "You're a magician. And the hologram. How did you?"

"A secret."

"I think it's real."

"It's not," Damian said.

Pavel tucked a blond icicle behind an ear and fixed Damian in hard blue eyes. "How much do you have?"

"Seventy-five."

"I'll take a million."

Damian shook his head. "One-hundred-thousand is the limit. And it has to leave the country." Pavel was never to discuss Damian's identity or even his existence with anyone, ever, under any circumstances without clearing it with him first. Damian gave Pavel the number of a bank account in Guatemala and instructed him to deposit Damian's fee on the morning of the exchange. After what happened with the Koreans, he didn't want to handle cash anymore. If it cleared, Damian would be in touch and they could continue doing business. He was being high maintenance but his product was worth it. And more. "If anything weird happens, so much as a misplaced sneeze, I'll pack everything up and you'll never hear from me again."

"Fine with me."

"I don't deal with anyone but you," Damian said. "You pick it up and pay me. No one else. We can meet here or at a neutral location, whichever you prefer. And I want fifty cents on the dollar."

"Be patient," Pavel said. "Forty is the best I can do."

Pavel wanted the seventy-five-thousand Damian finished the previous night and another twenty-five-thousand in April. It was going to Mexico. If it proved as clean as Damian's last batch, he could expect regular orders every few months, and might eventually make his fifty cent rate.

Outside, a chrome sun dazzled the early morning sky as

clear and hard as ice. The cold shredded Damian's lungs and breath plumed from his nostrils. Steam rose from his body, steam and smog evaporated from everything, until he could no longer be certain whether the cold source was around him or within him. Lunchtime was over and the sidewalk nearly empty. Suddenly, Damian knew he was being watched. He scanned the windows across the street and swung his head in both directions before walking toward Geary Boulevard. He half expected Nathalie to emerge from a nearby storefront. No one looked up and no one looked away but his skin puckered under his coat and the feeling persisted: someone was looking at him. He stopped under an awning and looked up and down the street. He wanted to hide but made himself stand there, glancing around, trying to see whatever could be seen. A few minutes passed and he couldn't remember seeing anyone on the street from a few minutes earlier. Everyone was on their way somewhere else. No one lingered. The only one looking was Damian. The oversensitivity of the paranoid and the paranoia of the career criminal, but he dared not laugh at himself. His dad taught him to love his paranoia. It was what kept him free.

Near the streetcar station he stopped an old man in a black overcoat and matching fedora for the time. The old man drew a nickel-plated pocket-watch from the folds of the overcoat and displayed it several inches from his eyes. His ears were mutilated and the skin angry pink where they should've been. "Seventeen minutes after six," he said, and nodded, and smiled, and Damian walked away.

◆ ◆ ◆

Albert's breath rises in firelight. Bitter cold in the mountains, and the peasants sparse this far from the village. Days go by without language soiling the forest. He has not laid eyes on a human being since Michaelmas. Poimandres, his only company, spends most his life asleep by the fire or purring in Albert's greatcoat.

The roof needs mending but there are no iron nails and no chance to get some before spring, so he does his best with peat moss and river clay. The daub mortar freezes and cracks. It falls off one wall and leaks what little warmth the hearth provides. Heat flies out the same way cold leeches in. On the worst nights he heats a lead bar until its belly turns purple. He moves it with a fire-iron to a leather pocket sewn into the mattress. Keeps the hay warm and the rot out. Sometimes in his sleep he kicks the lead and blisters the soles of his feet.

Mornings bring rime glittering on the furs he keeps for blankets. The days last only a few hours. Long enough to fetch water from the brook and chop enough wood to keep thawed another night. He works on the chapel until last light bleeds on the mountains round about.

Nights wiled by firelight over astrological charts. Reading the sky and writing it on paper with a square and compass. Light poured by the gods as they wander in heaven. It says the time is coming to begin again. Stars promise it will work this time. In a few months the Lord of Aries will bring a grand cross. Mercury in conjunction with Saturn opposite Venus and Jove. The sun and moon in the first and eighth houses trined to Mars. Time comes again to bend the elements. Make fire and water dance with earth and air.

The dance begins with dragon blood. The primary material of the cosmos. Taint in the heart of god. It existed at the moment of creation as the one and only substance. Prime matter. All the elements are born of its decay and atoned in its perfection. Every object and force, every emotion and thought are other names for the dragon. The thought and the thinker and that which it thinks about are symptoms of the blood.

When the ink freezes Albert sets the well to thaw on a flagstone above the fire and goes to bed. In the morning he fetches the dragon. He knows where to seek it. He learns it from the trees. Branches that groan under fresh snow. The muffled thump of downed deadwood. Let gray alders point the way. He follows the murmuring brook, whispering to rocks beneath a skin of flow ice, to a crag in the limestone face. Drawn like a migrant bird back to the place of his conception. Digging in snow-crusted muck. Midwife to the earth. Reading the stones, the shifting light slants in bald beech trees, deflected by the yawning crag. Numb fingers. Stiff as kindling despite leather gloves. Several times he stops and holds them in his armpits to bring them back to life. At the bedrock he wipes mud away, cleaning the wound to the bone, and the blunt end of his hatchet breaks off a chunk. He cleans it with snow and turns it in his hands for inspection.

A vein of oily lightning zigzags through the gray ore. Like a shattered mirror that drinks up sun and reflects midnight at the sky. Hermes' signature in the earth, as plain as if the god signed his name with quill and ink. The primeval chaos yearning for order and well-ordered nature ill for want of chaos. What Albert's master taught to him as dragon blood. It glistens in the forest light. He shaves flakes from the ore with a chisel and hammer and rubs them between his fingers, just to be sure, and he is sure. Fine black chaos, as pure as he ever witnessed.

He flees the ravine, chased by twilight, saying thank you as he goes to the brook water, the limestones, and granites. Thank you, peat moss. Thank you beeches, alders, and yews. The forest breaks on the horns of the waning moon. In the clearing Albert props the stone on the stump used for a chopping block. He dresses the ore into a rough oval, flat on the bottom, and places the chisel over its heart. A single hammer stroke splits the ore neatly in half to reveal its delicate striations. Prime matter black and grooved in its limestone prison. The soul of the elements bathed in moon milk. He will get the woman to bless it before the work begins. Slow Henry will need blessing too. Albert runs his fingers over the inky surface and pities it. How it will suffer in his hands. How Albert will torture it and love it at the same time.

The Great Work begins the same as it ends.

In fire.

ANDROGYNE OF
THE ANCIENTS

*"During this putrefaction, the philosophical male, or the sul-
phur, is blended with the female in such a manner that they
become one and the same body, which the philosophers have
named hermaphrodite; this says Flamel, is the androgyne of
the ancients, the head of the crow: the elements converted in
this way reconcile two natures which can make our embryo in
the belly of the glass and bring to birth a very powerful King
who will be invincible and incorruptible."*

—LOUIS GRASSOT, LA LUMIÈRE TIRÉE DU CAHOS, 1784.

January sealed the city under hazel clouds, which blushed
at twilight, and stung sharp and cold as menthol. But
underneath Nathalie was on fire. She was designing a
group choreography and a solo for a performance in March
and rehearsals were electric. Afterward, walking to the BART,
she loved crisp winter against her still-sparking skin, the hot
ache of wrung muscles and her whole body popping like static.
The world was cold and loud and she could find herself best in
these moments because she was not that. She was this small,
quiet heat buried inside it.

And she could feel Damian's heat too. She called to make
sure the number he'd given her was real and felt stupid soon as
his voice came over the phone. He wanted to know if there was
anything he could do for her, which there wasn't, and he asked

if she'd dreamt about him again, which she hadn't. He hadn't dreamt of her yet, either. "We should do something," she said. She invited him for coffee but his work was insane right now. He'd call soon as things let up.

The first Saturday in February she saw him without anyone needing to call. She took her two youngest sisters, Angela and Bianca, to a flea-market in Bernal Heights. At a stall selling hand-knitted alpaca sweaters, Nathalie picked up a beautiful yellow and red hat with ear flaps and a pom-pom on top, which she thought Angela would love.

"Oh my god, I want it," Angela said, and tossed a long black braid over her shoulder. Angela was sensitive to fabric and she caressed the material between her fingers, deciding if she could stand to wear it.

"Oh my god, me too," Bianca said. She picked up one of the hats from the display table and Nathalie warned her not to taste it. Bianca had a bad habit of putting things in her mouth, even inedible things, even in public places.

A tall shadow fell across the table from behind Nathalie, the way a shadow falls when someone stands behind you and looks over your shoulder, but when she turned around there was no one. She turned her head the other way and her eyes flicked just for an instant into the periphery beyond the stall, and Damian stood in the next aisle. He faced her without seeing her, holding what looked like a rubber machine belt, the kind of thing that might make a motor run, but bigger than anything she thought would go in a car. By the look of him, he was skeptical about this particular belt's ability to meet his needs, and intense bargaining ensued. Nathalie waited for him to glance up at her, but he didn't. After a minor haggle with the belt's owner he dropped a wad of bills on the table and without ever raising his eyes walked away.

A week later she saw him again. She was driving east on Market and traffic was slow and he stood at Thirty-ninth Street, leaning against the corner building, waiting for a bus. Two days after, again: Nathalie walking down Larkin Street, on her way to meet friends at the Orpheum Theatre, a limp but distinct sensation of being stared at, and Damian Lancaster, ten feet in front of her, jogging the stairs two at a time. It surprised her and she stopped at the foot of the stairs to watch him hurry into the main branch of the San Francisco Public Library. Foot traffic passed in both directions. No one looked at her.

She wondered if Damian was the man from her recurring dreams. She wondered if seeing him in real life might be the same as dreaming of him. Was it a warning? Had it ever really been a warning? She wondered if it was just a coincidence, and then a monstrous paranoia caught her by the throat, and she wondered what it meant if it was not a coincidence.

Was he following her? Could Damian be a stalker? But why stalk her when she made plain her desire to see him again? Unless for some reason, some creepy reason, he wanted to see her without being seen by her. For two days everywhere she went —every door she entered, every corner she walked around— she caught herself expecting to see him, a heady mixture of anticipation and despair filling her up as she searched for him across the landscape.

And then he called. His tone was angry but she could hear the panic it was masking, his voice low and too measured. It was the way she spoke when she didn't want people to know how scared she was. "Why are you following me?"

"What?" She didn't say anything else because the question knocked her off balance.

"You've been following me. I want to know why."

"I saw you," she said. "But I wasn't following you. Promise. I didn't even go to the library, I just saw you on my way somewhere else."

"The library?"

"And at the flea-market. I was with my sisters."

"What are you talking about?" he barked and now his fear was naked.

"I don't know what you mean."

He'd seen her twice in as many days, he told her, the first time at a BART station. He'd gotten off and saw her getting on. He told her how yesterday he'd been waiting in line at a drugstore to buy toothpaste. It was busy and lots of people were behind him, all pressed together pretty close. He had a feeling like being watched. He looked over his shoulder and his face must've been ferocious because the people behind him backed up a little bit and parted. Through the alley of bodies, which opened up behind him, he could see Nathalie at the other end. Holding a little basket of things, craning her neck to see far away. "Like you were looking for someone," he said. "Who were you looking for?"

"You," she admitted.

"But you're not following me?"

"No," she said, and hoped it sounded honest. She told him about the flea-market, the bus stop, the library, the feeling of being watched. She told him how she started to wonder if he was following her. More than ever she thought the dreams were important and she wanted to understand why. She invited him for coffee again. He didn't say no but he didn't say yes, either. He was still too busy but he'd be in touch. When he hung up she knew he was still trying to decide whether or not to trust her.

So she dealt with Damian the way she dealt with all things frustrating to her heart: she danced him away.

On nights she didn't have rehearsal and could reserve an empty floor she ripped all the second-thoughts and worry and curiosity out of her heart and gave it to her moving body: to her hips and back and limbs. She put it in motion and moving purged it. Leaping pirouettes across the entire floor, double-time chest pops and locks in combination with shoulder and hip isolations, and then a long sequence she'd been working on, some complicated Afro-bellydance fusion thing with lots of strange time changes and unintuitive transitions. And the whole time she thought about Damian.

Walking home near the bay and her surprise at the scene:

the near empty parking-lot, dark sedan and open trunk, four murderers and the rag doll at their feet. The indecision that twisted her up. Approach or flee. She'd wanted to escape but her conscience screamed at her and damned her to action. She was consumed by the memory of Damian prostrate and hamstrung. Men punching and men kicking. Fear in her heart, knowledge of how black a thing she discovered and how her mind revolted at running away. She danced that, too, and what dawned on her: she must do something or never tolerate herself again. And she was running and kicking. Almost in flight from those men. She struck them as much out of panic as aggression, as much to keep them away from her as to protect their victim.

And the confusion which followed, the mangled aesthetics of the not-choreographed, the unsymmetrical motion, how the center of her terror slammed with a brilliant point of excitement, the thrill of it, to anticipate, to predict what had not been designed. And this: how no one spoke, how she had not screamed, and how the men had not spoken, not to each other and not to her, how rhythmic their breathing and her own, and how such a simple thing drove them to flee. They saw her cell phone. She danced the mad dashing thugs and the bundle left for her discovery—the bound and bagged boy. She danced him out and danced him out and just when her instrument was clean of him, he called. To ask if she'd dreamt of him since they had met, and she had to laugh because, no, she hadn't dreamt of him but when she was awake she couldn't stop thinking about him.

He apologized for taking so long to call and asked to see her again. She said okay but after hanging up realized she didn't know if she wanted to anymore. She didn't believe what happened in that parking-lot had been a simple mugging. What was he doing there and why did those men almost kill him? How scared and at the same time untouchable he'd acted at her condo. So sad and dangerous. The shared dreams deepened the feeling. Rendered her experience of him more confused. More personal. Made it darker.

A white envelope arrived in the mail. About the size of a greeting card, sealed, with her name and address written in an attractive hand. Elegant but unpretentious. Strokes a mixture of thick straight lines and delicate curves. No return address. The postage cancellation stamp was made in Germany, which was odd since she knew no one there. She took it to the kitchen counter where she kept a letter opener. The slit envelope emitted a stench, subtle but nasty, like mildew. It was indeed a greeting card of sorts, a single sheet, gray, unevenly textured, stiff as cardstock but fragile too. The paper crackled between her fingers and felt as though careless hands might cause it to flake away, to crumble more than rip. It was folded in half to fit the envelope and she gently flattened it on the counter. It wasn't quite straight on one side, slanting slightly so the corner came to less than a ninety degree angle.

The image on the front was in black ink, an elaborate woodcut two-headed figure standing with legs apart and arms outstretched, Vitruvian-style, holding the sun in one hand and crescent moon in the other. One head male with short hair and a beard and the other female with long hair and a heart-shaped mouth. Both wore crowns. The figure was nude, ambiguously breasted, without genitals.

Beneath it a Latin inscription: *In hoc signo vinces.* On the other side, a type-set printed message, a longer one, in another strange language. German, maybe. She didn't know a lot about languages, but it didn't look like anything related to Latin. At the bottom it was signed in the same script as on the envelope. *Sponsus et Sponsa.* The bridegroom and bride, she guessed. There was a large dark splotch in the upper right corner, a blackening which left the texture slightly furry. Here the structural integrity of the paper felt thinner, more delicate, like a few sturdy fibers were all that held it together. Across the surface were several tiny holes, some only visible when held up to the light, circled in brown auroras like stains left by tiny coffee cups.

A cursory internet search revealed *In hoc signo vinces* was Latin for "in this sign, you will conquer," which according to legend was what the Roman Emperor Constantine saw written across the sun in a dream and inspired his deathbed conversion to Christ. It was used on early Christian battle-standards and the coats-of-arms of several noble families, from Portugal to Byzantium.

What the hell could it be? Who would send it to her and why? No one came to mind, but she asked her friends about it anyway, her sisters, even her dad. None owned up to sending it. She didn't press the issue because everyone seemed as baffled as she was, and anyway, none were likely culprits. She kept it in a clear plastic sleeve to contain the smell, which spread the longer it was out of the envelope. A smell she couldn't quite place, light but persistent, and evil, like rotting organic matter, like an animal a long time dead which never stopped decomposing. Every few days at a quiet moment the two-headed figure came into her mind and she retrieved it from its sleeve to study again. For the life of her she couldn't imagine why anyone would send it to her. It could've been a mistake, but no, the envelope was clearly addressed to her. Frustrating. Nathalie slid it back into its sleeve and put it away.

She met Damian on Potrero Hill, a coffeehouse with green stains on the floorboards and exposed pipes in the rafters. She inspected the back of his head and bruised ribs now nearly healed. The bridge of his nose wasn't swollen anymore and his blackened eyes, angry and blood-drunk the last time she saw him, were dried up and gray. He wanted to know if she'd dreamt of him again but only awake had she seen him since they'd met. "I've started thinking about the place in my dream," she said. "The room I walk into where I always see you. It's vivid in my mind. A café or a bar. I think if I saw it in real life I'd recognize it. So I'm going to start looking for it."

He nodded, as if to approve her decision, but he looked embarrassed by the notion, and he didn't say anything. "I thought we might do the same thing with your dream," she added carefully. "If you're willing. We could walk along the pier. See if we spot your white bench."

"It's a dream bench," he said. "I've dreamt that bench for more than ten years. I've only lived here for two. It's not any particular place. Just a bench in a dream."

"I'd still like to look for it."

"Even if we found it, I don't know what it would prove."

"Me, neither," she said. "But I want to try."

He agreed to help her and, encouraged, she showed him the strange letter she'd received in the mail. According to Damian, who apparently knew about the history of printing, the paper was handmade by someone who knew what they were doing. He couldn't say exactly what the document was supposed to be, but it looked old. The images were created using a woodcut, possibly on an intaglio printing-press, using a technique from the fifteenth century. He showed her what made him think this, the texture, how it wasn't quite even, wasn't quite the same density throughout the paper, how the ink was thicker in places and thinner in others, and yet the lines were perfect: no bleeding. The feel of it between the fingers. Light yet durable. Slightly spongy. Linen paper.

Otherwise, Damian seemed completely disinterested in the strange letter—if you could call it a letter. He wasn't curious about it at all, like he would be content if she decided to ignore the card, to stick it someplace forgettable, throw it away and never think of it again. This failure of imagination seemed more unpardonable to Nathalie than being a drug dealer. If he was a drug dealer. Because he wouldn't tell her anything certain about his job. Or his family. Or anything, she realized, he was a first rate listener, and she believed when he said if ever she needed him, for anything, he would be there for her. To repay a debt he insisted, against her protests, he owed her. She thought he wanted to know her, but he did not want her to know him at all.

Damian intrigued her and she wanted to like him, she did, but she believed in premonitions. She'd learned to honor her instinct about things even if it didn't seem to make much sense, and her instinct said Damian was bad news.

She didn't want to think about it too much but she must've been because the next day Rosalie, one of her sisters, came into the coffee-shop to see her and asked what had her looking so down. Nathalie shrugged it off at first, but ten minutes later decided what the hell and told Rosa about how she saved Damian in the parking-lot and spent the whole next day with him in her apartment, and how she danced to get him out of her system, and about the bad feeling it gave her.

"He's probably a criminal," Nathalie said. "Exactly my luck."

Rosa licked her lips and cocked her chin. She looked like she was thinking hard, but Nathalie knew different. Rosa wasn't thinking—she was looking. "Things aren't always what they appear to be."

Nathalie raised an eyebrow at her. "I found him in a parking-lot after midnight, hog-tied with a bag over his head, getting the crap beaten out of him. He's probably a drug dealer."

"Could be."

"But you don't think he is?"

Nathalie was the eldest of six sisters. Rosa was the second. She was nineteen and possessed a special talent: she could look at you and see your future. Sometimes. It was pretty hit and miss. Rosa inflated her cheeks like a bag and blew out the air, slowly, maybe feeling the pressure of the moment. "I think you're right," she decided. "You said so yourself: he was tied up in the trunk of a car in an otherwise empty parking-lot. He's probably some kind of criminal."

"Then what's not as it appears?"

"Your instinct," Rosa said, as if it were obvious. "Your bad feeling. Maybe it's not what it seems to be."

Maybe.

And still she couldn't get him out of her.

8.

Cold mornings dampened the potpourri of moo-shoo, coffee, and backwashed sewage. Fewer than normal street-barkers seduced tourists on Market Street, but the local carnival of eccentric costumes, glistening advertisements, storefronts, three-piece suits, vagrants, pressed on warmly as possible along the walk Damian made every day from bus stop to warehouse and back again. By midday it warmed a little and Bayview wore a shawl of muslin fog.

Nathalie picked him up in front of his building and told a funny story about a guy who came into the coffee-shop, high as she'd ever seen, wanting to buy sheet music. He didn't know where he was and when he left she didn't think he believed the only things she could sell him were coffee and baked goods. He kept trying to give her board-game money. "I think he believed it was real."

Together they braced against the icy sea-breeze to walk the Presidio coastline in search of the white bench where in recurring nightmares the dark-haired woman awaited his approach. They did not find it.

"We'll find it," Nathalie told him.

Dozens, maybe hundreds of white park benches littered the Presidio but none struck a familiar nerve. Nathalie chose one with a perfectly appropriate ocean view and made him show her exactly how it was in the dream. So he sat her on the bench, posed as best he could remember, explained the angle of the bench to the water—there was a sidewalk, or at least a path, a pier, pedestrians, the stars in the sky over there—Damian walking towards her from this direction. He crammed his hands in his coat pockets and stared out to sea because he didn't want Nathalie to see him upset. The search for the white bench distressed him and he didn't understand why. More than embarrassing or silly, it unnerved him, and he was pissed off at himself for being uncomfortable about something so stupid. The ocean did not feel sorry for him. It was overcast. Black pleats rolled and sank in the waxing tide.

Not the bench from his dreams, but there was a food truck selling kabobs, which was better as far as Damian was concerned, and they made a picnic on the grass. They ate with flushed faces, backs to the wind, and Nathalie showed him a trick with a paper napkin and plastic spoon. She let him see her put the spoon in her coat pocket and folded the napkin into a tiny square and pretended to eat it. "Where'd it go?" she said and let him inspect her pink tongue and teeth like stars, but the napkin wasn't in her mouth. He patted down her coat and jeans and watched her turn out the pockets, but no napkin. She suggested he check his coat and only when he pulled out the spoon did he realize it hadn't been in her coat when he checked it.

"What about the napkin?"

Nathalie grinned and tapped his foot. Between his sock and shoe he found it folded up like a stamp.

"Show me how you did it."

"Trust me, you don't want to know." Nathalie grinned slyly. "The illusion stops being magic when you understand it. This trick has been ruined for me ever since I learned how it's done."

Their second excursion to the Presidio proved equally futile. February pulled coats of frost over street-side vendors. More than a month had passed since Damian met Nathalie and neither dreamt of the other since. They trudged from white bench to white bench but none featured in Damian's dreams. Nathalie stood with her arms crossed and her mouth set hard while Damian shook his head.

"Would you recognize it?" Nathalie slumped on the bench

with her elbows on her knees and the wind standing curls on top of her head. "If we found it, would you be able to tell?" When the wind loosened she stroked her hair down and dragged a tress away from her eyes and looked into his face to show she expected an answer. Cold reddened her nose but she didn't shiver and she didn't look away.

"I don't know," he said when he accepted he must say something.

"Then it could be this one?"

"I guess."

"What makes you think it's this one?"

"I don't think it's this one."

"Okay," she said, and stood up. "That's all I wanted you to know."

Both of them hung their heads as they walked back the way they'd come. Two women stood in profile among a thin stand of cypress trees, and as he and Nathalie passed, Damian saw them kissing. They were the same height, petite, no more than teenagers, dressed in polyester coats and workman's trousers. Tongues lingered an instant between parting lips. They wore short hair, one shaved to her stubbly scalp, the other armored in blunt purple spikes, exposing delicate pixie ears. They kissed each other on the eyes and embraced again and their long necks churned as if drinking from each other's mouths. Nathalie stopped walking and Damian turned to find her watching the girls. Nathalie smiled at him and motioned to keep moving. She slid her hand inside his arm as they walked. "We should appreciate what happened back there," she said. "That was a gift, what we saw, and we didn't do anything to deserve it."

In the car Nathalie wouldn't speak to him. They pushed down

Highway 101 in stiffest silence and Damian thought she must be angry, but her voice was cheerful when she finally spoke. "We'll find your bench. We just got to be patient. Keep looking." She knew it because her seventeen-year-old sister, Eugenie, told her. "She could hear it," Nathalie said. "In my voice. I told her about you and the dreams and what we're looking for. She said we would find it. She heard it in my voice."

"The sound of your voice?"

"Could be," and Nathalie exited on Caesar Chavez Street. "I don't know. The sound or the tone or whatever. She just heard it in my voice."

"I'm convinced," Damian said, and Nathalie giggled. She didn't expect him to believe her, she hadn't meant to tell him until she did. Of course, it wasn't guaranteed. Eugenie heard things and sometimes they turned out to be true. Sometimes they didn't. It obviously wasn't an exact science but Nathalie had witnessed too many things work out the way Eugenie heard them to not believe she heard something.

"It would be stupid of me to ignore."

"And do your other sisters also have magical abilities?"

"Yes, asshole, as a matter of fact they do." She tried not to smile and lost. Damian smiled, too.

"So what's your supernatural power?"

There were thorns in the way she looked at him and he could tell he'd hurt her feelings. He apologized. He wasn't trying to mock her—he thought they were having fun together. By the time she turned onto Oakdale Avenue her look softened. "I've wondered about that a lot," she said. "Nothing special about me. My sisters must get it from our dad. He's not my biological father so that's probably why. Unless dreaming of you counts as a supernatural power."

"Maybe," he said, but he didn't smile. The mood for games left him. He hadn't wanted to offend her but her feelings were clearly hurt. He didn't understand why or how to make it better. He didn't know how to talk to her, he realized, and decided the best thing would be to shut up. When she stopped to drop him off, before getting out of the car, he asked if there was anything he could do for her.

"No," she said and her voice told Damian what she thought of him. "That's all for today, thank you." He understood because it was the same voice in which he spoke to the automated system when checking his bank account balance. Like she spoke not to a person and not to any other living thing.

Damian stood on the curb and watched her drive away. He questioned not for the first time what he was doing with her. He liked her but not all the time and he suspected she thought the same of him. He wondered what making love to her might be like, but thought she probably didn't want him to find out. He'd only had two girlfriends in his life and none since his stepfather died four years ago. Since then his romantic life had been a handful of casual encounters and he didn't want Nathalie to be one of those. Mostly, he felt indebted to her. She risked her life to ransom him from violent death and he knew keenly the meager worth of what she saved. He wanted to earn her courage, make his life equal to her value of it. But her original estimation of him would probably prove to be exaggerated.

Nothing but ads in the mail. Upstairs, he threw them on the kitchen counter and turned on a couple space heaters. The digital clock on the floor next to the mattress said 6:31. He heated a microwave pizza and disguised the cardboard taste with cans of beer and a bag of pretzels. He hadn't eaten anything since yesterday and he was starving. For half an hour he watched television but couldn't get into any of the network programming and turned it off. He sat on the mattress and tried to read a book but couldn't concentrate. Thought about Gangjeon instead.

This was the longest they'd gone without communicating in over a year. Gangjeon hadn't returned his message and it worried him. Damian wanted to know how much Gangjeon knew about what happened on New Year's Eve, if he planned it, and if so, why? Was Gangjeon betrayed by the two men in Forest Hill, or had he betrayed Damian? He didn't know if Gangjeon was friend or enemy or if his life was still in danger. Because someone was watching him, he was convinced, and the most likely suspects were Gangjeon and the other Koreans.

Briefly he'd thought it might be Nathalie—every time someone seemed to be following him he turned around and there she was, at the BART station, in the drugstore. But when he confronted her about it she'd been genuinely shocked—she thought the same thing about him, that he'd been following her, she'd seen him at the library, she'd seen him buy the belt for his printing-press at the flea-market. Why would she admit to more than what he accused if there was something sinister going on? No, he didn't think she was following him. If she were keeping tabs on him all she needed was to call him up. It was coincidence, unless you asked her, and then, like everything, it related to the dreams.

Everything had a hidden meaning to her. Warnings in her dreams and messages in her voice decoded only by her sister's ears. Gifts in the form of lesbians making out behind the trees. Her thinking was strange. Ludicrous at times. He was shocked at the gullible way she met the world, but he envied it too. There was a richness to her experiences, an awe in the pleasure of simple things, which he wished he could share. Another reason her life was full and his impoverished. She found a special magic in each of her five sisters and what proof had he against it? None. Only proof he was skeptical of anyone who discovered a method of seeing the world any way that wasn't fucked up.

She'd told him a little about her half-sisters but not much. He knew more about her dad, her fucking dad, she'd said, Sebastião Jevali, a dickhead and a feel-good story all at the same time. At least people liked to tell her. He'd actually come from an upper-middle class family in Bahia and amassed through a combination of worker exploitation and privatization of public resources one of the most lucrative steel companies in South America.

Nathalie told Damian about a series of mergers and corporate takeovers, which grew the business into a thriving international corporation, partially because her dad was so damn smart and partially because he was so damn ruthless. Interests in everything from real estate development to renewable energies, munitions manufacturing to pharmaceutical research, fiber-optics, textiles, genetically modified agriculture. He fantasized about leaving this empire in the care of a blood-heir, preferably a son. But as he constantly reminded Nathalie, he had six daughters and no sons. She had the misfortune of being the eldest and so was expected to be the surrogate son. She knew how stupid and old-fashioned it sounded, but her dad could get pretty stupid and old-fashioned about things.

"But I don't want it," she said two weeks later when next they met at her condo. She didn't want any of it. She'd seen how it made her dad a stranger to his family, she despised a great many things he'd done, terrible things, business things, money things, and she hated benefiting from them. She was ashamed of him, but she didn't care. She loved him anyway because he did terrible things on her behalf and she hated to disappoint him. She wanted to dance more over the summer, take some workshops, maybe even perform. "But my dad wants me to work for him again. The same thing I did last summer and the summer before."

"Poor you," Damian said.

She snorted and nodded and fell silent. Damian knew he hurt her feelings but right then he didn't much care. He had a headache and the leather squeaked as he lay back against the couch with his eyes closed. Damian was of the opinion if rich people did what they loved instead of what made them money, the world would be far better off. He had no idea what his great passion in life might be, but if he had one, nothing would keep him from it, especially not his dad.

"Are you asleep?"

"It's been like twenty seconds."

"Can I come closer?" she said in a voice so small he barely heard. She moved next to him on the couch, near enough to feel her heat in his lap. Her whisper soft as feathers on his ear. "Is it okay if I talk? You don't have to listen if you don't want to. You can even fall asleep. I won't mind."

She told him of a magnificent cherry tree at the house where she grew up. When she was a little girl she climbed it all the time, whenever she could get away with it. The maid and the nanny would beg her to come down but she always refused. If they wanted her down, they would have to come get her, and if they tried, she promised to bite and kick until they fell. She called them horrible names and shouted every swear word she could think of. This was fun sometimes, except she was playing this game with the maid and the nanny, and she didn't like playing with other people, especially not her sisters.

"Games are always more fun when you're the only one who knows you're playing, don't you think?" She would pretend to be a pirate and the tree was her ship, or she was a fairy princess and the tree an enchanted palace. Everyone thought she was lonely but she wasn't lonely. She liked to imagine from her throne in the highest branches she could see everything happening everywhere in the universe. That's when she became Queen of the Cosmic Sea, beyond good and evil, mistress of the seven worlds. She didn't climb the tree anymore—two summers ago her dad had it cut down to make room for a new boathouse—but sometimes, walking down a busy street or watching it rain out the window of a coffee-shop, she still liked to pretend she was Queen of the Cosmic Sea. "Do you think I'm weird?"

"No." Damian tried to keep his whisper as clear and fragile as hers. "I used to play that way, too."

Nathalie rubbed her nose with a fingertip. "Have you ever

seen a dead person before? I mean really looked at them?"

"Yes."

A couple weeks ago on campus a cat gave her a crow head. The cat was walking around with the head in its mouth. She'd always assumed death to be the absence of life, but that wasn't true. When she inspected the dead bird, the way it stared at her without being able to see, she could tell it was still in there. Nothing alive departed, but something else was in there, too. A tangible substance. Like death was this stuff that filled you up and made it so you couldn't live anymore.

Damian had nothing to add to this and so he said nothing.

"My dad can be pretty selfish," she said.

"So tell him to fuck off."

"It's not that simple."

"The hell it ain't," he said, but she only shook her head. She wasn't like that. She was a loyal daughter. What would she think, Damian wondered, if she knew about the things he did? Terrible things, money things. Would she find Damian as terrible as her dad? What if she threw him out and never spoke to him again? What if she called the police?

What if she didn't care?

9.

The next week Damian received his copy of the document. He'd worked all night at the warehouse before coming home after dawn with a vague plan to spend the rest of the day shivering in bed. The Pacific Ocean shouted twenty-eight degrees and ninety percent humidity. Its wet breath saturated Damian in bone-bitter chill, which clung on his clothes, and the bay as black as volcanic glass amplified the cold. Before going upstairs he checked the mailbox. There was the white square gift-card envelope with his name and address in the same handsome script he'd seen once before. International reply coupons lined the top and the cancellation stamp said it posted from Germany the week before.

"Holy shit," he said. He looked around the empty lobby and crushed the envelope into his coat pocket and went upstairs. The document was exactly like the one sent to Nathalie, the same paper and imagery and strange inscriptions. Signed *Sponsa et Sponsus*. The bride and the bridegroom. It made his mouth dry and his knees tremble because this was no coincidence. It was a calling card. One was sent to Nathalie and now one was sent to him. Someone was keeping an eye on them and wanted them to know about it. But why? If someone was following him they'd know about the warehouse and no one would be more interested in the warehouse than the Secret Service.

When he was a kid Damian often wondered at how calm his father could be in the company of policemen, even with the printing hole nearby, even with the press loaded with paper and plates on the rollers. If they made him nervous Damian never saw it. But his dad had said cops didn't bother him because he knew where they were. It was the ones you couldn't see you should worry about, the United States Secret Service, whose sole duties included protecting the President and the currency. That's all the Secret Service did: provide personal security to the President of the United States and hunt down and prosecute counterfeiters. And the President wasn't difficult to protect most of the time. That left a lot of days to look for counterfeiters.

Looking for us, Damian was proud to say. For both of us. But what he remembered most was how his dad hadn't answered, refused to answer, Damian thought. His dad smiled and Damian could feel in the warm gaze how much his father loved him. He messed up Damian's hair with his hand and smiled and squeezed Damian's shoulder, but he had not said a goddamned word.

If the Secret Service knew who Damian was they wouldn't advertise it with junk-mail. Maybe the Koreans wanted to clean up what they started. Definitely they'd be interested in Nathalie. Maybe when four grown men run away from a woman it bothers them.

He caught the bus south of Market and spent the afternoon watching his printing hole from a safe distance. Made a few laps around the neighborhood and browsed the cars in the parking-lot. Nothing came but the tang of goulash, salt water, marijuana carried on the wind. He stood on the sidewalk across the street and looked at the door of his unit. No one approached. The Secret Service would end up disappointed if they raided it. The reams of cotton-linen blend paper and the intaglio printer would be suspicious, but there was no hard evidence of counterfeiting on the premises, and the lease was in a fake name. Unless they busted him unlocking the front door there was nothing to connect him to it. But he had work to do and at some point he must risk it.

The next day he visited Pavel at the restaurant in Little Russia. He needed information on the Koreans and Pavel promised to ask a few questions around town on his behalf. There was an antiques dealer named Christopher a few blocks from the restaurant. A retired historian with the tweed suit and bifocals to prove it. He specialized in Italian Renaissance print culture. Damian consulted him several times last year over the technical details of the early modern intaglio printing-press, when he'd been building one of his own. Damian decided a walk might do him good and thought he'd drop in to say hi. After brief pleasantries he introduced Christopher to his card. He looked at it under a microscope and said it must be fairly old based on the discoloration and aging of the paper.

"And the damp," Christopher said, pointing to the dark splotch in the corner. "That's been there a while. Hard to fake mold." He indicated the Latin signature. "It seems to be some sort of wedding invitation. Perhaps. I really have no idea." He noted the ink was faded somewhat. The method was clearly early modern, though unlikely Mediterranean in origin, but the woodcuts, the materials and technique of paper-making, likely the ink, all looked authentic fifteenth century—sixteenth at the latest. "I can't say this itself is that old," he added. "Probably it's not. I don't know if they even used wedding invitations back then. But certainly whoever made it knows a great deal about this sort of thing."

Christopher's equipment wasn't sophisticated enough to say for sure what it was made of or how old it might be. That would take science more high-tech than an antiques dealer kept on hand. None of this meant much to Damian. He didn't especially care how old it was or what it was made of. He only wanted to know who sent it to him.

On the bus, a familiar figure: a small man, older than sixty, younger than seventy. Silver chevron mustache. Black overcoat. Matching fedora balanced on the stumps of his ears.

When Damian called to tell Nathalie what he found in the mail, it made her arms tremble. She told him to come over right away and show her. He couldn't, he was in the middle of work and he was starving, he hadn't eaten all day, he'd bring it over in a few hours. "Goddamn it, Damian! Get your ass over here now! You might not give a shit but it matters to me!" She shouldn't shout at him, but she was too excited to stop herself. He showed up half an hour later with an oily sack of Chinese takeout and the white envelope she wanted to see.

The documents were not, in fact, exactly the same. Nathalie noticed it right away. The male head on Damian's figure was on the left. On Nathalie's, the female head was on the left. Damian's figure held the sun in the right hand and the moon in the left. In Nathalie's, it was the opposite. Also, where Nathalie's was cut slightly crooked along the top edge, Damian's was straighter. Nathalie's was signed *Sponsus et Sponsa* and Damian's signed *Sponsa et Sponsus.*

"So they're not the same," Damian said.

"They mirror each other." Nathalie couldn't stop smiling. She looked at one document and then the other, explored the woodcuts and text and stains and tiny holes. All of it delighted her. The flat question on Damian's face made her want to smile even bigger and she had no idea why. When she was satisfied, she set aside the documents and they ate cross-legged on the living-room floor. Damian told her what little he learned from his historian friend: they might be fifteenth century wedding invitations. She could hardly sit still and eat, she was so happy Damian got one, too.

"Why are you so happy about it?"

"I don't know," she said. "It just makes me happy."

She wanted both invitations to stay with her, just for safekeeping, did he care if she held onto them? Fine, sure, whatever, they made her a hell of a lot happier than they would ever make Damian. When he went home she got them out again and sat on the couch looking at them, feeling the texture between her fingers, breathing their pungent scent. She slid Damian's into a transparent sleeve and put the two of them in the pockets of a laminated folder. For the rest of the night, and for a long time to come, she couldn't get the wedding invitations out of her mind. They wouldn't leave her alone. Perhaps her fascination was absurd—they didn't seem to have anything to do with her or her life or anything about the world she understood. And yet they felt important to her, for no reason she could articulate, just an important feeling she got. Her pulse quickened and a beautiful sensation came over her like endorphins flooding her brain. Excitement. Mystery. Anticipation. None of these and all of them at the same time.

The next day she took the invitations with her to school and showed them to Max, a doctoral student who taught an English class she'd taken as a sophomore. He'd been her favorite teacher that semester and they'd run into each other a handful of times since. He recommended she show them to Dr. Moira Sundstrom, a professor of medieval literature and an expert in early modern manuscripts.

After classes she visited Wheeler Hall and made an appointment with the department secretary for Dr. Sundstrom. Then she got up the hill to Foreign Languages in Dwinelle Hall. In the department lobby she checked the directory and found the German professors. She was lucky enough to catch a Dr. Heath Lunsford holding office hours. She knocked on the door and introduced herself and carefully removed the documents from their protective folder. She was trying to learn what language they were written in and thought it might be German.

"Yes," Dr. Lunsford said after a cursory glance. "It's German. Or used to be. Middle High German." It was hard to tell when it had been written with so short a sample but he imagined it was anywhere from the fifteenth or sixteenth century. Seventeenth at the latest. Vague, but like he said, it was hard to tell for sure with such a brief sample.

"Would you be willing to translate it for me?"

"Sure," he said and copied the texts into a spiral bound notebook along with Nathalie's university email address.

Dr. Lunsford told her it'd probably be a few days before he could get to it but she had an email from him the next afternoon. They were wedding invitations. Based on the dialect, they were probably younger than his original guess. Much of it was more archaic but some grammatical constructions and spellings weren't in common use until the early seventeenth century. The text was the same on both documents. Attached was a translation.

She showed it to Damian a few days later at a bar on Telegraph Hill. Not the place from her dream. It was on the roof and had wood floors and the lighting was too icy. Nothing seemed right and it depressed her. There were more than five-hundred bars in San Francisco alone, never mind the rest of the peninsula, never mind the east bay, and the idea of visiting them all seemed hopeless.

They pressed together behind a round table and silently read the printed sheet with their cheeks almost touching: *You are invited to the wedding of the King and Queen. If you are born for this, chosen by god for joy, you may ascend the mount whereon three temples stand, and bear witness to the holy union. Take heed! Prepare yourself! If you do not bathe enough, the wedding can work ill. Perils come to those who fail. Let the light beware!*

"Any of this make sense to you?" Damian asked.

It did not.

"But why would someone send us an authentic seventeenth century German wedding invitation?" she asked Damian on the walk back to her car.

"Wait for the manuscript expert to weigh in," Damian said. "We'll know more then."

"But even so," she said. "What could it possibly mean? What possible explanation could exist that isn't absurd?"

Damian smiled and shrugged. "Maybe the explanation is absurd. We'll have to wait to find out."

They visited three more bars, all crowded, none right. They ended up at a nightclub on Fremont Street with a posh cover charge and four floors, a bondage cabaret party, a drag-queen review. Forget it, Nathalie decided, it was Friday night and she wanted to dance. She believed you could tell a lot about a person by seeing how they dance and Damian didn't disappoint. She didn't think he would dance, but he did. He lacked anything like talent but made up for it by not giving a fuck, which oftentimes proved more interesting. He mostly danced by himself, free of the self-consciousness that censured most boys like him, so stoic and stuck in their own heads. He was lots of fun when he was willing to be.

By one in the morning she was done. She'd worn heels and held them in one hand by the straps while she danced in stockings. Her neck hurt and her ankles were swollen and she was starving. It was March now and getting warmer and she talked Damian into setting out on foot, drunk, the thrill of spring-time flaring her nostrils, in search of cheap food. She insisted on teaching him a game she used to play with her sisters when she was a little girl. She made him stand side-by-side with an arm and a leg locked together and jump from white bar to white bar of the crosswalks. He was half a foot taller than her, and at first they were a buckling pile of limbs and giggles, but by the third intersection they could've won a three-legged race.

They found an all-night diner on the edge of South Beach and waited twenty minutes for a booth. She wanted French-fries and a strawberry-banana milkshake. Damian had an omelet and pancakes. The nightlife crowd came and went while they ate. After, the stillness of early morning. Damian went to the bathroom and came back for a napkin and a pencil and went back to the bathroom. He returned with a *San Francisco Chronicle* he found in the garbage, and they quietly took turns at the crossword puzzle.

"I'm getting sleepy," she said. "You about ready?"

"I guess I should be," he said. They split the check and walked back to her car and she drove him home. He asked if she'd dreamt of him yet, which she hadn't, and if there was anything else he could do for her. There *was* something else she wanted him to do and she was surprised by it. She would be performing in a few weeks and wanted him to come. He looked shocked by her request, totally shocked, as if he never expected her to actually want him to do anything.

"Don't worry about it."

But he wouldn't let her let him out of it. "No," he said and the hesitation in his voice wounded her. "No, I want to go. I just got a thing I'll have to reschedule, but I'll make it happen."

"It's okay."

But he said, "Please. Let me come. I was only surprised to get invited. It would be my honor to see you dance." And the look on his face when he came off with that line—she could tell he wasn't being ironic. It was sincere and she could feel herself blushing, embarrassed to get such a gallant response for such a little thing.

Sweet and damnable. He seemed to want nothing more than to listen to her talk and she wondered if it was only to avoid telling her anything about who he was. His work was hectic and demanding but he wouldn't say what he did for a living. He was from Cincinnati but he would tell her nothing of his parents or what brought him to San Francisco. Like a ghost conjured out of nothing at all. As if Nathalie dreamed him into existence. To listen to him talk, you'd think he had no past to remember and no future to live for, and she worried about him all the time.

Dance distracted her. Three nights a week she rehearsed her group choreography with eight other dancers, the piece she was beginning to consider her best composition thus far for its gradual progression across the floor, how it filled the space, the marriage of content and form, the expression of feeling, it's timing and geometry, how the movement seemed random and at the same time symmetrical, like the patterns of blowing leaves. But the tricky thing was the articulation of some of the phrasing. There was a particular sequence she couldn't get right, it came out either too classical or too quirky. She often opened her eyes in the middle of the night, wide awake and anxious, the balls of her feet aching for the dance-floor, calves already stretching and thighs burning for flight. She would clear the living-room of furniture and rehearse in her bed-clothes.

These nights she was most obsessed with the strange phrase, its various access points and transitions, which she entered like secret passages in a maze, listening to her body, waiting for it to teach the sequence to her. Strange how the middle of the night opened up the work. The quiet and the dark. They made it possible to compose in a vacuum, disengaged from the world and her personality, out of context, distilled.

Nothing there but her body lit up with imagination.

Not so much the dancer as the dance.

10.

The quiet and the dark. Exactly what Damian wanted. All this bar-hopping overwhelmed him—he didn't have the personality for it. He just wanted to sit someplace still with a stiff drink and enough room to hear his own thoughts. This one was an improvement and so he was relieved when Nathalie said they should stay. It was dusk and early enough on a Tuesday night for the place to be nearly empty. They'd started almost an hour earlier working their way down Haight with brief digressions of side-streets such as the one they found themselves in now. They must've visited a dozen bars and this was the first time they'd stopped for a drink—mostly Nathalie walked into a place, glanced quickly around, and dragged him out by his sleeve before he could sit down.

He only saw her once every other week so he didn't know how many bars she'd checked without him, but she kept a wad of maps with every watering hole north of Daly City in her purse and when they stopped she pulled them out to eliminate a few more pretenders. He thought it was a fool's errand, seeking a place from a dream, but she wouldn't be derailed, and she seemed to think his being there made a difference. Like she wouldn't recognize the place unless she could see him sitting at the bar all miserable and broken, exactly the way she'd dreamt him.

They took a pair of stools at the end of the bar and ordered drinks and Nathalie went to the restroom. The bar-top was rustic in a hipster kind of way, aging raw beechwood, and the floor was the same. The ceiling and fixtures painted burgundy and the walls beige. It rained most of the day but the sky was clear now and the natural light added warmth to the colors and haloed the space amber and gold.

"D'you know. It's the last. The last night of the new moon?" said the man sitting on the stool next to Damian. He sounded like he'd been drunk for hours. Damian guessed he was in his forties, soft looking with wobbly chins, overweight but tidy, bloodshot, in an expensive-looking suit and boring tie. His hair was black and wavy and neatly combed. His drink was full, a mint julep, held loosely in both hands where it sat on a fresh cocktail napkin. When Damian didn't answer he hunched his shoulders and rolled a plump finger around the rim of his glass. "Forgive me, sir. I am distraught, sir."

Damian's drink came and he struck it lightly against his neighbor's glass and sipped it. The man acknowledged the gesture with a sad nod and dipped his mouth to the glass, still perched on its napkin, and slurped liquid over the brim. "Allow a poor soothsayer, sir, to harrow you with a... With my tale of incest, jealousy, and... Jealousy and heartbreak."

He must've understood the look on Damian's face because there was an apology in his smile. "It's early, sir. You're the first person that's sat next to me."

In a halting alto he explained how two months ago he came home, not even early, just at the normal time, to catch his wife engaged in sexual intercourse with her younger brother. From the bottom of the stairs he could already hear her demanding to get fucked harder. She hadn't spoken to him that way, even at the best times, in fifteen years. The children were now living with their grandparents in San Luis Obispo. The divorce already looked long and demeaning. "She's got a side, too," he said. "I'm sure there are reasons. How these things occur. It would be ungentlemanly to paint her in too mean of terms. Without. Without hearing her version of it."

But he didn't want to hear her version, he told Damian, he didn't care what she had to say about it. He didn't hate her and he didn't want to demonize her but he couldn't look at her anymore. Maybe not ever again. His therapist told him he was suppressing his emotions. Of course he felt rage, disgust, jealousy, betrayal, heartache. And how could he begin to properly process his feelings without getting fall-down shitfaced drunk at least once and maybe, the therapist recommended, several times.

"It's an infamous day, sir, do you know what day it is?"

Damian didn't know.

"March fifteenth?"

Nathalie returned and quietly sipped her wine. She swung her feet gently on the stool beside him and Damian thought it meant she was content to hang out a little longer.

"Beware the Ides of March," the soothsayer said. "Do you know the Ides of March?"

Damian shook his head.

"Pagan festival in Roman times, but it's best. Best known as the day one Gaius Iulius Caesar was struck down on the forum steps by his own. His own adopted son." And that, the soothsayer said, wasn't all. The abdication of Czar Nicholas II, the discoveries of SARS and the hole in the ozone layer, the Nazi invasion of Czechoslovakia, all happened on the Ides of March. Tsunamis, floods, sir, blizzards, by god. An inexhaustible list of outrages. "March fifteenth," the man said. "An ominous day indeed, sir. Beware. Beware the Ides of March."

The soothsayer stared at Damian with wild eyes and breathed through his mouth. He either forgot what he was going to say next or realized he had nothing left to say. He shambled off his stool and lurched towards the restroom and Nathalie said they could go now, this wasn't the place. She thought there should be steps and a railing inside the entrance and the bar was on the right in her dream. This place had no steps and the bar was on the left. They continued their dry crawl down Haight Street, more than twenty places in three hours, stopping twice more for quick drinks before forging on. At ten-thirty she had enough and asked if he was ready to go home.

"Only if you are," he said, and she invited him to her place to watch a movie. It was spring break at the university, she would graduate in the summer, and she'd spent the day catching up on schoolwork. She hadn't found the place from her dream and she was sick of the bar scene and this was her last chance to save a wasted day. They stopped at a corner store in Portside for red wine, chocolate covered raisins, licorice whips. Nathalie liked 1980s B movies and settled on a slasher flick with gratuitous violence and nudity.

They gorged themselves on junk-food, and, inebriated, delirious with exhaustion and high on sugar, bawled laughter at the movie and threw candy at each other. Damian barricaded himself behind a wall of throw-pillows on the couch and dropped chocolate raisins on her like mortar shells until she cried foul, no hiding behind pillows. He kicked the pillows away and faced her cross-legged with hands on hips and said if she really wanted to, she could take a free shot at him. She said no, she didn't want to, it was a stupid game, but when his guard was down, she pummeled him. "My kingdom for a horse!" Damian cried.

"Then yield thee, coward! And live to be the show and gaze of the time." Nathalie clapped her hands on her mouth and spun on her heel. "I knew I liked you for a reason," she said. Nathalie had taken theatre all through high school and performed in several plays. The theatre faded as her attentions turned more to dance, but her love of Shakespeare endured. For Damian, it was common as water. His mother had aspired to be a Shakespeare scholar and taught him to recite soliloquies like nursery rhymes. His head was a clearing house of half-forgotten sonnets and scraps of iambic pentameter. "We'll always have the Bard of Stratford."

"I guess that explains everything," Damian said. "The mystery of the recurring dreams has been solved."

They decided to make it a double feature and selected an animated adventure story about kitchen appliances that spontaneously break into show-tunes and because of shared adversity become best friends. Damian figured they must be pals now because Nathalie leaned against him on the end of the couch. When he couldn't feel his arm anymore, she moved so he could pull it out, and rested her ear on his chest, and he put his arm around her shoulders. She smelled like coconuts and geraniums. This was the closest he'd ever been to her and he could see her hair wasn't the tangle of curls it looked like from a distance—there was a pattern to it, an intricate design of layers and coils, the longest locks pulled by their own weight into thick spirals. He could see beneath the complicated knot-work the eggshell of her scalp, pale and vulnerable, which startled him to a profound intimacy. A closeness to her, and a trust, like she bore her head to him so he could know something private about her, a part of her body even she had probably never seen.

They watched the movie and she held his other hand in her lap, gently stroking the hair on the back of his wrist. After a while she turned his hand over and traced the shallow lines of his palm with a fingernail. He took her hand in his and squeezed it. She lifted her head off him and tilted her face to his and they stared at each other for a long time. His forearms vibrated against her shoulder-blades, his whole body shook a little, and he wondered if she could feel it. What did she think it meant? Damian blinked. A moment later Nathalie blinked. Her eyes were huge and brown. He looked at the fine constellation of freckles over the bridge of her nose and onto her cheeks, the bones high and thin, her dimples, her narrow chin and shut mouth.

He pulled her closer, brought his face to hers, hesitated. She nodded. They kissed, softly at first, taking turns holding the other's lips, and then deeply, tasting each other. Damian explored her mouth, the soft underside and ridged dental dam, running his tongue slowly along her teeth, and then she did the same in his mouth. She tasted like licorice and pinot noir, sweet and tart at the same time, and all his senses burning with her. He was aroused and she pressed his dick against his thigh, almost holding it, while his hand scaled her belly. She yanked beneath her shirt without releasing his lip and held his hand in hers and guided it to her breast.

His chest and arms hurt from trembling and there was a nauseous sore in his belly and he pulled away from her, stroking her hair as she curled her back into him on the couch. He kissed the back of her neck and tried to calm down. Nerves. The shaking in his arms wouldn't stop and all his muscles were exhausted.

"Damian," Nathalie hissed at him. "Damian, goddamn it, you cheater, you fell asleep! Wake up!"

When he finally roused she loomed over him, sticking her fingers in his ears and flipping his nose. He spent several seconds in a groggy huff rubbing his face and ears with both hands. "Don't be creepy," he said. When he was sufficiently awake, he looked up at her still lying on his back, where she crouched on her knees beside the couch. The clock on the wall said it was almost 8:30. He could tell by looking at her she'd fallen asleep, too. "What's wrong?"

She cocked her head to the ceiling, trying to decide how to tell him, he thought, or if she should tell him at all. "I've been waiting all night for you to kiss me again. But now it's tomorrow and I'm sleepy."

"It wouldn't be right. You're drunk."

She laughed at him. "I haven't been drunk for like six hours."

"Maybe *I* was waiting for *you* to kiss *me.*"

The look on her face told him she hadn't considered that particular possibility. "It's too late now," she said, and yawned.

"Sorry." He really felt sorry. "I didn't know. Should I kiss you now?"

"No," she decided. "It's too late. I fell asleep and now my

mouth feels gross. My breath probably stinks too. Anyway, I don't want you to do it just because I told you to. You should want to kiss me. I wanted you to think of it by yourself."

"I was asleep," he pointed out. This did not impress her. "I'm awake now."

"The timing's all wrong. It's a bad moment."

"I could do it later. When the timing's better. When I'm thinking about it but you're not."

"*Or,*" she said, "I could kiss you. Later. When the moment's right."

Damian laughed. "We could race."

"Sure. Whatever. Awesome. As long as it's because you want to and not because I told you to."

They had coffee and cereal for breakfast. Nathalie offered a ride home but he said he was fine with taking the bus and walked to the stop. Did he and Nathalie just make a formal agreement to become lovers at some unspecified future date, he wondered, is that what the conversation was about? The more he thought about it, the more he thought it was a bad idea. There were too many things Nathalie must not find out, too many secrets he must keep for it to work out well, and he didn't want Nathalie to be some chick he used to sleep with. Although he was assuming a lot about her. Maybe she wanted nothing more serious than a casual lover. Regardless, it made him nervous. His whole body felt weird. His belly was queasy and his muscles still ached. She gave him a hangover. He hadn't touched a woman in a long time, had not kissed anyone in years.

He thought about dying of thirst, how they say if dehydration is severe enough, when you finally get to water, your body wants it too fast. You want to gulp as much as possible. But your body is in shock, it's ready to die, it's already given up. So you throw all the water up and die of thirst. As much as you want it all, you've got to sip a little at a time for a while, until your body can handle it again. Too much too fast and the body rejects it, and he thought affection might be the same way.

Sages say the philosopher's stone is magnesia, azoth, divine ruby, elixir of life, miracle of philosophy.

It is a fire emitting no light, a water that is not wet, a stone that is not a stone, a tree with roots in the stars and branches in the earth. It is an alloy of soul and substance. The great mystery at the center of existence. Marriage of matter and imagination. Wedding of spirit and dust. It is food to the hungry and water to the thirsty. It has been used as a ship for sailing and a song for singing. Axes make it wood and flour makes it bread. The ill call it medicine and the weak call it power. In a farmer's hand it is seeds and in a gambler's pocket it is dice. It makes the slow swift and the wise foolish.

The stone is called ambrosia, cornucopia, sophic hydrolith, prince of metals, king of elements.

It turns cowards into tyrants and thieves into heroes. The peaceful wield it like a weapon and the selfish share it like alms. Ambition makes it a tool and poverty turns it to gold. It is a fraud to the cynical and a novelty to the bored. The blasphemous discover the art and fall to their knees in prayer. The pious witness the work and weep that god is dead. The virtuous shall be corrupted by it and the rational driven insane.

The true stone is quintessence, precious treasure, glorious phoenix, holy grail, child of sun and moon.

11.

Nathalie didn't see Damian again until the night of the performance and then only briefly. It was a special performance, magical in a way she'd heard other dancers talk about, the kind of experience many dancers never receive, and those who do, precious few times in their lives. And she knew it was happening. Backstage, getting ready, she could feel it. The whole routine in her fingertips. Humming an inch deep in her thighs like dogs jumping on leashes to be set free. And when she hit the stage the whole thing flowed out of her. The sequence she'd practiced so hard was perfect. She could picture every moment in her imagination and it happened exactly the way she saw it. In an odd way, there was no difference between the two experiences. What happened in her mind and what happened on stage: the two were the same thing. So caught up in each other, so intimately connected, she couldn't say for certain which one caused the other, or if they were coincident of each other. Her body was inspired and she did nothing to cause or anticipate it. It just was that way.

Damian stayed after to congratulate her, hunched over in a windbreaker with his hands in his back pockets. "Thanks for letting me come," he said. "What I saw tonight—I don't even know what to call it. I never saw anything like it before. Watching you dance is the only way anyone can see it. That's the only way it exists in the world."

He had this way of saying heavy things with such ease, like it was no big deal, like it was totally unrehearsed and even he had no idea how it would come out until he was saying it. It was corny as hell but he said it with such an open face, clear eyed, naïve, and she could see him transforming from cold and sharp and isolated from her and everything else in the world into a man deeply touched and hungry for connection. It made her wish she could know him. Really know him. She'd never experienced eye-contact quite the same, especially not with a man. It was disarming. Usually it was about intrusion, coercive, but Damian looking her in the eye felt more like an invitation than an advance.

She smiled and blushed and thought she should say thank you, but she just kept smiling and blushing. "I should've brought flowers," he said. "But I didn't think of it until I was already here." People were piling up behind him and he walked away. She looked around later but couldn't find him. He just left. And the mystery of Damian Lancaster grew in her imagination. It was just as well—she already spent several awkward evenings at home alone dwelling on what happened the last time she saw him. What did it mean and how would things change, as they surely must, in the aftermath? He basically threw himself at her and she'd been ready to accept. Until she fell asleep. She thought about what she'd said to him the next morning and felt stupid about it now.

At the after party, a plastic cup of red wine in one hand and a paper plate of exotic cheese balanced on her knee, she spoke to Kendra, the director of a small dance company called Strange Equinoxes. Kendra loved Nathalie's choreographies and hoped they could work together, might Nathalie consider joining Strange Equinoxes? They were a small troupe but performed a lot, and if she joined, Nathalie would definitely get opportunities to choreograph. Plus, she'd learn how a company works. Nathalie could hardly believe it. They arranged for her to meet the other girls. "Excuse me," she said. Joy vibrated from the center of her chest—excitement so intense her body couldn't contain it. Happiness could be ruthless sometimes. Her bones might crack if it didn't stop. "I need to find the restroom." But she didn't need to find the restroom, not really, she just wanted to get away before she started crying.

Two days later she met the manuscript expert. Nathalie liked Moira Sundstrom immediately, a tall woman with short hair and square glasses, a composed air of self-control, and a warm smile. It was infectious and made Nathalie want to smile, too. After handshakes and introductions, she showed Dr. Sundstrom the wedding invitations along with Dr. Lunsford's translation of the text.

"Of course, this is very exciting," Dr. Sundstrom said. She reminded Nathalie of a swan, awkwardly built but graceful. Her neck was long and lovely. A web of fine blue veins gave her tone a silvery pall. "Early modern wedding invitations—if that's what these turn out to be—are somewhat rare. We know very little about them."

She looked over both invitations before setting them aside and reading the translation. The paper looked right, the ink looked right—they seemed to be the real thing. On the other hand, early modern wedding invitations were a highly formalized genre with strict conventions, almost none of which were being observed here. There ought to be a formal address to the recipient, a record of the banns being read in church, a proper salutation. There should be some reference to the families involved, especially in connection to a royal wedding, which this claimed to be. Usually there was a long preamble with Bible stories about the importance of marriage. Adam and Eve and original sin in the Garden of Eden. A lot of misogyny. That sort of thing.

"Like I said, the extant record is thin, so it may well be there was a wealth of deviations from convention, or there could've been variations in conventions. We just don't know. But as far as what is known goes, this is totally unprecedented."

"So they're fake," Nathalie said. She tried not to sound disappointed but it was no use.

Dr. Sundstrom smiled. "Well," she said, "not necessarily. The peculiar thing is: a lot of authenticity has gone into faking these, if they are fake. The ink and paper. The woodcuts. Not easily done." A forger would have to use other old documents for the raw materials. Whoever might've faked them did a lot of painstaking, time consuming work. Expensive work. Why do all the research, the hard work, not to mention the monetary commitment, only to get lazy and completely botch the textual conventions? It didn't make sense. "Combined with the dearth of information available concerning these texts—if anything, I'd say it's an argument on the side of authenticity."

"Could someone fake them because they're worth money?"

Dr. Sundstrom seemed not to have considered the possibility. She looked stunned by the question, thought about it, and shrugged. "I guess anything's possible. Documents like these are of an exclusively scholarly interest. Someone's dissertation. These two documents alone could consume an entire career. But, I suppose, to the right collector, they might be worth some money. Not as much as you might think, though. Maybe a couple thousand dollars at most. Maybe less. A few hundred. The lack of an apparent motive is another argument for their authenticity. Usually, if someone goes to all this work and cost and risk to fake a document, they fake a Milton letter or a Shakespeare sonnet. Something sexy. Not wedding invitations. Nobody cares, or almost nobody. Certainly, nobody with means to pay a lot of money. As I said, they're wedding invitations. Who's going to care besides a scholar?"

"But you're not willing to say one way or the other?"

"Not with confidence. There are things to suggest authenticity. But some things raise questions." Dr. Sundstrom apologized for not being more helpful and suggested submitting the invitations for forensic analysis if Nathalie needed a better idea. "I could help you with it," she offered. "It's not exactly cheap, though." It wasn't cheap and her dad would not be pleased if he bothered to check on it but Nathalie didn't care. She left the invitations with Dr. Sundstrom after arrangements were made to send them to the lab.

Three days later she ran into Hector, the old boyfriend who lived in the same building as Damian in the Mission, and agreed to catch up over lunch. She was relieved when her dad called shortly after her Cobb salad arrived. Urgent news he must share in person. She must come to the house tonight, now, as soon as possible. It didn't matter this was a bad time, she was busy, she had homework tonight and class in the morning. She might've been angrier at his selfishness—how he demanded the whole world revolve around his convenience, the way her entire existence was but an extension of his will —but the interruption saved her from an awkward scene with Hector who promised not to be heart-broken and lovelorn but who after half an hour of conversation had obviously lied. She used the phone call as an excuse and escaped without eating.

By the time she reached her car she decided to tell her dad about Strange Equinoxes, that she was going to do it no matter what he thought. It was as good a time as any. She'd skipped breakfast, and now lunch, and she could feel her stomach cooking itself to feed her, and the pain was compounded by the coming confrontation with her dad. She worried about it while driving on the Eastshore Freeway, but by the time she reached her parents' house on Belvedere Island she was no more certain about what she would say or how he would react.

The original part of York House was a Queen Ann style mansion built in the 1880s by one of San Francisco's leading steel barons, an immigrant like her father. It suffered significant damage in the Great Earthquake and acquired a few Lakeside and New Colonial flourishes as a result. The extension, a three-thousand square foot wing, had been added a decade before her father bought the house. When Nathalie was ten it had been added to the national registry of historical sites, and before moving to the Portside condo it was the only place she'd ever lived.

Her dad bought it only partly to aggrandize his gothic ego and mostly to make Nathalie's mother feel safe. Her poor mother. She hadn't stepped outside this house in twenty-one years. Shortly after wedding she was attacked in the streets of Salvador, her hands and tongue stolen from her, and Nathalie's dad agreed to take her away from Brazil forever. Disfigured, she haunted the house big enough to protect her, a premature ghost, burying herself inside its walls and corridors and praying none of her demons could find her there. Nathalie's first education the fear of men, taught by a mute mother who could not hold her, and her only lesson was the fact not Nathalie nor any of her sisters ever heard their mother's voice or felt her fingers in their hair.

The housekeeper let her in and Nathalie ascended the central staircase to search for her dad's study. It was a big house and strangely lain and Nathalie had never confidently mastered its design. Always changing, hallways lengthening and shortening, walls sometimes widened and others narrowed, stairwells grew deeper or shallower—a quality helpful to her hiding mother who disappeared days at a stretch before being discovered. Its upper-halls were especially labyrinthine, obeying an internal logic all the house's own and not at all intuitive to Nathalie, transforming slowly but constantly like the synapses of a developing brain.

That's how Nathalie thought of this house: as a mind. Even now it gave her the creeps. When she was a little girl and the house was silent, utterly silent, she could hear it thinking. She and all her sisters were its thoughts. Her mother its broken heart.

"Glad you could make it," her dad said as she pulled a chair to the side of his desk. He considered her for a moment before looking through papers on his desk. He possessed the unnerving ability to pierce her with a gaze, focus the energies of the entire cosmos upon her, before turning to the business at hand without another thought of her. As if god cupped her in the absolute power and protection of an almighty hand only to fling her to the frigid emptiness of outer-space. A sensation like being stabbed and ignored at the same time.

"I'm happy you came," he said again, and without allowing her a chance to speak took off his reading glasses and leaned heavily back in his black leather office chair. "We lost Kronocell."

She arched her eyebrows and waited.

"That's all," he sighed and ran both hands through silver hair. "Thought you should know."

"You made me drive all the way out here and that's all you had to tell me?"

Suddenly the hot point of his attention drove on her once again and this time she wished he'd shake her off. He stared at her until she could no longer bear it, and she turned her eyes away to study the polished cherrywood of his writing-blotter. "It's a big deal," he said in a voice as calm and gentle as his eyes were furious. "We missed an important opportunity. A defining moment: gone. Two years planning. I worked on it—god—eighteen hours a day for the last six months." He put his hand on a portfolio. "Cost analysis for this Kronocell project. All for nothing. What a waste."

His interest in buying Kronocell had been marginal until a few months ago, just one potential asset among others, many others. It was no big deal. He won more often than he lost. In another month he'd be on to the next thing. Or not. She doubted this was really the end. Because once he had an idea in his head it was already a reality. He would pursue it with a tenacity bordering on idiocy until he accomplished it, and for no greater reason than because he decided and nothing on earth could ever—ever—prove him wrong. He would burn a hundred bridges, destroy a thousand careers, and alienate his entire household before he would see his own will fall short.

"I understand," she said. "But I have class tomorrow. I have homework. I need to study. How much sense would it make if I flunk out because you dragged me up here over every little thing you could tell me over the phone?"

He studied her for a long moment and nodded his ascent. Nathalie smiled. She'd been his daughter long enough to learn how to handle him. "Well," she said, "I'm glad you told me. And I'm glad you made me come because I also have news."

He arched his eyebrows and waited, which she supposed was as close to genuine interest as anyone would ever get out of him. She told him about Kendra and Strange Equinoxes, pretty impressive considering her limited training and meager experience as a choreographer. Rehearsals were three nights a week and Kendra already booked a few festivals for the summer. It paid, but not much for the hours she would put in, not even enough to call it a part-time job, but she decided not to say that part.

"Great, honey," he said and smiled. "Everyone needs a hobby."

"It's not a hobby. We talked about maybe touring."

His brow knitted and his eyes like searchlights swept the contours of her face. He shook his head, slowly, and said, "Not a good idea. You won't have time. And anyway I thought you wanted to work at the Gilman foundry over the summer?"

She didn't say anything. She already knew how this conversation would end, knew before it started, but like a total raging fool she told him anyway, even though it was begging disappointment to expect him to respond any other way, and now she saw no reason to make a scene over what she'd known would happen.

"I need your help this summer," he said and still she refused to answer. Her dad might be a tyrant and a bully, but at least he was honest about what he wanted. He ruled the world with wisdom and courage. Only Nathalie betrayed. Only

Nathalie was a fraud. She was sulking, she realized, and she didn't give a damn.

"It's important."

"I know." She hated the way she sounded. Like a chastened child. Like a spineless weakling.

"But I'm glad for you. The thing you did. It's good, right?"

It was good, she told him, and she'd work at the Gilman foundry over the summer. The experience would be important and she agreed it should be the higher priority. But it was getting late and she had class in the morning. So she kissed him on the head and left. Where she would go she had no idea but she didn't want to go home, she didn't want to go to class in the morning, and she did not want to ever spend another summer in a steel foundry.

12.

Damian owned an old-fashioned answering machine because he was paranoid about who might be listening to his voicemail—he wanted to know the messages were gone when he deleted them—and he could see the red light blinking on the windowsill when he came through the door. Pavel had found something. He would be at the restaurant in Little Russia all evening.

They sat at a table in the middle of the restaurant and drank vodka martinis. Pavel wanted him to try an imported Finnish gin but Damian hated gin, he couldn't stand the shit, he would stick with Absolut. He didn't want anything to eat when the waiter came but Pavel ordered a meal. The room was small, decorated in thick velvet draperies of damasked gold and icons of orthodox saints: Our Lady of Vladimir, Alexander Nevsky, Catherine the Great Martyr, George the Dragonslayer. Music came from speakers mounted high in the corners and occasionally violins swelled and expanded enough for Damian to recognize Tchaikovsky. *Swan Lake,* if he had to guess. "A little heavy-handed," Pavel admitted. "But Russian enough and probably it assists digestion."

Pavel hated serious conversation over food, Damian knew, but was enthusiastic about American politics, as absurd and outrageous as a soap opera plot, and he gossiped about cable news giddy as a fanboy. Damian showed him a paper napkin with a note written on it in Cyrillic letters. Graffiti on the wall above a urinal he found at the café where he ate the other night with Nathalie. "It made me curious and I thought you might translate it."

"Someone's a philosopher," Pavel said, and fought off the grin reddening his pale face. "It says: *I will find what I'm looking for where I least want to look.*" The waiter cleared the plates and Pavel ordered them each a coffee. When it arrived he told Damian what he knew about the Koreans.

Kim Hyeon-gi and Noe Gun, the two men Damian met in Forest Hill, flew in from Seoul December twenty-ninth on Asiana Airlines and missed their return flight scheduled January second. They hadn't been heard from since. Gangjeon Jae-kyeon left the country on December thirtieth. Pavel didn't know where he went but his departure wasn't unusual. He was apparently quite the world traveler: Berlin, Seoul, Melbourne, São Paolo. No one Pavel talked to thought there was anything strange about the way he left. Nobody thought he seemed anxious or in a hurry, and while they couldn't say when he'd be back, they didn't have reason to think he'd be away long.

The man Gangjeon was working for when he hired Damian proved more difficult to identify, maybe impossible. There was gossip Gangjeon bought counterfeit for a Hungarian or Bulgarian or something like that. An alchemist or something. Accounts were extremely inconsistent. He made fake gold and sold it for fake dollars which he converted into real euros on the European black market. They said he spoke perfect American English with no trace of a foreign accent, but none of this could be confirmed.

A few additional wrinkles: on January third Gangjeon started making phone-calls, no one knows from where, looking for Kim and Noe. The calls went on for about two weeks but no one could tell him where they were. Around Valentine's Day strangers started asking around Little Korea for anyone who'd seen Kim or Noe. There was a woman and at least one man, maybe more. No one Pavel talked to knew who they were. No one had ever seen them before. Most thought they were probably feds.

"What do you make of this?" Damian asked.

"I see three possibilities," Pavel said, and finished his

coffee. "One: Kim and Noe acted alone. Two: they were work-ing for Gangjeon when they tried to kill you. Three: The client ordered the hit. Maybe Gangjeon knew about it and maybe he didn't. But there are problems with all three scenarios."

Pavel waved the waiter over to refill their coffees and when they were alone again he told Damian there were plenty of amateur street urchins crawling all over the east bay happy to make a simple exchange for cheap. So why did Gangjeon fly two professionals in from South Korea for four days? That's what you did with specialist jobs. Assassinations, for example. Gangjeon obviously knew something went wrong because he was looking for Kim and Noe, who no-showed for their return flight. He never contacted Damian to find out why his order didn't arrive, so maybe it did, or if not, maybe he knew why. Everyone Pavel talked to thought Gangjeon seemed calm when he left. Nothing out of the ordinary. And if he was running away or hiding he was doing a piss-poor job of it so he must still be on good terms with whoever he was working for.

"It doesn't make any sense, though," Pavel said. "You're a valuable asset with a high quality product. It wouldn't be worth a few thousand dollars to get rid of you. Gangjeon is an intelligent businessman. He has nothing to gain by losing you. Likewise his employer. Kim and Noe are the only ones who benefit."

It was the only thing that made sense. Kim and Noe got a couple like-minded thugs together with a plan to steal money from Gangjeon and Damian. They split the proceeds four ways and went on the run. They probably missed their scheduled flight because they prearranged an alternative exit strategy, one not arranged by Gangjeon and therefore less likely to be traced. The strangers asking for Kim and Noe could be feds or they could be working for Gangjeon or his employer. "But really it's hard to say for sure. None of it makes clear sense."

"I'd appreciate if you would keep asking around," Damian said. "Let me know if you hear anything."

"Of course," Pavel said. "But only if it's convenient." People tended to notice when you kept asking for information about the same thing, especially when it didn't appear to concern you. It made people curious about you, made them wonder why you were asking, the kind of attention Pavel wanted to avoid as much as possible.

Damian wanted to avoid it, too.

He picked up the check for Pavel's meal and decided to look at the icons before going home. A portrait of the virgin with child was his favorite and Pavel joined him in viewing it. "Theotokos of Vladimir," he said. "This is a miraculous picture. They say she has saved Russia from siege and rape many times over the centuries. Our mother loves all her children."

"She's beautiful."

"She's actually Byzantine. A version of Our Lady of Perpetual Help. But she's spent most her life in Russia. This one's the same way," and Pavel directed Damian's attention further down the wall. "Saint George slaying the dragon. He's the patron saint of Moscow, but he has nothing to do with Russia." He was Cappadocian, Pavel explained, a soldier in the army of the Roman Emperor Diocletian. In Liberia there was a voracious dragon living in a lake and the local Christians worshipped the dragon as the second coming of the one true god. They made blood sacrifices to it like a god and fed their children to it one by one, in the same way people have always murdered their children with the one true god.

"For the journey home," Pavel said and handed him a small styrofoam to-go box. "Vatrushka. Cheese, raisins, and applesauce in a sweet bun. Homemade," and he squeezed Damian's shoulder in parting. "It's quite delicious."

Damian stood alone in the dining-room but hardly noticed. He was concentrating on the icon, captive to an ill emotion stirring for no reason he could comprehend. The oppression of it alarmed him. The crimson background and the virgin sacrifice looking on the white charger in mid-stride and the young legionnaire, serene, dusky, haloed by a circle of gold paint illuminating his short-cropped curls. And beneath the mount's hooves, impaled on the long slash of the hero's lance, the beast curled in some unnatural combination of joints and musculature like no animal Damian had ever seen. Black, winged, reptilian, rising from the shadows beneath the horse, coiled girth wet and spreading to engulf the bottom of the frame, too gigantic to be seen all at once. It just kept going and going all the way to the end of Damian's imagination. Down and down through the chthonic layers, all the way to the light-devouring bottom, to the black hole where gods come from. The place made of fear and wonder.

◆ ◆ ◆

Crows circle the mountain peak and Phaedra drops the sling to watch them. Three crows, like black flakes on the sky, blown hither and yon in a complex geometry of their own reckoning. Good omen. The gods are happy, the wheel of fate grinds its gears, and what fell apart for so long finally becomes ascendant. With a deep breath she hoists the sling onto her back and braces against the weight. It is late March and soggy. Wet kindling would produce too much smoke and harm the work so she must gather deeper in the forest where thicker branches protect underbrush from rain. Descending the ridge, she sees far below the muddy road gouged by wagon wheels and lined with men on tall spikes. Saracens. The Prince Lord Impaler has returned from captivity. In a few weeks it will be Easter Sunday, when the boyars will be sentenced to slavery and death in the construction of the dragon's palace on an island in a lake. Could it be that time already? Some centuries seem to fly away from her and others crawl like sloths. A thousand years ago they fled the burning of the great library to wander among the Persians. In less than two-hundred years the Winter King shall rule at Heidelberg, and Phaedra does not look forward to making that journey again.

She enters the clearing and knows the man has still not returned. What's that goat got up to? she wonders. He's usually standing in the yard, tapping his foot, wanting to know what took so long. Phaedra drops the sling in front of the woodpile and lays the branches out to dry in the sun. The woodpile is stacked in a spectrum, thin sticks growing into thick logs from left to right, breast high and the entire length of one flagstone wall of the chapel. She bundles dry wood into fagots and carries them inside.

The tower furnace stands next to the hearth. Slow Henry. Pink bricks of kiln-fired river mud. On the left side of its chest an accordion-bellows and on its back a swan's throat connects it to a stove-pipe vented to the chimney. Opposite the bellows a small spyglass for observation. A trap door at the base for loading the fire-box beneath a hermetically sealed hatch wherein the crucible suffers bad dreams.

The chapel has no windows and the interior pitch black. Phaedra's mind probes the crucible, urging it to wake, to reach out for her. Withheld breath waits for the silent plea like a baby's mewl, but nothing stirs. After lighting oil lamps, she squints through the spyglass to behold a harsh miasma, glowing and flowing red and orange around the silhouette of a cup. The crucible. The graphite uterus. Within it the seed remains lifeless and dark. The temperature stings her eyes but is still not high enough to make the ore molten. She considers adding more fagots to the fire-box. Better not. If the chamber doesn't get hot enough the ore will never flow, but if it gets too hot the stone could ruin before it has a chance to grow. Temperance is needed. For now. She flinches at the creaking door. The man enters, shrugging water-bladders off his coat shoulders.

"Where have you been?" she asks.

"Fetching water. As you see me."

"The brook? Nowhere else? You should have returned before now."

Albert arches his brow and stares. "Where would you have me be? Tell me and I will go there."

"Don't be cross—you'll make us start all over."

"It won't be my doing alone."

The water bladders lay sweating before the threshold and Phaedra hangs them from a nail in the rafters while Albert crouches at the athanor and inspects the fire-box. Poimandres stands up on the table where he's been sleeping, and stretches. He leaps to the floor and scratches on the door and Phaedra lets him out.

"Have you found them yet?"

Albert freezes on his haunches and cocks his head as though listening to the rafters. His eyes reticulate in the gloom, diamond pupils dilating in the lamplight. "No," he says and turns back to the pyramid of sticks and feeds them to the furnace. "Have you?"

Phaedra shakes her head. Albert can't see her but he knows the answer. No, she hasn't discovered any of them, not yet, and she searched several times. All day gathering wood she thought about them, looking for them, but she couldn't feel a thing.

"Patience," Albert says. "It's early. They'll come—I saw the crows. They're coming."

"Yes, and the Voivode has returned. I could see the pikes down by the road."

"It won't be long now," Albert says. "Shall we turn our thoughts to supper?"

"We'll prolong our fast another fortnight. Lend them our strength until they find their own."

"As you wish," Albert says.

It's getting dark outside. Phaedra shivers. Eager for the dreamers to awaken, but she dreads it too. The blackening shall be long and the crucible full of terrors.

CALCINATION

"This is our Fire always equally burning in one measure within the Glass, and not without: This is our Dung-hill, our Horse-belly, working and producing many Wonders in the most secret Work of Nature: It is also the Examiner of all Bodies dissolved, and not dissolved; a Fire hot and moist, most sharp, a Water-carrying Fire in its Belly; otherwise it could not have power to dissolve Bodies into their first Matter: This is our Mercury, our Sol, our Luna, which we use in our Secret Work. Take the Faeces left in the bottom, as soon as they are cold; for they are our Crowes-Bill, far blacker than Pitch, which thou mayest set on fire, by putting a kindled Coal into it; so as they shall be calcined of their own accord into a most Yellow Earth: But this Calcination sufficeth not for its perfect cleansing; put it therefore into a Reverberatory, with a moderate heat, for eight days, and so many Nights following, increasing the heat and flame, till it be white as Snow; they may also be calcined in a Potters' Furnace, being meanly hot."

—LANCELOT COLSON, PHILOSOPHIA MATURATAE, 1668.

W hen Nathalie called and asked if she could come over, there was a long pause, and she thought Damian might not have heard. He'd probably been asleep when she called. She was about to apologize and hang up, or maybe repeat herself, she wasn't quite sure which, when he said, "Okay." She looked at the clock on the bedside table. It was nearly one in the morning. "I'm not doing anything interesting," he said and she promised that was fine, she just didn't feel like being at home.

When she arrived he cleared her space on his only chair, a pea-green recliner someone left on the sidewalk beneath his window, and offered her a drink. While he made the drinks she did a little looking around. Obviously, he hadn't managed a girlfriend recently. The bed was a twin, unmade and uninviting, probably third or fourth hand. All the furniture, what little he owned, was probably the cheapest he could find at the cheapest thrift store he could find. In fact, she was surprised at how cluttered the space was considering how little he owned. It felt like those motel-rooms you rent by the hour. No nick-knacks, no little comforts to give a space your personality. Make a dump a home. No pictures of family or friends, nothing like that. Suggested transience. A temporary stop on the way to elsewhere. Wherever Damian's home was, this wasn't it—he was hunkering down for a while, a short while, she thought, before moving on.

He brought them each a coffee cup of whiskey and she asked for the grand tour. "It's a shitty studio apartment," he said. "This is the room." He pointed at the counter next to the sink where a hotplate and mini-fridge sat. "Kitchen." He pointed again, "Bathroom. Closet. That door you're familiar with," and he indicated the front entrance. She forced a smile and wondered why the hell she'd called him. Of all people. At one in the morning. Probably not such a good idea, but she refused to worry about it now because it was already done.

She sat in the chair and ignored the way it leaned heavily to one side when you put weight in it, and Damian sat on the unmade bed. "I caught you in the middle of something." Nathalie could feel how tight her face was when she smiled, how fake she must seem to him.

He'd been folding laundry when she called. He wore the same clothes as last time she saw him, three days ago. A rumpled wad of clothes on top of the unmade bed and a laundry basket half-full of folded clothes on the floor.

He kicked the basket. "The clean clothes got wrinkly in the basket 'cause I left them sitting there for over a week." He was trying to save the conversation, and she could see he felt bad for making her uncomfortable. "I hate doing laundry because I don't have a car and the nearest laundromat is over two blocks away, which makes the whole project a pain in the ass," he said. "But I also don't own an iron, which makes it a little easier."

She laughed and he apologized, he didn't mean to be an asshole, but it was a dangerous neighborhood, especially at night, and a filthy apartment, and he didn't want her to see the squalor he lived in. Nathalie apologized for calling so late, she just didn't want to be at home, and he asked how many people she called before risking a drive to Bayview in the middle of the night. "Six," she admitted, "but never fear. I took a taxi." They tipped their chipped cups to each other and drank and Nathalie choked on the liquor.

"Not a big whiskey drinker, I guess," Damian said and she agreed, still coughing. He fetched her a can of tonic water to dilute the taste and told her the best antidote was to drink more until it tasted good. He asked if she'd dreamt of him since they last spoke.

"No," she said. "Which reminds me. I talked to the manuscript expert about the invitations." She told him what she'd learned from Dr. Sundstrom and that she'd submitted the wedding invitations to a lab specializing in manuscript authentication. He refreshed their drinks and asked what she was doing out so late on a school night. She told him about her dad's failed buy-out and his reaction to her being recruited by a dance company.

"But it's good news anyway," Damian said. "You'll still do it, right?"

"Do you think I should?"

"Sure. If my opinion matters. I vote for dancing and to hell with a business degree from fucking Berkeley."

"Fuck it," she said and giggled.

"Your dad loves you. So he's mad about it, but he'll get over it."

"You don't know my dad. What you're saying sounds, you

know, *sane,* but trust me. He wouldn't take it as well as you think. And I'm not saying that just because I'm his daughter and don't want to disappoint him. If you knew him, you'd agree with me."

"It wouldn't change my vote."

She thought about this for a few seconds. "I couldn't. I'm just torturing myself. I keep thinking, like you said, maybe I should just say fuck it and he can deal with it, but I already know I'll end up working in a goddamn foundry over the summer."

"Then you're a coward," Damian said and saluted her with his cup of whiskey.

"Maybe. Or maybe you make sacrifices for the ones you love."

"The ones who love you don't expect you to sacrifice yourself on their behalf."

What he said put heat in her throat and a sour feeling in her belly. Her dad wasn't using her like that, was he? He was belligerent and narrow-minded, but she'd always considered his intentions good. The more she thought about it the more it grew and moved upwards until she could feel something—call it cowardice—boiling deep in her sinuses, and she could feel her face, how still it was, how placid. The insult stung, but the possibility of its truth pissed her off. Damian could see it, she could tell, miscalculation clicking behind his eyes. He'd pushed her in a way she could not be pushed, and regretted it. She let him look. She wanted him to watch her worry turn to hurt and then to frosted anger.

"You mean I should tell him to fuck off," she said coolly. "Would you tell your dad to fuck off?" And a chilling comprehension of him. "You did, didn't you. Tell your dad to fuck off. That's why you're so evasive about your parents."

"I'm not being evasive," he said but there was terror in his eyes. He wanted to hide, she could see, he wanted to run away, wanted her to go away. She felt sorry for him but her curiosity was more powerful by far than her compassion.

"Then tell me about your dad."

He was preparing to stonewall her, but then, inexplicably, he stopped. He relaxed a little bit. Not much. But something sharp in him softened like if she touched his skin it might not cut her now, like he was fortified for siege, and for no reason she could understand, decided what the hell, fuck it. "My dad's an alcoholic," he said. "He used to beat my mom. As far as I'm concerned he died when I was fifteen. But he wasn't an asshole. If it's possible for those things to go together. He was nice, probably too nice. And he loved my mom and me more than anything. In the end I think it destroyed him. So I feel guilty for hating him."

"And your mom?"

"Dead. I was seventeen." He shrugged and smiled. "She was beautiful. And vain. Her vanity might be what drove my dad off the deep end. Trying to provide for her, give her all the luxurious things she deserved. But she was really smart, too, and brave. So strong and brave in spite of everything, but not very confident in herself, you know. Always thought she needed a dude around. Even though she did fine for the two of us."

"That's the most you've ever said to me." Nathalie felt suddenly ashamed for forcing these confessions. That's what it felt like to her: confession. And she was startled by how what he said affected her, like she forced him to show her things she had no right to see.

He smiled and blew air out his nose and shook his cup to show her it was empty. "Well, I'm getting sleepy."

There was no way Nathalie could drive right now and he told her she could stay if she wanted. She couldn't possibly impose, and he told her to suit herself. "Where would I sleep?" she wondered, and waited for him to offer the bed, but all he said was she could crash in the chair. She looked at him, a little shocked and a little disappointed. It dawned on her she was probably drunk.

"Sorry," he said. "Did you want to take the bed?"

But now there was no way in hell she was going to sleep

in his rancid bed. "It's your bed," she said and asked if he at least had a t-shirt she could sleep in. Preferably clean. He found her a shirt and she changed in the bathroom quickly, stripping down in three brisk motions and redressing in one. She peed and washed her hands and folded her clothes, a little too neatly for the occasion, before emerging from the bathroom. She sat her clothes on the floor next to the armchair and asked if Damian had an extra blanket she could use.

He pulled the best one out of the covers twisted on the bed. "Sorry there's nothing fresh. I don't keep extra stuff around."

She was awfully drunk. She thanked him for the blanket and he turned out the lights and got into bed. A few minutes later she asked if he was really going to sleep in his clothes.

"Yes," he said.

Nathalie couldn't let it go. She tried, but her head was spinning and she couldn't feel the chair she was lying in, like she was floating, or falling, because suddenly she turned her head from one side to the other and it slammed into the wooden frame beneath the deflated cushion of the armrest, and the only thought she was able to fix on was Damian sleeping in the same clothes he'd been wearing for three days. She remembered her car was in the parking garage of her condo—she didn't need to drive home, she could just call a cab, but the task seemed impossible. She thought of all the things she would have to do, step by step: getting up and finding the light and fishing out her phone, finding the number for the taxi service, talking to the dispatcher, for hell's sake, and waiting for the driver. Maybe the most difficult thing anyone had ever done.

"Damian," she said. "Damian, you goofy bastard. Are you asleep?"

She strained to hear, through the dark room, through the spinning in her head. A moment passed. Damian said, "It's been like twenty seconds."

"Damian. I'm sorry, but it's disgusting to sleep in your clothes. Damian? Damian?"

He didn't answer. He must've fallen asleep. But a minute

later she could hear him grudgingly kick his shoes off the bed.

In the middle of the night Damian woke to the feeling that he and Nathalie were not alone in the room. Someone was watching. After his eyes adjusted to the darkness he propped himself up in bed to watch her sleep slanted akimbo in the pea-green chair. He was freezing but it was because the room was too hot and his whole body was covered in a thin glaze of sweat. He got up to turn the space heaters down and walked around the apartment to make sure nothing had been disturbed, inspecting the windows and the door. After returning to bed he heard a third breath in the room. The anxious thud of his own heart, swish of Nathalie breathing, and beneath that, another breathing, deeper in tone, but quieter. He held his breath and listened until he was convinced he'd made it up. Yet the feeling persisted: someone else was in the room. Paranoid, he thought, it's getting worse. For a while he watched Nathalie sleep, waiting for something to happen that never happened. He could hear the calm rhythm of her breathing and he could see her eyelids flutter and he wondered if she was dreaming about him.

He felt sorry for her. Her beauty and self-confidence, expensive clothes and privileged childhood, affluence and Berkeley education, none of these things could keep her from being the slave of fear, just as doomed as he was to a life she did not want. He had no idea why it was so hard for her to defy her dad, but he didn't doubt the thought terrified her. Fear was plain in her eyes when she considered the possibility. Out of nowhere he felt an overwhelming impulse to protect her. For no reason. The feeling was intimate and urgent, and he knew she was in danger, and she was his responsibility, and if he failed her it would mean devastation greater than any he'd so far suffered. He didn't have any family and he didn't have any friends. No one loved him and there was no one alive he loved. Since losing his step-father, Nathalie was already the closest thing he had to family. He knew how desperate this sounded and how pathetic and for the first time he felt the severity of his loneliness. He fell back to sleep pitying himself and angry for it.

14.

When he woke in the morning Nathalie was already gone. While brushing his teeth he decided to shave, chopping the black lawn with an electric beard trimmer and scraping it smooth with a disposable razor. He ate granola bars on his way out the door and took an early bus to the warehouse. He wanted to be there before sunrise because he must make a decision about whether or not it was safe to enter. It was April and if he was going to have twenty-five-thousand dollars ready for Pavel in three weeks, he needed to get to work. He still thought the wedding invitations were some kind of calling-cards though he had no idea who they were from. He long ago dismissed any suspicion of Nathalie—if she was spying on him, she did a bad job of it. Kim and Noe made the most sense, but their disappearance made him nervous—if they'd been arrested it was likely the Secret Service were aware of him. Someone, he felt sure, was keeping an eye on him. If it was federal agents this is how it would go down: the warehouse kept under regular surveillance, raided the moment someone put a key in the lock to enter the unit.

Damian had already staked out his printing hole four times since receiving his invitation to the wedding, a couple hours each time, once with binoculars. But he always arrived later in the day, when cars filled the parking-lot and surrounding streets. Several vehicles always seemed to be there, but it didn't mean anything. They could belong to people who worked nearby, tenants who leased the other warehouses. He wanted to get there as early as possible, before the traffic of the day. If he could see everyone who came as they arrived it would give him the best chance to decide whether or not his printing hole was safe.

By noon he felt little better. It was impossible to keep track of everyone who parked in the lot or on the street, but he thought he did a decent job knowing where people went after parking their cars and how long they took to return. He knew how long they lingered before driving away, who loitered on the street, where they went when they finally left. Every couple hours he walked around the block, checking cars, and crossed the parking-lot the same way. No one seemed to be sitting there. No one seemed to be watching the cinderblock row that hid his printing hole. At one point he risked walking down the sidewalk and stopping in front of his unit, turning his back on it, to see what could be seen. If anyone was watching he'd be able to spot them from this vantage point.

But if anyone watched he couldn't tell. Nothing happened. The only one who came and did not leave was Damian. He was the only one loitering and the only one watching the warehouse. It could all be over if he just put the key in the lock and turned it. Moment of truth. Hours passed and he thought about it a lot. But, no, he still wasn't desperate enough. It was better to go on not knowing than to know he was fucked.

When he checked the time again it was nearly three o'clock and he decided to call it off. His feet and knees were sore from standing all day and an ache grew in his back. He was hungry. At home he put four frozen burritos on a plate and listened to the answering machine while they microwaved. The Bayview Branch Library called to say the books he requested were in, he could pick them up any time before five o'clock. That was on Third Street and he calculated how long it would take to get there.

The laundry still laid where he'd left it when Nathalie showed up the night before, wrinkly and half folded in the middle of the threadbare carpet. Pale yellow nicotine scars streaked the walls and big water spots swirled in the low ceiling punctuated by the open sore of the light fixture, bulbless, uncovered, because the bulbs popped every time he changed them. Thus the mismatched standing lamps in two corners. He'd given up removing the stains. Every time he scrubbed them clean, they came back a few days later. It humiliated him for Nathalie to see any of this.

She'd worn a black jacket fragrant of animal leather, shiny buckles matching those of her knee-high boots, the toes as pointed as the high heels. Lipstick red enough to draw attention to her mouth but not enough to look calculated, hair straightened and pulled back in a ponytail to show off her beautiful throat, her ears, their silver hoops, which dangled above her shoulders and matched the buckles. It was all smart and tasteful, and as far as Damian was concerned, a great big waste of cash. Nothing else could've looked more out of place in his apartment than she did, and he knew everything ugly about the picture came from him.

The phone rang several times before she answered. He knew from the hesitation in her voice when she said hi she didn't want to talk to him, but the temptation to send his call to voicemail wasn't strong enough to stop her. She still gave him the benefit of the doubt and he felt damn lucky for it.

"You left before I could say anything this morning," he said. "I just wanted to make sure everything was okay."

A long pause. "I'm fine."

"I owe you an apology for the way I acted. You're not a coward—I was just embarrassed. It's stupid."

"I shouldn't have made you tell me those things," she said. "About your family."

"I'm glad I told you."

Neither of them had much more to say and the call ended. He ate the burritos standing in front of the microwave with a bottle of sriracha sauce in the other hand, and debated leaving the books until morning. There was nothing on TV and after flipping through the channels a few times, he turned it off and browsed the pages of a furniture catalogue he'd got with the rest of his junk mail, before deciding to go to the library.

He arrived with ten minutes to spare but hadn't realized how many books were waiting for him, thirty-three, or how big some would be. He brought bags to carry them but nothing like enough, and the librarian allowed him to use the phone to call for help. Nathalie found him forty minutes later standing on the sidewalk in a nest of books. "Traffic sucks. Sorry it took so long," she said. "Why do you need all these?"

"Research."

They loaded the books into her car and took them to her place. He was looking for the wedding invitations, he told her on the drive, the translation was useful and the chemical analysis would be important but neither of those things were likely to lead to who sent the invitations. Or why they were sent. He was sick of waiting for experts to figure it out. He thought he would do a little dense reading in his free time, but seeing the books, he realized they would take the rest of his life to work through alone. He needed Nathalie's help. "I thought you might know how to be organized about it," he said. "The smartest way to do it."

They stacked the books in the living room and Nathalie offered him coffee. "I'm in for a late night," she said and pointed at the table strewn with textbooks, post-it notes, index cards, a rainbow of highlighters.

"This is the organization I was hoping for," Damian said. They took coffee on the couch, side by side, and he asked about her classes. She answered his questions without much interest and when the conversation lagged she asked if he'd gone to college. "I thought about it. My step-dad wanted me to go. My mom would've wanted me to go. I guess making money was more important to me. I didn't think school would solve that."

"You think anything that doesn't make money isn't worth knowing?"

"No, I believe in those things," Damian said and frowned. The question cut him a little. "But I don't believe in paying for them. That's why I got a library card," and he pointed his coffee cup at the stacks of books on the floor.

At 7:30 she insisted on getting back to her homework. She said Damian should come the next day and they'd start organizing the books. Friday they could start working through them in earnest. Outside, springtime ruled the dark and it was like the bizarre winter never happened: sixty degrees, music of birds, scent of coming rain, fog knee-high and feathery. A nourishing quality in the night air which Damian rubbed like ointment into his barren face. He unzipped his jacket and walked to the bus stop with his hands in his pockets. It occurred to him what he was feeling was happiness and he had not been happy in a long time.

By the time the bus dropped him in Bayview the weather took a cold turn, global warming, melting icecaps or whatever. Winter evenings lasting into springtime. The news showed pictures of a tagged yearling fawn jamming traffic on the Golden Gate Bridge, driven by late snow to lower elevations in search of food. Damian made grilled cheese sandwiches on the hotplate, wasted a minute surfing TV channels, finished folding his laundry, and passed the rest of the evening with a book.

15.

It rained that night. The temperature dropped back into the thirties and hardly rose the next day. The first time on record such an extreme temperature fall occurred so late in the season. Nathalie didn't expected the cold to last all day and turned the heat off when she left for school. By the time she got home from work the condo was freezing and she left her heavy coat on to wait for it to warm up. She turned the news on TV and listened while she started going through Damian's books to a meteorologist explaining how the cold front attacked the west coast from the Bay Area up into Canada. It would pass quickly and temperatures should return to normal in the next few days. A research scientist explained the effects of climate change, how around the globe weather patterns were getting harder to predict and we should expect more bouts of strange weather in the future. A climate change denier offered a rebuttal.

Nathalie was skeptical of what could be learned from these books. Reading them all would take forever and probably end up a big waste of time. No way would she and Damian, a couple amateurs, find things in a handful of dusty old books a scholar like Dr. Sundstrom didn't already know. What was Nathalie looking for? She could be staring at the answer and not recognize the question. But she agreed with Damian about one thing: she was sick of doing nothing—this at least felt like action. And she wanted to learn about the invitations, where they came from and what they meant. These books might at least offer clues.

They ranged in size from ratty trade-paperbacks to oversized coffee-table tomes, all musty with a downy layer of dust along the top edge. Some must've been thirty years old, pages yellowed and curling with faded ink and disintegrating jackets. Others looked like they'd never been opened before, pristine no matter their age—certainly never read. And who would read them? High school students writing research papers, she supposed.

It seemed awful that a book—any book—should sit on a library shelf for decades, available free of charge to everyone, and never be read. It gave her a forgotten feeling, a sense of nonexistence. Who was it, she wondered, these books were intended for? Who ought to read them and never read them? Whose life might've been better if only they had? Probably no ones. These were not that sort of books. Books like these, she thought, weren't written to be read—they were written so the author could get tenured at some university and that was their only real purpose.

Her first task was to get a sense of the subject matter. She checked the author and title of each volume, making a list in a spiral-bound notebook, and glanced through the tables of contents to get an idea what they were about. Technical manuals on how to evaluate old books and manuscripts, a couple on the history of print culture, surveys on the history of marriage, and several on European cultural history seemed to contain pertinent chapters. She tabbed these with sticky notes for easy access. A feminist study of gender and marriage rituals in early-modern Europe intrigued her. Finally, a thick stack of art books. The coffee-table books belonged to this category. Medieval and early modern art, historical surveys of woodcuts, surveys of the human body in European art.

They were all logged and organized into piles by subject when Damian showed up. "Don't take your coat off," she told him and explained why it was so cold. She asked if he was hungry but he'd eaten an omelet before coming over. He sat across from her on the floor with piles of books between them and she caught him up on her work so far.

"Sounds good to me," he said. "What's the next step?"

"I think we should cross reference the indexes. Maybe it'll save time." They would each take a pile and start working through the topical indexes in the back, establishing key terms of interest and tabbing the appropriate passages. "Take notes on these," she said, and threw him a pen and a handful of index cards. "You're looking for things that connect to another pile. A book on marriage might have information on period print technology that isn't in the print books or the technical books. Stuff like that. It'll give us an idea how it all fits together."

If it fits together, she thought. She chose the feminist study to start with and located the index. They worked in friendly silence for several minutes before Damian took off his coat and laid it on the floor next to him. Nathalie was warmer, too, and followed his example. He worked on one of the histories of print culture, which looked brand new though it was catalogued twenty years ago, and she told him she felt sad for books no one read.

"We're reading them," he pointed out, and she knew that but it wasn't the same as loving a book, reading it for pleasure in your spare time. Who would read these books that way? "Me," Damian said and laughed. "I'm doing it right now."

"You really are one mystery after another, Damian Lancaster."

"I know, it's fucked up. I hate fun."

Nathalie laughed. She was in a good mood and it made the reading go better. She was to the M's already with a decent stack of index cards to show for it when she felt wet against her belly and realized she was sweating. "It's getting hot in here," she announced and went into the hall to turn the thermostat down from seventy to sixty-five degrees. She was filling out her next index card when Damian asked if she'd made a decision about Strange Equinoxes. She ignored him but it couldn't heal her broken concentration. "I don't want to talk about it."

She felt him staring at her. When she looked up, he said, "It would be a great tragedy if you quit dancing. A terrible tragedy." His eyes were fixed hard on her but his expression was placid, like she was the focal point of a meditation. It felt the same as when her dad looked at her. Opened up like that. "There's plenty of wretched shit in the world. Plenty of people making money. It could use more dancers." Heat charged through her. They both wore long-sleeved shirts and sweat darkened Damian's chest. The temperature hadn't dropped—if anything, it was getting hotter. "If you want to work for your dad, do it. If you want to be a dancer, there's nothing else on earth you should be doing," he said, "and I admire your courage. I hope that's clear between us. That I admire you."

"I like the way you talk to me," she whispered. He'd hit a nerve inside her and the heat was getting unbearable and if she spoke any louder it might come on a sob. "You always say what you're thinking like that, like you're not afraid of anything."

He scoffed and looked away, tried to recover, but couldn't bring his gaze to meet her. It was his turn to be shaken. "I'm afraid of everything," he said. "God, I'm roasting," and he pulled his turtle-neck over his shoulders. The plain white t-shirt he wore underneath was completely drenched and clung, translucent, to his navel. Nathalie went into the hall again and turned the thermostat down to fifty degrees. The digital thermometer on the unit said the current temperature was eighty-six. She tapped on it a couple times, hoping she might knock loose whatever was stuck. A few months ago her dad sent a repairman to tinker with it and she wondered if he'd broken whatever was causing the problem.

"I think there's something wrong with it," she told Damian. He stood in the living room fanning his body with the hem of his shirt. A slick line of black hairs dove from his belly-button into his cargo pants. Thick stripes darkened the sides of Nathalie's sweater. Maybe they could work outside, but no, they walked onto the patio and knew immediately. It felt wonderful, but only because she was so hot. The breeze upset the books and it couldn't be forty degrees outside. After a minute she was already shivering. They went back into the condo and it was like walking into a furnace.

She left the patio door wide open and asked Damian to help open the windows. Maybe they could cool it down that way. She called the repairman but they were swamped, he said. He would come as soon as he could, but it would be pretty late. Walking down the hall she noticed the thermometer. Eighty-eight degrees. "It's okay if you take your shirt off," she told Damian. She took her own shirt off and used it to wipe down the tops of her breasts, the shallow dish of salt water in the bottom of her sports bra. Damian thought they should try again another day, but she wasn't ready to quit. He could go home if he wanted but she would keep working. She found mason jars in a cupboard and filled them with ice and mineral water. They drained them and refilled them and drank half again standing in front of the open refrigerator.

Shirtless, mason jars full of ice water, they returned to the living room floor. The reading went much slower this time. Pulsating heat made it impossible to think. Nathalie felt baked. She caught herself staring into the middle space, not thinking anything. She studied the pale wood of Damian's bare flesh, the broad line of his shoulders, musculature slender but hard, the apostrophe of his spine curled over his lap as he read.

Sweat dripped from her hair onto her clavicle and brought her back. "Why won't you tell me what you do for work?"

He looked up and frowned, as if he'd forgotten where he was, and shook his head. "Not today," he said. "Maybe another time."

"Is that what you're afraid of?"

He ran a hand through his soaking hair and wiped it on his pants. "Yeah. I'm afraid to tell you."

"But why?"

The glaze came over him, a plastic look she was used to seeing by now, the signal he was shutting down, closing her out whenever she brought up things he didn't want to talk about. But this time he shook it off and sighed. "Because it's illegal."

She let that sink in for a long second and nodded. "I knew it. Are you a drug dealer?"

"No."

"It doesn't matter to me, so you know. I already figured you were probably a drug dealer and decided if you were it wouldn't make a difference."

"I need more water," he said, and got up. Opening the patio door and windows made a difference for a while, but now the heat was overpowering. The letters of Nathalie's book smudged where she touched them, margins embossed with her grimy half-fingerprints. Sweat ran freely into her eyes. She ran upstairs to her bedroom, stripped naked, and looked at herself in the twin mirrors of the sliding closet doors. She looked like a clown. Makeup was smeared all over her face, more lipstick on her chin than her mouth. Mascara gauged her eyes and ran down her cheeks like black rain. Sweat curled her hair which stuck out every direction in a frizzy mess. She got a towel from the clothes hamper and wiped her armpits, crotch, thighs. She put on a thin summer dress with spaghetti straps and ran down the hall to the bathroom for makeup remover, cleaned her face, pulled all the hair off her neck, and wound it on top of her head in a black tie. She felt disgusting—already fresh perspiration made the dress stick to her breasts. The dark buttons of her nipples showed through the fabric but she was too thirsty to care. When she came back downstairs the indoor temperature reached ninety-one degrees.

She found Damian in the kitchen. He'd loosened his belt and was shaking the top of his pants around, she guessed to move air through the dense canvas. "Go ahead and take them off," she said. "I won't mind."

Damian dropped his pants in a puddle on the kitchen floor. He wore plaid boxer shorts with a little fastener over the fly. When she looked up his eyebrows were arched. "What?" she said. "I can ogle just as well as you."

"You still want to do this?" he asked.

She crossed her arms over her breasts and looked at the

books. "What if we put this aside for now and look through the art books? We might find the figure on the invitations."

They refilled their waters and spread the coffee-table books out on the floor. This was much easier than reading in the heat—she could gather the focus required to look at pictures. A few minutes later Damian made the first discovery. A glossy page of six black and white engravings. In the upper right corner a figure with two heads, nude but for a loincloth, standing on the stylized face of a crescent moon, arms extended to either side. It held in one hand a large bird and in the other a chalice sprouting three snakes. Next to it stood a tree with a smiling face at the end of each branch, twelve in all, and one radiating rays on top. A gentle mountain slope crossed the background, populated by a few desolate looking shrubs. Damian read the note under the image. "Balthazar Schwan, *Philosophia reformata,* Frankfurt, 1622. Hermaphrodite with tree of sun and moon. Emblem 10 of 20 (second series, after *Rosarium philosophorum*)."

Nathalie took the book from him and checked the index but there was no other reference to *Rosarium philosophorum.* She checked her own book, but no luck. On the fourth try she found it in a collection of woodcuts and flipped to the page. "Look at that," she said and sat the book down in front of Damian. "What do you think?"

"They're not the same as ours," he said, "but they got to be related."

Nathalie leaned forward on her hands and knees so they could study the picture together. *Rosary of the Philosophers.* Emblem 10 of a series of 20 woodcuts. The print was less detailed than the Schwan, more primitive, but the imagery was similar. In this one the hermaphrodite wore wings, stood on the face of the crescent moon, to its left a tree sprouting thirteen moon flowers. No sunrays this time. In its left hand a coiled serpent, three snakes rising from a cup in its right hand. A bird—a crow, according to the description—stood on the ground to the figure's right. *De alchemia opuscula complura veterum philosophorum...* Frankfurt, 1550. MS Ferguson 210. She didn't know what everything in the citation meant but it wouldn't be hard to find out.

Then she glanced past the page's edge and saw Damian's erection pressing against the front of his shorts. The fastener kept anything from getting out, but sitting cross-legged like he was, it didn't hide much. Through the opening she could see the tender muscle lit up by a flash of fine blue veins. She looked up and knew she wasn't caught: her dress fell open when she leaned forward to examine the book and gifted Damian a perfect view of her breasts. She sat back on her calves and smiled at him. He blushed and looked away but she kept grinning like an idiot. She tried to stop but the corners of her mouth fought harder to widen.

For a second they looked at each other. Nathalie thought, it's not the biggest mistake I'll ever make. She strummed his erection between two fingers and it sprang up again. She told him to open it. He obeyed. She leaned into his crotch and kissed it on the head and sat up again. They looked at each other, a little shocked. Damian leaned over the book and she raised her face to his and he put his sweaty palms on her sticky shoulders and she opened her mouth, only a little, and he kissed her. He tasted sulfuric, greasy with a hint of old eggs, the omelet he ate before coming over, but she didn't care. She kissed him harder, running hands up his neck, grabbing his hair softly against the back of his head, pulling his mouth to hers.

"Did you see that coming?"

"Yep," she said, kissing him along the collarbone. "And now I want you to pick me up and throw me on the bed and ravage me. But first let's brush our teeth."

They showered with water just warm enough to rinse the copious soap they coated each other in. She had only the one toothbrush and insisted they both use it. His mouth wouldn't get as clean if he rubbed on toothpaste with a finger and it didn't make sense to want his dick in her body if her toothbrush in his mouth was gross. They took turns, and while he brushed his teeth she chewed his earlobe and whispered in graphic detail things she hoped he would do to her, and in what order, and also things she wanted to do to him.

When their mouths were clean, she locked her hands behind his neck and jumped into his arms and wrapped her thighs around his hips. "Slowly at first," she said as he carried her down the hall. "Really take your time. But then much, much faster. I'll tell you when." They were sweaty again by the time they reached the bedroom and their naked skin glistened in the wall-sized mirrors of the closet doors. But the wind blew through the open windows and a delicious cross breeze eddied the surface of her bed.

Later, they lay on top of lavender sheets, her back curled against his chest, not talking. Her head rested on his bicep and she held his hand in both of hers and kissed each knuckle while his other hand stroked her pubic hair. They watched out the picture window patterns of sunlight and shadow creep over neighboring buildings. Almost dusk. They couldn't see the sun but they could see the effects of its motion through the sky mapped onto the wall opposite the window.

"You sure had a lot of it," Nathalie said and rubbed it into her skin like lotion. She wanted him all over her, his smell and his body and everything.

"I want to do something for you," Damian whispered into her hair. "To prove I'm worthy."

"You're worthy," Nathalie promised, but he seemed less convinced.

"Give me an errand or whatever. A test. I want to prove it to you."

But she insisted he didn't need to prove anything to her or anyone else. He was worthy because she said he was, not because of anything he might do or not do. Her body and her love were hers to give, freely, to whomever she chose, for no reason but that it gave her joy to give them. It was impossible for him to earn love. She would either give it or not, and there was nothing he or anyone could do about it. "I'm not that kind of girl," she said. "I can't be earned. No matter what."

They made love again and drowsed for the rest of the evening. Around 11:30 the repairman woke them and they scrambled to dress and let him in. They were beyond starvation and ate pears, blood oranges, whole avocados, plain wheat tortillas. When the repairman left they made love on the kitchen floor.

The next morning Nathalie let Damian sleep while she made breakfast. She would have to get a morning-after pill. Maybe make an appointment to get back on birth control. Or would this not turn out to be a regular thing? Rosa had a theory you were officially lovers after the third time you had sex, so they should be lovers. She'd know when Damian woke up, she decided. How he acted would tell her. More importantly, she was hungry. She started the coffee and put bread in the toaster. But when she cracked the first egg on the edge of the frying pan and split it open, what came out was black. It was the consistency of an egg and scentless and it sizzled like an egg on the teflon surface, but the runny part was like dirty motor oil and the yolk as black and thick as tar.

Thirteen hours later she started her period.

On clear nights the disc of the Milky Way soars like a dragon above the treetops. The cosmos wracked upon the breaking wheel forever turning. From earth the rest of the galaxy blurs and bleeds together on the sky like a pale river made of starlight. Titans roam. The wheel turns. Albert gazes into the center and sees his fate, the brooding end-time, and the world-eating monstrosity that slumbers there.

16.

Whoever was responsible for the invitations, it wasn't the Koreans. Pavel called to tell Damian that a couple weeks after missing their return flight to Seoul, Kim Hyeon-gi and Noe Gun were arrested in a motel-room outside Los Angeles. Scared stupid over what they'd done and in a panic over what to do next, as relieved to get caught as they were terrified of it. They'd been looking for a mule to smuggle them and the money over the Mexican border and weren't too discrete about it. Pavel knew someone at the State Department who said the arresting officers found more than sixty-thousand dollars, cash, in the motel room. It was taken into evidence and inspected. Twenty-thousand was phony. The rest came back bona fide U.S. currency.

"No, that's backwards," Damian said. "Fifty-thousand dollars was counterfeit. Twenty-thousand was real."

Brief silence while Pavel checked his notes. "Maybe I wrote it down wrong," he said. Thankfully, the Koreans took credit for the counterfeit, so there was a chance the Secret Service wasn't turned on. Kim, Noe, and their two accomplices were held for several weeks by Immigration and extradited at the end of February.

Still no word on Gangjeon. Pavel figured he left the country on legitimate business, heard the news about his couriers, and decided to lay low offshore until he knew if he would be a person of interest. Probably, he wasn't—the State Department didn't know him, at any rate. It looked like Kim and Noe half-cocked a scheme on the fly, went on a spending spree, and lost their nerve. "Fucking poseurs," Pavel said and signed off.

Of course it couldn't be that easy. Kim and Noe lifted fifty-thousand dollars of Damian's money and twenty-thousand of Gangjeon's. They were brought in with sixty-thousand dollars, most of it legit, so what happened to thirty-thousand dollars of the counterfeit? Maybe they sold it, but that would be difficult on such a grand scale without prearranged contacts, and Pavel didn't believe either of them had prior experience in the Bay Area. If they spent it, Pavel would know. Damian couldn't make sense of it. He recalled the night of the exchange in Forest Hill, Kim and Noe obsessing over the c-notes, checking serial numbers, Damian thought. It bothered him.

But whether Damian was being followed by the Koreans or the Secret Service or someone else or no one at all, the fact remained he had bills to pay and a payload due in two weeks. He spent a few more days staking out the printing hole, casing the parking-lot, and still nothing proved he was being watched. He should get back to work one way or another. Nothing for it but to chance the warehouse and see what happened.

No sirens erupted. No unmarked cars charged the lot, no plain-clothed horde scaled the fence. Only business as usual. So. He set up and shot the bill and modified the pictures on the computer. There were a couple features of the composite Damian didn't like and he reviewed the images to find a better original to work with. He didn't have time to take new pictures and he didn't think he should have to because what he had was damned close, he just needed to get a better focus on the right edge of the bill and blend the background—where he deleted Franklin's face—to the surrounding pattern with a more regular resolution.

He needed to hurry but he also knew if he became careless he could ruin a whole night's work, and then he caught himself thinking about Nathalie and his recurring dream of her, the emotional texture of her eyes, the wordless exchange between them and the familiar tenderness of his hand in hers. He exhaled halfway between frustration and paranoia and got up to reshoot the bill on the process camera.

Counterfeiting was as much an art as a science, Damian's dad used to say, as dependent upon inspiration as craftsmanship. The objective wasn't to recreate the genuine article but to simulate it. It's not a copy of real money—it's an illusion of real money. But his dad was full of bullshit most of the time because the art of successful forgery lay in the ability to manufacture the original article. Damian didn't make fake one-hundred dollar bills—he made real ones using most of the exact materials and techniques as the Treasury Department. The only difference was the money he made was unauthorized.

At first, when Damian was twelve, his dad would only allow him the most menial tasks. Mop the floor, scrub down the surfaces, eliminate fingerprints, dispose of the evidence. The rest of his studies were conducted through observation and listening to his father explain in exact detail how to perform each operation, what their purposes were, possible complications and what to do in each event. Then his work included setting up the process-camera and babysitting the arc-light burner, monitoring the press, cutting the sheets. Finally, he was taught how to mix inks and load them in the press.

Since then, the counterfeiter's apprentice overtook the master. The watermark was Damian's first true innovation, much better than his dad's clever but hackneyed method. On genuine currency the watermark was designed into the actual paper, before ink was ever applied, through an intricate combination of denser and thinner weaves in the pulp. Several crude methods had been developed by counterfeiters to suggest the presence of a watermark, but Pavel said Damian's was the most believable he'd ever seen. It looked real. Making his own paper with a cylinder-mould watermark was too expensive so Damian developed an ironing stamp technique in which paper was dampened, stamped, and cauterized prior to inking to simulate the watermark. The results lacked the clarity and tonal depth of a true watermark, a subtle deficiency mitigated by a special layer of inking. It took a microscope to tell the difference.

Once Damian was satisfied with the graphic results he went back over the last few hours' work, point by point, to make sure the composite was perfect, before saving to disc and transferring to the arc-light burner. There would be no going back once the images were burned onto aluminum plates. If he bit the plates too long he would lose detail, not long enough and they wouldn't hold ink. If the acid solution was too concentrated it would dissolve too much of the resin base on the plates. The slightest flaw could result in a finished product obviously fake, all his hard work ruined, and there wouldn't be enough time to start over. The old man gave a lecture about it. How old had Damian been? Thirteen? Fourteen? His dad recited a whole series of lectures he liked to quiz Damian on, to make sure he was paying attention, but the proper biting of aluminum plates had always been one of his favorites.

Never give in to selfishness, his father would say while they were scrubbing the lab. This is important. Remember everything I say. And in the years since, Damian did his best to remember: don't let yourself get greedy. It starts with making too much. Never move more than a hundred-thousand at a time. Never make more than you need. There will come a time when you want to, for whatever reason, it'll sound like a good idea. Maybe you got bills to pay or you see a good opportunity or there's something nice you want. Maybe you want to buy something for a woman. Don't do it. Are you listening?

I'm listening, Damian would say. But his dad was just getting warmed up. Never work under a pressing deadline. Never rush yourself. Don't lie to clients, don't cheat clients, don't steal from clients. Never work tired—whatever you think you're getting for it isn't worth the risk. That's how you get sloppy. It takes discipline and attention to detail. Not every once in a while for a few hours here and there. At *all* times and for the *rest* of your life.

Damian had learned how right his dad was. How it starts small and with the best intentions and pretty soon you've got counterfeit stashed all over the house and you're passing it at the grocery-store and your real money is mixed up with fake. That's how you get caught—or killed.

This was a regular staple of Damian's middle school education, what his father code-named the book business. Geometry, chemistry, and history during the week and forgery over weekends and summer vacations. Sometimes his dad would make Damian repeat the lecture and his dad's nostrils would flare as he listened to make sure no point was left out. It seemed nothing could possibly frustrate him more than Damian not paying attention.

What his dad did for a living—what Damian did—was illegal. This was the only ethical difference between counterfeiting and most jobs. No less honest than most 'honest' work. Damian had worked some jobs, respectable jobs, which made him feel a hell of a lot greasier than counterfeiting. In four short years you'll be an adult, his dad told him. Fully grown, all done. And from that day forth the whole world will line up and dangle a couple lousy bucks in front of your nose. The only thing you'll have to do to get them is sell your soul into slavery.

He remembered that too.

Research clients before picking them up. A lot. You got to make sure the money won't hit the street in the city where you live. Best if it leaves the country. You want to make sure whoever puts it into circulation has no idea who it came from. If you're smart and careful you can create a good life doing this. Raise a family. Enjoy your time. You figure out how to get both of those things in the same room and talking, you'll have figured out something not many men ever do.

Sounded fine to Damian. Perfect. The school-year started and he went back to helping his dad on the weekend. But a few months later and long before his dad ever thought seriously about teaching him how to move the money they made, he dreamed of the dark-haired woman. The midday stars, the stoic sea, the bench painted white, and her matching dress. Pluming black curls. Velvet in her eyes and silk on her hands. He'd forgotten all about her in the six years since she gave him fever, but seeing her again, he remembered vaguely knowing her from somewhere, if not this same dream, one that made him feel the same.

A week passed, two, and then one day his dad didn't come home from work. How they found out he'd been arrested Damian could no longer remember, if he'd ever known. His mother called everywhere she could think and finally the police. Was that how she found out? The cops told her? Sometimes when he was too drunk to know better Damian took the question through his mind but always came out empty. Not the arrest or the attorneys or the trial. He'd been so naïve, so stupid and sheltered, and his mom did everything she could to keep him that way. He hadn't understood the significance of what was happening nor grasped the finality of it. He'd thought it meant they wouldn't be able to counterfeit anymore. As it turned out, counterfeiting was the only thing from that life that didn't die.

What came next, though, he remembered. Seasons of moving. Changing schools. His mother taking a two-dollar-an-hour waitressing job against a column of foreclosure penalties and overdraft fees and bankruptcy. Housing-projects and social-workers. Nights lying awake at three in the morning listening to his mother weep through the hollow drywall between their bedrooms and police sirens beneath his window. Gold-toothed prostitutes on street-corners with distended bellies and glaucoma-ravaged eyes. And in the stairwell crackheads sleeping swaddled in semen-stained overcoats and plastic grocery bags. He remembered very well. Too well. Long days alone in the apartment with nothing but the sinister sounds of adjacent apartments for company. Or sitting on a barstool in the diner sucking shirley temples until two in the morning while his mother finished the second shift of a Friday night double. The highlight of a weeknight taking his mom's tip change to the convenience store for a licorice-whip and soda-pop. Coming home to a pink eviction warning wedged under the doorknob.

How the same as any other addiction hunger stretched the seconds of his life and forced his thoughts as small and mean as his body's chronic ache. How it made him plot every inch of his day. Lies he would tell. Who he would hit and what he would steal. How much food he could get for it, and where he would hide to eat it, and how long he might make it last.

Eighteen months, prison incubated his father, and what emerged languished for the rest of Ronald Lancaster's life. He was never himself and never Damian's dad again. They let him out eighteen-and-a-half years early in exchange for his trade secrets and cooperation as an expert witness in counterfeiting trials. He moved his family to a slightly safer block of the South Fairmount neighborhood and got a job as a gas-station attendant. Regular appointments with a probation officer and weekends devoted to community service. Once in a while the Secret Service came around with a search and seizure warrant to make sure he wasn't counterfeiting in the apartment and once in a while he testified in court.

He drank a lot. Damian remembered the juniper stink of his gin sweats, the feral knife of his eyes, the nervous laugh of him and his trembling hands. The clink of ice in the glass and the glass on glass chirping of the bottle dipped in the tumbler. If his mother wasn't at work she sat in a corner of their small front-room, blanket and rocking chair, dry red-eyed stare equal parts gratitude and terror. She looked at her husband the way Damian thought people would look at ghosts. Or car-wrecks.

Months passed this way. A year. Damian couldn't imagine a colder hell than his fifteenth year on earth. And then he dreamed again of the white dress and sweet smile and freckled skin of the dark-haired woman. Was it Nathalie? His nose twitched at the thought. He still hadn't dreamt of her since they'd met and she hadn't dreamt of him. His body thrilled to wake with her in his arms and he was terrified of seeing her in his sleep.

Damian cleaned the warehouse and locked the unfinished bills in the safe and walked to the bus-stop. As promised, the weather returned to normal: sixty-two degrees, partly cloudy, eighty-six percent humidity. Muted light softened the early morning hour and painted the industrial neighborhood pastel. Dark and greasy colors, blurry edges, thick shapes of buildings like smudged mistakes on a brighter background. Boarding the bus he happened to glance over his shoulder and saw ascending from shadows a neutral figure, unnerving for its indistinctness, its initial shapelessness and the way it seemed to glide from shadow to shadow without touching the ground before emerging in the morning light neither tall nor short, neither dark nor fair, in a black overcoat and matching fedora.

Maybe he'd noticed this coat months ago in Bayview scurrying out the doorway of his apartment building as he approached on the sidewalk. He recalled stopping this man to ask the time outside the restaurant in Little Russia. And on the bus going home from the antique shop this man had sat two rows in front of him. Ducking, Damian thought. Not wanting his face visible. The way the coat shuffled out of shadows as Damian entered the belly of the bus. If he were hiding he might move that way, too.

"Wrong bus," he told the driver and walked in the direction

of the black overcoat, around the corner and down Howard Street. Ornate Victorian facades stood cheek to jowl between cement lumps and brick monoliths in a frenzy of color: blue, purple, gray, orange, white. A procession of disparate architectures lined both sides of the street. Panel siding and shingles and bay windows and adobes.

It was a long block and the traffic was thickening, but there were few pedestrians, which made spotting the black overcoat easy. It turned at the corner of Ninth Street and Damian followed a hundred yards behind. Cars checkered the four lane street. He passed two homeless men squatting outside a welfare office. The black coat disappeared around another corner and was gone when Damian reached the intersection. The old man couldn't be as old as Damian's first estimate. He was far too fast for nearing seventy. Fifties at the oldest. And fit.

Parked vehicles lined half the narrow side-street made of industrial warehouses. Commuters loped the sidewalks. Damian looked through the bars of a gated parking-lot and scanned half the block of doorways but couldn't find the man in the black coat. He'd given up and started walking back the way he'd come when he saw the man looking at him from the opposite side of Ninth Street. A wide river of cars separated them, and without knowing how he would get across or what he would do on the other side, Damian stepped into the asphalt vein, and the man broke for a side-street. "Fuck it," Damian said and sprinted after.

Somehow he lost the coat in a maze of byways. At first he could just keep up, coming to a crossroad and looking down it in time to see the black hem flash around a corner, but after a few minutes there was no trace. He was sweating and when he wiped his face the skin was hot. He didn't understand how the old man could vanish. The blocks were long and there were no alleyways between the buildings to hide in. He wondered this for several blocks before reaching Ninth Street again. On the other side of the traffic stream, on top of the roof of a four-story office building, stood the man in the black overcoat. He was looking at Damian. For a few seconds they inspected each other. The man doffed his hat. Then he turned and walked once more out of sight.

17.

Nathalie got a call from the Haas School of Business at UC-Berkeley. She'd been accepted into the graduate program beginning in the fall. "Great," she said, but she could hear in her own voice how little she felt it. She accepted the offer, she didn't need any time to think about it, she said, and listened without paying attention to the instructions for enrollment, matriculation, tuition, fees, class registration. A packet with the full details would be coming in the mail. She thought about calling her dad with the news but decided no. She really didn't want to go to graduate school, and once her dad knew she'd been accepted there would be no getting out.

The second week of April brought back the wedding invitations and their analysis results. Dr. Sundstrom sent a text message saying they would be available for pickup with the department secretary. Nathalie stopped by Wheeler Hall after class and left a handwritten thank you note in Dr. Sundstrom's faculty box. The secretary gave her a manila legal-sized envelope with the invitations, the data printout, and a brief summary of the findings.

The invitations were printed on high quality linen paper and cut in octavo pages. The molecular content suggested a carbon ink, most likely lamp-black, with a binding agent composed of turpentine and walnut oil. Consistent with incunabula dating from late fifteenth century Germany. The depths of the typeface in the paper surface confirmed a fifteenth century letterpress technique using moveable typeface cast from molten lead. The image of the double-headed figure was almost certainly a woodcut, as opposed to wax or metal, based on the texture and coverage of the ink and dimensions of the lines. But the big thing was the staining and deterioration of the paper due to age, suggesting it was made between the last decades of the fifteenth century and the early decades of the sixteenth. This, however, wasn't corroborated by the rate of fading in the carbon-based ink, which should've been significantly more advanced.

The paper also showed evidence of exposure to damp, which tended to speed the deterioration process and skew the chemical analysis. Probably, the ink was either added at a much later date or else touched up after extreme fading occurred. Tests to ascertain whether or not the ink had been reapplied were inconclusive, and x-rays failed to confirm the documents as palimpsests, scraped and reprinted, but aging on the typeface suggested the original pressing to be more or less contemporary with the age of the paper. In the opinion of the forensics lab at Riverside the documents were twins from the same printing, made no later than 1650, and likely a little older, and subjected to skillful restoration at some point in the last fifty years. As no similar documents were known to exist, authenticity would be impossible to verify through comparison.

"Does any of this make sense to you?" she asked Damian over dinner.

He furrowed his brow and shook his head. "A little," he said. "But I still don't understand why someone would send us three-hundred-year-old wedding invitations."

That was the heart of the question, and Nathalie was starting to lose hope of ever finding an answer.

"Someone could've done touch-up work on the invitations. We could take them to a professional bookbinder. Or a rare books dealer. They know what to look for with this sort of thing." Damian got up to load the dishwasher. "Spotting crafty forgeries is part of the job."

She didn't see anything to lose and Damian made a consultation appointment for the following Monday.

Talking to Rosa didn't clarify things. She couldn't see much over the phone. "There's a wedding, but it looks more like a funeral." A long silence, and over the distance between Portside and Palo Alto, Nathalie could feel her sister concentrating. "What the invitation is and what it means aren't the same thing. I'm sorry. I can't see more without looking at it."

Damian took her skydiving for their shared birthday. He'd always wanted to try it but the idea excited her less. Only a week before there was an accident involving a skydiver in Newport Beach. A parachute caught in a wind gust and a woman smashed into the air-traffic control tower. She was already dead when the tandem instructor landed, her neck broken in the collision, witnessed from the ground by her husband and two children. The tandem suit didn't make Nathalie feel any better about it, strapped to a stranger and falling in a clumsy tangle of arms and legs like a two-headed crab from the ribcage of a Cessna. But she was glad Damian talked her into it because it was wonderful to fall like that. Swimming in the sky. She felt more like flying than falling, like she was perfectly still, the cold air flashing upwards all around and the earth spreading out like a blanket to catch her.

She loved falling. Maybe that's why she loved dance, for even walking was the recovery from a controlled fall. Every dancer must learn to embrace falling, to know she was going to fall and let her body fall anyway. Don't be afraid. Even if nothing would catch her it would be okay because the earth would support her. It helped to think like that. Sometimes she spent her entire rehearsal time practicing falls straight from her feet onto her back, side, knees, belly, sliding falls and rolling falls that brought her back to the balls of her feet, gripping the floor like talons. There was a physical grace to falling and a subtler grace in the submission to falling. Surrender to grace. Confident the floor would gently keep her, the earth would cradle her, and the universe honor her willingness to descend. She knew how to help the ground catch her and years of practice taught her it works the same in the opposite direction. She could fall from a prostrate position to an erect one. She could lie down and fall onto her feet. Until the ground came up there was no difference between falling and flying and she was ready to fly.

Only her dad didn't see it that way. She met him for lunch a few blocks from his offices in the commercial district. "You're too compulsive," he said. "As stubborn and proud as your mother and I fear for you. I would die if anything happened to you, my love, I would kill somebody."

"It's my birthday," she said. "I don't want to fight."

The way he saw it, duty as her father compelled him to forbid this nonsense. He wanted her to work for him. She'd interned at one or another of his companies all through high school and he knew she was cut out for it. The fact was she had the intelligence, talent, and determination to be successful at anything—absolutely anything. Three generations of Jevali's came before her and she was made of the same stuff. If she wished, she could add her name to their legacy—she would make a lot of money for the company, her philanthropic spirit would make real strides, meaningful progress, in the lives of people. She would become the greatest Jevali of all because she was smarter than all of them put together. She had the aptitude but lacked the ambition.

"So fine," he said. "The heart wants what the heart wants. There's no forcing it." Now she was on the verge of a degree from one of the best universities in the world. She had a promising portfolio and applications placed at the finest business schools in the country. Only the most visionless hacks among them wouldn't accept her and she could choose from the rest. Doors would open, opportunities would come, and in a few brief years her talent, perseverance, and hard work would be rewarded with a brilliant career. Her desire to be a dancer was the only thing standing in her way. She was a Jevali and the world would know it. Unless her father didn't love her enough to stop her from throwing it away. Because she couldn't expect to be anything if she gave up. "You're turning into a quitter, Nathalie. It shrivels an old man's heart."

"I'm not quitting—I'm choosing a different path," she said and immediately regretted it. She felt her face blush under her father's blank gaze. He believed success in anything was the result of struggle and proven with material rewards, and he hated any suggestion the difference between success and failure amounted to a difference in perspective.

"A different path," he said, and the muscles in his jaw flexed tight around contempt. "You'll end up a cocktail waitress. Or worse." She would end up working seven days a week and dancing a few weekends a year at cultural festivals and charity benefits, he warned, performing to cow-faced crowds of apathetic suburbanites gaping at her with one eye and with the other wrestling the obnoxious demands of slack-jawed children for ice cream or cotton candy. "You deserve better than the life of a performing artist."

"You mean *you* deserve better."

"You don't owe me anything," her father said. "Do you owe anything to yourself?"

She didn't know the answer but she sure as hell wasn't going to give him the satisfaction of admitting it. Sullen, she finished her meal, skipped dessert, and excused herself without deciding one way or the other what she would do. Only she knew something delicate inside her charred over the dinner table and no one gasped, no one even noticed. But she felt sick. A cauterized feeling in her heart, like it had been cut out of her, and she recognized the phantom beating of its absence. A numb tingling sensation beneath her sternum. And then she went home and discovered more bad news in the mailbox. Her official letter of acceptance to the Haas School of Business. She read the letter once and buried it in a kitchen drawer under a stack of take-out menus.

What her dad wanted for her was wrong, all wrong, and Nathalie couldn't pretend it would work out. Her dad, the world, the very earth, if they couldn't love her for who she actually was, they would never love her at all. If she didn't want to despise her life she must stop using it to tell a lie. Even if it meant burning love out of her heart. If it meant this agony. She didn't need her dad to accept her—someone else would do it.

She used to wake in the middle of the night overwhelmed with the urge to dance. Now she woke up in the middle of the night for a different reason. She was angry Damian wouldn't tell her about his job or his past or really anything about himself, but he believed in her and her dad did not believe in her. All she needed was a little protection, a safe feeling, and she would be fine in her dangerous new life as an aspiring dancer. Nothing to it. She kept the wedding invitations close all the time now—they were the last thing she looked at before bed and the first thing in the morning—because they would protect her. How, she had no idea, but the moldy paper mattered less than what it represented: someone else believed in her and his believing made her brave.

Damian couldn't sleep, either. He lay in the dark staring at the midnight glow of streetlight out the window, neon and halogen bright and sweet as candy, and listened to the comforting sounds of his adolescence: the posturing of rival street gangs and the peel of car alarms, stray cats meowing, and the solicitors' shop-talk of drugs or sex hushed by passing police light.

He thought of Nathalie because he thought of her all the time. Fingernails cut short and painted plum to match her toenails. Front teeth shining like twin stars between her lips, merlot-stained, the lift and pout of them, the slope of her jaw and pitch of her nose. All the swells and planes of her face. The coiled seashells of her ears and light spray of freckles across her cheeks. Wide black slashes of eyebrows and black rug of hair matted and wild and fragrant of violets. He didn't think these things so much as feel them. Sentimental and nonsensical but it was also the only way he could describe it: her hair, teeth, freckles were not thoughts—they were emotions. And once he was this far gone to them there was no getting back to sleep and nothing for him to do but shower and dress and get some work done.

He spent twenty minutes walking the neighborhood but it was deserted. He didn't know who the old man in the black trench-coat and fedora might be, but he was beyond the pale of suspicion: Damian knew he was being followed. He didn't know why or by whom but the more he thought of it the less he believed it could be the Secret Service. They utilized strict protocols, sophisticated surveillance methods, highly specialized investigative teams. This old man was too conspicuous to be a cop. Damian had no idea who he was but he'd clearly tracked Damian for some time, he'd followed Damian to and from the warehouse, his cover was blown and if he were gathering evidence for a bust it would've happened by now. It was stupid of Damian to go anywhere near the warehouse until he knew for sure, but he was in a tough spot. His deadline was up and if he missed it everything he'd spent the last four years building would be finished. Pavel wouldn't trust him anymore. Damian's reputation would be ruined all over the Bay Area.

The noise generated by the intaglio in full gallop made it necessary to print only at night. While the press warmed up Damian loaded the first plates on the rollers and used a turkey-baster to measure the first ink recipe and loaded the cartridge into the printer. He checked the calibrations of some of the presses moving parts and made sure the paper was properly damp. He put on earplugs and test-printed several sheets, which he threw in the wastebasket, before adding a little lime-green to the ink and tightening the rollers. Another test run and three-tenths of a centiliter more forest-green ink and he was happy enough with the results to open up the press. It roared like a monster and bucked furiously against the cement floor and Damian stood before it perspiring with his arms folded on his chest and his knees shivering over the vibrating earth. He set up industrial fans around the presses motor to keep it from overheating and watched sheets of greenbacks pour into the receptacle tray.

When the ink started to fade he added more to the cartridge and threw away the defective sheets. The run finished and he reloaded the paper, switched the plates, changed the ink to new colors, recalibrated the pressure of the rollers, and checked the motor temperature. Through a series of runs a palimpsest of features and colors emerged and the paper began to resemble—to transform into—money. First pale green and then darker greens, followed by blues and reds and purples, one layer on top of the other, until the foundation was completely covered, invisible but never destroyed. It's always there, buried underneath, even if you forget about it, even if you never knew it existed, it's still what holds it all together. That's what a palimpsest is, his father had told him, and people work the same way. That's what history is. That's what memory is. However you change, it merits remembering what you used to be is still there. Buried underneath.

Damian's biggest breakthrough had been the press. Buying a real intaglio was price-prohibitive so he homemade one from an assortment of presses and other industrial equipment. His father's printing-press preserved some of the tonal subtlety and topographical texture of an intaglio but had been based on a completely different printing method. A perceptive sales clerk might not be able to definitely identify it as counterfeit but they might discern something weird about it, more by the way it felt between the fingers than by how it looked. And brief suspicion often proved the difference between getting rich and going to prison.

How Damian spent his father's prison sentence: dumpster diving behind the projects or behind his mom's restaurant for half-finished food. Stealing lunch-money from smaller kids. The whined sobs of how sorry he was to the older siblings of his victims, three and four of them at a time, in the few seconds after they confronted him and before they reaped closed-fisted vengeance on his jutting hipbones and bas-relief ribcage. A loaner and a provocateur, defiant, hostile, made the target of bullies and showoff thugs. He learned to avoid isolated spaces, always stay within view of an adult, walk with his back to the wall. Pussy, they called him. Faggot. Dicksmoker. Everywhere he went he assessed the possibility of getting jumped. Any motion in his peripheral vision made him flinch, accustomed by now to getting his ass kicked, but he always fought back. On principle. No thought of fending them off—two of them, five of them—it wasn't the point. He knew they would beat the shit out of him but someone would pay for it in blood. He got suspended from school so much his mom lost her job for taking too much time off.

One day he jimmy-rigged a skeleton key to pulverize a bank of vending machines, lock by lock, and took the pile of change to the grocery-store. He walked to spare bus-fare for an extra loaf of stale bread from the expired-goods rack. The comforting weight of his father's pocketknife, he remembered, meant to protect his stash on the walk home should someone tough show up. Hunting and gathering to provide for his mother and she in hysterics to know how he got the food and Damian threatening her—*threatening* her—not to ask where the money came from and sobbing as he told her what a helpless bitch she'd become, how worthless she was without his father to take care of her, how she was unfit to care for anyone. He'd told her she was an idiot for working sixteen hour days and having to choose between food to eat and electricity to cook it, especially when women on this block twice her age were a lot better off selling nothing but the cunt between their legs. She'd used it to get what she wanted from his dad, she sold it to him for years, so why stop now?

Yes, he'd said those things to her and he was still ashamed. Not until later did he understand her courage. He thought she was a weakling because he was too stupid to see her feeding herself to violence, to poverty, to death, as a way of protecting him. His father's job had been to teach him how to live in the world, how to take advantage of it, exploit its stupidity and cowardice. He'd taught Damian the best way he knew, but sometimes Damian caught a sense of how crippled he was because of it. His mother, on the other hand, only wanted him to be a person she could admire, someone brave, creative, kind, intelligent, capable. A good person. Her real tragedy had been wasting her love on such a mean-hearted fucker as her only son. He could only see her loss of dignity.

Seven years she'd been dead. Sometimes he thought about what he would say to her if he could. He wanted her to know it wasn't true, what he said that day. It had not been she who was unfit to care for anyone—he was unfit to be cared for. No one liked to admit it but love and dignity had always been poison to each other. You only get one or the other. Or maybe it wasn't true—maybe some people got both, but his mom sure didn't. He knew he wasn't a person she would admire. He knew he was damned sorry for it. He knew the day he fucked up those vending machines and went to the store, those things he said to his mom, the way she doubled over and wept. That was the worst day of his life.

Remember, his dad had pleaded, and for whatever it was worth, Damian remembered.

18.

And how memory gets entangled with fate. Sometimes Nathalie thought remembering doomed her to repeat the past. She believed in fate but often wondered if dwelling on the past had a way of influencing what would happen in the future. Her attention to memory was the reason the past tended to repeat, sometimes in small ways, sometimes in large. All she knew of the world was school and dance and her father's stubborn will-power, all lead and tenderness, the soft bully in her conscience. Remembering and soldering her future to her past so the more she thought about it—the more she worried—the harder it became to tell if maybe she was remembering the future and imagining the past.

"So what I imagine that I remember becomes a blueprint for the future, and in this way I create the future for myself, which I remember, even though I don't really remember it. It was all in my imagination. Or something like that."

"Remember when your dad wanted you to work for him but instead you followed your heart and became a dancer?" Damian said, and kissed her hair. They sat against the headboard of her bed, covered to the waist by a single sheet. The bedroom window was open and the scent of rhododendrons pushed the curtains like a sail. "Remember how scary it seemed, back then?"

Was that how it would be? Everything turning out fine like that? She hoped so but she had second thoughts about it all the time. Maybe she could tell her dad she wasn't going to work for him anymore. She could ask for more hours at the coffee-shop, or pick up a second part-time job, and throw herself into

Strange Equinoxes. She'd hinted at it many times before but always he'd been able to talk her out of it, and he'd probably do it again.

Most of April was spent making love, primarily in Nathalie's condo, though occasionally elsewhere, but never in Damian's studio. Nathalie knew he kept her away from his place on purpose. He didn't want her there. He was embarrassed to live in Bayview. The ugly studio apartment, underfurnished and filthy in a way cleaning couldn't mask. It depressed him. But no. He *did* compare his place to hers, he *was* ashamed of where he lived, but that wasn't why he wanted to keep her away. There was something he was hiding. Something he didn't want her to find, or something he didn't want her to discover about him.

How much should this feeling bother her? Probably not at all. She was still unknotting a tangle of emotions for Damian. Her future was as yet undecided, but almost certainly it would take her away from here. Strange Equinoxes had created an underground stir in the local dance community, a lot of interest, and if things went well this year they planned on touring next summer. There was talk of relocating to Austin, Texas. She didn't see Damian fitting in her future, but she loved the way he made her feel and she refused to cheat herself of love. It was what it was. No need to get complicated. If he didn't want her in his home, that bothered her, but it was his business. She still had no idea what he did for a living. Since the night she'd slept at his studio he hadn't been willing to tell her anything meaningful about his past. How he felt about her was clear enough, if never made explicit. She would enjoy him for now and when it was over she'd make herself feel better by remembering how it wasn't going to work out anyway, how he didn't want to make her a permanent part of his life.

"Come," she said, and took Damian's hands off her breasts.

"I want you to come, little wasp."

Nathalie giggled. She loved this game. "If I was a wasp, you'd have been stung by now."

"Not if I took your stinger."

"You'd have to find it first."

"Everyone knows where a wasp wears its stinger," Damian said and dragged her lip between his teeth. "In the tail."

"Tongue," Nathalie said and kissed him.

"Whose tongue?"

"Yours, if we're talking about tall tails." She could feel him hardening again beneath her hand. "I'm leaving."

"With my tongue in your tale?" he groaned.

"We'll be late." She got out of bed and went to the shower.

Celsius Antique Bookbinding and Restoration was in the Dog Patch off Seventeenth Street. The man who met with them, Ferdinand Sobraille, was tall and thin as a mantis, with a great wedge of nose and matching ears, which stuck straight out from the sides of his balding head. After shaking hands all around, Sobraille took his turn with the wedding invitations, perused the chemical analysis report, and asked what, exactly, did they want to know?

"Have you ever seen anything like them before?" Damian asked.

Sobraille shook his head. "They're new to me."

"Do you think they could be fake?" Nathalie asked.

He raised his eyebrows, half perplexed by the question. "You mean forgeries? Not according to this," and he held up the analysis report.

"But what do you think?"

Sobraille thought about it for a long moment. Too long, Nathalie thought. She could tell he was doubting. "The thing is," he said, "I've seen wedding invitations from the time period this is supposed to be. They're quite rare. The ones I saw were Hungarian, but these things have pretty strict conventions, which were rarely deviated from, and never this radically. There should be something scriptural, for example, a preamble with a kind of defense of marriage as being ordained by god, maybe a synopsis of the story of Adam and Eve, something like that."

This was nothing Nathalie hadn't heard already and she decided to change tacks. "Would it be possible to fake them? Well enough to fool analysis?"

"It's been done before. It would take a great deal. It wouldn't be easy. You're looking at a lot of expertise, time, money. Not cheap, but it's definitely possible."

"But the aging of the paper," Damian said. "The typeface marks and water damage?"

Sobraille nodded. "Difficult to reproduce artificially, but not impossible. Reams of period paper have been known to resurface, paper made in the early modern period and never used, sits neglected for hundreds of years, and then is discovered. So the paper itself could be authentic without the documents necessarily being so as well. This is rare but not unheard of. More likely, the paper was made recently, using early modern papermaking techniques. The same with the typeface. It would be expensive but not difficult to make a set of type from molten lead by following period recipes. The discoloration and damage can be faked by staining the paper with tea. Certain chemical treatments make paper appear older than it is, even under professional chemical analysis, unless the technician knows exactly what to look for."

"And why would someone do it?" Nathalie asked.

"That's the intriguing question," Sobraille agreed. "With the proper education, determination, and resources, the how of it is easy to answer. The big mystery is why. In every case of forgery on this scale, as far as I'm aware, the answer has been money. But these wouldn't be heavy hitters, even among the biggest spenders. Almost certainly, the forgeries would cost twice—even three or four times—what you could expect to make from the best sale imaginable. So why do it?"

"Wouldn't that, along with the chemical analysis, suggest they're most likely authentic early modern documents?"

"One thing you've got to understand," Sobraille said. "What you've got in the analysis are two different things. First, the raw data. Just the facts, ma'am. It's about numbers. Elements, compounds, chemical reactions. Second, you have an interpretation of that data. A narrative written by a human being, a story explaining to you what the raw data might mean, or probably means, or ought to mean. Hidden in the data, there are always anomalies. Stray bits, which don't disprove a theory of interpretation, but don't support it either. Usually, the analyst will explain this data away, or pretend it's less significant than it might turn out to be, or ignore it all together. The data is always useful. The interpretation should never be taken on faith."

"So your vote would be forgeries?"

"Yes, because this image—do you know what this is? It's called a Rebis. It means 'double thing.' You see a fair number of them if you deal in this period long enough, usually associated with alchemy." Sobraille swept an arm around the room, indicating the books. "I've spent my life immersed in this stuff," he said. "I understand the medieval mind. I understand the Renaissance mind. I've learned, a little at a time, over the course of a career, how to think like them. This," he said, holding up the wedding invitations. "This is not the product of an early modern psychology. It can't be. It makes me think of someone now, someone from the twenty-first century, imagining how a fifteenth century mind works. It's anachronistic. It takes for granted ideas about the visual image as art, as symbol, as a vessel for meaning, which simply did not exist in early modern Europe. The whole point of an image like this, a document like this, would've meant something different to early moderns than to post-moderns like us. But the design doesn't get that. The design thinks like we think."

"For example?" Damian asked.

"Well, everything about it. But for example, the lines are

wrong, the details of the faces, how they're composed, the style of the eyes, the way the hair is done, the impression of musculature, the way joints fit together. It's stylistically anachronistic. If you want a better sense of it, you'll need to consult an art historian. Not my area of expertise. But like I said, I've spent my whole professional life around the genuine article. I know it when I see it. This is not it."

Textual content was also not Sobraille's area of expertise, but he could say right away the documents weren't actually meant to be wedding invitations. Obviously. There were no salutations. They weren't addressed specifically to anyone. No particulars, the names of the bride and groom, anything about their families, no date or time or place where this supposed wedding would occur. "So they're bending genres, they're something other than wedding announcements pretending to be wedding announcements. Do you see?"

That kind of genre-bending existed in early modern Europe, for sure, but not so blatantly, with so much self-awareness, an object so self-conscious of not being what it claimed to be. "You see? Very post-modern. And the gendering of the invitations. His and hers. That would never happen in a formal document. Absolutely never. Not before the eighteenth century."

They thanked Sobraille, asked if it would be alright to call on him again with further questions, which he said would be fine, and took defeated leave of Celsius Antique Bookbinding & Restoration.

"So where does that put us?" Damian asked on the drive back to Portside.

Nathalie could only shrug. "We have two documents, one mailed to each of us, without explanation, either made in the fifteenth century or the twenty-first century. If they were made in the fifteenth century, they're so rare and idiosyncratic as to be the only examples of their kind and therefore impossible to verify through comparison to any others. Or we have twenty-first century originals made using fifteenth century technology but discarding fifteenth century conventions of art and language. Forgeries that cost way more to fake than real ones would be worth. Plus, if they're real, why would someone send them to us? Plus, if they're fake, why would someone send them to us?"

19.

Of course the invitations were real—Damian could hold them in his hand, couldn't he? He knew Nathalie meant whether or not they were authentic. Real as in really hundreds of years old. Not whether or not they existed—whether or not they were forgeries. But the way she talked about it irritated him. As if the mystery would dissolve if the invitations turned out to be forgeries. Damian understood better than most the ambiguous line between real and fake. The distraction from the much more serious question of authority: who gets to decide what's true and what's false? He didn't care about whether they were genuine or not—he cared about the truth and the truth was someone sent these invitations and they had a reason for doing it. Who and why mattered more to him than what.

He delivered Pavel's order on time, in the out of service men's room of a Pacific Heights dentist's office. He had no more orders due to Pavel until July—he still had a few jobs to do for other clients, but they were small scale and wouldn't require much attention. In the meantime Damian plowed through the library books and renewed the useful ones, including the art books. He didn't expect to find the answers to his questions. A clue would show up sooner or later, maybe in his mailbox—it didn't make sense to send the invitations unless they were the preamble to something else. Damian hoped whatever it was would make sense because of something he'd read. He would know what it meant, how to interpret it, if he were thinking about it the right way. The more he knew about the invitations, the better his chances of identifying possible clues.

Iohannes Danielis Mylius. Author of *Philosophia reformata*

and as good a place to start as any. Born around 1583 in Wetter, in what is now Germany, and educated at the University of Marburg: physician, composer, alchemist. Balthazar Schwan engraved three series' of alchemical emblems for the project, commissioned by Lucam Jannis, publisher. Nathalie found an internet archive that included high resolution scans of them all. The double-headed hermaphrodite—the Rebis, Sobraille called it—figured prominently in several. Damian couldn't quite articulate it but the images were definitely telling a story. Two figures, one male, one female, crowned, fully clothed, shake hands. In the other hand the man holds a spear, the woman a branch. A bird descends upon them. Before them are two lions conjoined at the skull, sharing a single head, vomiting blood.

Next, they are nude from the waist up but for their crowns, indoors, approaching a man who tends a lit fireplace. Then they bathe in a shallow pool, framed by two trees, only one bearing fruit, the sun and moon in the upper corners, the same bird descending upon them. In another, they lie in bed together, side by side, beneath a tree. The sun and moon are both visible in the sky, accompanied by two birds. Then they lie side by side again, this time in what looks like a glass coffin. On the left a peg-legged man, swaddled in a loincloth, points at the coffin. On the right, a skeleton holds a scythe. Finally, the Rebis appears, nude, two-headed, crowned, lying upon a sarcophagus. Overhead a thick roll of raining clouds. Then the Rebis lies covered in a canopied bed. Then it lies nude beneath a tree. Then the figure lies upon a coffin. The bird, crowned now, descends. To the right a winged figure points at the Rebis whose human heads have been replaced with the sun and the moon.

"Looks more like a funeral than a wedding," Damian said. The wedding of the King and Queen, the invitations called it. Hochzeit. German for both wedding and marriage.

"Are these the King and Queen?" Nathalie asked. "Or is this not what we were invited to attend?"

Damian didn't know but he wanted to find out. He wanted to read *Philosophia reformata,* but it was more difficult to find than he anticipated. After a couple hours search Nathalie found a pdf, but it turned out to be scans of the original Latin. The next morning, after breakfast, Nathalie located an English version but the file was corrupted and wouldn't open. She found a commentary on a blog dedicated to Hermetic philosophy and the occult sciences. "Not what my professors would consider a reliable source," she said. "Lock the door if you go out. I get off work at three," and she left him alone.

It wasn't listed in the public library's catalogue either, but the Leonard Library at San Francisco State had an anthology of alchemical primary texts in English translation which included *Rosarium philosophorum.* Damian wasn't a student but for an annual fee he could become a friend of the library with full rein of its services. He requested the Mylius through interlibrary loan and walked to the Embarcadero rail station.

He'd never been to the Leonard Library before and it took the better part of half an hour to get his bearings. He didn't find the anthology right away but picked up a few other books he thought would be useful, *Psychology and Alchemy* by Carl Jung and Mercia Eliade's *The Forge and the Crucible.* A few aisles down a library assistant shelved returns and he got help looking for the anthology. Damian had the call number written on a scrap which the assistant checked and together they searched the nearby stacks but neither of them found the book. Downstairs, the assistant consulted a computer at the help desk and said the book hadn't been checked out—it should've been on the shelf. Probably sorted wrong. Or it could be missing. It could be anywhere.

Someone had stolen it. Damian knew it was stupid but he couldn't help thinking this was not a coincidence. That anthology wasn't misplaced. Someone prevented him from checking it out, someone who didn't want Damian to read it. The man in the black coat and matching fedora, possibly, or Gangjeon Jae-kyeon. Pavel had said there were rumors Gangjeon purchased counterfeit on behalf of an alchemist, a Hungarian, who spoke English without an accent. At this point no one was above suspicion. It could've been Pavel, for all Damian knew.

But if someone was purposefully keeping him from reading these books, the whole goddamn world must've been co-conspirators. *Rosarium philosophorum* was of unknown authorship, collected as the second volume of a larger work, *De alchimia opuscula complura veterum philosophorum.* He bought a used copy over the internet but a week later what arrived in the mail was a grimoire of herbal medicine, astrology, Kabbalah, and spells for conjuring angels, *De occulta philosophia libri tres* by Heinrich Cornelius Agrippa. At first he chalked it up to an honest mistake on the seller's part. Confusing 'De occulta' for 'De alchimia' was understandable. The original publication date of 1533 made the two books roughly contemporary, and the introduction informed him Agrippa had been an alchemist as well as a magician. They were probably sitting next to each other and the retailer accidentally grabbed the wrong one. Then the Leonard Library sent an email notification. His interlibrary loan was available for pick up. He got the book and was home again before realizing it was not *Philosophia reformata.* He held a paperback edition of the newest English translation of *Rosarium philosophorum,* according to the glossy cover, by Johann Mylius. But that was ridiculous. Mylius had been born circa 1583, *Rosarium philosophorum* first published in 1550. Unless Mylius was a fucking time traveler there was no way in hell.

The content made about as much sense. A kind of recipe for the philosopher's stone, though there was no list of ingredients, quantities, temperatures, instructions. The author promised to speak plainly and honestly and to hide nothing, before proceeding in riddles and contradictions and gibberish. The stone of the philosophers was decocted of metal, it claimed, not common gold but philosophical gold, and mercury had nothing to do with it—it was all fire and water. Later it was a mixture of red sulfur and white sulfur putrefied in stinking water, and at another part the stone was made of salt, and elsewhere vinegar and elsewhere nothing but argent vive, Latin for 'living silver'. Quicksilver. The medieval name for mercury. It was a thing possessed by rich and poor alike but the author warned it was a foolish thing for the poor to seek and would never be discovered by any mere laborer, only a true philosopher, and only then if it be the will of god. There was a green lion and an eagle that devours its own wings. There was a child born of incest and there was a great dragon that could not be slain by the sun or the moon but only by both of them together. The stone was of one substance but it was both fire and water, hot and cold, dry and wet, male and female, sun and moon, poison and medicine, red and white, and this, Damian read, was what is known as Rebis, the twofold thing. The author claimed whenever the book seemed clear, it spoke only lies and wherever there were riddles, there was also the hidden truth. And so he who knows not the beginning shall obtain not the end, and he who knows not what he seeks is also ignorant of what he finds.

This Damian underlined in black pencil and added a cursive note to the margin: *Pretty sure this part's about me.*

He didn't have the first suspicion what the philosopher's stone might be or how to make it or why anyone would want to. He didn't know what *The Rosary of the Philosophers* meant and he didn't especially care to find out. It told him what he needed to know: the Rebis of the wedding invitations was a symbol for the philosopher's stone. He could appreciate the significance of someone sending him something to do with turning base metal into gold. Someone was saying hello, someone who knew he held the secrets to transforming paper into money. Just wanted to let Damian know he was being watched, he wasn't so alone in the big, cold universe after all. That had to be what it meant. Cold beads rolled down his spine because he wanted things to start happening now. He'd been scared of his own shadow long enough. It was exhausting and he was ready for all this bullshit to come to a head.

He woke in the night to pee and laid down unable to sleep for a length of time he could not measure. He was wide awake when at last he gave up and checked the time. Quarter to four in the morning. Christ. He sat on the bed in the dark deciding what to do. His stock of inks was running low and he needed a new set of aluminum plates for the coming weeks, so he had a busy day of shopping planned, but it wouldn't be time to get started for hours. He could shower or make coffee, but those were admissions to the new day, and he still hadn't given up on sleeping. He could eat or read. Maybe that would make him tired again.

He turned on the corner lamps and gasped in the sudden light and steadied himself with a hand to the wall. Something startled him and gooseflesh puckered his naked arms. He giggled, relieved, and sat back down on the bed. The familiar sense of not being alone. He'd just become aware of someone he hadn't known was in the room until they noticed him turning on the light, but this time it was different because he knew who was with him. *Rosarium philosophorum.* He was aware of the book's presence as if it were a person sitting on the floor next to the bed waiting for him to wake. He picked it up and let the pages flip through his fingers until they stopped on a folded piece of paper, which he'd already discovered. It was a standard sheet of lineless rice-paper so thin the black handwriting was visible through the repetition of neat folds, which shrank it to the size of a credit card. He unfolded the note and read it again.

Wherefore, work your earth gently and not over hastily, from eight days to eight days, decoct it in dung and calcine it, until it shall imbibe the fiftieth part of the water in it. And know that after the imbibing, it must be mois-

tened inwardly the space of seven days, therefore begin the work again many times, although it be long, because you shall not see the tincture until it be accomplished. Study, therefore, when you shall be in every work, to record all signs which appear in every decoction and search out the causes of them, and bear them continually in your mind.

It was copied from the same two pages that hid it more than halfway through the book. Lies, apparently, since this was as lucid as *Rosarium philosophorum* got. Someone had written it recently—nothing suggested it was more than a few months old—in the sort of cheap ballpoint pen available anywhere with small office supplies. He could see the impression of the ball at the end of some words, the shallow streaks of cheap ink. The same person who addressed the wedding invitation envelopes? Damian doubted it. The hands were nothing alike, this one smaller, lighter, less fluid. Normally, he would think nothing of it. People forgot such things between the pages of library books all the time, but strange shit had been happening and the note was strange. It seemed meaningful.

Toward the end of the book, in the margin, he found a symbol. An upside down V beneath a cross beneath a horizontal figure-eight. Small and light, probably in the same hand as the note, hastily scratched with a dull pencil. It could be foreign writing, Chinese or Greek, maybe, or an astrological glyph. He couldn't help thinking what it looked most like was a stick figure of a person with two heads. His imagination, paranoid, twitchy from chronic worry, kept trying to connect it to his dream of the dark-haired woman, the Koreans, Nathalie, the wedding invitations, the man in fedora and trench-coat. An encoded message he must decipher. Omen. Threat. Like the book was telling him something he didn't understand.

He refolded the note, put it back in the book, and put the book back on the floor. Started coffee, took a shower, fried eggs with tater tots and sriracha sauce for breakfast. He tried to ignore the book, even moved it from the bedside to a drawer beneath the counter so he wouldn't be tempted to look at it while he ate. He watched TV, face flush with hot sauce, and thought about the book because he knew it was in the drawer, under the microwave, on the other side of the studio. It was waiting. Damian knew it was thinking about him.

There were plenty of places in San Francisco to buy aluminum etching plates but he took the bus across the bay to Concord. Except for the rolls of paper shipped from China, none of his supplies were delivered. He bought them as far away from the warehouse and as far away from each other as he could manage, in modest quantities, always with cash, and never from the same store twice in a row. He visited an etchings supply store in Concord and took the bus to Fremont for dry color pigments and stopped for lunch at an oyster bar in Mountain View overlooking the bay. Oils and diluting agents in San Jose and extenders in San Mateo. Astringents in Hayward for cleaning the press and replacement injector heads at an industrial supply store in Alameda. The especially thick printing inks were brutal on Damian's equipment and required regular replacement of several smaller parts. He didn't know the secret recipe used by the Treasury Department but it wasn't difficult to mimic. After a few months experimentation he'd developed an identical mixture, indistinguishable to the naked eye, even an educated one.

He dropped his purchases at the warehouse and arrived at home a little after eleven o'clock, sunburnt and sore and starving from fifteen hours of cramped buses and scorching asphalt. For a while he accepted exhaustion, not bothering to turn on the light, with his elbows on his knees and his hands in his hair. His calves felt atrophied from so much sitting and his neck spurred from so much walking. He undid his shoes and kicked them away and laid out straight on the unmade bed.

Heat droned steadily beneath the right side of his face and his arm from the elbow to the seam of his short-sleeve. He'd spent most the day on that side of one bus or another with the sun looking right at him, its reddening stare magnified by thick windowpanes. He hadn't thought much of it at the time, but now he shivered with sun-sickness. He should eat before he fell asleep, he thought, but got up to look at himself in the bathroom mirror instead. His face divided almost symmetrically in two. One side pale, the other bloody pink and angrier toward the ear. Rebis. The double thing.

Tomorrow he'd buy aloe but now he needed to eat. He was too tired to cook and thought of the bananas sitting on the counter beside the mini-fridge. When he turned on a standing lamp, the bulb popped and died. He was pretty sure he had extras in a drawer and turned on the other lamp. He opened the drawer under the microwave and jumped back. "Oh! Shit, you scared me!" he yelled. There was *Rosarium philosophorum,* right where he'd left it that morning, looking at him, as startled as Damian. "I forgot you were in there," Damian said. "Tomorrow you're going back to the library. I can't start talking like you have fucking ears. I wouldn't be able to stand myself."

◆ ◆ ◆

Phaedra wakes from nightmares she cannot remember, chased with clammy palms and a clenched jaw, chased with a galloping heart, but she does not flee by herself. In the stillness and dark she hears her own frightened breath and the man's gentle snore. Slow Henry huffs. And beneath that, barely, light and quick as courting mayflies, more breaths.

They are awake.

They are with her.

She reaches out to them with her imagination and caresses each of their faces. Oh, my darlings. Precious babes. She wants to protect them, but there's no protection from the coming ordeal. The best she can hope for is to prepare them. Teach them to love and to endure. She wants to say don't be afraid, but she does not dare. There are reasons to be afraid—Phaedra is afraid.

She dresses in thick darkness, careful not to wake Albert. Now they are roused, she must not tarry if she is to reach them first. Albert deploys his own minions abroad. Working to martyr everything he's striven to bring to pass. She must not let him do it. Already she has put a charm on him. Bound him in a cage of books. Surely, in the end, he will see why she must act swiftly to stop him. Surely he loves her that much. And she loves him. Too much. More than the wedding, more than the stone. She will not stand aside and play witness to his ruin. Part of him must know. She need not betray him—he is so intent on betraying himself. He knows. He knows she will destroy for him, she will summon fire, drown the seven worlds, swallow light, rain death from the center of every nucleus, in order to prolong his life a single hour. Only love can make this hatred bloom. Only love can stay the executioner's hand.

Phaedra draws a stub of chalk from her apron and creeps to the chapel door. Poimandres follows, phantom eyes haunting the darkness, black tail flicking as he runs like liquid across the stones. "This is our secret," she whispers. "You mustn't tell anyone." Poimandres rubs his ears on her shins and purrs into her skirts.

Soon the tortures will begin and she has no idea if her darlings will withstand them. She must do all she can to help. She must teach them how to love this world and its broken king. But to accomplish this she needs time. Another charm, she decides. That will work, at least for a little while. That will protect the work from the alchemist's folly.

A charm will do it. Yes. Kalemaris. A single word chalked to the outside of a door.

The portal creaks open and Poimandres disappears into the starlit clearing. Phaedra turns to the ancient wood and begins to write.

Precious darlings. They will not be subjected to anything Phaedra and Albert do not suffer with them. Small comfort, she thinks. When they are purified by fire, our flesh will bear the burns. When they are dissolved in acid, it is our bones that will melt. As above, so below. What takes place in the crucible transforms Phaedra's soul, and what happens in her heart is endured by the living stone.

CRUCIBLE

"Amalgamate Luna with Mercury, to which add as much Saturn, as there is Luna; put it into such a Crucible that a fourth part of it may be empty: Assuse on it Oyl of Sulphur, and decoct it unto the consumption of the Oyl: Afterwards keep it for two hours in a moderate fire; and there will be generated a black Stone, with a little Redness."

—PSEUDO-JABIR IBN HAYYAN, SUMMA PERFECTIONIS, 1531.

Nathalie woke before dawn from a dream she could not remember. Only the Rebis lingered. Damian's heartbeat beneath her ear, the rise and fall of his lungs beneath her face, the plate of his chest as white and cold as limestone. Musk and soap and a scent she thought might be ink. His skin was always so cool. Even in this unrelenting heat he felt almost cold against her slick belly. She peeled off him and sneaked down the hall to the bathroom to pee. The Rebis shimmering on the cusp of memory, a mirage emergent between every other thought. She retrieved the wedding invitations from the bedroom, careful not to wake Damian, and crept downstairs to the kitchen counter. Naked, no longer sleepy, not yet ready to be awake. Slipped the invitations out of their sheet-protectors to reexamine while waiting for coffee to percolate.

A few things struck Nathalie about Dr. Lunsford's translation. First, she had no idea who might've sent one of these invitations to her, even as a joke, which surely it was, or else it was sent to her by mistake. She'd hoped the translation would suggest an explanation but it didn't. Sobraille had pointed out these supposed invitations contained no date and no address for the wedding. She'd noticed, too, and now her curiosity ached over what it might mean. She started her laptop and read through the translation, not knowing what she was looking for. The tone struck her as menacing, too, the excessive exclamation points and the warning—*Take heed! Prepare yourself!* —seemed to imply a threat. The total lack of irony, the self-important earnestness of these declarations, should've seemed comical. But they made Nathalie nervous.

A wooden sigh broke her concentration. Weight shifting in the building's foundation. She looked up to find Damian standing at the doorway rubbing his eyes, naked body smooth and angular in the soft halogen light. She hadn't expected him to be so beautiful. A body cut from balsam wood, white and hard, but pliant under her fingertips. "Come back to bed," he said, and she could see in him the small boy he must've once been. Blue eyed and blurry with sleep, tousle-haired, sunburnt from play, pale and thin. For a moment she wanted to weep for celebration of him. Delicate as a fallen twig and as easily broken in half. She wanted to meet the naked boy before her, this vulnerable thing, but she didn't know if she'd ever get the chance because Damian wouldn't let her. In a while he would fully wake and he would be a secret to her.

"Soon," she said. There were a few more things she wanted to look at. Damian nodded, sniffed, and with his eyes half open stumbled back up the stairs. Nathalie remembered one of Sobraille's last remarks. The data was always useful. The interpretation should never be taken on faith. That's what she'd been trying to say to Damian the other morning, about remembering the future and imagining the past, only she couldn't articulate it at the time. She didn't make the past up. That's not what she meant. The facts were the facts. What happened. But the meanings of events were her own invention. An interpretation of the data. And if she reinterpreted the past, she could change what the past meant. Her dad wanted her to be like him but he'd taught her to be something else. Her studies were preparing her, but not for graduate school. She had a new fate now, one she didn't understand, but authentically hers and out there waiting to be discovered. A transformation as mysterious and illogical as turning lead into gold.

Sobraille said the Rebis had to do with alchemy and she'd spent several hours the night before investigating alchemical allegory and symbolism. She sipped her coffee and closed the translation file and opened a folder of the digital images. A bizarre world of medieval magic and dark science in which the boundaries between philosophy, physics, cosmology, chemistry, religion, nature, magic, medicine, mathematics, myth, had not yet been delineated. A language of imagery. The hallucinations of a primordial fever dream, she thought as she clicked through the scans, all blood and earth and awe. Profane geometry. Holy nightmares. The King and Queen inside a circle inside a square inside a triangle inside a circle. Fantastical furnaces and ovens, mythological beasts of every imaginable mutation imprisoned in glass beakers and retorts and alembics of exotic shapes and designs, long stems twisting like rollercoasters, and all manner of weird scientific instruments, morbid torture devices, lurid sex acts.

Lions eating the sun and lions eating one another and dogs fucking one another and serpents eating themselves. Swans, doves, crows, peacocks. Phoenixes and unicorns and dragons and angels. A knight cracking a giant egg with a sword. A knight, fully armed, charging into a great wall of fire stretching all the way up to the horizon, naked woman in pursuit. A naked woman breast-feeding the sun. A naked woman astride an enormous sea-monster spouting cascades of gore from twin blowholes and breaching an ocean of milk that pours from the woman's breasts. A naked woman copulating with a dragon in an open grave. The King and Queen copulating in an open grave. The King and Queen beheaded with an axe. The

Rebis roasted on a spit above an open fire. The Rebis stretched upon the rack. The Rebis, prone, sprouting a tree from its navel. A field of corpses lying exposed beside their open graves and a murder of crows descending to pick clean the carrion.

Nathalie rinsed her coffee cup and put it in the dishwasher and shut down the computer. For a few minutes she searched for her hair-pick. She didn't know when she misplaced it but it had been missing a few days and her hair showed it. Combs and brushes were useless against the dense cloud of curls. Only the thick-toothed pick could strain snarls out of it. Damian helped her look for it the night before and promised to pick it up if he spotted it. She was in the habit of taking the pick from one room and setting it down in another, and lost it often, but this time she must've accidentally knocked it in the garbage or something because it hadn't come back.

Upstairs, Damian drowsed, naked, splayed upon the bed-covers. She licked his hipbones and ran her fingernails down the fence of his ribs and aroused him with her mouth. Memorizing his curvature, learning with her tongue the slope and diameter of him. She loved how elated it made him. The way he gasped and writhed made her generous toward him. And he was a generous lover, too. Humble. Willing to learn the cravings of her body and to feed them. She taught him to use all five senses. Smell her hair, taste her pussy. Kiss the backs of her knees and stroke her neck. She wanted to look in his eyes. She wanted to come all over him.

They held hands while she drained him until she knew he would stay hard. Damian shook all over and she held him in her arms and kissed his forehead. "Thank you," he said, "thank you, thank you. I never felt like this before."

She wanted to know what he felt but he couldn't explain it. "Wonderful," was all he came up with. It frustrated her a little —she wanted to understand his wonderful feeling, if it was the same thing she felt, or different. Thoughts dissolved when Damian dipped his nose to her crotch and arched her back, made her squeal, made her squeeze his head between her thighs and cry the world's oldest love song. They made open-eyed love, mouths glazed and kissing, moaning shared wonder. Nathalie felt plugged into him, her belly on fire with his belly, her knees lit up with lightning, she could feel between her fingertips the hysterical muscles of her uterus shuddering in Damian's throat. Bleating like a dying animal the arrival of orgasm into the soft flesh between his neck and shoulder, and Damian singing the same song to her. For a long time they trembled like that, lying in a heap, welded at the groin.

Seconds melted in a blaze of full daylight and wore out the morning. Heat stacked on top of demented heat and drove them apart. They lay side by side with Damian's fingertips skiing the sweat on her breasts and his thigh clasped between Nathalie's shuddering thighs, neither willing to surrender the other's body completely.

"Are you falling in love with me?" Damian asked.

"Maybe," she said. "I haven't really thought about it."

"Have you ever been in love before?"

"I don't know," she said. "Probably not. You?"

"No."

"And? Are you falling in love with me?"

Damian shrugged and ran his hand over the stiff branches of her hair. "I guess where I'm at right now, I could go either way."

More questions than answers and no answer definitive, only probabilities, only possibilities. A week later, after rehearsal for Strange Equinoxes, she took the invitations to a professor of art history at Cal State East Bay, Dr. Anjelica Singh-Velasquez, who more or less agreed with the bookbinder: the woodcuts were clearly made by a master artisan, not merely proficient but also technically innovative. A true artist. And that's where Anjelica, as she insisted Nathalie call her, added another wrinkle to the source of the wedding invitations. There was evidence of styles and techniques that didn't exist in Europe among woodcarvers before the mid-nineteenth century. Especially the influence of Gustave Dore was subtle but distinct in several details. Anjelica pointed them out with examples from a book of Dore prints she used for comparison. It didn't take an art expert to see how they were similar. Nathalie saw it right away and her heart sank.

Anjelica also found it difficult to believe the invitations were made anytime recently. She could think of only two working artists with the necessary skill, but stylistically the woodcuts didn't match up with either of them. She found it hard to believe an artist of this magnitude could've gone undiscovered. If whoever did this had been working in the last fifty years she would know about it. Her theory was that the woodcuts were made between 1875, when Dore was at the height of his powers, and the beginning of World War II.

It didn't make any sense to Nathalie and she was starting to wonder if Damian was right when he said the answer might be absurd. She was a wreck. Finals were coming up, she was getting ready to graduate, and all she could think about were those damn wedding invitations. At night she lay awake turning and turning everything she knew about them over in her head, hoping some clue might present itself in the dry facts. The chemical analysis said they were made in the fifteenth or early sixteenth century, the language specialist thought early seventeenth century at the latest, the bookbinder said they were made in the late twentieth or early twenty-first century, and the art historian said they were made in the mid-to-late nineteenth or early-to-mid twentieth century.

Sobraille was right about one thing: the crucial aspect wasn't the data but the interpretation, and Nathalie had no idea what any of it meant.

On a Saturday night Rosa came to the city for a concert and they met up for coffee before the show. Nathalie took her wedding invitation out of its acid-free sleeve and flattened it out in front of her sister. "It's not fake," Rosa announced, although she couldn't say when it was made. The document was hidden under layers, which made it difficult to see clearly. There were a lot of bodies on top of it.

Nathalie arched an eyebrow.

"Forms." Rosa hesitated, reaching for the right words. "Kind of like shadows. Some are human and some are—creatures. Entities. A lot of intention has gone into it, but I don't see anything like deception."

"On the phone you said what it is and what it means are two different things."

Rosa held up a hand, as if the answer was obvious. "The invitation isn't the important thing. The wedding is what matters. Once you get to the wedding, it'll make more sense. Or something. Maybe."

Nathalie didn't understand why it mattered if she went to this wedding. What's so important? How was she supposed to get there? Rosa's attention slid from the document to Nathalie, eyes flitting left and right, pupils going in and out of focus as she searched Nathalie's face, looking for things no one else could see. "What's that?" Rosa said and frowned. "You've got something lodged right in the middle of you." She pointed a purple fingernail at Nathalie's breast. Nathalie started to object. And stopped. She hadn't noticed before, but once Rosa pointed it out, she could feel it in her chest. Right where Rosa pointed, deep in her ribcage, between her lungs and her heart.

"It's a jar," Rosa said. "It looks like an egg cup, but there's no opening and no lid. Not even a seam. It's perfectly sealed, like it was never meant to be opened, but—why can't I see inside?" She looked at Nathalie like it was an unfair trick.

Nathalie crinkled her face and shrugged. She was just as clueless as Rosa. "I don't know."

"Well, something's got to be locked up in there. What about this wedding you're looking for? Do you think it could be in there?" Rosa stood up and walked in a semi-circle until she stood behind Nathalie. "There it is," Rosa whispered. "I think that's it. Way out in front of you. So far away I can't make out the details, but I recognize the shape. It's going to take you a long time to get there." She sat back down and sighed. "Sorry I couldn't be more helpful. It's just too small to see right now. You'll have to get closer to it. Then I'll be able to tell you more."

Nathalie tried not to look disappointed. She drank her coffee to keep Rosa from seeing her face.

"I know it's a lame gift," Rosa said. "I can't see well enough to tell you what's going to happen. Just well enough so that after it happens, it'll look like I saw it coming."

But that wasn't what Nathalie was thinking. She was thinking about the cup inside her and the wedding. What was the connection? "What does the shape look like? Maybe that'll help me find it."

"The wedding? It's not really shaped like anything else," Rosa said and shrugged. "I don't know. I guess it kind of looks like destiny."

21.

And then catastrophe. The last week of April, two weeks before finals, all her end of quarter assignments coming due, and hard as she tried, she couldn't summon the ambition to focus on school. It gave her a headache. She tried to convince herself it was important but the blunt truth was she didn't give a shit anymore. Her dad called to take her to lunch but the idea twisted a knot in her spine. She begged off and he told her why he really called. Her summer internship started the Monday after graduation, in three weeks, working with the COO of the Gilman foundry.

"Okay," she said. She couldn't even fake interest.

He knew it wasn't where she wanted to be this summer, but the foundry was adding an aluminum division, they were going through organizational changes, restructuring the corporate model, he'd thought about it quite a bit and the opportunity was too good for her to miss. He wanted her to learn how all those things were done. "It'll be more interesting than you think," he said. "Try to sound excited."

He hung up and she was just getting back into her homework when the phone rang again. The Booth School of Business at the University of Chicago congratulating her on being accepted into the MBA program. She jotted down tuition costs and registration deadlines. A package with full details was coming in the mail, along with her official letter of acceptance, and a formal declaration of her intent to enroll, which she would have to mail back. She put the notes in the kitchen drawer with half a dozen other offers, all of which she'd accepted over the phone, none of which she wanted to attend.

Those acceptance letters were in the back of her mind all day. Leering at her. As long as she kept her attention on her homework she could pretend to ignore them.

The assignment was to create a fictional business and put together a mock proposal for potential investors. Her idea was for a dance company that worked with high-risk inner-city youth. The kids would learn dances from all over the world and receive education on everything from college prep and family planning to job interview skills and domestic violence awareness. The professor refused to approve her project because it sounded more like a non-profit, which Nathalie admitted was true, and helped her brainstorm better options. Nathalie picked one but scrapped it a week later and went back to the dance company. She didn't care how it affected her grade —this was the only way she could give a damn about the assignment enough to finish it.

At eight o'clock she stopped work for the day, turned on music, made dinner, but all she could think about were the acceptance letters. Strange Equinoxes had a performance in a few weeks and she pushed the furniture out of the way to rehearse her choreography but everything came out flat. All she could see when she closed her eyes was expensive matte stationary, flowery letterhead, crisp sans-serif fonts: *we are pleased to inform you...* It threw her anticipation off, all clunky footwork and stiff timing. She turned on the TV, which couldn't distract her, either. She thought of her dad and the bleak Monday morning he'd promised her. How excruciatingly short the next three weeks would be. Every day of it hardening the pit in her gut. Filling her lungs a little bit each day with scalding lead.

She imagined laying out her clothes the night before, the monotone peal of the alarm at six in the morning, showering, brushing her teeth and fixing her hair, her makeup, the lonesome silence as she ate breakfast, the brisk walk to the rail station, crossing the Bay Bridge into Berkeley. Handshakes with the office staff and the plaster feeling of her own smile. She cried thinking about it. She texted Rosa to call her, but she was busy with a study group, could it wait 'til tomorrow? No big deal, Nathalie replied, she just wanted to talk. Kendra didn't answer her text. Finally, she called Damian. It was almost midnight. "Sorry about the hour," she said. "I thought I could handle it until morning, but I was wrong, and no one else can put up with me. Please, will you come over?"

"Call me first next time," he said.

When he arrived she told him about the phone calls from her dad and the Booth School of Business. She showed him the acceptance letters—Harvard, Wharton, Fuqua, Stern, Ross—and explained how she'd committed verbally to them all. "I don't know what I was thinking," she said. "It just felt like there was no way out of it."

"So which one do you want?"

She blinked back at him. It took her a second to understand what he was asking. "I don't want any of them."

Damian looked through the letters. "I don't know how much these applications cost, but there's gotta be over a thousand dollars' worth here."

"I sent them in January. It just seemed like I had nothing better to do, so why fight it? But it's not what I want. It never was."

"Did any reject you?"

"Stanford and MIT," she said. "Assholes."

Damian walked to the wastebasket beneath the kitchen sink and filed the letters. "Problem solved."

But that wasn't good enough, they were still in there—it seemed effective and she couldn't explain why, but throwing them away wouldn't work. "It's like they're looking at me."

"Would it be better if we took them out to the big green dumpster?"

She thought about that but, no, she still didn't feel safe. They were too dangerous to throw away. "I would know they were out there. I feel stupid, but it's true."

"This is a bigger problem than I thought," Damian said

and sat down on the couch to mull it over. Foolish, but her heart raced and she'd never get to sleep until the acceptance letters were truly gone. She folded her arms over her chest and watched Damian mull.

"We could burn them?" Damian offered, but she didn't know about that idea. "I burn things all the time. To get rid of them. It works really well."

"Worth a shot," she said. There was a butane lighter she kept in the hall closet in case of power outages. She held up the first letter and lit the corner and laid it in the sink. She lit the next one and laid it on top of the first and when they were all at the bottom of the sink she and Damian watched them curl and shrink like snails. A long feather of gray smoke stood up in the chrome basin. When the fire went out she pulled the faucet and turned the ashes to mud.

Days she brooded on what Damian said, how she should do what she wanted, how her dad had no right to expect her life in his image, and in the end her life was her own responsibility, however heavy, and what became of it would be her fault, no matter the excuses. It put blisters on her heart, made her even number, until she couldn't take it anymore and called her dad. Nathalie didn't worry he might answer—he almost never answered his cell phone, especially during the day—he'd call when it was convenient for him.

She left a message that she'd made up her mind about the summer. She wanted to concentrate on Strange Equinoxes, which meant she wouldn't have time for the Gilman foundry, because she hated school and she hated working in the office and what she really wanted to do with her life was dance. She hoped he understood. She wanted him to support her, she said, she knew it was difficult news for him to hear, but in time she hoped he would understand because she loved him and she knew, no matter what, he loved her, too.

The first call came a little after four o'clock. Way too early for it to mean good news, so she stood in the kitchen staring at the display in her hands and watched it go to voicemail. She would listen to his message, see how he sounded, and decide what to say before calling back. But he didn't leave a message— he called again and she refused to answer again. In ten minutes she had half a dozen missed calls from her dad and she was paralyzed. She could not answer. Could not speak to him. If she gave him the chance he'd talk her into doing exactly as he pleased.

The calls got worse before they stopped. At three in the morning he called four more times, one after the other, like gunshots. She held her phone to her breast and cried until the calls stopped. When he finally left a message all he said was she hadn't been answering his calls and he was getting worried. She thought she heard resignation in his tone. She'd almost talked herself into calling when he left another message saying she should talk to him so he could help her make the best decision for her future. Then nothing for a month, perhaps the longest time ever without talking to him, then he was screaming and cursing and demanding she knock off this foolishness immediately. Nathalie was sick to her stomach. She wanted to cry. He was only acting this way because he was hurt. But it was impossible for Nathalie to save herself without hurting him. It made her nauseous. Devoured by guilt. Terrified of what would become of her. Elated enough to make all her suffering beautiful and, she realized, the kind of pain that made life worth living.

Damian spent the hottest hours working on the printing-press, greasing bearings, changing out injector heads, washers, cleaning the ink trap. It was Friday and the foot traffic thick in front of the payday loan service when he got home in the early evening, broken windshield glass scattered on the sidewalk. No sign of where it came from, no cleanup crew or cops taking statements, no sign of the assaulted car. Nothing in his mailbox. He unlocked the studio door and braced himself against the wave of hot air that rushed out. The first week of May and it already felt like August. Eighty degrees and no air-conditioning, all the heat of the first two floors rising into his apartment. He left the window open all day, an electric box-fan propped against the screen to blow the air out, but it did no good. The stale heat was difficult to breathe. Most days he avoided home between the hours of ten and six.

There was something else in the room, buried in the heat, his constant companion: the sensation of being looked at. He ignored it and went to the bathroom to rinse off under a cool shower. He was used to the feeling of someone watching him —it didn't frighten him anymore. What frightened him was his worsening paranoia. Obviously, no one was watching him, not in the shower, but he couldn't rationalize the feeling away. He felt accompanied all the time, a presence, no one in particular, just someone else with him. He'd returned *Rosarium philosophorum* to the Leonard Library but the feeling hadn't diminished. He should've burned the goddamned thing, like Nathalie burned her admission letters.

Later, after full dark, when the temperature outside got lower than inside, he turned the fan around in the windowsill to blow the cooler air in. He made cold sandwiches for dinner and ate them, shirtless, on the floor. That's when he noticed the books.

He was a poor housekeeper but liked a tidy stack of books and kept a regular rotation always at his bedside. Sitting next to them on the floor, he could tell they'd been tampered with, spines slightly askew, two of them facing opposite the others. He always lined the spines up straight, facing the same direction, so he could easily see their titles. And they were out of order. Last night he'd read Jung and sat it on the pile before going to sleep, but now Agrippa lay on top. *De occulta philosophia libri tres* was thinking about Damian. He picked it up and sifted the pages until he found a piece of folded rice paper. In the margin a two-headed stick figure. The note copied from the same pages of its discovery.

The Philosophers, especially the Arabians, say, that mans mind, when it is most intent upon any work, through its passion and effects, is joyned with the mind of the stars, and intelligencies, and being so joyned is the cause of some wonderfull virtue be infused into our works, and things; and this, as because there is in it an apprehension, and power of all things, so because all things have a naturall obedience to it, and more to that which desires them with a strong desire. And according to this is verified the art of characters, images, inchantments, and some speeches, and many other wonderfull experiments to every thing which the mind affects. By this means whatsoever the mind of him that is in vehement love affects, hath an efficacy to cause love, and whatsoever the mind of him that strongly hates, dictates, hath an efficacy to hurt, and destroy.

Damian didn't know what to think except it was intended for him. He hadn't read more than a few random pages of this book since receiving it, he'd supposed, by mistake. But he'd looked through it a few times and it was impossible he could've missed this note before. Someone had broken into his apartment to hide the note in the book.

His skin crawled and he realized he'd been holding his breath. He got up and paced the little room, trying to decide how anyone could've come in without his finding out. Not for the first time he inspected the front door and even the third-story window, the fucking air vents along the base-boards, in the bathroom ceiling. Nothing betrayed forced entry. As far as he could tell nothing else in the studio had been disturbed. The only keys belonged to him and the superintendent, a stuffy Indonesian woman with a hard-on for every article of the lease agreement. She wouldn't let anyone in without giving Damian twenty-four hours advanced written notice of intent to enter the premises.

He asked her about it anyway, first thing next morning, but he didn't mention a break-in because she would definitely report it, which would mean cops, and Damian didn't want anything to do with cops, not even for help. His electric razor was missing, did she know if anyone had been in his apartment? She did not. "Thought I'd ask," he said. "Don't know what I did with it."

Pavel would require a totally different approach. He wouldn't want anything to do with Damian if he thought the Secret Service was interested, but he was also a man who knew how to learn things and Damian needed information. "Courtesy call," he told Pavel over the phone. "Someone broke into my place last night and stole shit. Looks like a random burglary but it makes me wonder about some things."

22.

Pavel met him at the peace pagoda in Japantown. Heat kept people from staying too long and created a meeting place both public and secluded. The two men admired the cherry blossoms lining the cement terrace and spoke openly beneath the stupa's five umbrellas. "I don't keep anything incriminating at home," Damian said. "Nothing connects me to you or anybody else."

"You never struck me as a stupid man." Pavel had a gold ring on his right hand and Damian watched him slide it off between three pale fingertips, flip it over, and slide it back on, over and over like that. He could do it very fast and Damian found it hypnotic, strangely soothing, the repetitive motion, the deftness of Pavel's long fingers, twinkle of sunlight on precious metal. "I'm not worried about you compromising me," Pavel said.

"Any word on Gangjeon? Or the others asking around about him? The woman?"

Pavel shook his head. "You think one of them broke into your place?"

"No," said Damian. "I'm covering my bases." He was struck by Pavel's exquisite hands, the nails clipped straight and white, the unblemished milk of his fingers, palms pink and scalloped with callouses. Everything about him was tidy, the black wraparound sunglasses, blue polo shirt freshly pressed and neatly tucked into black slacks and matching belt. Damian bet women adored his angular accent and fluid gait, almost feminine, the slinky way he rolled his shoulders when he walked.

Pavel slid the ring down his finger one last time and put his palms down at his sides. "No news on Gangjeon. Even if there were, I don't know it would get back to me. The strangers were only interested in Kim and Noe. I've asked about them here and there but they disappeared. I don't believe they were cops, though, and nothing makes me think they knew anything about you or counterfeit. I think they worked for Gangjeon but there's no proof."

"What about Gangjeon's alchemist? The Bulgarian or whatever?"

Pavel laughed. "I don't think he exists. That's a myth."

Damian leaned back on his elbows and looked up at the steel gills on the underside of an enormous mushroom cap, the repeating tiers of the pagoda. None of this was what he wanted to hear. He must take a risk if anything was going to come of the conversation. "I think someone's been following me. No idea who. Maybe you could find out?" He described the earless old man with the chevron mustache, black trench-coat, and fedora.

"If there's trouble, I'll sell you out. I won't hesitate."

Damian let that settle between them before he sat back up and looked at Pavel. His voice was calm and he didn't seem agitated. He'd merely stated a fact.

"It's nothing personal," Pavel said. "Just good business. I'm telling you this because I like you. Otherwise, I wouldn't bother." Damian wished he'd take off the sunglasses. He'd be able to read between the brittle words if he could see better. Instead he looked at his own negative reflection shining off the black surfaces covering Pavel's eyes. "You're of great value to me, so I'll do it. But understand I don't need you the way you need me. There are other sources of money. Not as good as you, but cheaper, and less dangerous if you're under government surveillance. If that's what I find out, I'll cut you loose, and I don't want you to feel betrayed."

Pavel stood and put his hands in his pockets and rocked on his heels. Damian followed him in the direction of Geary Boulevard, unable to speak. "You might notice someone else following you in future," Pavel said. "Don't be alarmed. They work for me. If you're being watched, I'll find out who they are and where they live. What you do with the information is your own affair." He stopped at the park's perimeter and the two men stood in the small shade of pink flowers. Pavel broke a blossom from a low branch and inhaled. "Scent of cherries," he muttered and offered it to Damian. The silky texture of flower petals. So delicate and luxurious it made his fingertips want to cry. In his hand the tiny flower looked like a crushed fairy, pink wings ruined with the grime and oil of Damian's skin.

"I brought you a gift," Pavel said. A replica icon the size of a poker card. Our Lady of Vladimir. The Holy Mother covered in black hijab trimmed in gold against a gold-leaf background. The child swaddled in white, body disproportionately long for his tiny head, neck craned at an anatomically impossible angle to gaze upon his mother's face. Her expression an agony of compassion and sorrow, the narrow European nose and slight mouth closed with resolve. Or was it more like resignation? Her eyes, hooded and dark, watched Damian. He recognized those eyes, the worry and ferocious love they conveyed. His own mother had often looked at him the same way.

Pavel took off the shades and hooked them on his collar and showed Damian the blue sparks of his eyes. "Theotokos of Vladimir," he said. "It means 'the one who gives birth to god'. You admired her beauty at the restaurant. Are you religious?"

Damian shook his head.

"Me, neither," Pavel said. He smiled. "But if you pray to her, she will protect you."

At home Damian found another note, this one written on his front door. White block capitals. A single diminishing word shaped like an inverted triangle:

KALEMARIS
KALEMARI
KALEMAR
KALEMA
KALEM
KALE
KAL
KA
K

He ran his fingers over the bottom letter and rubbed them
together. Dry and gritty. Chalk. Slowly he opened the door and
slid in, ready for a fight, but there was no one there. Nearly
eleven o'clock but no chance of sleep now. The Leonard Library
was open twenty-four hours and he took a taxi. Kalemaris was
of unknown etymology, most likely a nonsense word, similar to Abracadabra, used in written protection spells. It first
appeared in a Danish grimoire, *Sybrianus P.P.P.,* published in
1771, though variations date back to ancient Alexandria, before the destruction of the Great Library. It could be worn
about the neck to cure disease and ward off evil spirits. It could
be written down and gifted to protect someone else. It could be
written across the top of the inside of a doorway for domestic
protection. Damian didn't especially care about magic words
on his door. The intention behind them, however, he wanted to
understand. Was danger implied and if so what kind? A protection charm must mean someone was looking out for him.

He took notes and requested *Sybrianus P.P.P.* through interlibrary loan, less confident than ever of figuring this thing out,
and went home to his copy of Agrippa because he remembered
seeing something in it about Abracadabra. He found a similar diminishing triangle in the third book, a chapter dealing
with the divine names of god. Agrippa credits Abracadabra
to someone called Serenus Semonicus, who claimed if a diseased person wrote the charm on a piece of paper and wore it

around their neck, the illness would wane little by little until completely gone. Before going to bed, Damian wrote down the name on one of Nathalie's index cards and set it aside. He would see what there was to learn about Serenus Semonicus the next time he visited the library.

The next evening he knocked up and down the third floor of his building and asked the neighbors if they knew who vandalized his door, but nobody saw a thing. Of course. He worried about washing the message off but he didn't see much point in leaving it. Not like the chalk could actually keep him safe, but what if the messenger took its removal as a slight? Except it would be gone as soon as the superintendent found out, anyway, and he preferred her not to know, so he wiped it off with the same rag he used for washing dishes.

He'd made a mistake with Pavel. Should never have told him about the trench-coat man. The risk was miscalculated and only made his situation worse. Someone was interested in him. There was no denying it. Before, he could dismiss it as stress and hyper paranoia, but Kalemaris was objective proof. The Secret Service were unlikely suspects but it was stupid to discount them—the consequences for being wrong were too dire. He brooded on it over breakfast, keenly aware of the other presence in the room. *De occulta philosophia libri tres* was thinking about him again. Then a sickening thought: no one was protecting him—they were trapping him. The other night at the library he'd read Kalemaris was a protective charm when the diminishing triangle was applied over the door on the *inside*. But it appeared on the *outside* of Damian's door. Did it change anything? If writing it on the inside was supposed to keep evil out, what did writing it on the outside do? Contain something within? And what was being contained inside the studio? Damian?

Or something else?

"I might be going away pretty soon," he told Nathalie the next time they were together. They drank vodka gimlets on the condo's patio beneath an acrylic sky. Mediterranean blue. Spritz of sea salt. They sat at a round table near the sliding glass door, but Damian didn't have the courage for this conversation so close to her. He stood and walked to the sandstone wall separating the patio from the communal courtyard and touched his drink against his forehead. Heat radiated from the concrete floor and pressed the sky down like a grill on his bear skin. Damian could bear to press his palm to the wall for only a second before the nerves hissed, the skin pink and swollen as braised veal. He swore under his breath and squeezed the full tumbler hard until the dewy glass relieved the burn.

Nathalie was motionless but for her eyes which slid slowly from his face to the glass in his hand. Bunched her shoulders and spoke. "I figured this was coming. Sooner or later." She picked a cucumber wheel out of her glass and sucked the vodka off. "Can I ask when you'll be back?" She bit the cucumber and laid the remaining crescent on the ice-cubes in her glass. "Will you be back?"

"Twenty-five years, minimum," Damian said and shrugged. "No possibility of parole."

"That bad?"

He sipped his drink and squinted against the heat. "My dad got two years, but he made a deal. I won't be making any deals."

"Why are you telling me this?"

Not a question he'd anticipated but it didn't matter. He knew the answer without much effort. "So I can enjoy the time I have left with you without feeling guilty. So I don't feel like I lied to you."

She guffawed and rearranged her weight in the wrought-iron chair. Smiled a pissed off smile. "You'd have to talk to me in order to lie, Damian. You'd have to—what?—fucking—tell me. Something."

Damian nodded and emptied his drink and said he needed another. Really, he needed more time. To think. When he decided to broach this conversation he knew there was a chance it might be the last he ever had with her, but he hadn't believed it. Not really. Now he saw her anger, her hurt at his secrets. She was helpless to make him trust her. He'd put her in an unfair position and he knew there was a serious possibility it could all be ending on the patio.

In the kitchen he took his time with the drink to give them both a chance to calm down. Outside she cleared tears and running makeup away from her eyes. "How do you see this playing out?"

Damian shrugged. "I don't want you to hate me. I want to mean as much to you as you mean to me. Not because of a stupid dream. If something happens to me, I don't want you to feel deceived or betrayed. Whatever it takes for that to be the case."

"I don't know what that'll take."

They looked at each other for a minute. Damian wanted to touch her. Hold her hand—something—but he didn't dare. He didn't dare tell her about the Rebis and the philosopher's stone and what the wedding invitations were about. A threat or a warning. Because of Damian someone was keeping an eye on them both. He wanted to tell her but he was too much a coward to trust her.

"Does this have anything to do with the guys who mugged you?"

"I thought so at first, but it's not them. I don't know who it is."

She crinkled her nose and drummed glossy fingernails on the ironwork tabletop. "It occurs to me," she said, "you want to be honest without exposing yourself. You want intimacy but not vulnerability. It doesn't exist. There's a simple solution."

"Which is?"

"You could trust me. Tell me what you got yourself into. Whatever happens, I won't be betrayed and I won't be deceived. Because I'll know what's going on. You'll see I don't hate you."

"I hope that's true."

"We could find out. Right now."

Tempting, but he already knew he wouldn't do it. He licked his lips and cleared his throat. He wanted to tell her about Kalemaris, Pavel, his dad and the man in the black trench-coat and the whole ludicrous mess. He fucked up, he wanted to say, he might've kept enough distance to know her for an ally but instead he'd fallen in love with her. She was like the printing-press now, the same as his mother and his father and his step-father: one more thing he depended on and would lose. "Sorry," he said. "It's not because I don't trust you. I don't trust anyone."

Her nostrils flared and for a moment he thought she might weep, but instead she bolted forward in her chair and picked the cucumber sliver off her drink and threw it at him. It bounced off his face and landed on the table and both of them looked at it.

"Tell me something," she whispered.

"What?"

"Anything. Tell me something you didn't think you would ever tell me. Something you don't want me to know. Tell me that. And make it good."

A long time passed. He thought of the invitations again and *Rosarium philosophorum.* His dad teaching him to make counterfeit and the wreck prison made the son-of-a-bitch. The notes left for him in books. In the end he told her he didn't know what to say.

"Fine," she said and stood up. "That's your task. You said you wanted a quest. Some errand to prove yourself worthy. Here it is: tell me whatever the hell it is you pray to god I never find out."

The holy trinity of Our Art is made of mercury, sulphur, and salt. They are the black dragon, which enslaves and nourishes the white queen, who is the only one able to heal the red king, who alone can slay the dragon. When the king and queen are wed the fruit of their marriage bed will be our precious stone. Secret fire stolen from the gods. To capture it, heaven must be combined with hell and cosmos divided from creation. The earth must be brought above and the sky must be brought below. The fixed made to flux and the volatile dense. It begins in the dark. Discovered where no one wants to seek it. Marked by the appearance of a crow's head.

23.

Through Nathalie's first eleven quarters of college she'd never earned less than an A-minus but her final term grades were straight B's. She was ashamed not because they were so low but because they were higher than she deserved. She skipped out on commencement but walked in the departmental ceremony. Her dad didn't attend, but three of her sisters—Rosa, Eugenie, and Carolina—sat with Damian throughout and even had their pictures taken with him in the lobby. Afterward, everyone celebrated with sushi and sakē in the Castro. Gold and crimson dining-room. Razor white and blue backlighting the sushi bar. Composite stone path, coy pond, bonsai saplings. Damian was quiet but gracious to her sisters. Polite. Effusive in praise of Nathalie's accomplishment. Mostly, he observed the four women and stayed out of the way. When the meal was finished he picked up all five checks and excused himself. He needed to get to work, he'd call when he got home.

"He's cute," Rosa said when he was gone.

"And nice," Eugenie said.

"And potent," Carolina said. "Dad'll hate him."

"Dad's not going to meet him," Nathalie said. "Spit it out before it chokes you. I can tell you don't like him."

"I like him," said Carolina and sucked her lemonade through a straw. Nathalie looked at her but said nothing. Carolina was only stirring the storm, egging them all on, that's why she said it. She liked to start fights. Rosalie and Eugenie looked at each other, mouths half open, each begging the other to sooth Nathalie.

Finally, Rosa said, "I think we're just surprised. The way

he affects you. He barely touches you and you light up like a Christmas tree."

"I can smell him all over you," Carolina agreed. "You've got pubic hair breath."

"Shut up," Rosa said and glared. Carolina concentrated on her lemonade.

"We didn't think you'd be this way about a guy," Eugenie said. "You're always so responsible. So in charge of yourself. But god. When you finally fall you fall hard."

"And that's a bad thing?"

Carolina shrugged but kept her mouth shut. Rosa and Eugenie shared another cagey glance. "It's dangerous," Rosa said. "When people get like you are, sometimes they lose themselves. It's hard to explain."

The insinuation exasperated Nathalie. She knew what Rosa was talking about. Nathalie's eyes might be ordinary but she could see as well as Rosa the simpering cows who forget who they are whenever some jackass at the other end of a dick shows the least bit of genuine interest, changing their appearances, bodies, plans to better accessorize the animus of their pathetic princess fantasies. Nathalie was not that woman. The idea lit a smoldering coal in her belly. "I didn't plan it. I never said I wasn't the stupidest one of us all." She actually had claimed to be the smartest, many times, but not since they were little girls.

"Your vocal pattern's changing. To match his. Your tones harmonize when you speak to each other. Your breaths sound the same," Eugenie said.

"When you stand next to each other, it's hard to see where he ends and you begin," Rosa said.

"You smell like him. Not just your mouth. All over," Carolina said. Her nostrils flared. "Is your arm hair burning?"

"I'm getting upset," Nathalie said and held her arm to her nose. She smelled nothing unusual. The waiter brought small porcelain bowls of green tea ice-cream and Nathalie asked for another hot sakē.

"Let's change the subject," Eugenie offered, but Nathalie didn't think so. There were still things she wanted to know.

"So the problem isn't him—something's wrong with me."

"It's happening to him, too," Rosa said. "You're blending into each other."

"You sound like each other," Eugenie said.

"His breath smells like your hair," Carolina said. "His skin smells like your breath. Like he's sweating your saliva."

Across the table sat Rosa and behind her stood a mirror on the wall. Nathalie's hair tamed by oils and conditioners, the laces of her French braid further tightened with hairpins. None of her sisters were cursed with this impossible mane and she guessed it must've come from her biological fathers. In the spirit of celebration she still wore the black graduation gown but she didn't feel like celebrating anymore. The matching black hat sat on the table beside her, tasseled blue and gold. She looked like a kid playing dress-up, taking romantic advice from three teenagers, still kids themselves. She wished she could hear her mother's opinion but that was impossible. Her mother would only worry and feel bad about herself, which would accomplish nothing.

Carolina said, "She's going to combust," and Nathalie took a languid spoon of ice-cream to cool down. For the sake of the brat's poor nose.

"He loves you," Rosa said. "I'm certain. Thick cords connect him to you."

"Maybe," said Eugenie, "but it's distant. Far away. I have to strain to hear love. He's got many secrets. From you and from himself."

"But he's not a liar," Carolina said. "At least I don't think. His voice—it's sour but not disgusting. More curdled milk than bullshit."

"I don't know," Eugenie said. "He believes the things he tells you. But some of them aren't true."

"What does that mean?"

"It's ambiguous," Rosa said.

"It's like he doesn't recognize himself," Eugenie said.

"He thinks he's one thing but he's really something else," Carolina said.

"He believes in you," Rosa said, "but he doesn't believe in himself."

"He's rank with fear," Carolina agreed. "That's not strange. Everybody stinks of fear."

"Shatter and howl. Terrible noises in his past and more in his future," Eugenie said. "Grinding and scratching."

Rosa nodded. "He's got a wound in his heart. There's blood all over him and he can't heal it here. He's got to leave or he'll die."

"It's not a long term thing," Eugenie said.

"Enjoy it while it lasts," Carolina said.

"But that doesn't mean it's bad," Rosa said.

"I can't make out yet what you're doing, but this is an important part of it," Eugenie said.

"Just know it's coming to an end," Carolina said.

Rosa nodded again. "Brace yourself."

Nathalie hadn't known what to expect, but never this. She wanted to ask if he was leaving of his own choice or if he was going to jail, but in the end decided against the question. Damian already didn't trust her. Stupidly. She didn't want to ask her sisters anything that would support his fear, even if he would never know about it. She shouldn't put too much stock in anything her sisters had to say anyway. They were children after all, and they weren't psychics. Not really. They were wrong at least half the time. Rosalie and Eugenie were the first to admit they didn't always understand what they were seeing. Or hearing. Nathalie supposed even spooky data was vulnerable to interpretation.

But whatever Damian was dealing with, he wanted to go through it alone. She couldn't forget that. His privacy fetish went beyond suspicion or distrust—it was a crater in his heart, so precious to him he didn't seem to recognize it as an injury, deep-seated and irrational, fundamental to his worldview, and someone taught it to him. Who? Probably his abusive scumbag father, a man Nathalie had never met and knew almost nothing about, but she hated him. Whatever Damian was caught up in he learned from his father. Damian let slip his father got a reduced sentence for the same crime. He'd told her his dad hit his mom but the fucker probably beat up on both of them. That would make it hard to trust, she thought, that could make you cling to lack and fear. Damian was the prime mover of her decision to face down her own lifelong fear, and she wanted very much to mean the same thing to him. Something else they shared in common, she realized. Constant fear.

She made a point to see him less over the course of May, cooling only half deliberately, like something inside understood the departure would hurt less if she paced herself. Best to start detoxing from him now, best to quell the fire he fed in her until she could control its hunger. And so as the temperature of northern California continued climbing, the temperature in Nathalie Jevali chose a gentle descent.

One day in the middle of May Damian came unannounced to the condo. "I'll do it. But it'll take time. I'll need your help."

A hard tension lined his voice, prolonged in the dead air between them by Nathalie's confusion. Furious heat thrumming the open doorway and the persecuted look of him ate the room. Nathalie opened her mouth to ask what in god's name he meant and then closed it. Her face flushed. He was accepting her trial by quest.

"Shut the door," she said. "You're letting the cold air out."

She offered iced-tea and he sat on the couch with the tall glass standing on the coffee-table clutched in both hands. "The thing is, I promised myself I wouldn't lie to you and I wouldn't involve you in anything illegal. For your own good as much as mine."

Nathalie stood on the other side of the coffee-table with her hands clasped over her sundress, unwilling to commit either way. "I give you permission to break those promises," she said. Maybe kinder than he deserved, but Nathalie didn't think so. Damian wanted to tell her everything and it terrified him to want surrender. The way he hid from her under his hands, the way he couldn't look at her for trembling, how he licked his lips and choked on words stuck in his mouth. Fear held him back and she would be a major league hypocrite if she thought less of him for that.

"If you're arrested, I'll find out anyway. And you'll lose your chance." More than ever she felt silly for her own fears, petty superstitions, reflected back to her by Damian. He thought she could hate him. Reject him. Only she knew his monstrous dread amounted to nothing. He was too frightened to believe her. She'd laugh if it wasn't cruel.

"We'll start small," she continued. "Tell me something you've never told anyone. It doesn't have to be important."

The words flickered first, small and halting and weak. Once he got going they blew out of him, breathless, famishing, all of a piece, he told her about the word Kalemaris written on the outside of his door, its associations with Abracadabra and an assassinated second century Roman physician and scholar, Serenus Semonicus, whose works were influential among medieval herbalists and cunning-folk as well as with the renaissance alchemist and mage H. Cornelius Agrippa, author of *De occulta philosophia libri tres,* which, along with *Rosarium philosophorum,* this edition spuriously attributed to Johann Mylius, thought about Damian night and day and never rested, like an old man with a chevron mustache who always wore the same black overcoat and black fedora and had been following Damian for at least four months, why, he had no idea but thought it had to do with the wedding invitations.

"That's enough for today," she said when he'd burnt it all off. "You did well. We'll try again another time."

He'd said nothing of his family or his past or his illegal dealings, but she didn't have the nerve to push him. He was embarrassed enough, so miserable she dared not speak again for a long time. She only sat beside him and held his hand. To reassure him but as much to comfort herself. Whatever else might occupy her, the invitations were always a happy thought, and now she saw a negative reflection of them in Damian's horrible books. It reminded her of how her dreams of him were protections while his dreams of her were sinister. Alchemists and magicians and thinking books. Mysterious lurkers dressed like villains of film noir. What if he's ill? She dismissed suggesting he see a doctor—he was in no state to hear that, at least not now. Any illness affecting his brain this way would surely require a specialist. If he had any medical insurance it probably wasn't enough.

Looking in Damian's eyes, cradling him in the center of her body, she made a decision. The consequences wouldn't be comprehended for years to come. That night Nathalie knew what it meant to be cleaved unto. One flesh. For twenty-two years she'd been half. Now she was whole.

24.

The invitations changed for Nathalie. She wanted them to be real but her desire to learn about them and who sent them had so far been driven by curiosity. In the glow of Damian's revelations they took on a new importance, a more serious shape in her mind, and her search renewed with purpose. She couldn't shake the feeling the invitations were not forgeries—they were old and the wedding was real and somehow she and Damian must find a way to attend. It was a rash fantasy and she didn't know why it persisted like a tune stuck in her head.

A week later she read the death knell in a historical survey of European marriage. She and Damian sat side by side in her bed, propped up with pillows, each with a book. It was past midnight and cool enough outside to open a window, the breeze laughing in the curtains.

"Listen to this," she said. Apparently the modern concept of a wedding was relatively new. It was hard to pin down exactly what sort of event they'd been invited to. The reading of the banns at church? The civil and religious ceremony? Or a wedding feast? All were cause for formal announcement. Well into the early modern period weddings were simply announced publicly by the town crier. The printing-press was invented in 1447 but its dissemination moved slowly, and even among elites private invites were handwritten throughout the sixteenth century by a hired scribe. Printing with lead type was expensive and inelegant and by the time printed invitations came into vogue in the eighteenth century, engraved metal plates were the preferred method. There was no history of movable type wedding invitations to speak of. None. "So it's settled," she told Damian. "They're forgeries."

She'd been so focused on proving the invitations authentic she'd paid little attention to the much more disturbing question: why send them? It opened up a void she could not hope to penetrate, not even through sheer speculation. It might be true, the answer to ninety-nine out of a hundred questions was money, but it was not the answer to this one. The invitations cost several times more to make than authentic ones would be worth. If money had something to do with it, why send them to Nathalie and Damian, neither scholars nor collectors, for free? Who made them? Who sent them? And might those questions possess different answers?

All her questions were consternated by unremitting heat. The most hateful summer in years with seven straight days of July over ninety degrees and the barometer bottoming out, the morning fog shriveled to the coastlines, hugging the Embarcadero to the east and Marina Avenue to the north, replaced farther inland by dust clouds ankle high. The city dried out and stared like an unlidded eye into a blue sphere, cloudless to the Pacific horizon, the broad scudding arc at the end of the world. Sunlight conducted through hundreds of thousands of tons of dense steel and magnified by hundreds of thousands of feet of double-paned glass upon tens of thousands of square miles of black bitumen, melting tar, asphalt, petroleum, concrete, cement, insulated by seven million people and their three million machines converting daily eight million gallons of fossil fuels into two million metric tons of carbon dioxide, and flushing eighty million gallons of wastewater through twelve-hundred miles of plumbing. On the Barbary Coast Nathalie watched a dwarf with mutton chops and back hair, naked but for a jock strap and rubber hip-waders, ring a silver Santa Claus bell and sing a song about how our god has gone insane.

"None of these," Damian said, and this time Nathalie didn't argue. Her purse carried two sets of maps now, one of eateries and watering holes and one of the coastline used for Damian's white bench. She marked the map and stashed it and left the pier without a word. He ran to catch up and the two of them emerged from the Pier 1 dock-house and gazed up at the proud granite and stately geometry of the beaux arts façade. They stood in the shade of a slouching palm tree and waited for a procession of fire engines to crawl down the Embarcadero and they made west on Washington Street.

She was angry at him and trying not to be. He knew it, too, she could tell, but he dared not break the lead silence between them and risk getting his ass chewed. He avoided it by walking faster. Damian was a hell of a walker, half a foot taller than her and much of it leg, and she had a hard time keeping up. She thought he didn't even want to find the bench from his dreams. He *refused* to find it. No, no, no, he said to every offered bench, nope, without even sitting on it, without even tossing a half-assed glance at the ocean view. It was a waste of time, and if he thought he was getting laid after this performance he was a moron as well as an asshole. Like she had nothing better to do with a Saturday.

When she turned to tell him as much, he was gone. A brisk current of bodies flowed all around her. She drifted to the sidewalk's edge and craned her neck but couldn't spot Damian up ahead. Behind her, a hundred feet, a blonde man, darkly tattooed, smoked a cigarette on the curb and looked for something on the other side of the street. Everything else was in motion, automobiles lurching in the street and the human swarm rushing west at the declining sun and the vanishing point crowded by skyscrapers.

Maybe Damian turned at the last street and she'd been too caught in her thoughts to notice. She backtracked and walked a block and a half north on Battery Street before giving up and returning to Washington. At the intersection, a stalky man with a shaved head and chrome sunglasses leaned against the traffic-light pole and stared across the street. This time Nathalie bothered to see what he was looking at and found it right away. A tall transvestite, short black hair, white smock, nestled in the glass shoal of an office building entrance. She was familiar, though Nathalie couldn't place her right away. Angular and slouched with wide shoulders and narrow hips, black bra visible through the thin fabric top. She was looking intensely a little farther west on Nathalie's side of the street, completely unaware of being watched. Nathalie tried to follow her line of sight and discovered Damian, half a block away, walking toward her. They made eye contact and Nathalie went to meet him. "Good thing your hair's conspicuous," he said. "Otherwise I might not have found you."

"I'm hungry," she said.

And there it was. They stood in front of the enormous bronze doors of the Washington Street entrance to the U.S. Customs House. The ornamental filigree green with age and exposure to the sea, the focal point a pair of verdigris lion heads with door-knockers hanging from their jaws. The green lion. It was a small moment. Insignificant. She made the connection but it's not like it mattered, it's not like she thought anything important of it, and she would've forgotten all about it if not for a second alchemical experience two days later.

Monday morning she opened the coffee-shop, turned on the lights, and clocked in. While putting down chairs she noticed on the community bulletin board her own flyer for a Strange Equinoxes performance from two months earlier. She pulled the tacks to take it down and hidden beneath it on thin pink paper, a homemade advertisement for a spagyric healer.

Experience the hermetic medicine of the ancient philosophers, it announced. *Bring the five elements of your personal life-force into balance and harmony with the universal Prana. Gain access to the Akashic record through personal transformation, transubstantiation, and transmogrification. This is not a hoax, people! Apotheosis awaits! The gnosis of spagyria! The wisdom of Thoth!*

The message of that Hermes known as the Thrice Great! I'm selling the secrets to the Elixir of Immortal Life Made Flesh!

It listed an address in Pacific Heights but no name and no phone number. And this, too, would've meant nothing if her dad hadn't called a few hours later. She hadn't spoken to him since April and he hadn't called in over a month. She almost answered but the thought gave her a bad feeling. She would call later, when she was with Damian, whose faith in her was enough to fortify her spine, even if her own was not.

During her break she listened to the voicemail and endured the rest of her shift flung to and fro by white hot rage and soul mourning, fugue and anxiety, cruel relief and swallowing darkness. After work she went to Bayview. Damian wasn't home and she waited over an hour in the lobby of his building, pacing among the mailboxes, biting her fingernails, talking under her breath. When he finally showed up he checked his mail before recognizing who she was. Shock scored his face and eroded slowly as he looked her over. Her fear reflected on his face pale as ash.

"He's evicting me," she said. "I have to be out in a week or start paying rent." Damian didn't seem to understand what she was talking about. "He says since I'm not going to school anymore, it's time I started taking care of myself. There's no way I could afford the condo."

"Your dad's kicking you out?" Damian said.

"He says since I'm not doing anything important, I don't need to live in the city. It shouldn't be a big deal. He offered my old room, if I need it, at the house."

"Is that what you want?"

"I don't know what to do," she said, and the truth of it made her feel utterly useless, like it was her own damn fault she ended up this way and she hated herself for laying it at Damian's feet. She wanted to cry but it was too late. The whole time waiting for Damian she'd wrestled it, gagging on sobs until her throat hurt, until she was no longer capable of crying and sick to her stomach because of it.

"Of course, you're welcome here," he said. "If it's not too gross. At least until you figure out what else to do."

It's not a big deal, she thought. She had a week to find other arrangements, but it was nice to know she could stay if she needed to. It would only be for a couple weeks, tops. A few girls from Strange Equinoxes made similar offers, a few friends from school, the assistant manager of the coffee-shop. But their help was temporary, nervous, spiked with unspoken conditions. If nothing better showed up her best bet might be to move in with Damian while she sought more permanent accommodations, but only as a last resort. He was a criminal of some kind, the less Nathalie knew the better, at risk of arrest any day, and then what would she do? Nathalie talked to a woman with a room to sublease on Russian Hill, who sounded enthusiastic to meet, but when Nathalie arrived the mood was icy and the room unavailable. The woman wouldn't look Nathalie in the eye, wouldn't open the door more than a crack, refused any explanation. Disappointing, but Nathalie gave it no thought until it happened again.

Every classified she answered showed promise until at the walk-through she learned the rent had doubled, the prior tenant decided not to move, the apartment already leased, her application had been denied. She got the distinct feeling these people were afraid of her. Something happened between her phone call and appearance. They couldn't get rid of her fast enough and no one would tell her what had frightened them. For forty-eight hours it seemed as though every vacancy in the Bay Area had been filled. Finally, she called her fellow dancers, school friends, co-workers, but their offers no longer stood. They'd thought about it and decided they didn't really have the space, or their roommates were against it, or they hadn't actually meant the offer in the first place—they were only being polite. All Nathalie needed was a couch to crash on, only for a week or two, but to no avail. Her time was up and her only options were Belvedere Island or Bayview.

Her dad didn't really expect her to move out and fend for

herself—he wanted to make her uncomfortable, squeeze her a little. He thought she would sublet a couple rooms. Trust-fund students at one of the universities, a young careerist with a sweet-tooth for night-life in the city. Portside was becoming a chic neighborhood. She could probably split the cost between her roommates and continue paying nothing at all. Eventually, she'd get back in line like she always had before, her dad's good grace would descend, and she'd get the condo back to herself. But the way his voice sounded on the message, the authority and the lazy triumph. She could hear it. The no big deal monotone, the way he could turn her life upside down, order another round of layoffs to cut labor costs for his shipping company, dump a thousand shares of stock in a startup by text message. All the same to him. The passive-aggressive coercion of it hit something weakening in her past, something umbilical, and it snapped off.

Fuck it.

The thing was, Nathalie owned everything in the condo but she hadn't earned any of it. The wage-slaves of several companies worked for it and her dad paid for it but she thought of it as her stuff. She felt keenly all of it pushing her down, telling her who she was and what her life meant, and she wanted nothing more to do with it. Damian offered to put it all into storage—he promised he could afford it and he wanted to help—but she said no thank you.

She wanted to keep the car. It was paid for and titled in her name. But she had nowhere to park anymore and it wouldn't last intact on the curb in Bayview longer than a weekend. If she sold it she could live on the money and what little she made at the coffee-shop for most of a year before she really had to buckle down and sort out her shit. And it's not like she bought it, she kept telling herself, she didn't deserve a car, she wasn't entitled to it. More burden now than luxury, and selling it was bound to scare the hell out of the smug bastard.

"You're not being rational," Damian pointed out, but that was on purpose. If she were rational she would wilt. Part of her wanted to be mad at Damian for saying such a thing, but he was right, she was being irrational, which felt good. Sometimes you need to be irrational in order to do the right thing.

Eugenie called because her dad knew Nathalie wouldn't answer if he called. "He says even if you don't want to move back home, you can store your stuff here. Until you get room for it. He'll pay for the movers."

"Tell him to raise the rent," Nathalie said. "It's a furnished condo now."

Her mind made up on Wednesday and her life moved into Damian's life on Friday. Damian took a taxi to Portside and paid the driver to wait while he helped her finish packing. It didn't take long. There wasn't room in Damian's apartment for a tenth of her things even if he threw away everything he owned. The sixty-four inch flat-screen TV, queen-size mattress with oak bedstead and matching dresser, energy-efficient dual washer-dryer unit, leather sectional couches. All of it belonged to her but she belonged to very little of it. The few objects she loved were sentimental, worthless, non-functional. Her first ballet slippers, a worn-out yoga mat, the wedding invitations. A closetful of dance costumes she'd paid a fortune for and worn once. Romani scarves and harem pants and saris. Ridiculous layered skirts and chainmail bras. Flamboyant headpieces with feathers and seashells and flowers. Plain tunics, spangles, and sequins. Hers no more.

She packed tight a deluxe rolling luggage carrier, gym bag, backpack, bathroom kit, a paper grocery bag with two changes of bed-linen and her favorite pillow, a canvas sack filled above the handles with library books, and five pairs of shoes: house slippers, sneakers, high-heels, sandals, knee-high boots.

"At least keep those," Damian said and pointed at textbooks on the coffee table. "The campus bookstore will buy them back."

Nathalie found another paper bag and loaded it. "Anything else in here you want?"

Damian looked through the kitchen cupboards. "Keep the

ban-marrie," he said. "And the juicer."

They put everything in the taxi and drove to Bayview. It struck Nathalie as funny. Four years she'd lived free of charge in a place like the VIP suite of an extravagant downtown hotel. It felt like real life and moving to Damian's crusty studio apartment with no air conditioning, black grouted tiles, threadbare carpet, and stained walls, felt more like going on vacation. Which in a way it was.

25.

Forest fires applied steadily increasing heat. The worst raged out of control in Lake County to the north, Calaveras County to the east, and Fresno County to the south, and the peninsula cowered in the middle of the ring, whichever way the wind blew. Over two hundred acres turned to dross thanks to freak lightning storms, high winds, prolonged drought. Smoke clawed Damian's throat and singed his nose hairs and filled his sinuses with charcoal. Against the skyline he could see it hanging, the burnt flesh sky, the tender brown and yellow of fresh scabs. At night the haze rolled across the bay, storm gray, and girt the moon in diseased clouds which could not rain.

Pavel collected his July order on the sixth level of a parking structure in Palo Alto. They made the exchange in Pavel's car where Damian learned his tail had spotted his secret admirer and it wasn't an old man, hatted, coated, or otherwise, but a cross-dresser, mannish but not ugly, tall, Caucasian, thirty-something. They'd seen her a couple times but could tell no more because they'd lost her before she—or he—could lead them to a residence. "We'll figure out who she is, though," Pavel said. "Sit tight."

"The same woman looking for Kim and Noe?"

"The human mind can be a tricky fucker," Pavel said and shook his head. "There's no reason to think that. You want everything to be interrelated and connect up all nice and neat. But that only happens in stories. Real life is complex. There are red herrings. Most leads go nowhere. Not every piece of information is a clue."

News of Kim Hyeon-gi. According to Pavel's guy at the

State Department, Kim was interviewed by the National Security Agency while in custody in Los Angeles. The subject
of conversation was unknown, the records requiring top secret security clearance, but it seemed strange to Pavel people
drawing interest from the NSA would be processed so quickly
for extradition, and he did some digging. It turned out Kim's
South Korean charges included arms dealing, drug-running,
white slavery, smuggling. Plenty to make the South Koreans
exert pressure to get their hands on him. A big deal, a real professional, and a dangerous man. Pavel was right to suspect Kim
and Noe were more than grunts for moving funny cash. They
must've been hired to move something important, either to
get it in or get it out. Guns or drugs or pussy. Maybe something
else.

"Money."

Pavel nodded, thinking, but he didn't look at Damian.
"Why not just make the exchange if money's what they were
after?"

Something had gone wrong but Pavel couldn't figure it
out, some miscommunication with Gangjeon, if they'd ever
been working for Gangjeon, which Pavel started to doubt. They
hadn't shown up at any of Gangjeon's usual safe-houses. No
one who knew Gangjeon knew anything about Kim or Noe.
Could be a case of honor among thieves or it might be the
truth. Maybe Gangjeon thought they were making a pick up for
him but they were really making a pick up for someone else.
Maybe Gangjeon and his employer were just as double-crossed
as Damian. Without talking to Gangjeon it was impossible to
know, but the more Pavel thought about it, the less he thought
it had anything to do with Gangjeon. Kim was a professional
smuggler, so why did he make such a jackass of himself in Los
Angeles? It was almost like he got caught on purpose, like it
was planned. No way could Gangjeon use the American government to get them out. It would take big power to pull off.
Serious muscle. Multinational influence.

"You think the NSA purposely helped to extract them with

whatever they really came for?"

"Of course not," Pavel said. "I'm merely thinking out loud. The human mind can be a tricky fucker."

None of it added up for Damian. The cold blooded smuggler Pavel described had nothing in common with the itchy and cocksure impression he had of Kim Hyeon-gi. The angry little man Damian encountered in Forest Hill would never last long as a professional criminal. He was more like a jackass who couldn't get across the border and fell apart when cops knocked on the door.

Pavel shrugged at this. It turned out LAPD worked cheap for guys like Pavel and he sent a blue shirt by the motel, where the four Koreans had been taken into custody, to pick up copies of their messages and phone records. It confirmed the story of four lost pilgrims with their dicks in their hands hunting coyotes and having a hard time getting their heads all the way up their asses. One number stuck out, pretty popular the Koreans' first few days at the motel, for a botánica in West Hollywood. Pavel's cop spoke impeccable Spanish and swung by to ask a few questions. Alas, the Brazilian matron spoke only Portuguese. Lapis exillis, she kept saying. He tried to talk to her but Portuguese and Spanish must be more different than Pavel would've guessed because lapis exillis was all the cop got out of her.

"Lapis means stone," Damian said, but Pavel already knew that and figured the real reason Kim and Noe were in San Francisco could be a rock of some kind. A diamond maybe. Or a jewel. "Anyway, I thought you'd be interested. If anything else turns up you'll know about it."

When Nathalie moved in, the first thing she'd insisted on after a deep cleaning was a wi-fi connection. At home Damian found lapis ex ellis on a Latin-to-English dictionary translated to "stone of they," which was nonsense, and he thought he must be spelling it wrong. A basic search linked the phrase to Rosicrucian lore and Illuminati conspiracies, as well as the holy grail and, of course, lapis philosophorum, the stone of the philosophers. At this point the connection hardly surprised him.

The earliest known use of the term appeared in *Parzival* by the twelfth and thirteenth century German knight, poet, and romancer Wolfram von Eschenbach who associated it with the holy grail, brought to earth by an escort of neutral angels, those who favored neither side in the heavenly war between Christ and Lucifer. A grail, or greal as it first appeared in the Old French *Perceval* of Chretien de Troyes, is a long shallow dish or platter used for serving fish. Though paintings discovered in Pyrenees churches of the Virgin Mother holding a bowl issuing flames suggested the idea of the grail predated Chretien's romance. Variously, the holy grail had been equated with a Welsh pagan myth of a magical life-rejuvenating cauldron, the communion cup of Christ's last supper, the Shroud of Turin, the black stone of the Islamic Kaaba at Mecca, and the holy womb of Mary Magdalene, which grew the mortal descendants of god on earth.

Lapis exillis might be a contraction of Lapsus ex coelis, meaning the stone fallen from the sky, or lapis elixir—elixir stone—a term used by Arabic alchemists to describe the philosopher's stone. Or lapis exilis—stone of little price—as the philosopher's stone is described in the fifteenth century treatise *Rosarium philosophorum*: Hic lapis exilis extat pretio quoque vilis,/Spemitur a stutis, amatur plus ab edoctis. Damian knew this couplet. He recognized the English translation from the copy he'd checked out from the Leonard Library. *This stone is poor and cheap in price/It is disdained by fools but loved more by the wise.*

It added up to nothing he could name, untouchable, ephemeral, an answer without a question, a clue without a seeker. The dreams, Nathalie, the wedding, the Rebis, Johann Mylius, Cornelius Agrippa, Kalemaris, the black trench-coat, the cross-dresser, the Koreans, lapis philosophorum, lapis exillis, the holy grail. All so random and interconnected at the same time. He felt like he could solve it if he had the slightest idea what he was supposed to be putting together. Like he sought something he'd never thought about. Like his mind would not know it until it was already in his hands.

When Nathalie arrived from work he was making dinner and she offered to help. This was one of his favorite rituals of the day, the two of them preparing their evening meal, kitchen-less, pressed to the counter, silent but synchronized. He chopped onions while she boiled pasta, she grated cheese while he sautéed asparagus. They negotiated each other gracefully, choreographed, contorting around each other in the cramped space.

He'd never thought of himself as much of a cook but recently discovered a talent for it and a pleasant satisfaction improvising dishes to share with Nathalie. He never planned them—the fun was in taking what he found on hand to create the unexpected. The experience was new—his dad had taught him not to be a creative thinker, not to trust himself, to remain objective, empirical, immune to hubris. The good counterfeiter, his dad often announced, is an illusionist who never believes his own illusions.

Nathalie shaved carrots for a salad while Damian sliced a lemon. He turned around, looking for canned tuna, as Nathalie reached past him for a lemon wedge and rubbed her breasts against his chest in the confusion. She wore no bra beneath her tank-top and he could feel her nipples through their thin shirts. Damian smiled gently as he worked, the savor of a cheap thrill just one of the small pleasures of domestic life he now cherished every day. Made him almost think he could be a normal person.

"What's it called when something seems meaningful but is really just a coincidence?" he asked. "A synchronicity? I had one today."

"You got it backwards," she said. "A synchronicity seems to be a coincidence but is actually meaningful. Something that seems meaningful, but really isn't, is called a coincidence." She asked what happened but he grimaced, shrugged it off, it didn't matter, it was only a coincidence, not a synchronicity. She looked at him sidelong, not believing him and unafraid to let him know. It dazzled him the way she could read him with a look, and how he could tell she was doing it without a word passing between them. He swore she could read his mind, the way she anticipated all his motions, and he was surprised to see how well he knew hers, too.

Cohabitation agreed with him, he was shocked to admit. He never would've thought so, but living with Nathalie suited him. When he was fifteen he'd thought getting away from his dad would make him happy. At twenty, fleeing Puget Sound and the deaths of his mom and step-dad was all he'd needed, or building a strong clientele when he'd first set up in San Francisco, making piles of money. He'd thought once he was established, once he could afford a nicer place and comfortable things, better food, a real kitchen, then he would be content. But at twenty-five Damian was content to sip whiskey and watch Nathalie at the scummy bathroom mirror, coifing her hair, plucking eyebrows, putting on make-up, lotion, polish, perfume. A flower growing through the cracks of his dross garden. All he needed to be happy was to love this woman and for her to love him, too.

At first Nathalie tried to find another place, but it was more difficult than she'd expected. It became clear she needed either a full-time job or a second part-time job in order to afford something decent, even with roommates. The coffee-shop couldn't spare extra hours and every part-time job she found had a schedule conflict so she would have to quit the coffee-shop to work there. She sold her car for enough money to live a while, but Damian suggested she sort out her income before making another move. He secretly hoped by the time she got it organized he'd be able to convince her to stay.

Nathalie prepared their paper plates and brought them to the studio floor where Damian waited. "Thank you for the pains," he said, and winked at her.

"If it was painful I wouldn't do it."

"So you liked it?"

"Yes," Nathalie said and turned on the news. "As much as I like choking a bird at knifepoint."

"There's a double meaning in that," Damian said. "If I figure it out, you'll probably be in trouble."

Nathalie watched the news and Damian opened on the carpet beside him a thick volume of Jung's essays on alchemy. He loved this ritual as well, the quiet way they ate, he in the world of the dead and she in the mad thrall of the living, and yet this hour he felt more than any other they were together, the two of them almost one, exquisitely aware of each other, sensitive to the subtlest shift of body or thought or mood. He half listened to the weather—more heat—until the reading absorbed him.

Transformation was the ultimate goal of all alchemical practice. Lead into gold, base matter into the philosopher's stone, exotic herbs into medicinal panacea, common minerals into the elixir of immortality. The coarse ego of the human animal becoming the noble heart of an enlightened being. The alchemist, Jung thought, yearned to change himself and projected this desire onto the molten rock in the crucible. The perfecting of the material would be mirrored in the perfecting of the alchemist's soul, and the perfecting of the alchemist would in turn influence the transformation of the material. All of it connected, linked, a communion between the human mind and the physical substance of the universe. Meditation and prayer, and the scientist would recognize samadhi in what emerged from the fire. There was no such thing for these people as impartial observation, no distance between subject and sage, because part of what the alchemist created was himself. It made Damian think about how light traveled in particles or waves depending on how it was being studied, how the presence of an observer affected the behavior of electrons.

Damian cleared their plates and washed the dishes while Nathalie cleared the remaining supper things. Afterward, they sat on the twin bed and painted their toenails. Nathalie told him about her day at work. He told her about Jung's work on alchemy. They undressed and brushed their teeth and lay for a while side by side reading in bed. Nathalie asked if he was ready for sleep, the signal she wanted to turn the light off. In the dark he groped her breast and she took his hand between her hands and kissed it. "Not tonight, babe," she said, and he kissed her hair. Damian lay on his back with one arm behind his head and stared at the ceiling without seeing it. A long time passed. As he drifted off, coasting through the in between places, still conscious but no longer awake, a question startled him back to the sultry night.

"Have you dreamed about me again yet?" he asked out loud. His voice sounded like thunder inside his head. His eyes were open but he could see nothing. Nathalie must be asleep, he thought, and made up his mind to join her. Nearly there when the answer came out of the blackness.

"No."

This is how Damian glided through the summer: counterfeiting and cooking, reading and painting his toenails. Making love or not making love. Half a dozen rich clients and a dozen humbler ones, Damian delivered the product on time either way, each batch more believable than the last. Months ago he stopped being able to tell the difference between what came from the warehouse and what came from the bank. Another hundred-thousand dollars for Pavel in September and his offshore savings bloated to $371,206.15. Nathalie slung coffee for college kids and looked for better work. They spent a lot of time sunbathing on Ocean Beach, walking in the knee-high surf, the cold shock of water a blessing in the lunatic heat. Sometimes they brought a picnic and sometimes they joined a bonfire already in progress.

These nights he lay awake deep into morning, the marrow

hollowed out of all his bones, the small of his back screwed to the wet spot, the hot weight of his lover's belly against his belly as she drowsed perpendicular upon him. He ran his fingers over her body, feeling along her flanks the last remnant of baby fat, toned muscles taut beneath the thin layer of cream, over the shelf of her rump, tracing with his fingertips her bikini tan-line, the pale milk trapezoid on her bottom bright in the rich bronze frame of her back and thighs. It amazed him the thirsty way her skin drank up sunshine and turned it into lacquer—he only reddened and peeled as white beneath his skin as an apple. He thought about the great big pile of money sleeping in the bank and the filthy apartment, the lumpy mattress and ill-fitted sheets. He thought—not to himself and not to god or anything else he could name—please, let it stay this way. Please let this last as long as possible. But it was no use. Sooner or later everything would change.

26.

By October the sun surrendered a few degrees. On the television news distant wildfires made candles of evergreens and the smoke evaporated into hazy stratus above the bay, echoed below by fog creeping in from the coastline. One day in November, Damian came home from the warehouse to the panicked trill of his telephone. "Mr. Lancaster?" The androgynous voice was rich and smoky, deep if it belonged to a woman, thin if a man. "Damian Lancaster? I am called Phaedra. We have a mutual acquaintance who might interest you. Elderly gentleman. Black coat. Mustache. Black hat. I thought we should meet."

The description stopped his breath and his real name turned over in his stomach. They arranged a rendezvous the next evening for a coffeehouse in Potrero Hill. "You might be familiar with it," Phaedra said and indeed Damian remembered taking coffee there with Nathalie.

Twilight and the sun slouched out of sight. A pink shadow melted on the skyline. What lingered was lavender and soft light but his skin was cold and getting colder. The days were scathing but in the evening fog-banks rolled as thick and gray as wool, low to the ground and blinding black as thunderclouds, and the humidity stung like lightning in Damian's bones. He shrugged deeper into his coat and ducked into the shop where he found the woman, Phaedra, as she said he would. In the corner, coatless, hatless, wearing glasses and on the table before her: two cups.

"Mr. Lancaster? You have good timing. Your coffee's still hot."

"Cream?" he asked and they shook hands.

"Cream, yes. Sugar?"

He sat across from her and sipped coffee and waited. She waited, too. Cropped hair listed above her ears, too black not to be dyed, and matched the form-fitting slacks and suit jacket. He imagined it was the kind of overdone getup Nathalie would show up for coffee in. Her eyes were more gray than hazel and composed her face in a way that suggested to Damian both wisdom and innocence. Seeing himself reflected in her eyes showed him those two things were not contradictory. Striking eyes, not for their size or shape or color but for how they saw him, so he felt it wasn't her eyes that were out of place, but the rest of her.

Finally she said, "I know who is following you."

"So you said. On the phone."

"Yes. It's risky for me to speak about but I needed to see you. To ask you something. To tell you something, in fact. About a bison."

She seemed to wait for a response. Damian returned nothing but raised eyebrows. She was a slender woman but not angular, with broad shoulders and a wide jaw, long, graceful neck. Older than Damian but otherwise he couldn't place her age. She might be in her thirties, or just younger, or not quite fifty, or anywhere in between. She drummed her fingernails, short, manicured, maroon, on the formica tabletop, thinking, and staring sadly at Damian the whole time. She said, "I wonder if you have ever heard of the great white buffalo?"

"Sorry," he said and drank his coffee. He was beginning to warm up and the hot coffee pricked the nerves of his fingers and toes like fishhooks.

"White Buffalo Calf Woman is a kind of Prometheus figure to the Lakota Sioux. She brought important spiritual implements, such as the sacred pipe, medicine dances, and other rituals. She was a teacher, like Jesus or Buddha, and a goddess." Phaedra stopped talking for several seconds, and as Damian waited for her to continue he realized she wasn't so much staring at him as she was staring through him, or maybe in him. "Some stories are completely different," she said. "In some versions the white buffalo is prophetic of events to come. Peace. Renewal. A gathering of nations and a new unity among the peoples of the earth. It means a return to balance. Harmony in the universe. It is a sign from the spirits that everything is going to be okay."

Damian asked the server for more coffee and the exchange seemed to bring Phaedra back to herself. He nodded to show he was paying attention. "Modern science has made white bison easy to produce through artificial insemination," she said. "But naturally occurring non-albino white bison are extraordinarily rare. They say at any given moment there might be between six and ten of them on the planet."

She paused to sip her coffee and Damian studied her mannerisms. There was something strange about the way she moved and the way she held herself and he was having trouble articulating what it was. Despite her manicure and clothes and prim elocution, she slouched in her seat, like a man, with her legs parted, she expanded to inhabit the whole booth. Her voice was deep and not at all melodious. She was unusually skinny but definitely female, lithe but hardy, and strangely—what? Not asexual, for he was acutely attracted to her, but the attraction alarmed him. From a distance, from the other side of a busy street, for example, he might confuse her for a lovely boy in drag.

She wiped her mouth on a paper napkin and continued. "In Wyoming, not far from the Wind River Indian Reservation, a white buffalo was recently born. All of these animals are sacred but this one is especially important. Its name is Brother Sun Sister Moon. It is a naturally conceived full-blooded American bison and neither of its parents are white. It was born under a full moon in the middle of a thunderstorm in which its father was killed by lightning strike. These details are all significant to the prophecy of the great white buffalo, but the most important part, what makes Brother Sun Sister

Moon unusually important, is she—or he—is intersexed."

"Intersexed?"

"Yes," Phaedra said. "An hermaphrodite."

The word drove panic through his septum. Inside his coat his sweat-soaked shirt stuck on his ribs and he clamped his face into a calm he did not feel. "Why is that important?"

"The calf personifies balance in the energies that move the universe. Male and female. Light and dark. Subtle and gross. Sun and moon."

"So," he said, "why did you want to tell me about this?"

"Brother Sun Sister Moon was born completely white. During the winter she has darkened and turned yellow. According to legend she will turn brown, then red, then black, then white again. I want to hire you. To protect her. Keep her safe until her coat is pure white once again."

"I thought the reason you called had to do with the asshole in the black coat."

"He wants to stop you," she said, "to prevent you from doing what I ask. Listen to me carefully. He is dangerous and he means you harm. You must not pursue him and if he approaches you, you must not believe anything he says."

Damian shook his head. He thought about it for a few seconds and shook his head again. "Sorry," he said. "I don't think I'd be interested."

"Mr. Lancaster, you must."

"But I'm not going to."

She smarted at the briskness in his tone. Weighed him in the sea-swell of haunting gray eyes. "If you have no interest in hearing my offer, I guess we are done. I would still like to hire you. If you could use the money. One-hundred-thousand dollars."

"I don't need the money."

"Right," she said. "I forgot. You make your own money, isn't that right?"

Damian couldn't breathe. He felt punched in the guts and a thin ringing in his ears. It took his eyes several seconds to focus and when Phaedra's cool smile sharpened on his retina his arms and shoulders softly quaked.

"How did you know about that?"

"Mr. Lancaster," she said, surprised at his ignorance, and her voice turned breathy and smooth. "I know a great deal about a great many things. I know Kim Hyeon-gi is not who you think he is. I know the whereabouts of Gangjeon Jae-kyeon and the man who's been following you. I know about your copy of *De occulta philosophia libri tres* and why it affects you the way it does. I can answer many questions about many things. About Nathalie and the invitations. And I will. After you do this for me."

He was shocked. Numb. Equally fascinated and terrified, no longer capable of hiding any of it from her.

"Don't worry," she said and winked. The most coquettish gesture he'd ever received and more natural on her than he would've guessed. "Your secret's safe with me. I have no intention of blackmailing you. It is of absolute importance your decisions in this matter not be coerced."

He didn't believe her, not about blackmailing him or about the white buffalo or even about the man in the black overcoat. He didn't believe her and he didn't trust her and he knew he must find a way to dissuade her interest in him. "What would I need to do? After the buffalo turns white again?"

"Give her the crow's head."

He didn't know what that meant. For the first time since meeting she seemed to doubt her absolute control over the conversation. He sat back on his chair and folded his arms, happy to see her thrown off script. She didn't try to hide it.

"You haven't received the crow's head?"

He shook his head and she frowned, confused, drumming her fingers on the table. "It doesn't matter," she decided. "I don't understand, but it doesn't change my offer."

"What if I won't do it?"

She sighed and fixed him under a hard stare. "I have no idea what would happen. But fear not, Mr. Lancaster. If you won't do it, someone else will."

"Give me time to think about it."

"Of course," and her eyes poured compassion upon him. Suddenly he understood why her eyes seemed so familiar. They were the eyes of Theotokos of Vladimir, exactly the same, like his mother's eyes. "Oh, my dear," she said, "I know it seems difficult. But you want to do it. And you've been preparing yourself for it. You've had a premonition this was coming."

"A premonition?"

"In the middle of the night. When you woke up and wanted to protect Nathalie."

Damian scoffed to keep from trembling, beside himself with this outrageous woman. "It wasn't a premonition," he said. He knew the night she meant, months ago, when was it? March? April? Nathalie had stayed at his place and he'd awoken in the middle of the night convinced he must protect her—hadn't the sensation of someone watching woke him? Lots of things could explain it, he insisted. Loneliness and probably pheromones and brain chemistry—because he was a young man and Nathalie a beautiful woman—and socially prescribed gender roles, which made him feel powerful if he could be important to a woman.

Phaedra laughed. "Yes. All those things, I'm sure. It was also a premonition."

Damian blinked. Phaedra stared expectantly.

"By when do you need my answer?"

"I'm afraid I don't know the exact date. You have until Nathalie begins her menstrual cycle under the sign of Aries."

She nearly reeled him in, but that broke the spell. She must be crazy. Damian was relieved, yes, and he would've expected as much. What he couldn't predict was how disappointed he felt too. He looked at the tabletop for a minute so she'd think he was taking her seriously.

"We done?" Damian said.

"For now, yes, Mr. Lancaster, we are done. But remember what I said. You must protect Brother Sun Sister Moon. It's your destiny."

The phrase shocked him. He narrowed his eyes on her and anger fermented his blood. He wanted to laugh at her, to embarrass her with how corny and melodramatic she sounded, how pompous her whole story had been. He wanted her to see, however creepy she was, she could not intimidate him. But her eyes met his and the impact ignited all his anger and it burned painfully. He could feel his mouth tremble and he knew he must flee now or she would see him weeping, because she chose her words on purpose. She knew his father sent him on an errand. And she knew her claims might turn out to be the truth of that errand.

Aries approaches its zenith. Albert eats naught and drinks naught three days and three nights. Hours devoted to constant prayer. Sunup to sundown on his knees. Imploring favorable intercession from the gods. Blind in the windowless chapel. Weak with hunger and half mad with thirst, lost in evanescent passageways betwixt oratorium and netherworld, hard floor on sore shins, and after amen lacks strength to stand. The rest of a fortnight nourishes him once a day on broth. Roots and greens boiled in water. His prayers begin before first light and stretch deep into midnight. Beyond the tabernacle drift sounds of Phaedra's dance and cackle beneath a waxing moon. Sleep dreamless and exhausting. Over, it seems, before it has even begun.

On the fifteenth morning he emerges from solitude to behold the woman crouching between Henry's legs. The rump of her homespun dress up in the air and her eyes screwed to the fire-box. "Something's wrong," she says and looks up at him. "I needed your help and what was more important?"

"What you bid me. Petitioning the gods."

Phaedra excavates a pile of unburnt wood and pushes a fire-iron into the box to rearrange what remains. "Pray and work," she mutters under her breath. "Work and pray."

Slow Henry belches and blusters. Its stomach rumbles. The furnace is congested—Albert knows by the cough—he's heard that dry hack a thousand times. More.

"Hungry, old friend?" Albert kneels next to Phaedra at the grate. The fire shrivels to a single ribbon. Henry can't breathe. If it can't breathe it can't eat. Finicky eaters, tower furnaces. Circulating the heat has everything to do with the proper balance of fuel, fire, and air in the earthenware bricks. Too thin and the chamber starves for lack of heat. Too dense and it chokes, full of wood it cannot digest, bricks hot enough to melt flesh and the crucible cold as bedrock. Slow Henry is easily confused. Struggles to breathe and eat at the same time.

"Did you remember to bless the work before we began?"

"Of course I remembered," Phaedra says.

Albert chops sticks into splinters like long ice-sickles which melt as Henry licks them. He hand-feeds several through the fire-box until Henry's tongue gets up and he pushes in fagots with a fire-iron.

"Feeling better?" he asks and shuts the door. Phaedra hurries out to the woodpile for more fuel and Albert looks into the spyglass at the mist swirling in the athanor's belly. The shadowy crucible still too dark to see but for a blood red vein of liquid running through its heart.

The man and the woman toil in silent sympathy, taking turns chopping wood, drinking water, feeding the furnace, pumping the bellows, resting blown muscles. Their labors divided and coordinated with glances and gestures, pats on the back, squeezes of hands. Frenzy of sweaty hair and sooty faces. When the fire circulates Phaedra shuts the vent. Slow Henry shakes and rumbles. Black smoke seeps from its fixtures. Flames blow out the fire-box and a terrible groan comes deep within the bricks as the dragon slowly rouses. It beats its wings and the tower bulges and throbs. Henry gasps for breath, its stomach slowly turning on itself for nourishment, chewing carbon locked inside the crucible, throwing off strange isotopes in the hazy atmosphere within the tower.

The tantrum subsides and Albert opens the vent in the pipe. The dragon roars and a pillar of flame erupts from the chimney. He hurries to the spy-hole again. The chamber glows like a nebula. Volatile clouds of pink and red undulate and fold around the black cup. The crucible's mouth shines star white. The matter has come to flux. Heat dries Albert's eyes to scales and makes him flinch away. Phaedra flings open the grate and stabs the box with an iron, breaking up the chary wood to regulate the temperature at a middle place between hot and cold. Henry sighs contentedly and nurses the infants.

Albert lies in a heap next to Phaedra on the chapel floor,

heaving breath, both of them too exhausted for jubilation, soaked in sweat, black crust, mud of ash. The oppressive heat. Throbbing like a blasted nerve.

"All is well," Phaedra says when they recover. "The wheel of fate turns in our favor. Next time could be different."

We brought this on ourselves, Albert thinks. That's what she means. Poison in our thoughts. Ill emotions. Deceit and mistrust. Could she be right? Did he allow baser desires to convince him of his virtue? It was possible. His worst instincts strive to infect the world at every turn. Only a fool thinks it impossible. Fear. Blame. Corruption lurks in eddies of the mind. Harms the work. Assaults its growth. "We must be more cautious from now on," he says. "The work requires constant purification."

Phaedra turns to face him straight. All her features smooth like a calm sky and she looks into his eyes. "Tell me, have you found them? Tell me and tell me true. Do you know who they are?"

"Why ask what you already know? Or is there another reason your spies follow everywhere I go?"

Phaedra smiles but holds his eyes in hers. "What makes you think I have spies?"

"Because you're not very good at hiding them. You never have been. Which is why they never learn anything I don't want you to know."

Her smile dissolves and becomes a frown, but she doesn't break the bond of eyes. Albert feels her reaching into him, probing his mind for secrets. He snaps his eyes away, pushing her out of his head, and stands up. Walks to the other end of the chapel and Phaedra casually follows.

"You found them, didn't you? Are you sure this time? You know who they are?"

Albert cocks his head to the rafters and weighs his answer. "No," he decides. "I'm not certain it's them. But it could be. It's possible."

"You shouldn't approach them like this. Casting spells.

Breaking into their homes."

"What makes you think I'm casting spells?"

"It's not so hard to figure out—I know you better than you know yourself. You think I haven't noticed books missing from the library? It's too soon."

Albert doesn't argue. It's probably true she knows him better than he knows himself. His own mind confronts him like the walls of an impossible labyrinth. His motivations elude him. Only after the fact, when it's too late, does he realize the reasons for his actions are not what he thinks they are. But Phaedra is clear to him. Almost always. He can predict her thoughts. He anticipates her deeds. They're not ready yet: Albert knows what she will say before she thinks it.

"They're not ready yet."

"They will never be ready if we don't prepare them."

"You'll get them killed—and then what shall we do?"

"I will not abandon them to face greater danger alone."

"I? Dangerous?" Phaedra's eyes widen and she flinches away from what's repulsive, Albert's words or the contents of her own mind, there's no way to be sure. No way to foresee what she cannot admit to herself.

"Protecting them from the world. It cannot be done. The only thing you will accomplish will be to destroy them, and us, with your avarice."

Anger darkens Phaedra's eyes. Nostrils flare. She struggles to keep her voice from shaking. "They have *seen* you. You *spoke* to them. This recklessness threatens the work. It does violence to their souls and ours."

"And you have a favor to ask."

"Take pity on them. Spare the nightmares and let me nourish them. Intercede with the gods on their behalf. You and I can break with the past. We can find another way. Only shed mercy on this Æon."

Albert takes her chin in his hand and strokes her face. "Only one can make me. Only one. And the shadow of that one."

Phaedra smiles. Tears stream down her cheeks and gather in his palm. "Bless your majesty."

"Promise. Do not betray me this time. Please."

She takes his hand in both of hers and kisses the leathery skin. "Bless you, my king. Ten times ten and a thousand times more, bless you."

THE UPPER WORLD
& INFLUENCE OF
THE PLANETS

"The metallic seed of our prime philosophic matter is nothing but an oily vapor created by God, nourished by the sun and moon, and which, being in the earth, is specified through the action of the universal menstruum, the circulation or motion of the upper world and the influence of the planets, by moving through the mineral kingdom and transforming itself into a metal or mineral according to the quantity, purity and condition of the Elements it meets."

—BARO URBIGERUS, HOW TO PHILOSOPHICALLY PREPARE
THE UNIVERSAL MEDICINE, 1690.

N athalie checked the time on her phone and clapped it face down on the table. This place had a jazz sextet dressed in identical tuxedos sound-checking at one end of the club. They would be starting soon and Nathalie could stop listening to Rosa's witch hunt.

"It's like he put a curse on you," Rosa said. Nathalie scowled back at her sister. "No, really. You're covered in black guck." Rosa described Nathalie's skin, cracked like a desert landscape, fissures oozing sludge, bleeding a shiny black net over her whole body. "He's got you caught."

"Would you knock it off?" Nathalie was tempted to flag the waiter and tell him her sister wouldn't turn twenty-one for four more months. She was supposed to be hunting the bar from her dreams. Damian had said something came up—an appointment he couldn't get out of—and she'd started stag in Laurel Heights. It depressed her spending so many evenings in bars and never having any fun. Rosa called and offered company and met her for a cocktail.

"It doesn't hurt?"

Nathalie sipped her wine flute. "You mean the enormous liquid spider-web which striates my astral body and suffocates the very essence of my being? It feels great."

It truly did feel great. Much as Rosa didn't want to hear it, this time with Damian had been nothing but precious to her. When she first moved in he told her to save her money, he had to pay for the studio whether she lived there or not. But she'd been kept by a man long enough—she hadn't escaped the thumb of her father only to live under the thumb of her lover, no matter how noble his intentions. It mattered to her to pay her own way, and she made him let her pick up half the rent and utilities. Damian mostly cooked and Nathalie mostly cleaned and they took turns shopping. He bought a secondhand armoire cabinet for her personal things because even in this dismal cranny they deserved a little privacy. The armoire was hers and the coat closet was his. He would never go through the armoire without her permission, and she must never, for any reason, open the closet. Odd enough, but the next day when Nathalie came home from work she noticed he'd put a padlock on the closet door.

"What do you think's in there?" she asked Rosa.

"Isn't it obvious?" Rosa scoffed. "That's where he keeps the corpses of all his previous girlfriends."

Nathalie hated the studio apartment. They'd wasted a long weekend cleaning on their hands and knees. Damian protested it would do no good but she insisted. In the end he was right. The carpet trampled by decades of traffic in places thin as a single sheet of paper, punctuated by decaying rosettes of red wine and white bleach. Once a week she scrubbed the sepia streaks off the walls. A few days later they seeped through and ran down the lead paint like yellow tears. The countertop a whorled patina of coffee stains. Chipped bathroom tiles tinted like smoker's teeth. There was no bathtub, only a standing shower stall. The ventilation was poor and the circulation fan often stopped up with lint. Black mold grew along the baseboards, the hem of the shower curtain, the wall behind the toilet tank. It was impossible to eradicate. Bleach cleansers only dyed it platinum blonde. The mini-fridge was barely big enough for one person and there was no extra cupboard space for food—they had to go to the market every other day or watch their money spoil on the countertop. She couldn't imagine one person living there without withering, let alone two, and it pissed her off how little Damian seemed to mind.

It was more than culture shock or class shock—it was a physical shock too. The limited space swallowed her up. She couldn't move around. The room made her claustrophobic, gave her a feeling like she must sit still. It followed her everywhere, as if invisible walls restricted her body all the time, cramping her posture, shortening her stride, binding even her thoughts to what she could see in the moment, until she could barely turn around, until she felt she must stop moving or avoid the studio altogether.

Unable to practice at home, she spent more hours at Strange Equinoxes' leased practice space in Oakland when she wasn't at the coffee-shop in Berkeley or looking for another job, an abysmal failure at every turn. Either she didn't have enough experience, or the wrong kind of experience, or she was overeducated or undereducated or her degree was wrong. None of the part-time work she found would cooperate with her coffee-shop hours. Lots of opportunities to work her way up as an unpaid intern, but that was no longer an option Nathalie could afford. She needed to make money. Now. Damian assured her she was welcome as long as it took, no hurry, better to make the right decision than be forced back to him again a few months later. And the fact was she adored him. Living together made her want to be with him even more, not less, but she wanted to move.

"We're looking for a place together," she told Rosa. "A one-bedroom in a cleaner neighborhood on the east bay." Her suggestion had been to move after she found full-time work and could pull her weight. Damian admitted they might not need to wait if she was serious about living with him. He had the money. He'd wanted to save a while longer, but if they could stay together he'd gladly break into it.

"He's got you right where he wants you," Rosa seethed, and ordered another round of white wine. "I'm getting you drunk. Hopefully it'll improve your judgment." Her dad, it turned out, was covered in the same black slime and Rosa was convinced it came from Damian. "Dad's having a hell of a time with this misguided phase you're going through. He's a mess." And Nathalie was glad he was a mess. "Don't get the wrong impression. I bear Damian no ill will, and god knows Dad's getting what he deserves. He's a cretin when he's like this. But it makes me nervous. You're different now and it's making Dad different."

Good, Nathalie thought. She shouldn't be happy for her dad's suffering, but it was the best way to cope with her own pain. Muffle the burn in a layer of spite like scar tissue. It would never heal—she didn't want it to heal—but she would learn to live with it. Comforting to know she was still connected to her dad, if only through shared hurt.

The jazz sextet galloped into an acid bop number, all high-hats and alto saxophone. Serpentine time signatures mellowing, half speed, clarinet and trombone driven, fronted by an obese baritone crooner. The small dance floor quickly packed and bounced. Nathalie tapped out the polyrhythms on her knee and watched the dancers slither. When the band took a break Rosa ordered Nathalie another glass of wine and told her about their ornery father, distant, fanatical, shorter-tempered than usual. He often worked twenty hour days, either downtown or in his home office. When Nathalie didn't move back in he went on a firing spree. Like an Old Testament god he delighted in torturing those most dependent upon him and demanded they adore him for it. Their mother was missing again, Rosa added. Carolina told their mother about Nathalie getting kicked out of the Portside condo, and no one had seen her in weeks, disappeared into the depths of the house.

In the corner a tall man in shirtsleeves, slacks, and suspenders skipped a few melancholy chords over a piano surface before picking out a Beethoven concerto. He wore black wraparound sunglasses in the single ruby spotlight, blonde hair combed straight back in rows of icicles.

"And Bianca's started eating dirt again," Rosa said into the bottom of her glass.

This caused Nathalie pause. When Bianca was eight she'd started eating soil from the garden behind the house. It was the only thing that made tastes go away. Nathalie empathized —it must be traumatic to taste so much: fairytales, arrogance, telephone static. Everything tasted to Bianca. Only earth offered relief, Bianca said, because it was the source of all flavors. All other tastes were small pieces of the taste of the earth and if she could savor everything at once it was enough to overwhelm her mouth for a little while. It took months to get her to stop. Now she was ten and doing it again.

Similar things had happened before. When Carolina was twelve she'd been obsessed with the scent of glass. To this day Eugenie became lightheaded, sometimes fainting, at sounds made by particular shades of green. At four Rosalie was terrified of natural sunlight. For a full year every window and door of the house snuffed out with thick black curtains, the poor girl convinced if the house leaked it would fill up with light like a bathtub and drown her. Certain fabric textures gave Angela stomach ulcers, made her scream and weep, a condition for which she still met twice a week with an occupational therapist. At home she was naked nearly all the time.

The band got up for a second set and Nathalie decided to dance. She rocked and swiveled and swayed until she found a nook the size of her body in the elongated rhythm and big brassy tone. A perfect fit and a total accident. She just started moving, trying to make sense of the music, and discovered a tentative form to inhabit this silky off-kilter soundscape. She swung her hips and strutted, twirled and high-stepped, shifted her balance from heel to toe on the offbeat. The dance floor was full when she started but now she felt the crowd thinning. Distant catcalls and soft laughter. From toe to knee and knee to hip and hip to chest, and down her spine again, up and down the curved line of her she pushed the sound, twisting with the horns and breaking on the symbols, snake arms drawing out the dizzy scales. The dance floor was empty, she realized, it was just the music and her crashing heart. Her movements expanded to fill the space. She saw faces in the periphery, seated patrons and harried waiters, bodies and windows and bar-back lights. She saw the drum-kit and the fat man grinning at her, sweat beading on his nose, alternating between singing to the mic and blowing a trumpet.

The music stopped and she clapped for the band while they stared at her. All the former dancers stood in a chorus along the edge of the floor and stared at her. Four men knelt to one side and stared. Behind them people sat around small round tables and gaped over forgotten drinks. Purposeless waiters watched with trays under arms or hoisting glasses aloft. A row of bartenders leaned on their elbows and looked at her. She smiled in the unnerving quiet, flush faced, and watched the room of eyes follow her back to Rosalie.

"Where did that come from?" Rosa asked. Her question was the only sound in the club and she immediately put a hand to her lips as if that might dampen it.

"I wanted to dance," Nathalie whispered. "What are they looking at?"

No one looked at her anymore but the silence held. No one moved, no one spoke. They all looked dazed. Sleepy. As if everyone had recently woke up but not yet risen from bed.

"I don't think they know," Rosa whispered. "I've never seen anything like it. What happened to you?"

Nathalie didn't know what she meant. For a second the two girls blinked at each other. Then a waiter walked up to the bar and the bartenders went back to work. Someone spoke under their breath and a cautious layer of conversation rose to break the hush.

"I wasn't showing off for these people," Nathalie hissed, still unwilling to raise her voice. "I don't give a damn if they think I looked like a fool."

Rosa snorted. "No one thinks you're a fool, I promise. I don't know what you *were* out there but a fool is the farthest thing from it."

Finally the band started playing again and the waiter brought them two fresh wine flutes. "Was it good?" Nathalie asked when he'd left. Rosa didn't answer. Nathalie listened to the band and finished her wine. The dance floor remained barren on their way out. The wall next to the entrance was plastered in ads and notices, band posters, instruments for sale, calls for auditions, an old Strange Equinoxes flyer, and next to it, the same pink ad for a spagyric healer in Pacific Heights. "I'm having déjà vu," Nathalie said, and Rosa dragged her through the door onto Geary Boulevard.

Later, when they were saying goodnight, Rosa told her the dance hadn't been good or bad. A month later, apropos of nothing, walking out of a bookstore, Rosa said what Nathalie did that night in the jazz club might not have been dancing at all. She couldn't say what it was but it wasn't like dancing. She texted Nathalie the morning after: It should've never been seen, what Nathalie did at the jazz club. It wasn't meant to be touched by human eyes.

Seven days before Thanksgiving Pavel offered Damian two more jobs. Special orders for a new client, one for fifty-thousand dollars due in April and the second for eighty-thousand in August. The first would go to Saint Petersburg, the second to Damascus. If the April order cleared as expected Damian would make fifty cents on the dollar for the one in August. With Pavel's regular clients and Damian's other jobs he stood to net more than $200,000 for five months of work. At that rate, if he lived frugally, he could expect to be a millionaire by his thirtieth birthday.

The winter, like the summer, proved unusually hot with temperatures in the low seventies. The worst infernos were contained but random pockets continued to flash and smolder among the dry foothills of the Sierra Nevada's. The summer's devastation had been vast: on the news a refugee mountain lion crouched, ready to spring, atop a power-pole in Oakland, displaced from its natural habitat as much by smoke and ash as flame. Its eyes shined in the klieg lights, its whole body emerald green in the night-vision cameras. In Nathalie's dreams it stalked her among the bookcases of the San Francisco Public Library. A shape-shifting labyrinth, which grew dead-ends where previously had been open aisles whenever she turned around. Blind passages and complicated switchbacks drew her deeper into the stacks. When the green lion finally cornered her she leaded her body against its pounce, but instead it only lay down, paws folded beneath its great muzzle, and guarded her until she woke.

She discovered another pink ad for a spagyric healer in Pacific Heights next to a Strange Equinoxes poster at the San Francisco Public Library. Another on the glass doors of a dance auditorium beneath a flyer listing Strange Equinoxes' upcoming performances. On her way to a job interview in Pacifica she saw one stapled to a telephone pole, half covering a promotion Nathalie hung months ago for Strange Equinoxes' Oktoberfest performance. It seemed every Strange Equinoxes promo in the city accompanied a pink notice for the secrets to the Elixir of Immortal Life Made Flesh. No name, no phone number. Only an address.

From the internet she gathered the green lion symbolized the philosopher's stone in its immature state, green the way unripe fruit is green. Or it referred to the oxidization of copper compounds in silver and gold alloys. Or it could be vitriol, an acid capable of dissolving all metals except gold. Possibly it was a catalyst for chemical reactions which occurred several times throughout the work. Even the alchemists couldn't agree on what the green lion meant. Spagyria was a little clearer. A branch of alchemy developed by Paracelsus in the late medieval period. Instead of transforming metals it dealt with plant extracts for medicinal purposes. Worth a trip to Pacific Heights.

28.

The two story stucco house teetered on a hillside and featured two offset French windows. A semicircle parking veranda showcased a late model SUV and a BMW convertible. A young woman answered the door, blonde, tan, in a cream cashmere skirt-suit and white headband. Nathalie showed her the pink paper and she called for Giles on an intercom unit mounted in the foyer. "He'll be down," she said. "I've got to run." She jingled her keys as proof and walked down the steep incline to the BMW. A moment later Nathalie was met by a pudgy fellow about her age in thick black-framed glasses and a scarlet kimono. He was barefoot and a tick shorter than Nathalie, hair epoxied into a shiny black carapace meticulously parted down the side. He held a plastic bottle of mineral water like it was a highball glass. "How have you discovered the true and ancient science of spagyria?" he asked.

"Synchronicity," Nathalie said. "I'm interested in the good news of Hermes Trismegistus."

"Then you shall hear it," he said and invited her to join him in the athenaeum. "There's no need to fear me," he promised. "I'm not dangerous."

Nathalie sucked her lip and sized him up. The idea this guy could be dangerous almost made her guffaw, but she didn't want to hurt his feelings. "I guess I believe you," she said, and he led her upstairs.

"What should I call you," he asked as they walked. Razor rash reddened his throat. Faint alcohol scent of aftershave. She told him her name and he said, "You may call me Frater Theophrastus Ashoka."

"I thought your name was Giles."

"Only my great-grandmother calls me that. Giles Combey. Frater Theophrastus is my alchemical name."

"She's not your great-grandmother," Nathalie said. She didn't laugh because she wanted to stay on his good side, but this kid was really too much.

He smiled politely and asked how old Nathalie thought the woman was. Twenty-five, she supposed, no older than thirty.

"One-hundred-and-twenty-three," Frater Theophrastus said.

The athenaeum was actually a bedroom with a vanity, bookcase, and daybed, decorated in a Hindu theme of mass-produced statuary and tapestries, which Frater Theophrastus gladly identified for her: Nataraja dancing the universe to life. Vishnu dreaming on the back of the cosmic serpent. Elephant-headed Ganesh, remover of obstacles, seated in lotus position. Lord Krishna making love to Radha. Kali cutting off her own head with a pair of shears to free devotees from her bondage. He offered chai with goat's milk, which she declined, and brought her a swivel chair to sit on. "Now, then, my friend," he said and made himself comfortable on the daybed. "How might I be of service?"

She took a deep breath to summon all her patience—she had a feeling she was going to need it—and recounted her recurring dream of Damian and his dream of her, the wedding invitations, the Balthazar Schwan woodcuts, the green lion on the customs house doors, the mountain lion stranded up a telephone pole and her dream of it in the library, and now Frater Theophrastus' pink flyers posted tandem, it seemed, to every printed mention of Strange Equinoxes. "You don't seem surprised," she noticed.

"I'm afraid I'll be of little help in this matter—I have no idea what it means. I wasn't conscious of placing my flyers close to yours. Synchronicities occur all the time to just about everybody," he said. "The only thing surprising about it is that you noticed. Suggests you're a strong candidate for spagyria."

Herbal homeopathic supplements, Frater Theophrastus explained, arrived at through alchemical means. He fermented his own alcohol. All his plants were organically grown and spiritually as well as physically prepared for consumption under beneficent astrological conditions. After distillation, the tincture was augmented by recombining the plant essence with its calcined body.

Nathalie wasn't sure herbal supplements were what she needed. She thought of her heart in cinders, her dad dug out and infection rotting the cavity. Her conflicted feelings for Damian on a smoldering nerve, how he made her blood smoke and sing and seep and weep all at the same time. The jar Rosa saw in her, the sealed cup and the secret it kept, which she could feel all the time now, swollen and feverish, burbling like a cauldron. What could help? What she needed was therapy, but there was no way she could pay for it, not without her dad, and she refused to ask for his help. It didn't matter if spagyria wasn't as good as modern medicine—it was what she could afford.

Frater Theophrastus smiled sympathetically. "No need to fret. If you come to Our Art with an open mind and a dedicated heart, I think you'll be pleasantly surprised by the results."

"Can it help answer my questions about the dreams and the invitations?"

"It would require time and attention," he warned. "Our Art knows nothing of quick fixes." The whole patient must be considered, body, mind, and soul brought into balance. Mercurius, Sal, Sulphur. The philosopher's stone was potable gold but it also must become a work wrought within Nathalie's own heart. She could not expect it to work for her if she would not work for it. Enlightenment could not be found in any one place —the tincture was but one aspect of a holistic spiritual practice. "And even then it doesn't always have the desired effect," he said. "More of nature's bounty is available if you don't torture it out of her. But sometimes you ask nicely and she still says no."

He wrote down her birthdate, place, and time so that later he could cast her horoscope, and recorded notes from a series of tarot spreads. He questioned her habits and preferences in order to determine her ayurvedic dosha and consulted botanical almanacs cross-referenced with astrological charts. Most of this work would be done at his leisure but it was good to get a few preliminary ideas while she was present.

"This is a seeker's elixir," said Frater Theophrastus, and pushed his glasses up on his nose. "We need wisdom, mental acuity, vibrations for discovering mysteries, learning secrets. Detective energy."

Nathalie nodded.

"We'll need help from Jupiter and Mercury, a little Saturn, a little Pluto. A lot of Uranus. The seeker is The Fool and The Fool is Aquarius. That means Uranus."

"Okay," Nathalie said.

"I'm thinking lots of oak. Nuts, bark, leaves, roots. And elder—that's the seeker of the Celtic zodiac. Mulberry leaves, ashberry leaves, carrots, radishes, hibiscus, sage, kiwi, persimmon, olive, echinacea, cinnamon, cloves, star anise, lotus blossoms, nutmeg, rain lilies, peonies."

"Sounds great," Nathalie said.

"A little basil, a little oregano. Any allergies I should be aware of?"

No allergies. Of course some of these ingredients were toxic, especially in high concentration, and she must observe his instructions with extreme care or risk a lethal overdose.

"Good to know."

"You should start the meditation and cleansing regimen immediately. I'd like to get started while we've still got Jupiter on our side. Under Sagittarius. Don't forget to fast for twenty-four hours first."

Any all-natural cleanse would do—lemon water, parsley or dandelion tea were all great. Good idea to get a massage first, too, work those hard to break toxins out of the deep tissue. Hatha-yoga or trance dance could help with meditation. He prescribed a strict vegetarian diet for a full moon cycle and told her to start writing down her dreams. "It's best if you record them first thing when you wake up, before the conscious mind has completely ascended. I find it convenient to keep a journal next to my bed. Don't leave anything out. Write it all down. You never know what might turn out to be important."

He penciled her in for an appointment in two weeks. They were getting ready to say goodbye when Nathalie noticed on top of the bookcase, between a *Farmer's Almanac* and *Advanced Techniques for the Master Tantric Lover,* a small framed photograph. A kitchen with a long banquet table overflowing with the kinds of finger-foods you expect to find at an intimate party. Wine bottles and half-empty glasses. In the foreground seven or eight people, men and women, younger and older, press silly poses together for the shot. Frater Theophrastus is among them, obviously inebriated, wearing a white pork-pie hat with a black t-shirt boasting I AM A JEDI KNIGHT LIKE MY FATHER BEFORE ME. Several more blurry figures mill in the background. One of them stole Nathalie's attention, an elderly man with a gray mustache. Black fedora. Matching raincoat.

"Synchronicity," she said. "My boyfriend's been looking for that man."

Frater Theophrastus frowned. "You have a boyfriend?"

29.

The man in the black coat had a name and his name was Albert. Damian felt sick to his stomach. The witchdoctor Nathalie visited didn't know if it was his real name—probably it wasn't, Albert being a pretty popular alchemical name among those inclined to assume one: Frater Albertus, Albertus Magnus, Albertus Magus, Le Grande Albert, Petite Albert. This one, so far as Frater Theophrastus knew, was just plain old Albert. He didn't know Albert well—he'd told Nathalie he couldn't recall Albert being at the gathering in the photo until she pointed him out. He turned up a lot at The Green Thorn Brier's Metaphysickal Bookstore & Cosmic Consciousness Emporium. If you hung out there you'd run into him sooner or later.

"It might not be him," Nathalie said. "The picture was blurry and I couldn't make out his face, but the basic facts are certain: it was an old man. He wore a mustache. His hat and coat were black. How many people could it be? Plus, he's an alchemist. It might be the same guy."

Damian was inclined to agree. He didn't tell Nathalie about Phaedra, partially due to his trust phobia, partially because he didn't know how to parse Phaedra out. What would he say? How could he explain things he didn't understand himself? Once he knew who Phaedra was, her connection with the man in the black coat, the meaning of the crow's head, and why he needed to protect the great white buffalo, he would explain it all to Nathalie. If they were in danger, Damian needed to account for who knew what, and the less Nathalie knew the safer she would be. He needed to control the flow of information, which meant hiding things from her. His research found the crow's head was a symbolic motif in alchemical imagery. What it referred to was vague and convoluted. Something to do with creating the philosopher's stone. The man in the black coat—if he really was this Albert—was supposed to be an alchemist, so there was a potential connection.

The Green Thorn Brier's occupied a converted house on a flagstone courtyard in Cole Valley. Damian and Nathalie dropped by the next morning. Spicy incense and Gregorian chants. Glass display-case with tarot cards and crystals and scented candles. Behind the counter a stereo deck and a stiff middle-aged man with russet skin and a collared shirt, black hair freshly cut, pomaded, graying at the temples. They traded nods and Damian moved into the store while Nathalie perused the display case.

The wall between the living-room and kitchen had been knocked out, the tiles replaced with hardwood. Double-sided bookcases divided the enlarged space. Where the kitchen used to be, a steep slant in the floor pulled toward the far corner and the sunken foundation. A sliding-glass door in the back opened onto a narrow patio and a Zen garden surrounded by high wooden fences. A narrow hallway connected the main showroom to two smaller rooms lined with bookcases. Damian looked through open baskets of gemstones and incense, a rack of pendants, cheaply made and overpriced ritual implements: gaudy daggers and pentacles and goblets and magic wands. Three other customers browsed the store. In the alchemy section he ran a finger along paperback spines and whispered titles beneath his breath. A good selection of classics. Frater Albertus, Fulcanelli, Michael Sendivogius, Michael Meier, Elias Ashmole, Paracelsus.

He pretended to read the introduction to *Le Mystères des cathédrales* and listened to Nathalie chat with the man behind the counter, the easy friendship of her giggle and the seductive Mumbai sing-song soughing the cadence of his impeccable British accent. When she joined him, Damian said, "Knows our guy?"

"Knows him," she said. "But hasn't seen him in a while. Several weeks." Nathalie nodded at the attendant. "His name's Bharat and he's a minority owner of the bookstore."

They browsed for another two hours, taking turns monitoring the entrance, before breaking for lunch. There was a bistro on an adjacent side of the courtyard with a small outdoor dining area and a perfect view of the bookstore. Nathalie wanted to know what now and Damian said, "We wait."

"You do this a lot, don't you?"

"It becomes necessary from time to time. How'd you guess?"

"We spent half the day in that bookstore. We're going to spend the other half there too and you're not even bored."

"I like books," he said, and bit his sandwich.

This time Bharat narrowed his eyes on Damian as they came into the store, obviously disappointed to see them again. Or just annoyed, it was hard to tell. Damian returned to the alchemy section. While handling the books he could feel the black shadow cast over his back by the proprietor's gaze. On the bottom shelf he discovered a book out of place. *On Formally Undecidable Propositions of Principia Mathematica and Related Systems* by Kurt Gödel. He knelt on one knee as he turned the pages. The acid in the paper had begun yellowing the edges. He put them on his nose and his heart quickened to the musty fragrance of an old book. Like the best part of childhood. More enchanting than any incense, Damian thought, and he took in stride the discovery of the thin folded sheet of rice paper buried halfway through. More like he remembered he would find it there than he discovered it for the first time. Like he'd come here looking for it, which was ridiculous.

In particular c (like any recursive class) is definable in P. Let w be the propositional formula expressing Wid (c) in P. The relation Q (x, y) is expressed, in accordance with (8.1), (9) and (10), by the relation-sign q, and Q (x, p), therefore, by r ë ê é û ú ù since by (12) r = Sb è ç œ ø ÷ ö q 19 Z (p) and the proposition (x) Q (x, p) by 17 Gen r. In virtue of (24) w Imp (17 Gen r) is therefore provable in P67 (and a fortiori c-provable). Now if w were c-provable, 17 Gen r would also be c-provable and hence it would follow, by (23), that c is not consistent. It may be noted that this proof is also constructive, i.e. it permits, if a proof from c is produced for w, the effective derivation from c of a contradiction. The whole proof of Proposition XI can also be carried over word for word to the axiom-system of set theory M, and to that of classical mathematics A, and here too it yields the result that there is no consistency proof for M or for A which could be formalized in M or A respectively, it being assumed that M and A are consistent. It must be expressly noted that Proposition XI (and the corresponding results for M and A) represent no contradiction of the formalistic standpoint of Hilbert. For this standpoint presupposes only the existence of a consistency proof effected by finite means, and there might conceivably be finite proofs which cannot be stated in P (or in M or in A). Since, for every consistent class c, w is not c-provable, there will always be propositions which are undecidable (from c), namely at, so long as Neg (w) is not c-provable; in other words, one can replace the assumption of w-consistency in Proposition VI by the following: The statement "c is inconsistent" is not c-provable.

Reading it made his hands clammy, the vivid line of perspiration beading along his hairline. Damian knew Bharat stared at him. He could feel the man's eyes digging the back of his head. He turned on his knee to stare back but there was no one standing behind the glass display-case. Damian stood up and looked around, calmly, perfectly comfortable with being watched by someone he couldn't see.

What did it mean, the rice paper transcription in this book, in this place? The copy of *Rosarium philosophorum* was an interlibrary loan from Ohio State University, *De occulta philosophia libri tres* from a used bookstore in Oregon. A sixteenth century alchemical treatise, a fifteenth century grimoire, an abstract mathematical proof. What did the three books have in common? He didn't know, but it might feel like remembering when all the pieces finally added up to a sum that dawned on him for the first time.

Bharat came down the hall from the back rooms and smiled stiffly. "Maybe there is something I could help you find, sir?"

"I'm looking for an old alchemist called Albert. Likes big coats and old-fashioned hats. You know him?"

"As I told the lady. We've not had the pleasure of Mr. Albert in many weeks. I don't know when we might next expect him, sir."

"Frater Theophrastus said we could find him here."

"Who?"

"Giles Combey," Damian said. Bharat nodded but said nothing.

"You know whose handwriting this might be?" Damian held out the rice paper note he found in Gödel's proof. Bharat flinched and his eyes widened before narrowing to slits. He took half a step away from Damian.

"Sorry, sir. I have never seen it before."

"You didn't even look at it."

Bharat made a big show of looking at the paper and shook his head. He wasn't smiling anymore.

"There's a symbol I'm curious about too." Damian showed him the stick figure with an infinity sign head in the margin.

"Recognize that?"

"It's unfamiliar to me," he said, but he was lying. Damian weighed the advantages and disadvantages of calling him on it. Nathalie had been watching them and now she stood next to Damian. He said, "Any clue why this book would be shelved with Alchemy?"

Bharat looked from Damian to Nathalie and back again, trying to decide what answering the question might give away. "A mistake."

"What time does Albert usually come?"

"Pardon me, sir." Bharat smiled again. "I'm not sure what you mean."

"Am I more likely to catch him at one hour than another? He a morning person, maybe?"

"Late, usually, sir. Just before closing. When he comes. Which is rare. Now it grieves me to insist, but I cannot assist further on this matter. If there is nothing else, I'll have to ask the gentleman and the lady to please leave."

"Let's go," Nathalie said, and put her hand through Damian's arm.

"Any day of the week he favors more than others? Really, anything would help."

"Let's go," Nathalie said again.

"No," Damian said. "I'm not done yet."

"Sir, if you don't intend to buy something I must ask you to leave," Bharat said again. He was still smiling. He looked at Nathalie and he looked at Damian and he smiled.

"I intend on buying something," Damian said, and raised the copy of *On Formally Undecidable Propositions of Principia Mathematica and Related Systems*.

Bharat's smile broadened. "I'll ring the gentleman up at once."

"Not ready yet. Still shopping."

Bharat frowned.

"Well, I'm going home," Nathalie said, and released his arm. Damian tore his eyes away from the smug attendant to look at her. "Do you want me to come?"

Nathalie thought about it for a second and sighed. "I guess not," she said. "If you want to stay, suit yourself."

Damian grinned at the frowning attendant. "I'm sure there's something else here I couldn't live without," he told Bharat. "I just got to find it."

Nathalie kissed him goodbye, made him promise not to get into trouble, and left.

"What can you tell me about the crow's head?" Damian asked.

Bharat lit a brighter smile, bowed, and pulled a book out of the shelf. "Modern alchemy doesn't have much to do with laboratory work. It is more speculative than practical. Over time, alchemists stopped trying to perform physical transformations and gradually began focusing more on personal transformation. Instead of turning base metals into gold, they were trying to become better versions of themselves. The crow's head represents breaking down your ego. Losing your identity. It has to do with burning off the personality and washing away everything you thought you were so you can become something else."

"Like a self-help thing."

Bharat laughed. He was all smiles and customer service, but his body was too stiff for comfort and there was an edge to his voice. Trying to be helpful enough to make Damian leave but not helpful enough to give anything important away. "It would be more like a mystical spiritual practice, sir."

"What does the crow's head have to do with the great white buffalo?"

Bharat didn't know what he meant. Damian explained what Phaedra had told him about Buffalo Calf Woman. Bharat was at a complete loss. He didn't know Phaedra, never heard of her before. There was nothing, to the best of his knowledge, about alchemy in Native American lore. Crows were a different story. He couldn't say off hand which tribe it belonged to, but he knew a myth about a dead crow who served as a psychopomp, or guide through the land of the dead. Bharat didn't believe it connected to the crow's head in alchemy.

Once he was alone, Damian amused himself with the book Bharat had taken from the shelf, a beginner's guide to modern alchemy. Apparently, the age-old cliché of transforming lead into gold dropped out of style among cutting edge adepts. Nowadays, the discriminating mage chocked physical transformation up to charlatans and crackpots—"puffers" in the specialists nomenclature—all the relevant research was going into psychoanalysis, homeopathy, self-improvement as a strictly psychological adventure. The philosopher's stone was a metaphor for the politically correct, ecologically sensitive, spiritually elitist and socially well-adjusted personality. The gold standard of high quality American living. The initial phase of which was referred to as the Nigredo, or blackening, and symbolized by the image of a raven's head or crow's head. He was just getting fed up when Bharat wandered over to inform him of closing time. It wasn't quite five o'clock. "Four more hours," Damian said without looking up from his book.

Bharat made an extravagant sigh: Damian was a huge pain in his ass. Point taken. "Terribly sorry, sir, we're closing early tonight. I have an appointment with the dentist."

"The dentist," Damian said.

"Yes, sir. A healthcare professional specializing in the maintenance of teeth."

"At five o'clock."

"Six o'clock, in fact, sir."

He was serious, Damian could see, the store was empty but for Damian and Bharat, the closed sign already turned on the front door. He tried to pay for the copy of Gödel, but there was a problem.

"There's no record of this book in the system."

"Just charge me something," Damian said, but no, Bharat would need to receive it into inventory first and it wasn't worth the bother.

"Consider it a gift if you like, sir," he said. Damian thanked him and promised to return tomorrow. Which he did, shortly after seven o'clock, and waited until closing at nine, but Albert the alchemist didn't show up.

Damian came a few hours before closing every day for a week. No luck. He toured the city's similar establishments, anything to do with the occult, alchemy, magic, the new age, asking about Albert and Phaedra, the crow's head and the great white buffalo, but no one could help. Bharat was telling the truth: he couldn't find any reference to the great white buffalo in alchemy. He searched websites and library stacks and shop shelves. Who was the man in the black coat and what did he want from Damian? How did the Koreans fit in and what did it have to do with counterfeiting? What part did Phaedra play and how did it relate to the buffalo? Nothing offered the slightest explanation. He read primary texts and commentaries and the hippy drum-circle fluff peddled at the Green Thorn Brier's. The clue was probably in front of his face. He was staring right at it, only he didn't know how to recognize what he was looking at.

30.

They got used to having him around the Green Thorn Brier's Metaphysickal Bookstore & Cosmic Consciousness Emporium. One of the part-time clerks, a scrawny hippy a few years older than Damian, took a liking to him. Brian. Big dreadlocks wrapped up in a blonde cable on the back of his head. Hemp vest worn over homespun sweaters, which left spindly fibers on everything he touched—the glass display-case, the stereo deck, the sales racks, the front of Damian's shirt. The guy was a hugger. "Namaste," he whispered, and wrapped Damian in a hirsute embrace. "You're a warrior of the light. I see it in your eyes."

"Stop it," Damian said. "I don't want anyone else to find out."

Albert came in once in a while, Brian admitted, but no one knew him well. He'd be there four or five nights in a row and then disappear for months. There were rumors. He was a practicing alchemist, one of the last of his kind. He had a laboratory in a warehouse somewhere in the city, a real museum quality athanor-and-bellows operation. True old school. No modern chemist's lab for him. Damian asked for pen and paper and Brian promised to deliver the note to Albert next time he came in: *I want to talk. I guess you know how to find me. –DL*

Pain wrenches Phaedra out of the other world. She lies doubled over the ulcer in her stomach, gasping between gritted teeth, tears stinging her eyes. Concentrates on breathing slowly, slowly, around the stabs, slowly and controlled, until it eases enough to open her eyes. Bones brittle and raw. Guts twist over a trickle of breath. Waiting for the next spasm to clench her like a fist.

It's happening. Sulphur mingles with mercury. Our Art quickens. The one thing. Phaedra would praise heaven if the birth pangs were not this brilliant fire ripping her in half. They are out there somewhere, waiting for her, needing her guidance and protection. But who are they? She thought she knew but was mistaken—the crow's head has not yet appeared. She feels the children, senses their presence, their panic and longing, but she cannot see them. It bodes ill.

Waves of despair emanate from the crucible—fear and lust and melancholy—sink her heart in a mire of dross. What's awry? What if the matter suffocated in the crucible before she and Albert could regulate the heat? The children stillborn. There's no way to know for certain. One can only work and pray, pray and work. But each day that passes without the arrival of the crow's head makes it less likely it will ever come. Only grace conceives the stone. Only the worthy heart confects it. Phaedra's heart harbors too many resentments. Dark hungers. Violence. Avarice. Too much selfish love. She can blame failure on the choked furnace if she wants, but she knows the true cause lies with her and Albert. The chemical marriage. All their passion and suffering end in nothing if hope is born dead.

Another crash shatters her thoughts. Phaedra clasps the blanket hard enough to blanch skin. Veins stand up on her hand like fat worms. The chapel utterly black at the witching hour. Slow Henry gurgles and sighs, incubating in its belly the black egg. The straw next to her empty and cold. She sips breath and swallows the urge to cry out. Counts her sins and smiles. As long as the torments do not stop there is still a chance. Phaedra listens beyond the walls and the clearing. The man rutting with ewes in mountain pastures. Horns like the waning moon, shape-shifting, running with wolves, killing the sacred deer. Burnt offering. The long night of flesh and teeth. A canticle of ash and embers. Howling to inter-dimensional chaos gods. Shudders charge through Phaedra and she moans. Blood mixed with lead makes smoke.

Alchemy and the Rebis. Green lion and philosopher's stone and marriage of the king and queen. They were not mere symbols, at least not of chemical reactions or psychological mechanisms. Nathalie didn't know what the wedding invitations meant, but unlike Damian, she didn't believe the answer lay hidden in books. The meaning wasn't a rational construct —it was more real than that. In the weeks after her trip to the Green Thorn Brier's Metaphysickal Bookstore & Cosmic Consciousness Emporium, she followed the preparations prescribed by Frater Theophrastus for her spagyric seeker's elixir.

Meditation was the hardest part. She wasn't a natural meditator, not versed in emptying the mind, observing her own thoughts, lulling consciousness to sleep so her subconscious could speak. The stillness made her intensely aware of the strange thing in the middle of her. Rosa had described it as a jar or a cup. Nathalie imagined it like a black carbon egg, perfectly sealed and hollow, nestled between her heart and lungs. She didn't know what was in it, but she needed whatever was in there. If Rosa was right, it might help her find the wedding. She could feel it smoldering, scratching like an insect at the walls of the egg, and it terrified her. She hoped it would never hatch because she knew the contents might destroy her.

When she noticed these thoughts, she banished them and started again. After a while her mind would wander and inevitably settle on the wedding invitations. She tried to stop. She tried and failed and tried again, but it was no good. She tried yoga and trance dance, as Frater Theophrastus recommended, but nothing could get rid of the invitations. She couldn't help it. Thoughts of the carbon egg, her parents, sisters, Damian, cleared from her mind with a deep breath and focus of will, but her wedding invitation consumed her for hours. She didn't notice it happening until it was over.

It spread from her meditation practice to the rest of her life. In bed with the alarm clock blaring and no memory of waking, her mind full of the invitation. Coming to, standing before the armoire holding her invitation, no idea how she got there or how long she'd been stroking the Rebis between her fingers. The familiar reek of rot and earth pervaded the whole apartment and clung to her hands for the rest of the day. She filled the sink with hot water and soap and thought about the invitations, only to be roused from her reverie by Damian kissing her hair, her hands sunk to the wrists in cold water and unwashed dishes.

Kendra canceled the studio lease in Oakland, moved to Austin, and took Strange Equinoxes with her. She invited Nathalie to come, promised to help her find a job and a place to stay, but Nathalie didn't want to leave. It wasn't the right time. Damian encouraged her to go. He'd be broken-hearted, he said, but it wasn't right for him to be selfish. This was about her and dance and she should go wherever that took her. If she wasn't going to let her dad stop her then she shouldn't let Damian.

Rosa accused her of staying for Damian, which would've destroyed him if he'd suspected it was true, but he had nothing to do with Nathalie's decision to stay. The idea of Texas never got comfortable inside her. Nathalie didn't know why, she didn't know what it meant, but when she thought seriously about leaving, she understood she still had unfinished business in San Francisco.

Damian thought she should go to Texas with Strange Equinoxes because her dream was to be a dancer and so she should chase that dream anywhere it led. Rosa thought she didn't because she was stupid and in love. Both of them wanted her to be happy but neither of them noticed she was different now. A few months ago, she wouldn't have questioned the decision to follow the dance. But now the impulse felt small and distant. It wasn't as important to her as it used to be and the loss made her ache more than anything. The things that used to matter to her were spinning fast. All mixed up and changing and she had no idea how it would turn out. She wished she could tell her dad because she knew exactly what he would say, what he always said: everything would turn out fine, of course, because she was a strong woman and no matter what happened, she would find a way to make it fine.

She got a new job as a bar-back at the same jazz club in Laurel Heights she'd gone to with Rosalie. It was only three days a week but the coffee-shop refused to work around her schedule. She quit the coffee-shop and found herself right back where she'd started: underemployed and looking for a second job.

Her dad made Carolina call and invite her and Damian to Thanksgiving dinner. A pretty bald scheme to coax her home since they hadn't eaten a real Thanksgiving dinner in ten years. Her dad preferred to work.

"If you don't mind, I'd like to meet him," Damian said, and her spine ratcheted tight.

"I mind," she said. "A lot."

"In that case, I guess I want to meet him anyway." He held her eye, wanting her to know he was serious. Nathalie didn't want to see her dad again until she was in a position to take great delight in laughing, maniacally, in his face. She wanted to say I told you so, you self-righteous fucker, but so far, he would get to say it to her. And he probably would because she'd ended up exactly how he'd predicted: scrambling for work, impoverished, living off the benevolence of her boyfriend, who still hadn't charged her sex for rent, though Rosalie seemed convinced he would start any day. Dancing festivals here and there, paying for stage space to perform for other dancers, or barely making bus fare in front of disinterested trolls, with hardly the time or space to practice in between.

Damian squeezed her knee, pushed his fingers up the inseam of her jeans. Insisting on an answer. "Shut up," Nathalie said, even though he didn't say anything, and pushed his hand away. "I'm ignoring you."

Two nights later she came home from work at nearly three in the morning, the bathroom door locked and the light on, Damian's laptop open on the bed. She only looked for a second, only a glance as she moved it over to his side, but what she saw was a confirmation page for a bank in Luxembourg. Transaction fees and currency exchange rates. A savings transfer of fifty-thousand dollars from a bank in Guatemala. Another of two-thousand dollars to a bank in San Francisco. The account belonged to someone called William Coker. A second later the page timed out and she could hear Damian washing his hands in the bathroom. She resisted the urge to ask who William Coker was and why Damian had access to his Luxembourg account, but it nourished a bitterness at the back of her throat. For every secret Damian confessed, she discovered two more he kept hidden.

It had been eleven months since she'd dreamt about him and two days later found him mauled, face down and hooded, on a Portside parking-lot. She'd dreamt of him almost all her life and believed it mattered. It meant something. But it had been almost a year and she hadn't dreamt of him since. She supposed she might never dream of him again. If it was him. Maybe Damian was right—what if she hadn't been dreaming about him, what if it was her own sad, beaten imagination she'd seen and Damian reminded her of it? What if her connection to Damian was just a love affair after all and nothing more important?

At her next visit, Frater Theophrastus gave her a box of tiny dropper bottles. Tinted glass with white labels. Essential oils. Oak root, ashberry leaves, kiwi—dozens of them. She should keep them under her bed while she slept and she must talk to them, each one all by itself, explain to them what she was seeking. "Tell them what you hope this elixir will mean to you," he said. "Tell them everything. Don't hold back."

Nathalie talked to the essential oils because Frater Theophrastus told her to, because she didn't see any point in cheating if she wanted to try spagyria. She felt stupid, though, every day, when Damian left for work and she retrieved the box from under her side of the bed. She held the tiny glass bottles at eye level between thumb and forefinger, each one in turn, blushing and in spite of herself carrying on one sided conversations aloud with the essential oils. "I'm sorry I feel stupid," she said. "Please don't be offended. I am the seeker," she told them. "I'm the detective, coo-coo-cachoo."

After a few weeks it became habit and she didn't think about it much. She just did it. She stopped feeling stupid about it. She didn't think speaking to the essential oils was pointless and she didn't think it was meaningful. It was simply something she did every day. Cautiously, she began to suspect her body changing. A strange new awareness. Not an idea, but a sensual epiphany. That was the only way she could describe it: what if the oils were listening? It didn't make any sense when she articulated it, but her body asked the question. Even her hair follicles wanted to know the answer, the enzymes of her digestive tract, her corneas, plantar fascia, red blood cells. What if the oils—radish, elderberry, lotus blossom—what if they understood what she was saying?

Ludicrous. And she didn't exactly believe it, but the question changed her. In a disturbing and consequential way she was no longer the same person, not anymore the Nathalie who never wondered if the eviscerated fluids of vegetal offal might be conscious of her chatter. She could draw a line straight through her life at that moment. Before it occurred and after. A rite of passage as clear and powerful as menstruation, graduation, marriage.

Or death.

Frater Theophrastus collected the essential oils and told her to continue focusing on the elixir during meditation. At her most recent appointment, he gave her a thin dark liquid in a sealed mason jar and instructed her to sleep with it under her pillow.

"Hold it in your lap while you meditate. Focus on it. Think about it all the time. Leave it outside during the day when you're not at home. It needs lots of natural, direct sunlight."

She leaned it in the windowsill with the blinds up, a thick black scum congealing on the surface and mysterious motes swirling in the deeper light.

He read her dream journal too and recommended she continue the practice. It hadn't gone so well. Normally, she retained dreams after waking, sometimes several a night she could recount in detail. But since she'd started writing them down, they'd grown murkier, more elusive. The effort required to remember exhausted her and all she got for it was usually a single image. Scraps of nonsense. Moods. Most of what she could recall, though, were the butterflies.

"Find the butterflies," Frater Theophrastus said. "See what happens."

31.

The chrysalis, no bigger than Nathalie's finger, hung by a single hair. She could see its metallic gleam whenever the breeze ruffled eucalyptus leaves and let the sun through. Signs at the entrance to the grove warned of a thousand dollar fine for anyone caught harassing the butterflies, but she wouldn't touch the chrysalis anyway, certain the briefest pressure of her fingertips would damage the poor thing. Such delicate structures. They were everywhere in the trees, liquid crystals dangling like ornaments from the branches, but for some reason this one decided to transform low enough for close inspection. Adult monarchs gathered higher up in enormous orange and black leis, thousands and thousands, wings blinking from the treetops.

Damian lay on his back watching them with binoculars and Nathalie decided to join him on their picnic blanket, nestled between the trees, wading the short November grass and dappled sunlight. It was a weekday, the grove unadvertised and poorly known, and she'd hoped to tempt Damian to make love beneath bouquets of butterflies. But it was not to be. They found a secluded nook between the trees but Nathalie could hear mere yards away other butterfly watchers, and behind them, the bustling parking-lot and clogged highway. They might still get away with it if they were quick and quiet, but she didn't want to be quick about it. Or quiet.

"Hungry?" she said and unpacked their lunch of sandwiches, hard-boiled eggs, mixed greens, a cheap bottle of chianti, the sort with a screw-off top.

"Why don't you want me to meet your dad?"

"Not this again," Nathalie said and tousled his hair. "It wouldn't go well."

"You can't stay mad at him forever. I don't need you to protect me from him."

Nathalie giggled. "Maybe I'm protecting him from you. Did you ever think of that?" She chewed her cucumber sandwich and ate the mixed greens like chips with her fingers and passed the chianti back and forth with Damian, taking straight pulls off the bottle. She avoided the hardboiled eggs—the moon, she knew too well, waxing and gibbous in the final days of Frater Theophrastus' vegetarian diet.

Damian picked up the binoculars and rolled onto his back again. Nathalie watched him, sipping the dregs of wine and wondering what it would be like if he met her dad. Not good —each had his qualities but they shared none in common and yet they managed to be too much alike in all the worst ways. Damian didn't want to meet her dad anyway—she imagined he secretly loathed her dad as much as she did his. But he hated thinking he'd ruined her relationship with her dad and he seemed to think Thanksgiving might mend it. Maybe the invite was a peace offering, but Nathalie doubted it. More likely a lure with a barbed hook underneath.

Damian championed her when she needed his strength to defy her father's strength. She hadn't spoken to her dad since, and now Damian felt culpable. He'd admitted it in the car, he'd been admitting a lot lately. He still wouldn't tell her what he did for work or what all the trouble was about, but she knew, for instance, he'd moved to Oakland after the death of his stepfather, Jordan, a pharmaceuticals chemist in Seattle. His mom, Marianne, disillusioned with academia, disappointed with career-chasing and six months pregnant with Damian, requested a temporary sabbatical from the university where she'd been teaching, never went back, never defended her doctoral dissertation, and only regretted it when her bridges were burned and her husband incarcerated. Her ex-husband, Damian's father, Ronald, the convicted felon, alcoholic, and woman-beater, a rare books expert, had once owned a shop in Cincinnati. Explained how Damian knew so much about ink and paper. It was progress but probably not enough.

"What've you told him about me?" Damian wondered.

"Nothing. But my sisters probably have. I'm sure he would hate you. It's one of the reasons I fell in love with you."

Damian rolled over and regarded her tenderly. It was the first time either of them admitted out loud to being in love, and he wanted her to know he hadn't missed the moment. She knew he wasn't going to say it back. He was too scared, too worried about what it meant, what obligations he would be accepting if he were honest. Nathalie wasn't worried about any of that. The only reason she said it was because it was the truth. Damian kissed her on the forehead and turned his attention back to the butterflies.

There weren't many left. The number of butterflies reduced to a fraction of their usual splendor but still breathtaking, the canopy burning spirals of orange fire and black coal. It had been a tough year for them. The late winter ruined milkweed the caterpillars depended upon to grow 2,700 times their birth size. No rain since March and drought conspired with urban development to pinch their meager coastal habitats. Hot summers interfered with their metabolisms, confused their reproductive rituals and migratory patterns. These ones came from the Rocky Mountains: Colorado, Montana, British Columbia. The two-thousand mile migration would end in Mexico before heading north again in February.

But none would learn what Nathalie knew—they'd never been to the mountains and they would never reach Mexico. The life of a monarch butterfly a slim six weeks and the caravans never-ending. Months ago their ancestors started the long flight south for a destination they wouldn't live to see, and the ones Nathalie admired now wouldn't see it either. Each generation performed a small piece of the voyage but no single life could experience the whole thing. Cycle of an entire clan. Pilgrimage of a total species. And when it finally ended next spring, those butterflies would celebrate the realization of their great-great-grandmothers' dreams, feast on high mountain wildflowers, make love, lay eggs, and die. And their babies would fly south again, carried by faith in eternal spring. This grove. The Pacific Ocean. Mexico. Only the blood in their wings heard these rumors.

The blood in Nathalie heard, too. It erupted into applause, clapping hard on her ribs. She'd come because Frater Theophrastus said to find the butterflies, and she was shown a secret. Nathalie was part of a cycle greater than herself. It began long before her birth and would continue long after her death. She was a small but vital piece. Everyone was. Everyone mattered. Only most people didn't know how crucial a role they played. Nathalie couldn't understand the whole—far too vast to be grasped by a human mind—she needed only to learn her task and become the person capable of performing it.

Damian had helped her become who she was, but he couldn't help her anymore. If she was going to become the person she must, she had to keep changing, and soon Damian must change, too, and everything would be different between them. The cup inside her pulsated darkly beneath her breast. Throb and dense heat hardening. Sharp and brilliant as a knife plunged into her chest.

"You look sad," Damian said. He stood over her in the clearing, sunglasses tipped against his forehead.

"Nope." She smiled, sadly, to prove she meant it. He sat beside her and held her hand but neither said anything. The clearing glowed with sunshine. Columns of eucalyptus soared around them and converged in vaulted branches high above where stained glass wings cast orange and gold patterns upon the floor. It's like a gothic church, Nathalie thought. A cathedral made of the earth.

"After this, do you want to go to the movies?"

"Sure," Nathalie said.

Through the trees she saw the western sky stacked with charcoal clouds. She wondered what butterflies thought of caterpillars. Did they recognize their uninitiated selves in the black and white striped worms? Was a cocoon a death-shroud to a caterpillar? Did they feel the coming chrysalis hardening beneath their skin, and tremble? Nathalie's transformation would be terrible. She would not survive it—what emerged would be as unrecognizable to herself as caterpillars are to butterflies. What was it like inside that darkness? Did it hurt to transform, cracking and splitting like that—was it painful to become a butterfly?

Nathalie lay on her back and held Damian's hand and watched the monarchs. The sun sank in thunderclouds. Then the mass of wings blocked out the weakening light and faded to darkness.

Thanksgiving came and went and Damian didn't meet Sebastião Jevali. He and Nathalie made dinner for each other, served buffet-style on the kitchen counter and enjoyed on the studio floor. The turkey, a boneless precooked and processed half-breast, the only option fit for the hotplate, sliced and fried—neither had thought to save the toaster-oven from the Portside condo. Canned cranberry sauce and yams, instant potatoes with powdered gravy and diced canned mushrooms added to stovetop stuffing. Nathalie made an excellent garden salad and Damian added German potato salad, his mother's recipe, and a pasta experiment with corkscrews, roma tomatoes, parmesan, whole black olives, vinegar and oil. Whiskey and red wine. Pop tarts for dessert. Nathalie's verdict: a great feast. But for the first time Damian regretted hoarding money. It was a better meal than any Thanksgiving he'd spent alone but Nathalie's presence made him crave a celebration worthy of his blessings.

To compensate, he got drunk and told her about Thanksgiving traditions growing up. It was his dad's favorite holiday, though he would've been pissed to hear Damian thought so. His dad had sat at the head of the table and carved the turkey and recounted the first Thanksgiving. A shameful tale of how in 1621 Anglo-Christian fundamentalists were delivered from the shocking foolishness and utter incompetence of their faith and culture by Wampanoag heathens, and how in thanksgiving Wampanoag mercy was rewarded with the rape of a continent, the systematic genocide of its indigenous population, and more than two-hundred years of definitive proof to the world that white people, on balance, are simply too fucking stupid to govern themselves. After the meal, he recited love poetry to Damian's mother`, all her favorites—Shelley, Keats, Yeats, both Browning's, Saint Vincent-Millay, fragments of Sappho in the original Greek, which he didn't speak but memorized specially for her, even the Great Bard of Stratford His Holy Self—until the gin made him stutter. Then they went around the table and each Lancaster confessed to the others what things in the past year they were most grateful for. What they had glutted themselves on thanks to atrocity.

"What did your family do?"

Nathalie twisted her face up and thought about it. "Dad would go to work early. At six o'clock the maid and the nanny would come to work because my dad wouldn't give them the day off. I or Rosa would send them home and the six of us kids would cook."

"What about your mom?"

Nathalie shrugged.

"I'm grateful to you."

Nathalie said she was grateful for him, too, but he shook his head. "No," he insisted. "I'm grateful to you. Really, really grateful."

"I know," Nathalie said and stroked his face.

"I wish I could demonstrate my gratitude. But I think I'm too drunk now."

"I'm a spoiled girl," Nathalie said. "Tell me about your

company."

Damian laughed. "You're trying to take advantage of me while I'm too drunk to consent. I would never do that to you."

"Everything I ever wanted in a man." But she was teasing, more melodramatic damsel in distress than gushing adoration.

"I make money," he said. He thought, no, you stupid fucker, shut up! "In a warehouse." And then he fell asleep on the floor. She must've responded, there must have been more, but the next day, all he remembered was Nathalie shaking his foot.

"Take your shoes off," she said.

A few days later Damian slid the December rent check under the new superintendent's door. It would be the last one. Gentrification had finally reached Bayview. Rents soared to cover initial costs. Once the old tenants were all chased away renovations started in earnest. The studios converted into one bedroom luxury apartments for the tech geeks who could afford extravagant rent. Most of the neighbors were already gone, including the Indonesian lady who used to collect the rent.

There was no way Damian could stay now—too many raised eyebrows. Anyway, Damian planned on buying a house. Hiding money overseas was easy—getting it back was harder. He'd begun moving $300,000 from the Guatemalan account to banks in Luxembourg, Hong Kong, the Cayman Islands, gradually transferring amounts small enough not to throw red flags at the Department of Homeland Security to local credit unions in California, Oregon, Nevada, Utah, each account with its own fake identity.

Like counterfeiting, none of this was difficult, so long as you understood how the financial system worked, you were careful about the law, and patient as an iceberg. Damian had always been a voracious reader. He was developing into a proficient researcher. But his true calling in life, he was beginning to suspect, was for waiting.

He knew Nathalie had seen the foreign account on his computer, the long dollar amount, probably the fake name, and he wondered what she thought it meant. He'd left the laptop logged in and she came home while he was using the bathroom. When he came back, the page had timed out but he noticed the screensaver hadn't activated. Which meant it had been refreshed. It had been only a matter of time, anyway. Sooner or later she was going to find out, and he was glad—he wanted her to know. It felt good to tell her on Thanksgiving though panic itched a layer beneath his skin. But she had no sense of what he'd told her—she'd thought he was being facetious. She knew he made money—obviously—by doing what? Only fear of losing her kept him from saying it.

A year from now it would be time for a vacation. A roadtrip with his best girl across the west. Closing accounts. She would know the truth by then and if she asked him to quit, he'd already decided to do it. When they came back he would buy a house in Chico, maybe, or Eureka. Up north. Nathalie could choose and he would put it in her name. An investment his dad would've rather pushed a screwdriver through his own eardrum than hear. Damian didn't need to own a house. If he and Nathalie didn't work out, he still wanted her to own it. If she decided to sell it, she'd at least get something for her bother, and if she lived in it, so much the better.

At the warehouse he printed orders on the graveyard shift. As the raging press poured the first layer of inked paper into the receptacle tray he thought over what Phaedra had told him about Nathalie and his own destiny. The fact was he didn't know if Nathalie's decision not to follow Strange Equinoxes to Texas was right or wrong. He'd made her swear her decision to stay had nothing to do with him. She'd chosen a dream and he imagined that would be the easy part—the trial and consequence of her decision were still to come and she might learn staying had been a mistake. Sooner or later she would probably go. For her, dancing was a passion beyond wealth or poverty. It was a calling, not a career move and not a hobby. It transcended common sense. Maybe it wasn't she who chose to dance but dance that chose her and what expression that took was beyond his comprehension.

But around two in the morning while reloading the press an idea stopped him: if Nathalie moved to Austin he could go to Wyoming. It was as good a course as any. Damian had never been chosen by anything in his life and he coveted the possibility. Perhaps the great white buffalo Brother Sun Sister Moon chose him. Perhaps Phaedra was schizophrenic and all her oracle an accident of circumstance. Maybe, maybe not. Either way it didn't change the naked fact he could do it. It wasn't like he was doing anything more important with his life. He could go to Wyoming and hang out with the great white buffalo until it turned white again for no reason other than a crazy woman asked him to and he decided what the hell. It was an option.

Phaedra had said Albert wanted to prevent him from protecting the calf. The easiest way to find the old man might be through the buffalo. Damian still hadn't received the crow's head—he wasn't even sure what that meant, but it seemed important to Phaedra. It couldn't refer to information he needed to learn—she'd told him to leave the crow's head with Brother Sun Sister Moon, so it must be an object of some kind—a statue, maybe, or a picture—unless it was a message he had to deliver. He knew the crow's head was a symbol in alchemical imagery, but what it referred to remained elusive. A chemical process or developmental phase of the philosopher's stone.

An illness of the imagination now infected his loneliness with hope. Damian couldn't trust it. What if Phaedra turned out to be a swindling bitch scouting patsies for a rip off? Except she knew things he felt but was slow to articulate. He had four months until Nathalie started her menstrual cycle under Aries —and what kind of deadline was that, anyway? Damian happened to be an Aries and he knew it lasted from March twenty-first to April nineteenth. Unless you considered the sidereal method of reckoning the procession of the signs according to the fixed stars rather than the tropical method of reckoning by the vernal equinoxes of the northern hemisphere, in which case it lasted from April fifteenth to May fifteenth. So there was room for error.

Bianca called Nathalie to invite them for Christmas. "What kind of monster sends a ten-year-old to do his dirty work?" Nathalie wanted to know, but this time she relented. They would go to Belvedere Island on Christmas Eve and stay two nights. For the sake of Bianca and Angela, who hadn't seen Nathalie since she'd moved in with Damian, and missed her dearly.

Later that week he was supposed to deliver Pavel's December order but at the last minute Pavel called to abort. He wanted Damian to bring it to the restaurant, he'd be in touch if it wasn't safe to come. Pavel preferred to move money on mutually exclusive territory but weird shit was going on and they needed a safe place to discuss it.

"If I got you in trouble," Damian said and took a deep breath. "I understand if you need to cut me loose."

Pavel's laugh a little too keening for confidence. "I'm already too far in it," he said and hung up.

32.

At the restaurant Damian was ushered into the office behind the kitchen. No coffee this time and no pastries. The outdated fight promo on the door had been replaced with a lewd calendar: a lean banana-breasted girl with chicory skin and a ten-gallon afro squatted on a pool table with her knees spread and two fingers bracketing her vulva. She smiled and Damian smiled back. "The manager's," Pavel said and ripped the calendar off the door and threw it in the corner.

While counting counterfeit out of the briefcase he told Damian what he was too scared to say over the phone. The corpse of a tourist discovered last November stuffed into a plastic garbage can in a technology park in Wellington, New Zealand. A pathologist estimated the man had been dead since mid-October. Murder unsolved. Three months later, in February, a solitary four-sentence item from an Associated Press correspondent: fingerprints and dental records confirmed the man's identity, unreleased, and his remains shipped to Busan, South Korea. "In August," Pavel said, "the corpse's identity was made public. Kim Hyeon-gi." He needn't point out the question to Damian, who remembered what Phaedra had said: Kim Hyeon-gi isn't who you think he is. It made sense to Damian—no way the spastic shithead from Forest Hill accomplished the things Pavel said he was accused of. So who was pretending to be Kim-Hyeon-gi? Who met Damian at the house in Forest Hill? Did Gangjeon plant the usurper or didn't he know the man he hired was already dead?

Pavel returned the empty briefcase and turned his full attention on Damian. "It gets spookier," he said. No word yet on the woman who'd been following him. She disappeared. Pavel suspected she'd never been looking for Damian in the first place. Recently, he'd run into one of Gangjeon's circle in Little Korea. A mutual colleague. It had been hard as hell getting anything out of the guy when Pavel was asking questions about Kim, Noe, and Gangjeon Jae-kyeon a few months ago, but now he had plenty to say since it looked like Pavel was also involved. He said the mysterious man and woman looking for Kim and Noe in February had resurfaced, only this time they were collecting information about Pavel the Czech. This time, descriptions were much more helpful: there was only one man, for instance, and one woman, and no one thought they were working together. The woman was tall, broad, with jet black pageboy hair and big sunglasses. Matched the description of the cross-dresser observed by the shadow detail Pavel had assigned to Damian. And the man?

"Mustache," Damian guessed. "Fedora. Et cetera."

"Did you think of it? This fellow might only be following you as a way to spy on your poor friend Pavel?"

It hadn't occurred to him. Damian still didn't believe it, though Pavel seemed scared enough of the possibility. Asiana Airlines records proved Gangjeon purchased flight tickets for Kim Hyeon-gi and Noe Gun in early October. Pavel's counterpart in Australia made some calls and confirmed Kim flew to Wellington a few days later to do the early legwork for one unwholesome business opportunity or another—details were sparse and unreliable. Sometime the middle of October he got murdered and stashed for safekeeping. A month later, decomposed beyond visual recognition, the body was dumped in a public place, meant to be found.

On December twenty-ninth Noe and Pseudo-Kim had flown into San Francisco, met up with their accomplices, and robbed Damian at Gangjeon's prearranged drop-point on New Year's Eve. They lasted two weeks before getting busted in Los Angeles seeking safe passage to Mexico. Gangjeon called around his old haunts in Little Korea trying to figure out what happened. A pair of strangers started looking for Kim and Noe. Roughly the same time the man in the black trench-coat started keeping tabs on Damian. A few months later, the woman followed suit.

The NSA must've figured out Pseudo-Kim wasn't the true artifact, but they bargained him to the South Koreans anyway. Possibly, they discovered the real reason the four Koreans were over here. Eight months later, the South Korean government allowed the death of Kim Hyeon-gi to become official. The two strangers caught some version of this and returned to Little Korea, this time asking about Pavel.

"Competing theories," Pavel said: One. It all had something to do with Damian. He was the only material connection be-tween Kim Hyeon-gi and Pavel the Czech. Two: The strangers, looking for Kim and Noe, learned Pavel was looking for them, too, and decided to investigate.

"We got to find your jewel," Damian said. "The stone you think Kim and Noe were after. Lapis exillis."

Pavel agreed. "Makes me want to know what happened to the counterfeit. How did they convert thirty-thousand dollars of it into cash? What was their plan for it? Where's Gangjeon squirreled himself away to? Who're these other people sticking their noses in it?"

The human mind can be a tricky fucker, Damian thought. He caught a streetcar two stops for the BART and integrated what he knew of Phaedra and Albert with what Pavel knew of the strangers in Little Korea. Until now he hadn't believed one way or the other if Phaedra was the cross-dresser Pavel's people claimed had been following him, but now it looked like she was. He wasn't any closer to knowing if Albert the alchemist was the man who'd been following him.

He'd asked through Nathalie to see the photograph in Frater Theophrastus' athenaeum, but, she said, he didn't have it anymore. Apparently, Albert dropped by for a visit, first time ever, noticed the photo and asked if he could keep it. Frater Theophrastus handed it over without a second thought, too ecstatic for Albert to request a memento of him. The dipshit. But Nathalie managed to get a crucial detail out of him. Frater Theophrastus hadn't mentioned it sooner because he wasn't one to draw attention to misfortune, but, yes, Albert had a physical deformity. He didn't have any ears. It must be the same man.

Damian hadn't mentioned this to Pavel because he wasn't convinced it mattered, and he didn't know how much he could trust Pavel. When the shoving started, he wanted a few wild-cards in his hand.

He got off the BART at Carl and Cole. By quarter after seven he was hearing good news at The Green Thorn Brier's Metaphys-ickal Bookstore & Cosmic Consciousness Emporium. While counting the cash drawer Brian had found a commission slip made out by Bharat and clipped to a scrap of paper: *For Mr. Albert.* The commission came from a rare books dealer in the Dog Patch, Celsius Antique Bookbinding & Restoration. Bro-kered by Ferdinand Sobraille. Brian offered contact info, but no need, Damian knew Sobraille. "I owe you a kombucha tea. Or stronger."

"Namaste," Brian said.

Outside, twilight coming, black clouds lidded the sky and boiled the city. Damian hitched up his jacket and slung his hands in the pockets. He looked up and down the street. And stopped. For once he was all alone. No one was looking at him, no watchers beyond his reach. No one knew where he was but him. Walking down the sidewalk he glimpsed in the artificial light of near-dark a black fedora. Disappearing and reappear-ing moment to moment among shifting pleats of pedestrians. He lost the hat at the intersection of Cole and Willard and paused to search but couldn't pick it up again. After a minute he decided to go home.

But halfway down Cole Street the man in the black coat re-appeared. Standing before the darkened glass of an insurance agency looking at nothing Damian could imagine, perhaps his own reflection. Another few steps and Damian would've been on top of him without even realizing it, but he noticed in time to step into the cove of a neighboring storefront. Shortly after, the man resumed his walk toward Stanyan Street.

Damian let him get far enough to feel alone but not far enough to get lost again. They passed The Green Thorn Brier's and turned left on Clayton Street and right on Frederick Street and walked several blocks. The foot-traffic thinned and Da-mian was forced to follow from a greater and greater distance or risk detection. The neighborhood grew darker, idyllic, lined with Victorian row houses and box trees, until it occurred to Damian he wasn't entirely confident of where he was or how far he'd wandered. Were they in Ashberry Heights now? Or had they drifted into the Haight? He scanned the buildings for an indication but found nothing and the corners didn't have street signs.

The man in the black coat turned down a one way lane between two Regency-style apartment blocks which revealed a secluded courtyard and a short row of parking stalls. At the far end an alleyway connected to a parallel street. There was no sign of how far ahead the man was, and Damian gave a ten second head-start before slipping through the alleyway. He came out on a narrow service road pocked with grated storm drains. The street dead-ended at a concrete barrier-wall kept vertical by a padlocked dumpster. The backsides of high-rise apartment buildings held upright by new fire escapes. Win-dows braced with iron bars. The scent of brine on the heavy night and the man in the black coat turned to the sound of Da-mian's shoes on gravel and steel and slurry.

Light behaved strangely in this place, stirred up by his en-trance, and his five senses went on high alert. Like they knew they wouldn't be trustworthy in this place and wanted to warn him. Something to do with the way light acted, but wasn't the light. Not really. It was everything and nothing at the same time. A presence, invisible and diffuse, which caused the light to rise and displace, like lead dropped in a cup of water.

The man in the black coat bore Damian the same blank expression he'd made from the rooftop across Ninth Street. That April day they'd been separated by four lanes of traffic and three stories of brick. Damian would be harder to avoid in the blind access-road but the man in the black coat gave no indication of it mattering. The night was full dark, overcast, moonless, lit by a single streetlight pointed at the dumpster. In the silence Damian's footsteps clicked like stones.

"Who are you?" Damian said when the distance between them shrank to a few feet, but no reply came back. Damian held out his hands to show they were empty. He only wanted to talk. "Is your name Albert?"

The old man drew from the great black coat a meerschaum pipe stained black and amber with use. He loosened the draw-string on a leather pouch and packed tobacco leaf into the bowl and gripped the stem in his teeth. The glow of the matchstick lit the underside of the fedora and illuminated the scars where his ears should've been. Fire moved from the match to the pipe and smoke billowed from the old man's nostrils. Black fog filled the service road with a savory aroma.

"Did you get my note?"

The old man fixed Damian in a piercing gaze and smoked his pipe. Tendrils curled over their heads and rose above the buildings. "Could it be you? After all these years? Come to take my place at the end?"

"No," Damian said. "I won't hurt you if you tell me who sent you."

"Come with me and I will teach you."

"I'm not going anywhere with you."

The man exhaled heavily and looked at the sky. "In that case there's nothing more to discuss." He emptied ashes on the gravel and dropped the pipe in his coat pocket. "You still have much to learn."

"Tell me about the crow's head," Damian said. "What does it mean? Who is Phaedra?" His thoughts felt incoherent. He tried to reason, remain rational and alert, but his senses betrayed and his mind floundered. What he saw didn't agree with what he heard. What he tasted contradicted what he smelled. His skin couldn't make sense of his eyes and his nose didn't believe his ears.

"In time you will be instructed in many things but you are yet to ask the appropriate questions." And with that the old man made to leave. Damian held up a hand to stop him. The man darted around Damian, but before he could disappear around the corner Damian tackled him into the side of the high-rise. Damian was surprised at himself—he hadn't struck anyone in years, and only ever in self-preservation—but the thought of losing this man again screamed at him and panic triggered his body. Damian pinned the man face-down on the sidewalk, knees driving the black coat into his back, twisting his wrists to his sides. Adrenaline and fear caked Damian's esophagus and he swallowed before speaking.

"You've been following me," he said into the man's ear, "and you're gonna stop."

The man struggled and Damian wrenched his wrist until he cried out and went limp. "Please," the man panted. "I don't want to hurt you."

"Tell me who you are and why you're following me."

"You're in great danger," the old man gasped and Damian shifted his weight and drove a knee cap hard into the old man's spine and brilliant pain erupted between Damian's shoulder-blades. His vision didn't so much disappear as it just ceased to matter inside the excruciating flash. For an instant he lost his balance and his body slackened. His equilibrium pitched and he slid off the black coat. A film of tears condensed on his eyes. Through the blur he spun around with his hands up against whoever attacked him, but there was no one there, and he lunged back on the black coat.

The old man had managed to turn on his side while Damian was stunned. Cheek to cheek they negotiated a balance between the weight of their bodies and their scrambling limbs. They lay halfway in the street facing each other on their sides. Hands grappled bodies for purchase. The old man's face was lined like the inside of a seashell and the skin around his eyes deeply creased. The look of him was intense but it was not threatening or angry or even scared. Damian saw compassion and sympathy for shared suffering. The fear that moved the old man's eyes back and forth between Damian's eyes wasn't for himself. It was for Damian.

The old man blinked and tears spilled over his ringed skin. The wet brush of his mustache dripped and Damian wept, too. It overwhelmed him. Like something inside Damian swelled up and secreted every emotion he'd ever felt all at the same time. The two of them held onto each other and sobbed. The only thing that made grief and love bearable was another life to brace them. Absorb them and share them. Damian absorbed the old man's tears and the sharing made it sweeter.

In fits it receded and Damian wiped his eyes. He was embarrassed and confused and terrified but he also felt hollowed. Refreshed. Stronger somehow. Firmer. The old man stood over him with the black fedora back on his head, red-rimmed eyes and soggy mustache, but composure regained. "When the fire claims me. When the smoke comes, you will know the truth. You will learn what I am," he said. "You will be taught by the flames."

Several minutes passed before Damian was stable enough to stand. The briefcase had been crushed in the scuffle but he collected it anyway and limped back the way he'd come. Persistent pain stabbed the inches between his shoulder-blades and a hot ache throbbed in his left shoulder but there was no more adrenaline. No panic and no fear. He wandered the streets, lost for the better part of an hour, before gathering his bearings near Mission Dolores. Cooler now in the evenings yet balmy, clouds paving skyline, but still no rain, the uncracked storms drifting eastward. His lip was split and one side of his face felt rubbery. He had to flex to keep the eye open enough to see.

33.

He didn't want Nathalie to be alarmed by his appearance. He hoped a smile might help but his face hurt like hell and all he could manage was a wince. She cocked an eyebrow, not surprised, and pointed where he should sit while she fetched the first aid. His right eye was going to swell shut soon if it wasn't drained. Nathalie washed her hands in the kitchen sink and doused a razorblade in rubbing alcohol and wiped down the area above his eye socket. "I learned this from a movie," she said. "You should be nervous." After it was drained she wiped it with hydrogen-peroxide and used medical tape to hold the gauze in place. Nathalie got his split lip to stop bleeding and told him the bruise on his cheekbone was almost black. It was going to hurt like a bitch, probably worse than his eye. She assessed the bruises on his chest and side. Cracked rib, maybe, he might end up having to go to the hospital whether he wanted to or not. The pain would decide.

"I'm having déjà vu," she said.

"We've done this before," he admitted. "I swear I'm not making it a habit."

But that wasn't what she meant. "This exact moment. You sitting on this bed, me crouched beside you, saying you might need a real doctor."

"Whether I need one or not, I can't afford one," Damian said. "This is the first time this has happened."

"Even this conversation about déjà vu is familiar to me. I don't know what you're going to say before you say it, or what I'm going to say, but after it's happened I feel like I remember it. Like a question you can't think of the answer to, and once you hear it, you realize you already knew but couldn't come up with it right away. Like something I forgot is happening again."

"I must've forgotten it, too."

"It's still happening."

She got him a glass of water and he explained what happened. The black coat, the cryptic message, the brawl and how his emotions turned inside out and smashed his body. All of it. She wanted to know what trouble he was getting himself into and why he didn't want her to know about it, but he insisted he wasn't in any trouble, he was only jumped in an alley.

"Now I know we've had this conversation before." She wouldn't look at him.

"You don't believe me."

"It's getting harder. I don't want that to be true. I don't like how it makes me feel."

Suddenly there was a new awkwardness between them, some invisible obscenity, which could neither be articulated nor ignored. It was like Damian all the sudden understood her and understanding made him realize he didn't know her, never came close to knowing her, because she didn't want to be known. Not by him. But he couldn't bring himself to shut her out. So they sat together in uncomfortable silence, incapable of being together and yet unwilling to be apart. He wanted to be close to her but he'd never felt so distant from her and never felt so alien to himself.

He sat at the far end of the mattress leaning away from her with his elbows on his knees and his hands cupping his ruptured face. As if remaining perfectly still might hide him. Like if he didn't look at her she wouldn't be able to see him. He wanted to be close to her but didn't know how to make it so, nor how to tell her. But he knew he must try, somehow, and he put a hand on her shoulder. She jumped and made a sound halfway laugh and sob and grabbed him against her and his groin tugged at her fragrance: shampoo, ozone, sweat.

"I know," she whispered. "I remember this."

Damian knew the moods he caused to come and go inside

her, for she conjured them in him as well, until there was no distinction between what he wrought and what was hers. Only this undulation of bright expansion and dark intensity exchanged between them, cycling and cycling, but never the same feeling twice, until it was not caused by either of them but it was conducted through the closed circuit of their bodies. Damian could see in her eyes what it took to make his own eyes dense and penetrating. As if the Nathalie he'd known until now was an opaque mirror and his body clarified her some-how, filled her skin up with light until she reflected the image of Damian back at him. And looking at himself this way he saw things he'd never noticed about himself. And Nathalie saw them, too.

From time to time they shared a word or two of encour-agement or praise and each word rang the same breath. Every inhalation drew in heat from the other and Damian did not know how to name the thought-stopping smoke at her lips. He felt her changing him, discovering him, creating—something. A moment expressive and collaborative and whole. He could not bear how sharp her eyes and how deeply they impaled him. When he looked away he could still see her, and just as clearly.

A crow comes into the clearing. Several days it lurks in the trees, gazing sidelong at the windowless chapel, the covered woodpile, and blood-spattered chicken stump. If spied by Albert it recedes into foliage or flaps to higher branches. "Shan't be long now," Albert mutters and trudges off to the brook. When he returns the crow pecks in the grass. In the shadow cast by the axe-handle where it stands up on the stump. Albert thinks it a good omen. The sun transits the ram for the bull and the scorpion breaks the horizon. But in the morning two score birds roost on the chapel roof. In waves crows light on the clearing floor to forage before swooping back up to their new perch. The mob snaps and billows like tatters of black sail in a breeze, rolling from eaves to ground and back. Wave upon wave. Albert poses a questioning glance and the birds grimace at him. They're waiting, he decides. Worse than vultures. Something's getting ready to die.

Soon as Albert enters the chapel he knows the work has gone very wrong. The darkness dumb and empty. Albert holds his hand to Henry's mouth. "Too hot," he says. Conflagration in the grate and inferno in the spyglass. How was he so careless? How was she so negligent? He barricades the grate and shuts the vent to starve the fire of air. Otherwise nothing can be done but wait for the flames to exhaust their fuel. The only emotions in the chapel his own: panic, helplessness, guilt. He shuts his eyes and holds his breath and waits. Nothing comes back. No pain. The torments of the crucible ceased, replaced in his heart by massive silence resolved to grief. He wants to cry.

Instead he places his hand over the furnace again. Cooler now—there might still be a chance—but their thoughts do not return to his head. Albert rushes to the oratorium and flings the curtain. Prostrates on his knees and begs for mercy. But the gods do not know how to be merciful. It does no good to negotiate with fate.

STUDY OF BOOKS ALONE

"No one can exercise our Magistry in the absence of the practical teaching of experience, without which the most diligent poring over books would be useless. The words of the Sages may mean anything or nothing to one who is not acquainted with the facts which they describe. If the son of knowledge will persevere in the practical study of our Art, it will in due time burst upon his enchanted vision. The study of books cannot be dispensed with, but the study of books alone is not sufficient."

—PETRUS BONUS, THE NEW PEARL OF GREAT PRICE, 1339.

They returned to Celsius Antique Bookbinding & Restoration a few days before Christmas, the soonest Ferdinand Sobraille could offer an appointment. Nathalie brought the invitations in hope a second look might reveal clues he hadn't noticed the first time. They idled in a viewing room full of bookcases and natural light. After fifteen minutes Sobraille apologized for making them wait and shook hands. "To what do I owe the pleasure?"

"We're looking for someone," Damian said. They sat in leather-bound chairs around an antique oak table framed by tall windows. "First name Albert. Don't know his last name. Bharat at The Green Thorn Brier's said you might know how to get in touch."

"This is about your mystery invitations?"

Nathalie and Damian nodded.

"I know who you mean," Sobraille said. "I've been able to acquire a small number of rare books for Bharat over the years. Rare editions aren't a big interest among his regular clientele, but once in a while he makes a referral. Esoteric literary antiquities are tough to find, and always expensive, but occasionally I can help."

"What was Albert looking for?"

"*Le Véritable dragon rouge,* French, 1863. *The True Red Dragon.* Also known as *The Grand Grimoire.* I located a private collector in Scotland who owned two copies and was willing to part with one. I think $1,700, American, plus fifteen percent commission for us, plus five percent finder's fee for The Green Thorn Brier's."

"Grimoire?" Nathalie asked. "We understood Albert fancied himself an alchemist, not a magician."

Sobraille smiled. "Ceremonial magic. Black magic. The most infamous grimoire ever written, in fact. Divided into three parts. The first two contain instructions for summoning a demon called Lucifuge Rofocale for the purpose of selling your soul to Satan in exchange for a variety of services. One method is safer but more difficult. The other is easier and quicker but guarantees the conjurer less control of the demon once summoned. The third section is a hodgepodge of spells, which, I think, is why this Albert was so specific about the 1863 edition. Some editions include different spells than others, or different versions of the same spells. He hardly seemed interested in books as objets d'art. But then that's stereotypical of these New Ager types. Hotdog tastes on caviar budgets."

"You think he was looking for a specific spell?"

Sobraille shrugged. "I spoke with him on the phone twice to confirm his offer and I met him in person once when he collected the book." Bharat had called in July with the request. Sobraille would see what he could find. By October there were a few interested sellers. He requested digital scans and called Albert to discuss options. Albert wanted the scans sent to

Bharat. A week later he called to greenlight the sale. Not the cheapest choice or the cleanest copy or the strongest provenance. A rather forgettable book for a collectible, Sobraille thought, a rather arbitrary winner.

The book arrived in November. Albert came by the same afternoon, spent maybe a quarter hour with the book, right where Nathalie sat now, asked no questions, made comparisons to a cheap Italian paperback, and read a few passages aloud. "His reading of the French was exquisite," Sobraille said. "His Italian nearly so. He's obviously lived a number of years abroad in Europe."

"Why would an alchemist be interested in black magic?"

"One spell, if I'm not mistaken, 'The Composition of Death', is a recipe for the philosopher's stone, though there's hardly need for anything so obvious. Understand," he said, "the early modern mage didn't think the way we do. They didn't make a distinction between magic and natural philosophy. Science, as we think of it, did not yet exist. Occult forces are simply those which cannot be directly experienced through the five senses. Unempirical forces. That's what occult means. Astrology and cabala are no more occult than atoms and gravity."

Nathalie had read a little about this. Before the alchemists, the world was the way it was because Aristotle said so, or Plato, or Galen. Hippocrates argued there were obviously four humors of the body because Empedocles had said there were four elements of the universe. As above, so below. Order and interrelation. The alchemists believed in magic but sought, through investigation, to learn how it worked and, like the magician, how to control it. This kernel of observation eventually matured with the scientific revolution.

"The alchemist saw no disagreement between religion, magic, and the natural world," Sobraille continued. "Each proved and informed the existence of the other two. It's known as sympathetic magic. The belief in correspondences between the stars, the earth, the human body, nature, the spirit world.

Everything. All interconnected and interdependent like the strands of an invisible web. These connections could be discovered and manipulated through prayer and experiment."

"They were all of the same fabric," Nathalie said.

Sobraille raised his eyebrows. "Exactly. Until recently, alchemy and magic were deeply troubling to historians of science and medicine. Modern scholars, since the Enlightenment, promoted a teleological view of scientific development, from Aristotle to Copernicus and Galileo, Sir Isaac Newton, Einstein, and Nils Bohr. But the alchemists won't fit into that neat narrative. They're recursive and transgressive, and so they are dismissed as superstitious fools. But it's only true if you can also say anyone who believes in the internal-combustion engine, without understanding the physics and chemistry of how it works, is also a superstitious fool."

Damian said, "Can you describe Albert?"

"Sixties or seventies, middle height, relatively fit for his age. Gray mustache. Wore a hat and coat."

"Do you know how we might reach him?"

"I'm sure I have contact information. Of course I can't give it to you."

"Of course," Nathalie said. "Maybe he mentioned something, though, in conversation, that might help us. We really want to talk to him."

"About your invitations?"

Nathalie nodded and set the two sheet protectors side by side on the oak table and slid them over to Sobraille. "Since we're here, I thought you might take another look." Nathalie told him what Anjelica Singh-Velasquez had told her about the woodcuts and what she'd read about the dearth of period wedding invitations printed with the movable-type press. "So I believe you. Now. They're fake. Can you tell why they might've been faked? Or why they were sent to us? Even a guess would help."

Sobraille held them up, one at a time, and studied them in the skylight. Even in the sheet protectors he was careful not to touch them anywhere but along the edges. He rolled them like vinyl records on his fingertips and studied the backside, one at a time, like that, the fronts and then the backs. "Works of art in their own right," he said. "I have no idea."

"There's an alchemical symbol I wanted to ask you about. The crow's head. Do you know what it means?"

Sobraille smiled patiently. "It's a technical term. It describes the beginning of an experiment. Alchemists would heat their material in a crucible over fire and treat it with acids to remove impurities. These processes would turn the material black, and this is what they called the crow's head."

Nathalie asked if he had a sample of Albert's handwriting. Sobraille didn't know but offered to look. Alone, Damian and Nathalie exchanged wary glances and said nothing. Sobraille returned, frowned, shook his head. A receipt signature, but illegible, a capital A with a lot of scribbling. No bank transfer or credit card receipt. He'd paid cash, stiff new hundred dollar bills, all deposited at the bank the same evening. Damian showed Sobraille the copies of Gödel and Agrippa, the rice-paper transcriptions and their accompanying marginalia.

"Seen anything like this before?"

No, Sobraille had not. It wasn't an astrological glyph. Not kanji. One looked like an infinity sign, the other like the Greek letter omega, the two hoops not quite closed. What the symbol made him think of—and this was reaching—was a sigil. It reminded Sobraille of the hieroglyphic monad of Dr. John Dee. Not the same, but that's what he thought of. More esoteric hocus-pocus.

"Please excuse my bad manners," Sobraille said. "But our interview must be wrapping up. The vulgar dollar and all. I have a lunch appointment." He shook hands again and continued. "It goes without saying. If, by some accident, I happened to leave something lying around. A rolodex for example. And it happened to contain information pertinent to your little quest. It would be highly unethical for you to use it."

Damian and Nathalie looked at each other and back at Sobraille and each other again. "Of course," Nathalie said slowly.

"It would be a misunderstanding to think I'd given it to you on purpose."

"No," Nathalie said. "We wouldn't think you were trying to help us."

"Good," Sobraille said. "Because it would be a mistake."

"That's what we would assume," Damian said.

"Either way, you'll let me know how it turns out. I must admit my interest has been piqued." And then he excused himself once again from the room. Lying on the oak table where he'd been sitting was a small square of lined paper. A rolodex card. Damian looked at it and passed it to Nathalie. No name. A San Francisco P.O. Box. And a telephone number.

35.

Tall iron gates guarded York House—named for the nineteenth century captain of industry who commissioned it—overrun with rhododendrons and honeysuckle. The gates, Nathalie said, were poured at the first steel foundry her father owned, bordering a favela in Salvador. The estate sloped down to the bay, a rocky beach on the island's southern shore with a concrete dock and a 1,400 foot sloop. The seven acres featured a grape arbor, tennis court, carriage house, outdoor swimming pool, indoor sauna and hot-tub, and a greenhouse of flora native to the Brazilian Amazon.

Damian and Nathalie arrived midmorning Christmas Eve. The nanny and housekeeper were promised full pay and sent home. By early afternoon Rosalie and Eugenie appeared. Their father remained at his offices in the city and wouldn't return until late—their mother, Damian knew, hidden within the daunting lair, suffered vague medical problems and social anxiety. Nathalie told him she might not emerge to meet him.

The house looked like a wedding cake. Layers of windows in painted sash boxes. Creamy white sconces and baroque friezes. The grand entrance trailed a cape of long wide steps down from a marble door-case. Wraparound verandah, central rotunda with skylight oculus, attached gazebo, corner turret mounted by a glass cupola, all adorned with Corinthian columns. Nathalie brought Damian a hot toddy with a heavy dollop of scotch and he sipped it on a porch-swing behind the house. The six sisters roamed the grounds arm in arm, chatting quietly, or playing hide-and-go-seek among hydrangea bushes. After a while the older girls joined him on the verandah while the younger gamboled grass-stained on the unending lawn.

They were odd girls. Laughing at jokes they all seemed to get without needing to tell. The way they finished each other's sentences. Damian watched them exchange whole conversations with body language and facial expressions, never speaking for fear language might confuse their meaning. Or they spoke all at the same time about unrelated things, the din thick as brambles and the voices impossible to distinguish, but they all seemed to understand each other, even if Damian didn't. They communicated through skin strokes and sighs and looks. At any moment at least two of them were holding hands, sometimes fastened in daisy chains three or four girls long. But Damian noticed quickly Nathalie was the high priestess of their games and the other girls her disciples. They circled round her, the two youngest at her knees, and waited to hear what they would play next.

Saucer eyes and long limbs, thick-hipped but lithe, all variations of Nathalie. He'd been afraid of getting their names and faces mixed up in his head but in fact they were very different. Rosalie was bold, effusive in her recommendations for how to suck every second out of the afternoon. Eugenie was quiet, self-possessed, regal. Carolina lewd and brash but also self-conscious and tentative, trapped halfway between the little girls and the young women. Eugenie and Bianca were blonde and fair, the others sable and crowned in ink splashing to their waists. Nathalie's wild curls were hers alone.

Near twilight the wind bit hard and chased them inside. Mahogany doors and marble tiles, teak wainscoting and hand-glazed walls inlaid with alabaster and mother-of-pearl, fifteen foot coffered ceilings, herringbone floors, a spiral staircase with bronze balustrade in the foyer, two-story bay windows, a mezzanine, a movie theater, a marble spa. They ate cold-cut sandwiches and reheated soup on the kitchen floor before watching *A Christmas Carol* on a small television in the great room. The girls, indifferent to so much opulence, lounged in bedclothes, perfectly comfortable except when spoken to by Damian. Then they paled, rigid, and stared at him with huge eyes and porcelain expressions, seeming to him like fairy creatures captured in a bottle, like what most disturbed them about him was his ability to see them at all.

Jevali had still not arrived when Nathalie declared bedtime shortly after midnight. Damian slept deep and oblivious, Nathalie under his arm, in a king-sized canopied bed. When he rose late morning Christmas day and stumbled downstairs Sebastião Jevali held court among his daughters. He was a dense man, formidable, handsome, with large hands. Cobalt hair, weathered to gray streaks, combed straight back at the temples, top parted neatly to the side. Martial brown eyes sharpened on the whetstone of Damian's nose. They exchanged smiles and shook hands and everyone sat down for breakfast. Damian had thought this man, worth six-hundred-million dollars on paper, would meet him like a king in a reception hall, but in person he was closer to a pharaoh. If Nathalie were priestess of this house her father was its living god.

The girls adored him—that much was obvious. He made no requests and gave no orders, but one daughter or another ensured his constant comfort. Chairs were drawn and coffee poured, breakfast served, an electronic tablet produced for checking stocks or email and then returned to nowhere when he grunted and pushed it away. They knew if he required diversion or conversation or silence to gather weighty pause. And if somehow they missed his desire, the first mention met them all rising in unison to make it right again. He didn't ignore Damian but neither did he pay special attention. Jevali fixed him now and then in a broad smile and went on flirting with the girls. It awed Damian to watch these pretty girls suddenly thrilling when their father's full attention lit them up.

Even Nathalie illuminated when beckoned, relishing the hassle of serving him, and not out of fear. There was an argument over the housekeeper whom Nathalie wanted to send home again, but Sebastião insisted she stay until dinner was done. Nathalie called him cruel to make the housekeeper work on Christmas, especially since it wasn't necessary—everything was prepared, the oven cooking, and whatever needed last-minute attention could be done by the girls. But he refused because he wanted the girls with him, not in the kitchen. There was a tense standoff until, grudgingly, a compromise was reached: the housekeeper would stay and be paid triple-time for the outrage.

Once the housekeeper was left to the breakfast things they gathered around the Edwardian hearth in the great room. Jevali doffed a red and white Santa cap. Angela and Bianca gathered from a far off closet packages papered and ribboned, too many for display beneath a spangled spruce that crawled up one wall of the room. Damian received gifts from each of Nathalie's sisters, which embarrassed him, since each of them got a single inexpensive gift from him and Nathalie together.

"Open it!" Bianca commanded, and so he split the peppermint striped paper and drew out the box.

"Thank you," he said. "A flashlight," and he held it up for everyone to admire.

"You'll need it underground," she said.

"You'll need this, too," Angela said and laid on his lap a small purple box. It hid a pocket multi-tool, the kind with screwdrivers and knives and pliers folded into a stainless steel handle. "After the persimmons."

"It's just a mirror," Carolina said and gave him the plain white box dotted with stick-on bows. "For when you forget who you really are."

A small hinged box of black crushed velvet. The sterling silver ring within barely fit his pinkie. "I don't know why you'll need it," Eugenie said. "But you'll hear sirens."

Rosalie placed on his palm a soft-shelled box wrapped in gold with white snowflakes. A pack of cigarettes. "To pay the ferryman," she said.

After paper and boxes were cleared away each girl produced one final gift and stacked it solemnly beneath the tree.

"For Mama," Angela told him. "Every Christmas you leave presents beneath the tree and while you're asleep she comes and gets them."

"You and Bianca can play outside if you like," her father said. "Take Nathalie with you." He dropped a wide hand on Damian's shoulder and guided him toward the spiral staircase. Nathalie levied a warning glance. Be nice, the look said, and Damian hoped Jevali was paying attention.

On the fourth floor balcony the two men reclined in beach chairs, drinking cognac from stemless sifters and puffing whole leaf Dominican cigars. Jevali taught Damian how to get the full flavor out of cognac—you needed to swirl it in a wide-mouthed glass to let it breathe—how to cut the cigar at an angle and light it so the leaf burns evenly and doesn't taste like butane. "It seems we have a mutual interest," Jevali said once they were friends. "We both want my daughter to get the most from life. Except I know what's best for her and you don't."

Damian filled his mouth with smoke and nodded. The balcony was more like a suspended patio than a deck, the vantage casting a panorama of Angel Island, the bay, the city skyline.

"She's decided to pursue a dance career at the expense of her education. She could make a difference. Improve the world."

Damian looked at the opaque glass bay and the urban sprawl beyond, but he was listening.

"She would rather frolic mindlessly about a stage for her supper, half-naked and leered at, little better than a stripper."

"She's got a dream."

"I wonder what kind of dream makes her worse off—not better—for dreaming it? She's always fallen for—what? Fancy eccentricities? Her heart's big and deep. But she's always come back to what she knows is right. Someone's put this idiocy in her head."

"I only said she should do what she wanted to do," Damian said. "I never said she should be a dancer or make a million dollars. It's none of my business."

Jevali laughed amiably. "I know and you know. But apparently she listens to you. She's being foolish and you'll have to help her see it."

"I won't help her see anything." Marble clouds drove southwest dragging beneath them a cutting breeze which eroded the surface of the bay to unfinished stone. Damian sucked cognac over his teeth, the way Jevali taught him. His palette pressed down on liquor until his tongue stung. A dead minute passed.

"This is a warning, young man." Jevali's tone was still friendly. "I'm pointing it out because I wouldn't want you to miss it. You don't want me for an enemy—I'm much better as an ally. The kind that makes impossible things possible. I take care of my friends. It's a point of personal honor. You might need a favor someday. Any kind of favor. And I'll be enthusiastic for the chance to help you. To repay the favor you're about to do for me."

"I don't ask for favors," Damian said. "Point of personal honor."

"In that case you're forbidden from seeing my daughter. You're a nuisance and I want you to go away."

Jevali didn't sound like they were friends anymore. Finally Damian looked at him and blushed. He fought a smile tugging at his face. "You're something else," he said, and looked at the gritty water again. It was either look away or laugh in Jevali's face.

"I don't know what you do with Nathalie and I don't care. Frankly, the possibilities make me nauseous. But it's a big city with plenty of women for you to carry on with."

"I'm not carrying on with your daughter."

"Then it won't be difficult for you to knock it off."

"Sir," Damian said and bit his lip to keep from laughing.

"Really. If Nathalie says she doesn't want to see me anymore, I'll respect her wishes."

"That shouldn't take long. It's not hard to tell she's a lot smarter than you. She'll figure it out."

Damian emphatically agreed. He'd never considered whether or not Nathalie was smarter and he didn't care much for it now—either she was smarter than him or he was with someone who wasn't as smart. Either truth denigrated them both. It was a useless line of inquiry to a man who thought intelligence was a lot like love: words that held different meanings to different people. He knew she was a lot braver than he was, more thoughtful, creative, resilient, and tenacious than he had strength to be. These things seemed more important than being smart. So he admitted Sebastião Jevali was definitely right. Nathalie would tire of him sooner or later. The thought frightened him. He didn't want Jevali to see him tremble. So he bit his lip to keep from laughing.

36.

And there were other lines of inquiry. After leaving Belvedere Island it was time to follow up on the phone number Sobraille had given them. For a week Damian called twice a day with no response, no voicemail, the baritone skip of the dial tone extending as far as he would listen to it. The exchange was for a San Francisco landline and he called information for a reverse address request but the number was unlisted. His urgency fizzled in the face of yet another disappointing lead but he continued calling every three or four days throughout January.

The dead ends took a toll on Nathalie. Damian feared she would soon despair of the dreams, the invitations, anything to do with him. They leased a one-bedroom on the outskirts of an industrial complex in Oakland, a nicer apartment than the studio in a tougher neighborhood than Bayview. Gray cinderblock and black soot, chain-link fences, garbage piled on the sidewalks, barred windows and shuttered doors, lulled to sleep each night by ambulance song. Nathalie brought the armoire he'd bought when she first moved into the Bayview studio. Her personal space, he told her. The coat closet was for his private things and he put a padlock on the door. She must never open it and he would never open the armoire because it was her personal space.

Nathalie used her experience as a bar-back to get a second part-time job as a waitress at a chain restaurant closer to home. He hardly saw her anymore—if she wasn't at work she was dancing—and her dreams, she said, were of stabbings, lightless places, running away, hiding from things she couldn't see but could feel closing from every direction.

Damian's sleep was just as troubled. He woke one winter night fully conscious, panicking, sweat-logged and certain, absolutely convinced: he must get up this instant and leave California and never return or regret it forever. But he didn't. Looking at Nathalie asleep beside him made Damian ashamed of the feeling. What he needed wasn't to flee but to see this thing with her through, however it ended. And he harbored no fantasies it could end well.

He'd promised himself not to lie to her, and he'd kept that promise. He avoided questions or refused to answer, but he never deceived her. So why did he feel like a liar? Maybe keeping secrets was inherently dishonest and he'd just been fooling himself that it could be otherwise. He'd thought of telling her about Phaedra and the great white buffalo, Pavel and counterfeiting, but he didn't dare. To protect himself, but also to protect Nathalie. Until he understood what kind of mess he'd gotten into, he couldn't risk endangering her. But he hadn't foreseen the harm this would do to their relationship. If nothing else, it was a learning experience. Nathalie taught Damian it was more important to love each other than protect each other. He couldn't fall in love without surrendering all of himself, and he couldn't stay in love with someone who didn't share their whole self with him. He'd made a bitter mistake, but it was too late to do anything about it—Nathalie was keeping secrets, too.

Damian hadn't met Frater Theophrastus, didn't know where he lived or how Nathalie met him—only that he was a spagyric alchemist acquainted with Albert. Nathalie thought he'd already been as much help as he was going to be. A couple times Damian suggested paying a visit, but Nathalie laughed it off. Theophrastus was an idiot, wasn't very reliable, didn't know anything. She couldn't reach him or he wasn't home. After asking her to get the photograph and learning it had been returned to Albert, Damian didn't think about Frater Theophrastus again. Not until Nathalie started staying out late, hiding telephone conversations, leaving without letting him know where she was going or when she would be back. "Who are you talking to?" Damian asked. "Where've you been?"

"Nowhere," she said. "It's not important."

Fair play, he guessed. She was her own woman. He valued her autonomy as much as his own. It was important to be independent, he kept telling himself. Healthy, even. There were plenty of things he kept from her and he wasn't misogynist enough to think that should only apply one way. He wanted to trust her but she was too jittery. Wouldn't look him in the eye. Avoided him in passing. When he cornered her about it, she admitted to meeting with Frater Theophrastus. He was teaching her spagyria, designing an elixir for her, and she didn't want to tell Damian about it because she already felt foolish and she didn't think he would approve and too much negativity could ruin the work. "Besides, there's nothing wrong with having parts of my life that don't involve you."

"If you're not doing anything bad, why are you hiding it from me?"

Nathalie laughed and waved her hand in his face. "You of all people don't get to be upset with me hiding things. You forfeited that right long ago."

Damian ran his hands through his hair. He felt his whole life crumbling like ashes between his fingers and he wouldn't be able to hold onto anything. First his dad, then his mom, step-dad, and finally Nathalie, and Damian would be left with nothing. Worse than nothing. Handfuls of counterfeit— fake nothing. "Are you attracted to him?"

"Frater Theophrastus?" Nathalie asked and crinkled her face. "Gross, no. You wouldn't wonder if you knew him. If I wanted to sleep with someone else, I wouldn't cheat. I'd just break up with you and get on with it."

Damian believed her. The way she scowled at the question, without reacting in her head first, infidelity was a thousand miles from anything she'd thought about. She was an intelligent girl—if she wanted to deceive him, he wouldn't find out about it. But really, it didn't matter. If she was going to betray him, there was nothing he could do to stop it. His choices were to trust her, put up with it, or leave, and he chose to trust her.

Or at least he tried. What did she want a spagyric elixir for? What did she think it would do? What happened at her consultations with Frater Theophrastus? What did they talk about? How long did the meetings last? Were they alone? But Nathalie wouldn't answer questions. Damian had never been jealous before and he hated it. The way pictures fouled his brain, dark whimsy, sleazy imaginings. How jealousy made him hate her, made him hate himself. All his fault, these weeds sprouting between them. He'd been investigating without her and now wondered if she was doing the same thing. What if Nathalie knew who Phaedra was but wouldn't tell him? What if she knew the significance of the crow's head, the white buffalo, things Albert had said, the books and the invitations? What if Nathalie understood everything and was hiding it from him?

Damian lay awake and thought about the dream of the dark-haired woman and Nathalie's dream, she believed, of him, and the strange wedding invitations, Kim Hyeon-gi, Noe Gun, Gangjeon Jae-kyeon, Pavel the Czech, lapis exillis, Johann Mylius, Cornelius Agrippa, Kurt Gödel, Albert, Phaedra, Buffalo Calf Woman and her avatar Brother Sun Sister Moon. He thought of his mother and his father and Sebastião Jevali and his six daughters. What was missing? How did they all fit together, or was it all meaningless? He would be taught by the flames, Albert had said, but what fire was he talking about? How would he and Nathalie ever put the pieces together if they didn't talk to each other? And then an idea let him go to sleep.

"Tell me about your mom," he said to Nathalie the next morning over breakfast. Whole wheat toast with butter, grapes, and coffee. When they moved into this place Damian bought her a cheap dining set as a late Christmas present. A small table and matching chairs, which they kept in the living-room, the only civilized furniture they owned.

"What do you want to know?" Nathalie said. "She's not an interesting person."

"I think she's interesting."

Nathalie, freshly showered, ate nude beneath a bath-towel fastened under her arms. Her hair corseted into a tight French braid to wring water from her curls. She sipped coffee and looked at him.

"I've told you a lot about my parents. I know all about your dad and each of your sisters. I don't know anything about your mom."

"Sorry," Nathalie said around a mouthful of toast. "It's private—like your job."

"I already told you about my job."

Nathalie rolled her eyes. "You said you make money. That's not an answer."

"Let's make a pact," Damian said. "I'll tell you everything you want to know, right now, if you tell me about your mom."

"No."

Damian tossed his hands, disgusted, and retreated into the kitchenette where Nathalie cornered him, one accusatory finger thrust out, a heavy cluster of black grapes cradled in the other hand. She'd abandoned the towel but her nudity made her look dangerous, not vulnerable. "That's one thing—you won't tell me why your dad went to prison, what you do for a living, why people keep beating you up. And I won't tell you about my mom because there's a lot of pain on the other side. It hurts too much to dredge up just because you're curious. You keep secrets because you're scared and selfish."

"So how can we figure out what we have in common?"

Nathalie shrugged. "We share a birthday. It's like you said: serendipity. A fortunate coincidence. There doesn't need to be anything else."

"I don't believe that anymore."

"Fine," Nathalie said, batting her eyes. The signal of her annoyance coming to boil. She rattled off the trivia of her mother's life. For each item on the list she plucked a grape from the vine and threw it at him like a bloody stone. The grapes didn't hurt so he didn't try to block them. "Her name is Efigenia. She's from Salvador, Bahia. She has seven children. Her hands don't work. She can't speak. She never leaves the house. Sometimes she disappears for months at a time."

"Did something happen to her?"

"Fuck you," Nathalie said and threw another grape.

"Seven?"

Nathalie threw another grape and cocked her arm for the next.

"You said your mom has seven kids?"

Nathalie bounced the grape off Damian's shirt and put her hands down. "Bianca, Angela, Carolina, Eugenie, and Rosalie. Me. And Isador."

"Who's Isador?"

"My twin brother. He died right after we were born. Heart defect."

"Look at that," Damian said, more to himself than her. "Something else we have in common."

But what could it possibly mean? For weeks Nathalie sweltered under the bright light of her own gaze. The facts: she and Damian were born three years apart on the same day. For years they each dreamed recurring figures, if not each other, then resembling the other to an uncanny degree. Nathalie's twin brother died shortly after birth—Damian had a stillborn twin sister. Both of their mothers were victims of physical violence, though only Nathalie knew this. She had to work under the assumption there might be other commonalities Damian knew of but wouldn't share.

Harassed by bad dreams, burnt at the stake for a witch, Nathalie woke to mild fever, pressure in her chest, esophagus pinched, burning, and rolled over to an empty bed beside her. The digital clock said 3:04 A.M. Damian worked late sometimes, out all night doing god knew what. She might not have heard noises in the living-room if she didn't get up to retrieve antacid tablets from the medicine cabinet, might never have walked in on Damian rummaging in the closet. She didn't get a good look at what was in there—when he noticed her, Damian shoved everything back in and snapped shut the padlock. Hard to ignore how guilty he looked, sneaking around in the middle of the night, caught at his sins and scrambling to hide them from her. They stared at each other while her unasked questions hung between them.

"Sorry if I woke you up. I was trying to be quiet."

"Are you coming to bed?" Nathalie's gaze drifted to the padlock on the door.

"Soon," he said, and stood there. Waiting for her to leave the room. Aware of how guilty he looked but willing to help Nathalie ignore it. What's in the closet? Of course she would never open it, never considered it, not even in fancy. She'd promised not to, and knowing wasn't worth breaking her promise. It would only prove Damian right to not trust her. Nathalie didn't actually care what was in the closet—she wanted Damian to trust her enough to tell her.

Nathalie was surprised at herself for not telling Damian about her mom, but what she told him was the truth. It was too painful to talk about without a good reason and it just wasn't important enough to her that Damian know. Not anymore.

She was tired of waiting for him to share his life with her. She didn't care whether or not he ever told her about how he made money, whatever sordid business he was mixed up in. Not enough to tell him about her mom. She wasn't interested in telling him about the cup in the middle of her or the seeker's elixir or her consultations with Frater Theophrastus or her epiphany in the butterfly grove. The six month co-lease on the apartment was the most commitment Damian would ever be capable of, which was just as well. She didn't feel capable of more, either. She was sick of wanting him to let her in and she was sick of her own introspection.

She kept going through the motions because she wasn't ready to give up yet and she didn't know what else to do. She worked and she danced. She recorded her dreams in a journal: Nathalie opening an infinite procession of gift boxes, like nested Russian dolls, tinsel wrapping-paper and red ribbon bows, each containing an identical, slightly smaller box. Unfazed, she would set the outer one aside and open the inner one to reveal yet another box, and another, and another, forever. Nathalie dressed as Albert, the old man following Damian, in a black overcoat and black hat. Nathalie without a face, flat unfeatured flesh where there should've been a mouth, a nose, two eye-sockets. She woke with her mind on fire. Headache destroyed thoughts like burning flesh.

Frater Theophrastus called. Her elixir had ripened and she could collect it at her leisure. Soapy beads glided like translucent seeds in the oily black water. Six months' supply in a small glass jar fit neatly in her palm and cost a month's wages. Steep, but Frater Theophrastus vowed she would think it worth much more. A masterpiece of designer spagyria, he promised, the best custom job of his career. Truly inspired. Maybe, but looking at it, she permitted doubts.

According to Frater Theophrastus' typed directions, she must ingest one tablespoon three times a day—at dawn, noon, and dusk—on each day before, during, and after the full moon and the new moon of each month. If at any point the beginning of her menstrual cycle should coincide with the full moon, she should continue as directed but notify her personal spagyric practitioner immediately. "Don't expect any clear results for a few months," he said. "It usually takes time for the medicine to penetrate all your chakras."

Nathalie kept crossing bars off her city map and she kept glowering as Damian shrugged from park bench to park bench, insisting he'd dreamt none of them. She took turns with him asking after Albert at the Green Thorn Brier's, and she took turns with him calling the phone number they got from Sobraille, until one day in February a woman answered.

"This is Donna."

Nathalie was so surprised she nearly forgot what she'd planned on saying. "Hi, I'm looking for Albert. He gave me this number in case I needed to reach him."

There was a long pause before the voice came back small and helpless. "Who is this?"

"I work for Celcius Antique Books," Nathalie lied. "Albert's a client."

"You're helping find his books?" Still suspicious but less frightened.

"It's important I talk to him soon," Nathalie said, sounding urgent, she hoped, but Donna didn't know where Albert was, didn't know how to contact him. Albert used Donna's phone sometimes but he didn't live with her and there was no way to anticipate when he might show up. "Would it be possible to ask you some questions?"

"I don't know," Donna said, anxiety full blast in the pitch of her voice, the way she swallowed the words to hide the shakes underneath. "Not over the phone."

"Could I come see you, then? I promise not to take too

much of your time and it might help Albert a lot."

"I don't know," she kept saying, and Nathalie didn't believe Donna would go for it even after she agreed, even when Nathalie was writing down her address, she thought at the last minute Donna would change her mind and hang up.

Caws echo in the dawn light.

37.

Donna lived near Lake Merced a block inland from the Great Highway on a narrow avenue of grim row houses tucked between a golf course and the zoo. The ocean air, almost cold at the early hour, seeped over Nathalie's shoulders and played tricks on her eyes. Fog flattened the street and mangled perspective, buried morning colors in smoke, grayscale, dim, shallow, blurry. The street number came third in a long train of attached split-level homes. Clapboards the texture of gnawed rawhide, warped shingles, scabbed paint, one car garages. Bars on the windows. Dying weeds staggered in the cracks of cement lawns.

Nathalie regretted bringing Damian. Donna's face panicked the instant she saw him, but he introduced himself as Ferdinand Sobraille, and she recovered enough to shake hands without falling apart. She was in her forties, neat looking, the easy bearing of a woman with simple tastes and plenty of money. Sandy hair and thin lips. Pretty without makeup to hide the crow's feet and laugh lines. Her clothes were casual but expensive, well-worn jeans and a spaghetti-strap tank-top. She was scared, Nathalie thought, and she wasn't used to being scared.

"Pardon the mess," she said after inviting them in. "I just got home from a month in Malta and haven't had a chance to tidy up." The front-room dark and cramped. Stray clothes and blankets and pillows strewn willy-nilly over furniture, which covered every inch of wall: sectional couches and end tables and bookshelves and recliners. A restaurant booth filled the breakfast nook, covered in papers, envelopes, dirty dishes, paperback novels. "It doesn't look like much," Donna said, "but it's paid for."

She offered tea and told Nathalie and Damian to make themselves comfortable while she put on the kettle. "I don't have anything to serve with it. You wouldn't happen to have bread?"

"Sorry," Nathalie said. "We didn't think to bring anything."

When Donna joined them she said, "I don't know how much I can help. I don't know where Albert is."

"When was the last time you saw him?" Damian asked.

Donna shrugged. "October. Maybe November." She didn't know where Albert lived or how he made a living—he traveled a great deal, she knew that, and periodically showed up unannounced asking for a favor or a place to stay. One or two nights and then he was gone. He was what you might call an amateur scholar, which was how they met, through a shared interest in esotericism. Alternative spirituality. She'd known him a long time but she didn't know him well—he didn't strike her as a person who really had friends.

"But you're helping him collect books?" Nathalie asked.

"I don't do much." Donna aimed a generous smile at Damian. Nathalie could see she was used to having her smile appreciated. "I make my phone available." The kettle whistled. She excused herself and returned with the porcelain tea-service on a collapsible tray.

"Do you know what Albert does with the rare editions?" Damian asked.

Hesitation. The same fear Nathalie had heard over the phone and seen on the front porch. The woman didn't know how to answer, or whether it was safe to answer. Donna smiled again. "Research." She didn't know what he was researching or why he needed one book or another. As far as she knew, nothing was published—she'd never seen anything he'd written, if indeed he wrote anything.

Damian said, "Do you know anyone who might be able to help us find him?" and Nathalie knew instantly it was a mistake. She could hear the false step like a note in the following silence. For all the clutter, Nathalie found Donna's house cozy at first, but that was gone. It was too dark and hot, the curtains half pulled and fog blotting the windows. She could hear the tick and hum of baseboard heaters down the hall and the swelter added to the claustrophobic feeling of the room.

Donna looked nervously at Damian and Damian looked at Nathalie and Nathalie looked at Donna. Then the circle of eyes switched the other way. "You aren't booksellers," Donna said. "Are you?"

"No," Nathalie admitted. "Strange things are happening to us. We think they might be connected to Albert's research."

"He's been spying on me for several months and I need to know if he's dangerous or if he can help us," Damian said.

Donna nodded and Nathalie realized she'd been wrong about her. She'd thought Donna was afraid, and she was, but not of Nathalie and Damian—she was scared of disappointing them, failing to open them up. Now she'd unlocked them and all worry disappeared from her face. "I thought you would come. Sooner or later." She sipped her tea. "Albert said I should help you."

He always said things like that, weird stuff that made no sense at the time but one day, inevitably, terrorists would blow up a building, astrophysicists would make a discovery, earthquakes would cause tsunamis on the other side of the planet, and Donna would recall the offhanded allusion made long ago by an old man in a black coat. "Ten years ago, eleven years ago. He was only here for the afternoon. A few hours. He talked about my divorce and I hadn't even met my ex-husband yet, but what he said let me keep the house." There was an apology in her smile and she refreshed her tea from the still-steaming pot. "He said he was going away for a while, I wouldn't see him again for a long time. He said there might be interest in him. Two strangers trying to find him, and if they came, he asked me to answer their questions."

Nathalie handed over her invitation in its acid-free sleeve.

"Do you know what this is?"

"I've never seen it before. It didn't come from Albert."

Nathalie didn't believe her. The anxiety crept back into Donna's voice and she wouldn't look at either of them. Maybe she wasn't lying—not so simple—but the invitation made her think of something she didn't want to talk about.

"Have you seen this before?" Damian asked and showed Donna the rice-paper note from *De occulta philosophia libri tres.*

Donna's face paled. "Where did you get this?"

Damian explained how he'd found three in total, in books on alchemy, magic, mathematics. Donna hadn't expected this, Nathalie could tell. For the first time she was caught by surprise. It was Albert's handwriting, Donna was sure of it. When they'd first arrived, Damian lied about being Ferdinand Sobraille, collecting books on Albert's behalf. It looked like Damian was helping find Albert's books after all. He just didn't know about it. Neither did Donna.

"This doesn't make sense." Donna frowned. She didn't know how many books Albert owned—hundreds, maybe thousands—and she didn't know what happened to them, only that he lost them a long time ago, long before Donna met him, and he'd been hunting for them ever since. She'd helped track down several herself. Four times he'd brought her a book with instructions for delivering it. To whom and how and where. None were meant for Damian. "I should've known about it."

"What is it?" Nathalie wondered.

"A magickal talisman. Eyes and ears. He's grooming you. Preparing you. What for, I couldn't guess."

"If you had to try?" Damian asked, but Donna really didn't know. Albert had her send them to people he wanted to keep track of, but as far as she knew, Damian was never one of those people. Obviously Albert got up to things without her knowing about it. Likewise, the two-headed stick-figure located in the margin, which Donna had never seen before. She disagreed with Ferdinand Sobraille—it wasn't a variation on the monas hieroglyphica. It looked too much like a rudimentary

Rebis. The head reminded her of a lowercase Greek letter phi, whereas Sobraille had compared it to omega. It could be a sigil, she guessed. A symbol with magical power.

"A spell."

"That's one way of looking at it."

Nathalie waited for Donna to elaborate, but she didn't. There was a long pause and it seemed like the conversation could go in any of a thousand directions. A sense of limitless potential came over Nathalie. Anything could happen. More was possible than could be thought, and yet, she knew, time wouldn't halt on her anticipation. Something would happen, the exquisite moment would pass, and eternity would collapse into whatever form it took, and it would be like that was always the only thing that could've happened.

"I was contacted by a woman calling herself Phaedra," Damian said. It was destined from the beginning of time. Anything could've happened, but this was the only thing that was ever going to happen. "She told me Albert was dangerous and mentioned something about a crow's head. Do you know what she meant?"

Nathalie's heart sank. Donna wasn't the only one who admitted to less than what she knew. Who was Phaedra? What did she say about the crow's head and what else did she tell him? Damian hadn't shared any of this with Nathalie. He'd mentioned the crow's head to Sobraille, which Nathalie hadn't thought much of at the time, but now she saw he was keeping more secrets from her and she didn't understand why. Like a total moron she'd assumed they were partners, working together, but that wasn't true. Damian was investigating the invitations without her. Nathalie caught his eye. She was crushed and wanted him to see it, and he saw, but he shrugged it off like no big deal. Like nothing devastating just occurred.

"I've never heard of anyone called Phaedra," Donna said. She'd seen the slash pass between Nathalie and Damian—maybe she even knew what it meant, but if so she chose to ignore it. "Like I said, I don't know much about what Albert gets up to. He's probably involved with many people."

She was lying, Nathalie could tell. Again and again a recognition registered on Donna's face before she could hide it behind a mask of ignorance. Nathalie thought about pushing the issue but decided against it. She might need to talk to Donna in the future and she was wary of burning bridges over a hunch.

"The crow's head—I know a little about that. It means a transformation is coming." Donna refreshed her tea and blew gently on the steam. "The way the magic of alchemy works, in order to transform material reality, you must transform yourself. The change will be long and difficult. You will suffer. You will be forced to surrender. Your identity, your sense of self—everything you ever loved and everything you think you are will be taken from you, until you're reduced to your most fundamental essence. The crow's head is the first step toward achieving the philosopher's stone. At least, that's how Albert explained it to me."

38.

She'd been an undergrad at Berkeley when she met him more than twenty years ago, through Blitz, her boyfriend at the time. There'd been a thriving heavy metal underground in San Francisco, much more than now, and Blitz played guitar in a band. An aesthetic built on leather, spikes, Satanism, and Cthulhu. Most of it was gimmicky but the bands belonged to a larger subculture of anarchists, magicians, neo-pagans. For the most part a blue collar scene but they had a presence on the campuses. The student groups were more scholarly, more ideological. Donna and Blitz belonged to one of these groups. "A handful of burgeoning practitioners," she said. "More of a club than anything serious. It didn't have a name."

"A magician's club?" Nathalie wondered.

"Magicians," Donna said and flicked her fingers to expand the idea. "Religious reconstructionists, demonologists, witches, energetic healers."

"Alchemists?" Damian asked.

"Not until Albert."

She remembered seeing Albert at a few meetings, a lecture, and then more frequently. Sabbat celebrations and magickal workings. Functions leaned to the informal and it was common for diplomats to wander among the different groups. Only a few people knew Albert and he never came with anyone in particular. Always on the periphery, always silent. Friendly, the few times Donna managed to engage him in conversation, quiet but genuine, and exceptionally intelligent. Brilliant, even.

"Magickal workings?"

"Spells. In ceremonial high magick."

"And do you still perform workings with Albert?"

"Oh, no," Donna said and sipped her tea again. She held the cup in both hands, hard, like it could protect her. "These days I'm pretty much an armchair magician. I read a lot. Banter on the internet. I still believe things most people would call crazy. But the real thing—I didn't have what it takes."

"What does it take?" Nathalie asked.

"Everything." Donna shrugged. "Nothing. Something… exotic… happened."

Schisms in the group. People disagreed about magic's role in world affairs. They were all anti-establishment to some degree, Donna supposed, but beyond that the only thing holding them together was shared belief in a spiritual realm. Everything's political: that was the catch phrase of the times, and people started politicizing their magical practices. Most wanted a stronger political emphasis. Rallies, protests, party endorsements. Some were radicalized and wanted a revolutionary movement—fascists and feminists and everything in between—they couldn't even get along with each other. "We never had the structure of a proper organization. More like a casual network of worldviews. And then everything fell apart. Not all at once—nothing specific happened—but slowly, over time, it disintegrated."

"Why?"

Donna looked surprised, as though the answer ought to be self-evident. "Because it was based on a lie. If the personal is political, there's no such thing as the personal. It was a brilliant infiltration. Convincing people to turn their hearts and homes into the battlegrounds of a proxy war." She smiled bitterly. "I never believed in black magic until I saw how that idea poisoned everyone I knew."

Factions splintered off. People started hiding their true intentions. Secret societies and rumors of secret societies within secret societies. A kind of intellectual cold war set in. The borders closed between groups. Donna was left in the vast minority of those without allegiance. "The wackos got ridiculous. In the old days secret societies were necessary because occultists needed a way to protect themselves from getting burned at the stake by the bigoted mainstream culture. There are benefits to living in a world that doesn't believe in magic. It made it possible to practice in the open light of day. Except now we needed secrecy to protect ourselves from each other."

"How did Albert fit into this?" Nathalie asked.

"He caused it."

"I thought you said nothing specific happened. It just kind of collapsed," Damian said.

"Magic isn't like what you see in the movies. No one shoots lightning out of their eyes, no one heals the dying instantly with a touch. It's more subjective. It happens in the imagination." She paused for a moment to look them over, reading their reactions. "Magicians don't defy nature, they manipulate it. There are causes and effects, the same as with chemistry or physics. What makes magic different than science is with magic there's no evidence of the causes. They happen out there," and she pointed at the half-shuttered window. "In the other world. We see the effects in this world but they happen according to natural processes."

"How do you explain that?" Nathalie said.

Donna made an exaggerated gesture with her arms and shoulders. "I don't." She laughed but the subtle tremor of her voice betrayed the distress beneath her smile. "I can't explain it—that's the thing with magic. It assumes the existence of something fundamental to reality which is not only unknown, but unknow*able*. That's what's hard to accept—impossible for many. A talented magician can influence nature, but no one can control it. Not completely." Donna grabbed Nathalie by the hand and squeezed. Donna's hands were hot and dry, cracked with eczema. Nathalie could see in the poor light the shallow fissures like red string on her knuckles. "Anything can happen," Donna said. "You can intend a certain outcome, you can get pretty good at creating it, but you can't assume anything will work. So much is beyond your possible understanding. At least that's what I thought."

Until Albert changed her mind. That winter, in November, with the occult community in paranoid ruin, Donna was invited to a secret gathering, hush-hush, meant only for a small inner-circle of elite adepts. It didn't officially exist—no guest list, no formal announcements—if you managed to find out about it, you could come. She found out about it from Blitz, who found out about it from Albert. Blitz said it was meant to celebrate the wedding anniversary of old world aristocrats, grand masters of some ancient magical order or other, friends and patrons of Albert, who hoped Blitz and Donna would come.

She remembered the Mexican villa in the hills above Puerto Vallarta. The antebellum plantation house, a four-story square box with curved staircases, rows of balconied windows, and a screened porch, situated on a broad terrace, clear-cut and leveled into the lower elevation slopes of the Sierra Madre Occidentals. Isolated by subtropical cloud forest. Prehistoric thickets of giant ferns and bromeliads, spectral in the gauzy mists. Thick and hot and gray at high noon, like living inside a lung, and the black nights clung like phlegm to her skin, utterly lightless, pierced by stinging insects and the groans of humping frogs.

These were Donna's most vivid images of her trip to Mexico: suppurating darkness, wet heat, Paleocene old growth, the anachronistic slaver's manse in the clearing, waxy light and sticky fog. What followed unspooled in an addled smear. Sixty, a hundred people, mediums, mesmerists, mystics, ufologists, thelemites. Rosicrucians and Illuminati. Necromancers, hydromancers, geomancers, technomancers. The Bohemian Grove crowd and the Bilderberg Group. Rothschild's, Rockefeller's, Fugger's—even, she was told, the Comte de Sainte-Germain. Attended to by a full staff of liveried servants. The opulent house furnished in black hardwoods, luscious fabrics, pornographic tapestries, Grecian urns, flossy Rococo paintings in gilded frames, Egyptian statuary of hand-worked gold and lapis lazuli.

Four days and four nights guests glutted their senses in a pleasure palace of mysterious and carnal delights. Rich foods and rare wines. Ayahuasca, mescaline, opium, psilocybin. Poetry and music and dance. Even a laser light show. Ritual orgies, metaphysical debates, séances, oracles, blood magick and sex magick. Like a dour Gatsby, Albert presided over the festivities without indulging, observing from his station atop the staircase, one imperious hand gripping the balustrade, or shadow clad from an overstuffed wing-backed chair in the corner of the room. He gave instructions to the staff, managed the household, and did his best to accommodate the most decadent whims of the debauched.

Only once did the hosts appear, on the evening of the third day, so bent in half and palsied in their antique wedding clothes Donna thought they must've been married at least a century. The party convened in a basement chapel and a Mesoamerican priest, short, with small bones and delicate features, frocked and collared, presided over the Roman Catholic mass, delivered in Latin, and performed the nuptial rites. The bridegroom kissed the bride, led her out of the chapel to the marriage bed, and once more the congregation descended into ecstatic revelry.

"It happened on the fourth day," Donna said. Exhausted and dissolute, swampy minded and plowed raw in a place that winces at plowing, she retired to a quiet sitting room to catch her breath when Blitz came looking for her. He escorted her to the highest floor of the house. After passing through several chambers they came to a luxurious salon where Albert waited. One wall displayed remarkable artifacts. Terracotta mandalas and Bronze Age war regalia, Neolithic Venuses and scrimshawed whalebones. Museum quality pieces. Albert invited her to find an object that pleased her. She chose a silver bowl engraved with reformed Egyptian hieroglyphs upon a limestone plinth. It was filled to the brim with a thin black liquid in which she could see—ghastly, distorted—her own decomposing reflection. Eyes deeply recessed in empty black cavities. On the surface of the tranquil liquid she looked like a corpse. Bloodless and gaunt. Used.

She shuttered and came back to herself, unnerved by the hypnotic vision. It felt like she contemplated the pale face for a great length of time, but she couldn't remember. Albert stood beside her and the contents of the bowl became agitated. Liquid sloshed from one lip to the other. Turbulent waves assumed startling form. A human figure, female, with long red tresses, freckles, green eyes. The wraith looked directly at Donna and drew an index finger to her pursed lips, conspiratorial, urging silence. The image dissolved as the black water calmed, impenetrable once again, placid, revealing nothing but a reflection of Donna's wonder. It numbed her straight through. Everything she experienced thus far at the house was reduced to trivia and make-believe. After a few blundered attempts to describe her fascination, Blitz led her away from the salon.

"It was a test," Donna said to Nathalie. "I must've failed because nothing like that ever happened to me again. The doors to initiation were shut forever."

39.

Pavel wanted Damian to deliver the first of the two special shipments, the one due in April, to his colleagues in San Jose. Pavel had been summoned by his superiors to Budapest—he'd be out of the country and couldn't make the pick up. The cash was scheduled to board a flight the same night and couldn't be rescheduled. It was beyond his control. Damian said no way in hell, he would deal with Pavel and absolutely no one else, but Pavel begged him to reconsider.

"Look," Damian said. "We have an agreement. You're breaking your word."

"I know," Pavel admitted and blew frustration into the earpiece of Damian's phone. "It can't be helped."

"Sorry."

"I know these guys," Pavel said. "I've worked with them for years. And they already know you too. They've been following you for the last ten months. Nothing will go wrong."

"I don't care," Damian said. "This breaks our arrangement."

"And you'll be compensated for the trouble. Fifty cents on the dollar. For each shipment. And everything after this. If you drop product for me this way. One time."

So Damian would drop the first shipment to his shadow detail and improve profits thirty percent. It was a long time coming and he was left with hollow relief. He'd been working towards this for three years, but victory felt cheap. It figured his career would take off at the same time his relationship bled to death. Business was good and so busy he hardly had time for Nathalie. He was almost always at the warehouse and she didn't seem to mind, which worried him. She still didn't know what he did in the warehouse. Distance widened between them and he felt less likely to tell her now than ever before. It was a bad time. He needed to believe the rewards of confession were worth the dangers.

Later, when things calmed down and they got a chance to reconnect, he would tell her.

Donna Beckwith hadn't given them much to go on. She didn't know how to find Albert, didn't really know him well. He showed up sporadically over the years, without rhyme or reason, when he needed to use Donna, for what purpose he never deigned to enlighten her. She let him use her because Albert was supposed to be this super-powerful wizard, and to her way of thinking that counted in the world. She was able to connect Albert to the rice-paper notes but not to Phaedra or the invitations. It was possible Albert didn't have anything to do with the invitations but Phaedra had inferred otherwise. Donna's explanation of the crow's head was in line with what Damian already discovered, but it didn't tell him anything useful in terms of where to go from here.

The best he got from her were three names of people who knew Albert better than she did: Tommy "Blitzkrieg" Winnett, Vincent Chateaubriand, Carmela Talesco. What little free time Damian scratched up got spent flushing them out. He couldn't locate Chateaubriand. Blitz, Donna's ex-boyfriend, died a few years ago of a heroin overdose in south Florida. Talesco was a kindergarten teacher in La Jolla, didn't think Albert worth remembering until Damian described him at length, and dismissed him as an eccentric old coot like all the others. She'd known him a little, though it turned out to be less than Donna seemed to. She admitted to being at the party in Mexico. The night of the renewed wedding vows the ancient bride and groom had died in their sleep, undiscovered until late the following afternoon, which caused an early end to the celebration, originally expected to go on for seven days. She was surprised Albert was still alive—he must've been past sixty when she knew him and that was twenty years ago. After forty-five minutes on the phone Damian didn't think it worth the drive to La Jolla to know more.

It was March, the cusp days of Pisces, and the temperate winter looked like the prelude to a sultry spring and desiccating months to follow. The summer was supposed to be hotter and drier than last, with early water rations and air-quality warnings already in effect across northern California. Authorities expected the forest fires to be worse as well. Were those the flames Albert had told him about? Was he supposed to follow the Santa Ana's with soot in the sky to a place where the trees were red and black and the sun haunted smoke like a peepshow's neon sign? Damian was too busy for adventures. He had too many orders to finish one before starting the next, the warehouse chronically vulnerable, the safe stacked with currency in various phases of production. He liked to work early—watermarking paper, threading security strips, affixing holograms—before the worst heat turned his printing hole into a cinderblock oven.

At noon he set up the printer for the night-shift and went home for a few hours' sleep, a microwaved meal, and back to the warehouse to run the intaglio. Outside his unit was a wall and against the wall leaned an old man, finely wrinkled with flecked amber eyes and freckles on his balding scalp. On his back a black raincoat and in his hand a black fedora. He smiled. He winked. He nodded over his shoulder to the warehouse door. "I wouldn't go in there if I were you."

"No?" Damian looked up and down the row of warehouses but there was no one else in sight. "What would you do instead?"

"I got a good feeling about Brazil."

"'Cause I'm in such great danger. Is that why you've been following me?"

"You're the one who's been following me."

"I'm following you?" Damian's exasperation lasted a moment before he realized it was true. Damian had been following him, looking for him, chasing him.

"If you go in there," the old man said, "if you do the thing you came here to do, you'll be arrested. They have no idea who you are. They don't know your name and they don't know about this place. But they know where you're taking that money and they'll be waiting to meet you."

That got Damian's attention. "Why don't you tell me what's going on? Who's Phaedra? Tell me about the crow's head. You said I'd be taught by the fire—what's that mean?"

The old man, Albert, pushed his weight off the wall and considered Damian in the waning dusk. He put the fedora back on his head. The walls cast long shadows, and though they were less than a yard apart, shade obscured his face. A curious half smile played beneath the mustache. "You're warned," he said.

Damian risked a glance at the door. "How do you know what's in there?"

"I only want to help you. Don't make this delivery."

As Albert passed by, Damian caught a scent, weak and chemical, like ammonia and sulfur.

"What delivery?" Damian said.

Albert stopped at the end of the warehouses. "You know what delivery," he said, and stepped around the corner.

Damian worried about whether or not it was safe to enter the warehouse, but he'd already decided what to do. He ducked around the same corner as Albert and made way to the street. Albert had a two block head start but the bobbing fedora was tough to miss. On the north side of Market Street Albert lined up at a bus stop. Swelling darkness gored by racing headlights. The warp and weft of countless cars, buses, trams, pedestrians, cyclists threading the grand artery. Damian ran to hail a taxi and said he'd been separated from his friend and wanted to catch up with the bus.

They turned into Mission Dolores but were forced to stop a hundred yards before the chapel by protesters milling like lost cows in the middle of the road. Women in spandex shorts and hot pink halter-tops, mouths crossed out with black electrical tape. No one chanted slogans or waved placards and Damian couldn't tell what they were protesting. Standstill traffic honked. A few people rolled down windows to roar obscenities. The bus was separated from the taxi by three cars, and when its doors released, people splashed into the pink shirts. Damian squirmed to find the black fedora. He didn't see it but couldn't be sure if Albert was lost in the fluorescent mob or remained on the bus. He thought about abandoning the cab, feared what might happen if he was wrong, and decided to stay put.

The convoy shuffled to the end of the block and turned away from the Mission. For miles they caravanned and the fare meter added them up. Across Market again, meandering through narrow one-ways and down long, rolling hills, losing the bus in the troughs and spotting it again on the crests. A corrosive paste fretted in Damian's belly and convinced him he'd lost the old man in the Mission. He was ready to give up when Albert got off the bus.

On the next block he settled with the cabby and followed Albert southwest, losing him a couple times where the streets narrowed and the crowds coagulated entryways of theatres and night clubs. The hip and affluent disposing of income. Palm trees and laurel trees, renovated walkups, graffitied brownstones, signs in Arabic and Spanish, convenience stores beatific under pearls of phosphorescent streetlight. Albert ducked into a strip club between a Pakistani restaurant and an acupuncturist's office, and Damian kicked rocks on the sidewalk while he waited. He didn't want to go in because he didn't want to risk being detected by Albert. It took twenty minutes to call the decision stupid.

Inside, platform heels and ass floss, body paint and black-light. No one recognized his description of Albert. The bar-tender hadn't seen him, none of the servers knew him. "Shit," Damian said. No way Albert left the same way he came in— Damian would've noticed. Albert must've known he had a tail and slipped out the rear exit.

Damian wandered the artificially lit streets trying to get his bearings. The uniforms of students and protesters and prostitutes and peace-officers pushing every which way. He'd been in the taxi most of an hour with more turns than he could count and now he was lost. A few more blocks and the streets were quiet. Almost empty. He was hoping to find another taxi or a bus stop with a map to tell him where the hell he was, but there weren't even street signs. The farther he walked, the lonelier. He decided to double back to the stop where Albert got off the bus. And then decided not.

He knew where he was.

40.

The sidewalk ended at an intersection and shrank to an alley-way on the other side. The sign said DO NOT ENTER. AUTHORIZED PERSONNEL ONLY. Damian ignored it. The thin service road perforated with seepage drains. Against the dead end the green dumpster squatted under its lamp and the light spread just far enough to expose a black trench-coat slipping through a ground level door before it snapped shut. A high window on the opposite side of the street was open and played a piano concerto. Music and the sharp tang of brine infused the calm. Damian passed the little alley that brought him here the last time he'd followed Albert—through the aperture he could see the courtyard and parking-lot and Regency apartment block. Above the entrance street-artists had tagged the building in bright cartoon balloons: Lasciate ogne speranza, voi ch'intrate. Damian knocked on the door, just hard enough for anyone within a few feet to hear. No answer. The door wasn't locked. He slipped inside and silently pulled it shut behind him.

Darker inside than out. Stillness and Damian waited for his eyes to adjust in the half-light. He was knocked by waves of scorching heat and the sharp odor of rotten eggs and vinegar. The stench came from a vat in the corner next to the door. The heat came from a wood-burning stove ventilated by a chimney-pipe connected to the wall at the far end of the room. The gloom diluted by pale bars from open windows above the exposed rafters, maybe thirty feet up.

Half the room was storage space for industrial machinery, the other half divided between shelves and wooden pegs from which hung tubes of copper and iron and ceramic and glass.

Beneath them retorts, beakers, alembics, crucibles, other instruments Damian had no idea what to call. The shelves lined with clear vials of strange powders and crystals and fluids. Black glass jars of various sizes arranged single file. Damian inspected these and read the labels printed in a neat block script on white adhesive tape: aqua fortis, oyl of vitriol, ruber mercurius, black antimony, argent vive.

At the end of the shelf he discovered odd objects in an earthenware dish. Nathalie's missing hair pick and a sandwich bag with a tangle of curly black hair. He unfolded wads of heavy tissue to reveal a used condom and a bloody tampon. "Christ," he said under his breath and wiped his hand on his shirt though he'd been careful not to touch the contents.

In the far corner, next to the stove, was a pyramid of dry logs and a steel door with a window quilted in chicken-wire. Damian pressed his face to the window but all he could see was his own shade mirrored darkly in the glass. The pot-bellied stove stood on claw feet and radiated enough heat to sting Damian's exposed skin if he stood too close. Dry air scratched his eyes and burned his throat. The cast-iron glowed around the grate and from within the black bell he heard muffled screams of human voices.

This should have shaken him, he would think later, it should've sent him running for the door, the wind ought to be knocked out of him—but before he could react, light snapped on the other side of the steel door and the window revealed a concrete stairwell beyond. He started for the exit but didn't think he'd make it in time and hid among thickets of machinery, which filled the other half of the room. Menacing forms emerged from the dark. Monsters with teeth and talons, colossal in the distorting shadows. Lathes and sandblasters, steel-punchers and band-saws and drills, pressed tight together, either bare or covered with tarpaulins wooly with dust. There was the pneumatic hiss of the opening door and a starburst of electric light stabbed with a long hatted shadow like a dagger. Then the door clicked shut and Damian crept deeper into the mechanical forest.

A moment later Albert came into view. He checked on the stove and added more wood to the front grate and grew the sounds of torment louder. He was walking towards the exit when he stopped in the middle of the floor and quietly turned in a circle.

Who's there? Damian wondered. He recognized it was a strange thought but that's what he wanted to know. Who are you?

Albert walked to the edge of the machinery and tipped his head back. At first Damian thought he was looking at the rafters, but that wasn't what Albert was doing. He was sniffing. Smelling something. He lowered his chin and peered intently into the storage. Damian crouched between two machines and merged with their shadows. He knows I'm here, Damian thought, might as well show myself. Albert was looking right at him. If he wanted to hurt Damian he would've done it by now.

Who's there?

Albert, backlit by high windows, shuffled past the first pile of machines and squinted into the black. Damian thought he should speak but fought the urge. He hadn't followed Albert to confront him—Damian only wanted to see where he went, what he did, so why surrender? He should wait until Albert left and make his escape. But didn't it make more sense to come out now? If he declared himself, no harm would come to him. Just stand up. He didn't have to do any more than that.

Relief flowered in him as his thighs flexed to stand and reveal himself. He couldn't trust his eyes. His ears lied. His senses couldn't make sense and so he mustn't heed them. But immediately another idea made his knees limp: these were not his thoughts. They were in his head, they sounded like him, the puzzle of chemicals and dendrites and firing synapses, problem-solving, communicating without language in his mind, the logical sequences and random emotions as familiar to him as breath and hunger and lust. But the way he was thinking wasn't familiar. These thoughts were in his head but they didn't come from him. Totally irrational, and yet he was sure. His body knew the truth and there was no fucking way he was moving.

Albert flinched and craned his head left and right. He advanced another step and Damian didn't dare shrink any further for fear of detection.

A new awareness settled on Damian's heart. No less urgent and alien than what came before. A presence. Cold. Indifferent. The promise of profound violence. And he knew Phaedra was right about this man. He was dangerous and Damian mustn't approach him. If Damian showed himself, it would be the last thing he ever did.

Albert turned his head and Damian could see his profile. Flaring nostril and close set lip, heavy brow, mustache, wrinkles like wood knots in his ashy skin. And the reptilian eye. The gold and brown reticulations of the sclera and the black iris constricting and dilating the elongated diamond pupil. Trapping light. Searching the shadows.

I cannot hide from him, Damian thought. Albert turned on his heel and walked briskly out of the building and into the city. This isn't over, Damian thought. It was in his head, he was the one thinking it, but it did not come from him.

◆ ◆ ◆

What's wrong?" Phaedra cries, but she knows. Gleans the same way Albert knows. Anguish has gone out of her heart. She cannot hear them anymore. Her imagination searches the crucible but it contains only dead matter. Nothing alive is in it.

"I can't breathe," she whispers and stumbles to the chapel door. At the clearing's edge a crow laughs. How could this happen? When they did everything right, took all precaution, followed each procedure perfectly. And still the work is stillborn. Why? Desperate for answers but there's no one to ask. Only the laughing crow, blue sky, verdant forest. Only the silence of the gods. We're the problem, Phaedra thinks. It has to be—there's nothing else. She wasn't ready for the wedding, and Albert no better. That's why the children were born dead. Poor darlings. You can consult the books, account for the stars, master the crucible. Work and pray, pray and work. Know every correspondence and sympathy. You can bend nature but you cannot hide your heart from itself.

Still the crow mocks her. Phaedra points at the cackle. "You! Don't think I dismiss the role you played in this! I'm not above killing the messenger. Quite the contrary: I would take great pleasure in it."

But this only makes the laughter more gleeful. Now another æon must pass. Plenty of time for Phaedra and Albert to become worthy of the wedding. When the conjunction returns, they can try again. The cackling doesn't stop and Phaedra cannot ignore it anymore. "Foolish bird! I'll loose Poimandres on you. He'll rip off your head and eat your tongue!"

Fresh chorus of insults as the crow flies higher up the trees, safely out of reach. Phaedra scoffs, disgusted as much with herself as the crow, and storms back into the chapel, where Albert mourns.

For weeks it goes this way. Comforting each other. Weeping in unison or taking turns. Embraced in grief, or apart. "I should've trusted you," Phaedra says.

"You were right," Albert says. "I didn't do enough to protect them."

Sometimes Albert vanishes hours without end. She discovers him chopping wood or mixing mortar for the chapel walls. It irritates her, how easily he returns to common chores, and she must remind herself grief wears many cloaks. When he finally comes it is with a confession.

"This was my fault. I found them too late."

"No," Phaedra says. "I was arrogant and blind. I thought I knew how to prepare them but I was wrong."

Sometimes Phaedra stares into the fireplace with red-rimmed eyes, face wan from weeping, hypnotized by shadow-flames dancing on flagstones. What if this is her fate? Doomed forever to fail and fail again. Would the gods forsake her like that? Always hoping next time might announce the wedding. What if the gods are deaf to her prayers? Endless cycles of eternal return. Could they forget her so completely? Do the gods love her so little?

"You deserve better than me," Phaedra says.

"You're the best part of me," Albert says. "The work will never be complete without you."

Faces covered in kisses and tears. She needs his strength and he needs her courage. The work needs her and she needs the work. Next time will be different, she thinks. We will learn from our mistakes and in another æon the crow's head will appear.

"I swear to be more attentive to the fire," Albert says. "I promise to listen to you next time."

"Next time I'll be more temperate. I must learn to balance reason and emotion. I admit that now—it won't happen again."

Another fortnight passes. Sometimes she thinks the crucible stirs: sad voices, pleas, sobs. But it's her imagination playing tricks. When she clears her mind and waits, the only thoughts in the chapel are hers and Albert's and Poimandres'.

The moon changes. Nights getting shorter to meet the coming equinox. "We should think about burying them," Albert says. "Let earth become earth again."

The idea sheds fresh weeping in Phaedra. She hates it but when the spasm releases her, she knows what he says is true. They can't leave Slow Henry breached like that, halfway between worlds, and dead matter rotting in its belly.

They don leather gauntlets up to the elbows and together deliver the cup from the athanor and rest it on the stone floor. Slag gathers at the top of the crucible and Phaedra cuts it away while Albert prepares the shroud.

"Look," Phaedra gasps when she beholds what's underneath the shell. The tender body. She has never seen anything like it. A dull bog hot enough to singe the hair on her forearms. Every few moments it beats like a heart.

"Haste," Albert whispers. The matter must be transferred to the breast of a glass pelican, and Phaedra rushes to help. She doesn't know what it means, what could be happening, and her heart races. How could the voices fall silent when the matter quickens? She cannot say, but as long as black flame burns in the crucible, the work has not been lost. Its life can still be saved.

They move to the crypt far beneath the chapel, away from sunlight and subtle surface vapors, anything that could contaminate the egg. They work quickly in the damp, hunched beneath low ceilings, cold stones streaked with mold. Phaedra perspires heavily before heat throbbing from the carbon cup. What's inside it. A black lump without contours or textures, no depth, no perspective, erased by blackness so perfect no shadows mar its surface. It looks like a hole. As if the physical world was punctured to reveal the void beneath reality. Blackness makes candlelight sputter and snuff. Flame wriggling at its edges like caught prey. Blackness radiates a fever so intense Phaedra cannot look directly at it. If she tries, her eyes force themselves shut. Blackness transparent and shining. This fire emits no light.

FIRE

"Fire is the life of metals while they are still in their ore, and the fire of smelting is their death."

—MICHAEL SENDIVOGIUS, THE NEW CHEMICAL LIGHT, 1608.

W ho's there? Nathalie wanted to know. She couldn't quit the feeling of being watched. Whenever she caught herself alone in the apartment the thought arose. Who are you? The presence became impossible to ignore. Someone was looking at her, and drinking her spagyric elixir made it worse.

When she met Donna Beckwith she thought it might be proof of the elixir's effect. Since, she'd determined it was a coincidence. She couldn't relate the elixir or the feeling of being watched to anything Donna did or said. A dead end like so many others. Nathalie didn't think Donna's account of what took place at the Mexican villa outside Puerto Vallarta twenty years ago was a lie, but neither did she think it happened. The memory, Nathalie believed, was false, or Donna's interpretation was tainted by the passage of time, allowed to calcify into a drug-warped melodrama of what she'd actually witnessed. Transforming her youth to make better sense of her present disenchantment.

A few weeks later Damian told Nathalie about the kindergarten teacher in La Jolla, Carmela Talesco, who said the bride and groom had died the night before Donna's strange vision, cutting short the weeklong festivities. Donna seemed ignorant to this part of the trip—she'd mentioned nothing about it —and Nathalie thought this omission supported her opinion. Donna Beckwith saw the whole thing a little slanted. Damian thought the same and neither considered her reliable enough to bother with follow up questions.

And what of Phaedra? Who was this woman and why was she important? Was she connected to the invitations, or something else? Damian had asked Donna about her and the crow's head. Nathalie remembered shortly after meeting Damian a stray cat had brought her a decapitated crow's head and dropped it at her feet. She'd told Damian about it at the time, but he didn't seem to remember—he never mentioned it. The elixir was no help there and Damian even less. When Nathalie asked, he told her not to worry, it's nothing, but if so, why wouldn't he explain it to her? Fine, Nathalie thought. If he didn't want her help, she wouldn't remind him.

For the first time in almost a year she saw Damian shutting down right before her eyes, walls erecting around him, the distance between them greater than ever. Nathalie took it like an amputation, part of herself cut off, exposed nerves screaming fire. The pain was love. No other word would do. She recalled her sisters warning against falling too fast, too hard, for a guy not worth the trouble. It pissed her off. Realizing you're in love should be joyous, but on Damian it looked more like mourning.

After the story Donna gave them, Nathalie dropped the Albert connection and refocused her efforts on tracking down the bar from her dream. Her heart wasn't in it anymore but she was too stubborn to give up. Damian stopped accompanying her but she didn't stop asking him to come. They hardly saw each other anymore. Nathalie found a second job as a server at a family-owned Brazilian restaurant in Oakland. She worked the lunch shift before commuting to bar-back at the jazz club in Laurel Heights. Damian worked in the early mornings and late at night and slept in the middle hours. Each day of March was hotter than the one before and each day Nathalie found her life harder to hold together. She searched for the bar from her dream but her efforts were perfunctory and rudderless. Two jobs and a dance career competed for her time. Only enough money and leisure for precious few pursuits. It forced her to admit the dreams were no longer important to her. She stopped asking Damian to come with her and she didn't bother mentioning it to him when she finally quit.

She danced when she could, though without Strange Equinoxes she performed less. Haflas and smaller festivals, mostly. She wanted to get another group together but she worked every weekend, which limited networking opportunities, and she could barely put enough hours together during the week for practice. She took samba and bellydance classes two nights a week at a studio in Oakland. She joined a glamorless gym a few blocks from the restaurant, where she slashed out original choreographies in the funnel of a racquetball court. The concrete floor chipping the blunt bones of her feet and the next morning she could feel icepicks in her shins. Music mutilated in the echoey acoustics, like dancing in a chimney. Without mirrors she had to record herself on her phone to see what it looked like.

One night she came home from work convinced someone or something laid in wait. The rooms were empty. Unconvinced, she tore the apartment to pieces looking for a hidden camera or microphone. She took everything out of the cupboards, the refrigerator, felt along the baseboards and the space behind the toilet tank, pulled up carpet edges. She checked the air vents and the mouthpiece of the landline telephone. Nathalie was standing on a chair scrutinizing the ceiling when Damian came home at three in the morning. She refused to speak to him except in the bathroom with the door closed and the fan running. Damian wasn't surprised and he wasn't alarmed. He felt the same thing, the constant eyes, the certainty of never being alone. "Someone's watching us,"

Nathalie said, but Damian hardly seemed to give a damn.

"You get used to it after a while," he said. He nodded. He shrugged. "I don't even notice anymore."

But if that was the case, why the nonchalance? It implied he knew the source of constant watching. If there was something else in the apartment with them and Damian knew it, why wasn't he as frantic as she was? It made Nathalie's skin crawl. "What's going on? I have a right to know."

"Don't worry about it," Damian said, careful to keep his voice lower than the bathroom fan. "I'm taking care of it."

Nathalie abided all things and imbibed the seeker's elixir. A foul tincture, like vodka, topsoil, and unripe rhubarb. Astringent and gritty, she couldn't rid her mouth of the taste no matter how much she brushed. She diluted it. Chased it with water and milk and bread. Nothing took the venom out. The taste brought with it razorblade heartburn to shred her belly and cut open her sinuses. Frater Theophrastus said not to worry, keep quaffing, it was just the hard to reach dregs of her toxins getting worked out. Probably emotional residue, the real nasty bottom of the barrel sludge. It would pass, he promised, but she didn't believe him. A quack hawking snake oil, and Nathalie was the village idiot.

She shrank farther than ever from learning the source of the wedding invitations. No closer to discovering a significant meaning in her recurring dream of Damian. The location of the white bench or the dark bar-top. A reason for the dreams drying up since their meeting fourteen months ago. Instead, heartburn drove up her esophagus like a hot shank, acid cramping the muscles of her arms and legs, a taste like dirt and antifreeze. Nathalie fought through it—she was not a quitter—though the cramps contorted her limbs and the taste stayed in her mouth from new moon to new moon.

In April, only a few days before her twenty-third birthday, all of it sunk to the bottom of her gut and made her bowels splash. "For god's sake, stop drinking it before it kills you," Frater Theophrastus said, but she'd already given her remaining supply of custom-made spagyric seeker's elixir to Eugenie, who was intrigued enough to beg Nathalie for it if she was only going to throw it out. Nathalie warned her sister of the dangers and gave her the jar.

The rancid taste went with it but the paranoia kept with Nathalie. An invisible presence pressed down on her and the pressure turned her life to steam, scalding and shapeless. A dread she could not locate nor name nor escape. Her fear not so much of eyes as sight, not so much like being watched as like being thought, until all her secret parts were exposed, the dark places blinded with light and the wet places dried out. Every day less a person and more a thing. The feeling pervaded everything until she couldn't even think around it.

Each morning she woke feeling looked at. Nude in the shower or squatting on the toilet. Someone looking at her. Every day less a subject and more an object. Coming home from work she slammed the front door and flung open the refrigerator door, famished, stacking in her arms a leftover pasta salad, cheese, tortillas. She stood up and snapped around and gasped as the feeling swallowed her. Puckering her arms. Fanning the small hairs on her shoulders. Her heart beat faster, arteries thinning and widening to permit greater blood-flow, muscles filling with oxygen, pupils dilating and her whole body reacting to its own awareness, scouting the environment for sensory input, seeking instinctively what her mind already knew it wouldn't identify: who's there?

She gasped because it shocked her and it shocked her because it sneaked up on her. It wasn't there and then it was there. She didn't feel the presence before coming through the door, which meant it was in the apartment. Which meant it didn't sneak up on her—she sneaked up on it. Her body had always understood this but now her paradigm shifted and she thought about it differently. It was in the apartment and she needed to find it.

She started in the kitchenette, emptying cupboards, drawers, the refrigerator, the same way she'd taken it all apart before. Only this time she wasn't looking for a camera or a microphone—she was looking for whatever was looking at her. In the bedroom she flipped the mattress and piled on it everything from the closet and added everything from the plastic-ware bins she used as a dresser and sorted through Damian's laundry baskets. She inspected toiletries— loofah, shampoos and conditioners, hot oil treatments, skin creams, mouthwash, Damian's shaving kit, the grime at the bottom of the porcelain toothbrush holder—and reassembled the contents of the medicine cabinet item by item on the toilet seat. The hall closet's bath towels and washcloths and quilted towers of off-brand toilet paper, the disarrayed toolbox Damian crammed in the back, overfull of screwdrivers, socket-wrenches, nails, pliers, batteries. The shelf of sponges and brushes, latex gloves, cleansers for tile and porcelain and glass and wood.

When it was over she sat in a pile of books on the living-room floor, disheartened and wanting to weep. Where the fuck could it be, she wondered, *what* could it be? She'd looked every-where—what was she missing? "Idiot," she said because the answer stared at her the whole time. On the far wall, one of the few pieces of furniture she owned. Her armoire, the one Damian bought for her private things. And across the room, next to the front door, the padlocked coat closet. He would never open the armoire without her permission and she must never open the closet. The key to the padlock was one of the first things she'd found, in a kitchen drawer, underneath the flat-ware tray.

The key popped in the cylinder. The spring kicked out of the lock and Nathalie felt something precious inside her crack, some vague part of her she'd hoped would never break but once broken was like shedding a tremendous weight. Not her heart exactly, not her consciousness, and not her body. None of these and all of them at the same time. There was no name for it but it was the part of her that loved.

She tilted open the door and snapped on the overhead light. Damian's coat hung from a wire hanger. On the shelf, a sleeping-bag rolled up next to a tent in a canvas bag. A brown leather briefcase sat on the floor next to a black nylon gym bag. The briefcase was badly smashed. The brass lock was broken. Inside she found a photograph, thirty-thousand dollars, and a large manila envelope.

The picture was a sun bleached woman, blonde, wan, not quite forty, in a red and black striped dress, posing in the door-frame of a light blue house. His mother, Nathalie guessed. The money was in stiff new hundred-dollar bills, rubber-banded bundles of two-thousand dollars each. The envelope contained social security cards, driver's licenses, passports, and bank cards. Half a dozen names—William Coker, Lance Chevalier, Michael Pierce—but all the pictures were Damian.

Inside the gym bag were two paperback books. Musty, dog-eared and well-thumbed, with broken spines and damaged covers. *De occulta philosophia libri tres* by H. Cornelius Agrippa. *On Formally Undecidable Propositions of Principia Mathematica and Related Systems* by Kurt Gödel. These were what had been watching her. Poison leaked out of the gash in the egg-shaped cup. Viscous and acidic. It ate a hole in the middle of her, burned all the way through creation, and there was nothing underneath, just a godlike abyss. This is discovery, Nathalie kept telling herself. This is illumination. But the only things she learned were violation and loss.

Midnight, and the great work finished. What began as photographs and paper and ink transformed as if by magic into money. It would take a laboratory more sophisticated than Damian's to prove it wasn't real. If Pavel was right, not even a bank could tell the difference. Damian put the magnifying glass away and stacked the bills in ten piles of $2,500 and rubber-banded them and put them in his new briefcase with the $75,000 he'd already made and locked it in a titanium safe beneath the folding table. He defaulted the settings on the computer and erased the memory and shut it down. He changed to fresh latex gloves and fetched the bucket of cleaning supplies and turned the industrial fans back on. Because of his hurry he hadn't bothered cleaning up after himself as he worked, which meant he could expect to spend the next two hours sanitizing the lab.

He started with the darkroom and worked his way to the front. When he was finished he went back over the entire warehouse with an infrared wand to double-check for fingerprints, clothing fibers, loose hair, anything that might contain his DNA. His dad had been very clear about sanitizing the lab. It must be treated at all times as if it were going to be a crime scene. By 2:20 A.M. the mess vanished and with it all trace of Damian's existence. The lease was paid by automatic withdrawal from a bank account under a false identity opened with documents Damian forged himself. Unless he was physically arrested here, nothing connected him to the warehouse or anything in it.

It had been three weeks since Albert met him outside the warehouse and delivered his warning. Three weeks since he'd hid among the storage and waited for Albert to leave. Another half hour he'd crouched in the shadows for fear of Albert confronting him on the service road. Giving him enough lead to get far away before Damian escaped. His whole body screaming to flee and his mind screwing down on his hammer heart and snare drum breathing. What if someone else came in? What if Albert returned before Damian got away? But he'd made himself wait it out.

God knew how long he wandered for a familiar sight before stumbling onto Market Street below the civic center. Albert knew about his printing hole, he knew what Damian did in there and he knew the Secret Service was waiting for him. But how did the feds know? How did Albert know? The next morning he'd gone to a payphone at the Amtrak station and called all his customers to tell them not to contact him at home. It wasn't safe. He wanted to tell Pavel to put a couple of goons in that service road, he'd followed Albert and knew how to find him now, but Pavel cut him off. He didn't want Damian contacting him anymore, under any circumstances, for any reason whatsoever. Not until he figured out what the fuck was going on.

Pavel said he'd got to thinking about Damian's Korean friends. How nothing about the situation was as it appeared. How every fact he investigated turned out to be built of bullshit. The counterfeit especially bothered Pavel. He wanted to know what happened to it—how had Pseudo-Kim and Noe managed to exchange thirty-thousand dollars of it for real cash? They must've had contacts either in the Bay Area or farther south.

He called in a few favors, made some passive-aggressive threats, followed up on a handful of leads, and learned nothing. He switched tacks and asked his contact at the State Department to dig again. Not for information about the Koreans this time but for the cash in their possession at the time of arrest. Nothing. Every note checked out. Pavel read the report. Forty-thousand was genuine. Twenty-thousand was counterfeit. Ten-thousand was missing. Then he had an absurd idea. He sent a man to the bank with five-hundred dollars of Damian's February product to make a deposit. Guess what happened? Not a goddamned thing. The teller took the money, credited the account, printed a balance statement. So Pavel sent another man to another bank to make another deposit. Same result.

The Korean's didn't do anything to the money, Pavel

claimed. They'd brought twenty-thousand dollars of counterfeit to the meeting in Forest Hill, and Damian brought fifty-thousand dollars in genuine c-notes. Damian was selling real money and passing it off as counterfeit for forty cents on the dollar.

It created a delicate situation for Pavel. Damian needed to appreciate that. In the meantime, his job was to keep his mouth shut and his head down, make his deliveries on time, and stay away until Pavel sorted out the mess. The human mind can be a tricky fucker. Damian asked Pavel to let him know what he found out. One way or the other. Pavel had laughed. He would be in touch.

42.

When Damian finished cleaning inside the warehouse he sloughed the yellow jumpsuit and stashed it in a gym bag until he could take it to the dry cleaner's. He gathered wastebaskets of empty ink bottles, defective bills, ruined paper, and added to them gloves, etched plates, photographs and negatives, rags and sponges, ten-thousand dollars in perfectly good counterfeit—the extra made in case of large scale defects. All this he put in a steel fire pit and carried to the asphalt behind the warehouse. He built a fire in the pit and fed everything to it one item at a time, slowly, to make sure it thoroughly burned. Everything—every single thing, his father had taught him—must be accounted for and disposed of.

Baffling, what Pavel said about the counterfeit, but Damian didn't worry too much. He knew the source of his money, though months ago he'd lost the ability to tell the difference between his own work and the real thing. He empathized with Pavel's exasperation. Banks scanned the bills they collected to verify the security features and tracked the serial numbers through a Treasury Department database. Counterfeit would've been flagged and the account-holder questioned a day or two after making the deposit. None of that happened, which meant, according to the Treasury Department, the money must be real.

Damian didn't have an explanation but the answer would be something to do with Albert. Damian's thoughts turned to the old man in the black trench-coat and yet stranger things. Memories and the contorted specters of remembering. He knew what secret place he'd discovered the night he tracked down Albert. Brian at the Green Thorn Brier's had told him about it. One of the last true alchemists of the medieval tradition, Brian had said, with a laboratory hidden somewhere in the city. It was not a myth. Damian could vouch for it. Crammed low between the leering teeth of an upright circular saw and a vertical belt sander, he'd recognized the glaring eye —the serpent's eye—of Albert. A trick of the poor light he'd experienced once before with his father.

He'd been fifteen the morning of his final conversation with his father. Damian had lain awake in bed when the deadbolt unlocked. His father coming home for the first time in three days. Damian hadn't disposed of that memory. And the next morning when Damian woke for school his father was still up, soused and grimy in his bathrobe. Sitting at the kitchen table with two half-empty gin bottles and a filthy glass between his hands. Was that accounted for? Should he dispose of that memory too? His father's split lip and reticulated eyes and quaking hands as he splashed another shot down his throat. There was a single hundred-dollar bill on the table and his father sat the tumbler on it like a napkin. His fingerprints grease-stained on the glass. Sit down, he had said and kicked underneath the chair across the table.

Damian sat and stared at his father and his father poured more liquor and stared at the wall. After a minute Damian said, I'm sorry I hit you.

I wanted to tell you how proud I am. Of you. Not that it's worth anything.

It's worth a lot.

His dad picked up the hundred-dollar bill. Turned it between his fingers. I found this in an old pair of pants, he said. Miracle they missed it and now it's the last one. Before it was counterfeit, it was just paper, but it was always going to be counterfeit. I was always going to find it in my pocket. It started as a seed and then it was a sapling and then it was a tree. It didn't have to happen that way but that's how it happened. It could've been eaten by a bird or fell in the water. It could've grown too close to another tree and got crowded out. But that's not what happened.

He took another shot and squinted at his son in the weak morning light. The tree got cut down, he said. It didn't have to be that way but that's the way it is. Cut down and pulped into paper, though it might have been a chair or a table or a beam. It was paper and then I bought it and turned it into money. A coincidence. A matter of circumstance. Except it couldn't be a table or a chair or anything else. None of those things were ever going to happen to it. Because it was always eventually going to end up in my pocket. That's the only thing that was ever going to happen to it. Since the beginning of the fucking universe, that was the only possible thing. Because it's what happened. This and nothing other than this.

His father licked his lips. Listen to me, he said. This is important. I got to tell you I was wrong about the money. Making it. How the point is to find a way to make enough money that doesn't make you hate your life. None of it matters.

You can't buy happiness, Damian said. His father shook his head, frustrated, and coughed gin down the front of his shirt.

Couldn't be further from the point. That has nothing to do with it. Goddamn it, Damian, I wish you would listen to me.

I'm through listening to you.

Fine. Forget everything I ever told you. Only remember this: everyone has a destiny. Money has nothing to do with it and neither does happiness. Destiny is the only thing that matters. And as he spoke Damian perceived a transformation beneath the old man's sweat-glossy skin and liquor reek. The dying animal look of his eyes flickered and deepened and Damian understood what his father wanted to tell him was nothing that could be said in words because it was something you had to experience to comprehend, and Damian had not experienced it.

Take your mother and go far away from here, his father said. Never come back. Never think of me again. Only remember what I said. About destiny. You can choose it or you can ignore it. Starve if you have to, beg in the street, sleep under an overpass. Pick food from the trash. Spend the whole rest of your life penniless and alone and laughed at. Cheat. Steal. Murder if it comes to it. Do whatever you have to do.

Damian had said nothing, and over the years forgot nothing, disposed of nothing. He'd felt numb and frightened. He'd wanted to do exactly what his father said but he had not wanted his father to want him to do it.

And now Damian fed money to the fire behind his printing hole. He used to do it in a metal garbage can but the smoke was black and tall and he worried about the attention the beacon might attract. So he bought the fire pit at a hardware store. The wider mouth diffused the smoke and the coat of high temperature resistant paint allowed for hotter burning. Total incineration. Nothing left but black salt, chemical stench, and heartache. Salamanders leapt from the bowl and scurried toward the darkness at the edge of the parking-lot, chased from their hiding place by heat and flame. He used the poker to distribute the paper across the whole girth of the bowl and covered it with the spark screen.

Could this be the fire Albert had told him about? Damian wondered, peering into the glow. Was he supposed to learn something from these flames? Did Ronald Lancaster have one last lesson to teach his son?

Money curled and blackened in the canned light and as he fed the fire money, he fed his father to it too. Every time he burned the evidence he also burned his father. Let him go to ash and smoke and firelight. Let him combust and stink and dissipate across the whole city. Let his poison become transmuted medicine to protect Damian from his dreams.

The fire grew and burned high and hot and bright. Above it fog swirled like smoke and condensed rain beads on the outside of the steel pit and evaporated a white corona around Damian's clothes. The phantom flickering conflated with fog light and carbon particulates from the atmosphere above, and the ashy paper below, as well as city light and money light and ghost light.

Damian remembered. He had not forgotten. Sitting at the kitchen table in Cincinnati with the sodden zombie who was once his father. He took his father's hand in his own and dug his eyes deep into his father's eyes until his hatred catalyzed his heart and he sutured it to wounds buried in his father, stuck to the very nerve of mystery. His fingers trembled against the clammy skin of his father's hand and his father opened his mouth and Damian knew these were the last words he would ever hear him speak:

Hate me. It's a small price to pay. Turn your heart to lead. All that matters is you find and fulfill your destiny.

This and nothing other than this.

It happened on a Thursday in April. A few days before Damian and Nathalie's birthday. Walking in Golden Gate Park past flowerbeds of azaleas and buttercups, hand in hand, flushed from exertions and newly laid. They attended a matinee production of *The Importance of Being Earnest,* Nathalie's favorite play, at a small theatre in the Castro. Later they would splurge on dinner before going to a dance club on Fremont Street, one of the first places they'd gone together last March, where, Nathalie said, she'd first slid a little bit in love with him. There were a few hours to kill and Nathalie suggested a walk. The happiest week of Damian's life. He was ahead of his summer schedule and spending more time with Nathalie. Most days he slept in, rose midmorning to making love, cooked Nathalie's breakfast. The fug devouring her the past few months lifted. She spoke of the future, told him about her current choreography, the way she wanted to weld storytelling aspects of West African dance vocabulary to a Romani-samba fusion thing she'd been working on.

Nathalie led him to the lungs of the park and climbed him in the undergrowth of the tree fern grove, each holding a hand over the other's mouth, urgent and heady at the chance of getting caught—half wanting to get caught—but no one saw. They finished putting their clothes back together as they walked the path. Damian tucked his shirt into his pants, thought better, and pulled it out again. Nathalie straightened her skirt and ran a hand over black fronds of hair. They paused at the Shakespeare Garden to appreciate the bowl of manicured lawn, the standing sundial, statues on pedestals, quotations on plaques. Ruddy paving stones lined with trees and fresh beds of blue violets and red poppies. Something's wrong, Damian thought. The distance between them abruptly returned. Somewhere between the tree fern grove and the garden everything changed. "What's wrong?" he asked and Nathalie flinched as if the idea slapped her.

"I don't know." Her brow stitched like a wound. She held her left shoulder in her right hand and looked at her shoes. "I haven't been happy for a while but I don't understand why."

"Anything I can do?"

"I don't think so," she said and looked at him. It was early afternoon, hot, and they were alone in the garden. "Everything's so still."

She was right. It was the unnerving stillness that first alerted him. Something was wrong. Quiet and hot and still and wrong. A bumble-bee, fat as a blimp, trundled from one flower to another. It swayed as it flew, saddlebags so overstuffed with pollen it could barely stay upright. Poppies and violets. The city's heart stopped beating in this garden. Painted blood blue and blood red.

"I don't like my life anymore. All the things I used to enjoy. I keep doing them but I don't care anymore. Dance, my family, work, you—I lost the point. I keep going through the motions but there's nothing left."

A scratch cut the crystal quiet. A crow paced on the face of the sundial and its talons scraped the stone column. It spread its wings and opened its beak when it noticed Damian staring but it did not flee and it did not speak. That's why it was so quiet—crows had chased away all the songbirds.

"I wonder where all the crows came from," Nathalie said. "You used to never see them and now they're everywhere."

"We could use a vacation."

Nathalie shook her head. "I'm burnt up and dark. That's all I feel inside."

Damian knew the feeling she was talking about. On fire and black at the core. He'd felt that way after his mom died. Exhausted and anxious at the same time. Ruined. He studied her high-waisted skirt and knee socks, the arching palm branches of her hair. Pomegranate lipstick and tangerine fingernail polish. "Maybe you need time to yourself?"

Mascara streaked her face and she hugged herself. She couldn't afford to break the lease on the apartment but Damian promised to take care of it. She didn't know if she had anywhere to go but he said to take as long as she needed. "You've always been sweet to me," Nathalie said. She smiled sadly. Her thumb smeared charcoal tears into war paint on her cheeks. The crow screamed at them. "Last chance," Nathalie said. "If you're going to tell me how you make money, you'd better do it now. I think you should. Not because I want to know. It would be good for you to tell someone."

Damian hated this moment. He despised the universe and everything in it, everything that led him to this place on this day. He hated it but he didn't want it to end because he knew once it passed everything would be over. To make the moment last a little longer he studied the quotation on a nearby plaque: *Devouring Time, blunt thou the lion's paws, And make the earth devour her own sweet brood, Pluck the keen teeth from the tiger's jaws, And burn the long-lived phoenix in her blood.*

"I don't think so," Damian said. "I'll give you a few hours before I come home."

Nathalie kissed him on the cheek and left him in the garden. At the wrought-iron gate she hesitated and turned back.

"Have you dreamed about me again?"

"No," Damian said and shrugged with his hands in his pockets. "Have you dreamed about me?"

"No," she said, and then she was gone.

He wanted to tell her. For a second he thought he might. But if he did, his fate would no longer be under his control. He'd be vulnerable to her forever. His secret would be out there somewhere in the world with her, and he would have no power over who she told. For the rest of his life he'd have to trust her. Never a peaceful moment. Always wondering if she'd make him regret it.

For a while Damian wandered the park, his thoughts a surreal whir of nausea and vertigo, a feeling at the bottom of his solar plexus full of fumes and anguish. He studied the turning of fortune in the lethargic wheel of a Dutch windmill. He watched kissing couples, mothers pushing strollers, dog walkers, panhandlers, and daydreamers. The upwardly mobile crowd taking long lunches from important jobs to clear their heads. Joggers in streamlined air-resistant running suits and inconspicuous earbuds. Woolly black and brown bison keeping cool on blankets of jimson. He'd talk to Nathalie when he got home, he decided. He didn't want her to leave. Not what he'd meant to happen. It was early evening when he caught the BART to Oakland.

She was already gone. The armoire he'd bought her stood open and cleaned out in the living-room and she'd left the table and chairs. She'd taken most of the dishes and silverware but left him more than he needed. The juicer was gone but she left the ban-marrie he liked so much, even though it was hers. He didn't understand what the fuck just happened. He hadn't meant for her to leave. When she came for the rest of her stuff he would tell her, sort it out, but he knew she wasn't coming back. She'd left his wedding invitation in its acid-free sleeve on the dining table, and that more than anything else seemed final. She didn't care anymore.

In the bedroom her half of the closet was empty, drawers

cleaned out, things missing from the bedside table. But he could smell coconut oil, yogurt, lavender. Damian quickly shut the bedroom door: he wanted her scent to haunt this place for a long time.

The next nine days felt enormous. Silent showers fell straight up and down, thin and transparent. Gray skies blacked out the sun and in the mornings seeped into the brick and glass and concrete. Horizon sealed off by dark days and heaping fogbanks. When Nathalie left, Damian's life snapped shut like a trap. Isolation and paranoia. He was used to being alone but he'd always enjoyed solitude. He'd built a special place in his heart for Nathalie, a sacred place, unfamiliar even to him, rarely visited and then only in awe and praise. She was gone but her place in his life was still there, only now as an abscess throbbing all the time, and he hated his loneliness.

He read Michael Maier's *Atalanta fugiens* and Heinrich Khunrath's *Amphitheatrum sapientiae aeternae*. He fell asleep with a book on his chest and startled awake in the middle of a dream. Someone had been standing over him, watching him, but the sensation didn't come from the book nor anything else in the apartment. It was in the dream. Fragmented images and unconnected vignettes. There hadn't been a coherent plot and the only things he remembered were the crows. He'd been in the dream and watching the dream at the same time, but when he tried to recall more, it disappeared, like following the flight of a crow through thick fog.

He thought about Albert's warning not to make the drop, and the Secret Service, and Pavel the Czech. What if Pavel was setting him up? He didn't want to keep the appointment in San Jose but he didn't have a choice in the matter. Pavel wouldn't speak to him—he'd already gone to Budapest—and if Damian didn't show up for the drop, he'd never work in the Bay Area again. He must risk walking into a trap. Did it even matter, or was it already too late? He tortured himself because it was the only thing he knew how to do. He thought these thoughts because there was nothing else to think. The decision was made for him when he checked William Coker's Luxembourg account the night before the drop. Earlier that day a deposit posted for twenty-five-thousand dollars American.

Fifty cents on the dollar.

The stone of the philosophers is not a stone at all. It is solid fire.

43.

Black skies and heat. The day dark, muggy, steel clouds pinning carbon particulates to the concrete earth. The air quality index code red and Damian could taste ash in his sinuses. South of Market he secured the warehouse before entering to collect the briefcase. He thought about renting a car, weighed the pros against the cons in case of trouble, and chose the BART to San Jose.

The address was on a serpentine lane connecting two perpendicular streets of an industrial complex on the city's southern outskirt. He arrived three hours early, just before closing time, to take a long look around. There was a machine shop, an administrative building, a die-cast factory, a materials warehouse, a chemical treatment facility, an aluminum foundry, and a steel foundry, the last of which possessed the street address Damian wanted. Beyond this, the lane snaked back around to the main road where a sandwich shop stood at the intersection. The whole complex belonged to South Bay Investment Castings, a Pacific Structurals company according to copious signage. The irony wasn't lost on Damian: Pacific Structurals was a subsidiary of the Jevali Holdings Company. Nathalie's dad owned the foundry. Was it a coincidence or a synchronicity—or more sinister? Was the choice intentional, and if so, for what purpose? Damian didn't dare guess, but it felt like destiny.

After several walks over the grounds he decided to order dinner to go from the sandwich shop and ate it in the steel foundry parking-lot while he took a closer look at the building. His appointment was for 12:30 A.M. but he planned on showing up early. He knew from Pavel the day shift went home at nine o'clock and a skeletal graveyard crew started in the aluminum foundry, across the parking-lot, at ten o'clock. The steel foundry had operated in the red for years, Pavel had told him, and all production recently moved to a sister facility in Utah. The steel foundry offices were still in use but the manufacturing wing was closed for cleaning. Only a few cars remained. All lights were off and everything locked up tight. He counted three proper exits from the building, two emergency exits, plus four shipping bays. He finished up with the building and retreated to the end of the parking-lot, beyond the security flood-lights, and crouched in the dark to plan possible escape routes in case anything went wrong.

When he was satisfied, he took another walk around the complex, noting short-cuts, hiding places, the shortest escape routes. When he returned to the steel foundry the side entrance was propped open with a plastic bucket. It was a few minutes after eleven-thirty. Damian took a deep breath, squeezed the handle of the briefcase, and slipped inside.

And found himself enveloped in grasping heat, musty air, the stale scent of burnt metal. Darkness but for the thin knife of lesser dark cutting the cracked door-jamb from the parking-lot lights. He faced the clerk's station in a cavernous shipping dock, bay doors receding into gloom. A steel table, bolted to the floor, piled with computer monitors, plastic hard-drive towers, keyboards, power-cords, all willy-nilly, in various stages of disassembly. A three foot stack of flattened cardboard boxes furry with black mold. Over his head hung half a roll of bubble-wrap degraded into wispy plastic cobwebs and beside it the bare cylinder of an industrial packing-paper dispenser jutting out like an exposed femur.

He waited. He listened.

Pavel's cronies were supposed to meet him and obviously someone propped the door open for him, but he was alone. The drone of a generator undercut the stillness. The building was supposed to be abandoned but the power was on. On the far wall he came to an uncovered portal wide enough to drive a forklift through which led deeper into the foundry.

The next room hotter than the first, the cement floor pitted with bolt holes where machinery once stood. The near wall lined with a latticework of shelving, empty but for a few sunken cardboard boxes under white coats of metallic dust. Fetid air, thick and hard to breath, steeped in darkness. He could only see a few feet in any direction. He crossed quickly to the opposite wall, careful not to shuffle his shoes on the coarse cement and scratch the quiet. Feeling his way through the dark, he stopped suddenly and strained to distinguish a new sound from the generator. Voices. More than two. Tense but distant, murmuring under the constant hum.

Damian felt with his hands along the wall until it gave way to thick plastic curtains behind which emerged a much smaller room. On the far wall was a steel door propped open with a hunk of scrap metal. There was a round window on the door and a light on the other side. The voices were there, too, stronger but not clear enough to make out words, and another sound he wasn't able to discern before: hysterical weeping.

At the porthole he spied the heart of the foundry. A vast concrete pasture of massive furnaces, ovens, crucibles, ladles, heavy chains and ceiling-mounted pulleys, levers, complicated piping, propane powered forklifts. Damian counted four men, anonymous beneath heat-reflective suits and aprons and head visors. One of them held with gloves a leg-length metal rod ending in a spike that glowed red and white in the shadows. Pseudo-Kim removed his visor and spoke to the others in Korean. Another man lay naked on the slag floor, shuddering sobs and blood from one pulpy hand cradled near his chest. The old man was almost unrecognizable in such misery. Two captors kneeled on him and extracted his good hand and forced it flat against the floor while Kim Hyeon-gi advanced with the glowing rod. His back blocked the view so Damian couldn't see what he did with it, but Albert's scream, hoarse and insane, twisted Damian's stomach. He closed his eyes and swallowed bile in his sinuses. When he was able, he stepped away from the door and cast about for a weapon.

Next to the door squatted three bins. Ingots of steel alloy the blue of quail eggs. Leprous slurry shells of investment castings. Scrap metal parts bristled rust-red stubble. Damian felt nauseous. Sweat greased his neck and brow. He pushed backwards through the plastic curtains and felt his way along the wall further into the middle chamber. In the northeast corner he found a push-broom. Fear shook his hands and it took a minute to unscrew the handle, squeeze the hard wood, balance its weight in his hand. He didn't trust Albert but he knew he must help him, knew a year ago he would've suffered the same tortures had Nathalie not saved him. What the hell was Pseudo-Kim doing here and where were the Russians he was supposed to meet? He couldn't wait. He needed to raise the alarm at the aluminum foundry across the parking-lot.

But the bucket had been removed at the entrance and the door locked. He looked for a latch but found only a keyhole in the handle and cursed beneath his breath as he shook it. Another chill glazed his skin. He thought of the other exits and in his mind oriented where he was to where they should be. Several tentative steps into the darkness, hands feeling along the wall, and then, without warning, he heard the dry click of a chambered bullet. Sweet musk of gun oil. The smooth, cool barrel pressing against his head. The broom-handle was shaken loose from one hand and the briefcase from the other. Materializing on the edge of his vision the face of Noe Gun. He looked happy to see Damian. Excited, even, like they were old friends, a long time absent. Damian didn't understand Noe's Korean commands but figured out the gist. He walked slowly with his hands splayed at arms-length to either side a few feet in front of Noe and the death pointed at the back of his head. It was a slow walk until they were within sight of the porthole window. Then Noe called out to his companions and things happened faster.

Damian was searched and forced to sit on his hands near where Albert, naked and hobbled, lay on the floor. He couldn't look at Albert and he couldn't look away. Without his coat and hat the old man was the most pitiful thing Damian had ever seen. Skinny white arms red capped like bleeding matches folded protectively against his chest and one foot mangled the same way stretched out beneath him. Albert smelt like cooked meat. Sweet and hot. Cauterized blood and broken flesh. The vigor this man exuded while Damian had chased him through the city streets was gone. Albert looked frail unto death, a glistening white maggot, potbellied and sink-chested. His skin sagged like candle wax studded with wiry gray hairs. Liver spots browned his naked pate. Snot and tears dripped from the chevron mustache. Red-rimmed eyes rolled in his skull and slowly focused on his new companion.

"Idiot childe," he wheezed. "I told you not to come here."

"Sorry," Damian said.

Kim Hyeon-gi shook the leather briefcase in Damian's face. "Combination," he said and grinned as if he'd made a joke. Damian told him what he wanted to know and watched Kim and Noe count the counterfeit, sticking random bills up to the poor light. Checking serial numbers, Damian supposed. Testing for counterfeit. It was like Pavel said. They thought the money was real.

"I'm having déjà vu," Damian said but everyone ignored

him. Not exactly this way but he remembered how it was the last time he knew the paralyzing fear inspired by Kim Hyeon-gi and Noe Gun. The desperation and how hopeless he felt. All the numbing of that night came back to him, echoed down the corridor of months, and struck Damian with a queer warmth. There was comfort in this moment because it was familiar. Korean thugs would hood his head and hamstring his body and dump it in the trunk of a car. He'd be ferried to a black-top killing floor in some recurring nightmare, giftwrapped and delivered to Nathalie who would come to rescue him. Even as he thought this he heard the falsehood of it. Nathalie wasn't going to save him this time. Even in his nightmares the dark-haired woman was gone for good.

Kim Hyeon-gi spoke and two masked men took Albert up by the armpits. Kim spoke again and Albert answered in Korean. His chin shook and he began sobbing. The glowing spike was reproduced and passed to Kim who calmly stubbed it out like a cigarette on Albert's last good foot. The old man screamed. Flesh sizzled and cracked. There was the cloying aroma of seared pork. Albert writhed on the dirty ground, and when capable fixed Damian with tormented eyes. "Find the others," he said. "Find them and you'll know what to do."

Kim Hyeon-gi and Noe Gun argued quietly. When they reached consensus, Pseudo-Kim put his nose next to Damian's nose and said, "Don't move." Noe held Damian's wrists behind his back and unwound half a roll of duct tape on them. Kim turned his back away and walked towards the others. From the corner of his eye Damian saw Albert move. He scrambled, sobbing, on hands and knees a few feet and then seemed to waver off balance for a prolonged moment upon mutilated stumps, lumbering like a half-upright animal toward the door. There were noises like metal scraping stone. There were unintelligible voices. Noe sprang to his feet and pointed at the naked creature. Pop of gunfire. Tang of burnt nitrate. Albert lay on his side bleeding out on the black floor.

Damian couldn't remember his thoughts or emotions but

his whole body focused tight and small on his surroundings. The burnt smell of the bullet and the bite of the tape slicing his wrist. Snap and clatter of gunmetal as Noe dropped the weapon on the ground. Black soot on lumpy concrete. The smooth angles and elegant curvature of the furnace filled his view, and the beveled texture of the heat-resistant suits worn by his captors. Noe ran a hand through greasy black hair and for a moment Damian thought he might weep. Kim yelled but when it became certain Noe could no longer hear, he took up Albert's wrist and dragged him back to where he'd started next to Damian. Albert's eyes were alive but sleepy and his lips fluttered. Damian could make out only the strange gurgle of syllables trapped in the old man's throat. Damian didn't need to hear the words to know what they meant. Albert was begging. It was plain in his eyes. He didn't care about his life anymore—he just wanted the pain to stop. And still, the purple gouge beneath his ribs would not stop pouring red.

Kim and Noe walked away to discuss the situation. When they came back orders were barked and the masked men rolled Albert onto a large tray and tied his arms and legs to it with duct tape.

"Holy fuck," Damian said. He knew what was happening. When the fire gets me, Albert had said on the service road. You will know the truth. He'd prophesied his own death. He'd known this moment was coming and he would share it with Damian. The fire will teach you, and Damian gazed at the old man like an apprentice come to heed his master. Four Koreans rolled Albert onto a cast-iron grate and hoisted it onto their shoulders. On the wall directly before him the gigantic furnace door was dragged open. Ten feet wide and at least as deep, glowing red and white and vomiting invisible fire on Damian's face. It dehydrated his eyes and forced them closed. The pallbearers marched the funeral bier up to the pyre. Albert was sealed within and the men discarded the heat suits and went about cleaning the scene. Someone dragged Damian to his feet and marched him at gunpoint back to the parking-lot where they all piled into a minivan. It was starting to rain again.

44.

When they were moving, Kim Hyeon-gi pivoted on his armrest and sneered back at Damian. "I've been looking all over for you."

"I'm glad you found me," Damian said. "You still owe me thirty-thousand dollars."

"Dollars?" Kim said and shook his head. "If only you knew what I know."

"I know you're not really Kim Hyeon-gi."

"I know you're not really Mike Pierce."

Damian thought about that. "Are you gonna kill me?"

"No," Pseudo-Kim said. "I need your help. Find stone."

The stone they'd been looking for in Los Angeles, Damian imagined. He thought of Pavel's crooked cop and the botánica and the Brazilian woman who spoke only Portuguese. What did she keep saying?

"Lapis exillis."

Kim smiled and turned forward again in his seat. The minivan turned out of the industrial park and gained speed. Potholes jerked Damian like a rider saddled to a feral horse. Earnest rain, slow but thickening, polished the pavement in an ebony sheen. A police cruiser passed them in the opposite direction. The street was five lanes and lonesome at two in the morning, populated by sporadic pawnshops and peepshows haunted occasionally by a mercury-vapor lamp-post. It was a strange darkness, a positive, inky substance. Not the absence of light, but the presence of fluid nighttime. A gathering blackness with mass and texture.

After a while Damian said, "Your English is getting better," but the man who was not Kim Hyeon-gi didn't answer. It was a weird thing to say. Damian was acting strange but for his life couldn't think what he ought to feel or say. What happened in the foundry did something inside him. He felt far away, disconnected from everything around him and everything within seemed foreign, unrecognizable, like it was happening to someone else.

They stopped in the turning lane of a vacant intersection, following signs to the freeway, and waited for the light to turn green. It changed and they turned left and just as Damian felt the minivan accelerate beneath him, an oncoming car crossed the yellow lines and stopped in front of the minivan's hood. At the same time another car, overtaking them to the left, pulled alongside the minivan and stopped. Tires squealed briefly as the driver stood up on the brake and all the Koreans talked over each other at once.

The car in front of them turned on its brights and flooded the interior in white hot light. From the backseat Damian couldn't see but heard doors opening, and he recognized Pavel's voice. Kim Hyeon-gi and another Korean got out. Damian's eyes adjusted to the stinging light and he saw them on the sidewalk talking to Pavel and two more armed men. Negotiations concluded and Pseudo-Kim, furious, stuck his head in to bark orders. The Koreans on either side of Damian pushed him out of the van and waited next to Kim while Pavel looked him over. Pavel wore a black rain slicker but his hair was plastered to his skull and water shined on his pale face.

"He needs a coat," Pavel decided. "Can't you see its pouring? Give him something to wear."

Words exchanged among the Koreans and Albert's trenchcoat, folded into a puffy square, was passed out of the minivan. Damian caressed the fabric. The texture was stiff and smooth but he could not trust his senses. They were ill adapted to the task at hand and he thought only a fool could believe them sufficient to navigate a world like this. Everything happening to him was connected. It wasn't a rational thought. He'd seen it in Albert's eyes as his body was engulfed by foundry flames.

He'd thought the reason for the wedding invitations and the disappearance of Gangjeon Jae-kyeon, the reason Pseudo-Kim and Noe attempted to abduct him, why Albert was following him, why Phaedra contacted him, was due to his career as a counterfeiter, but now he saw that was a small detail in a much larger pattern. It wasn't even about him. He was just a thread of it.

The marriage of the king and queen and Pavel the Czech, the crow's head and Korean gangsters, Brother Sun Sister Moon and Sebastião Jevali. Frater Theophrastus and Damian's hatred of his father. His love affair with Nathalie and the philosopher's stone, the dancer and the dead alchemist. The double-headed hermaphrodite and Ferdinand Sobraille. The counterfeiter and the recurring nightmares of a dark-haired woman in a white dress. All of it interwoven, all of it the same thing, nursed by a common fate, and what it felt like was never being alone, always being watched, stared at by rice-paper notes buried in random books.

Find the others and you'll know what to do. Those were Albert's last words. Damian didn't know who he was supposed to find, but he wasn't being asked to understand. He was only meant to act. There wasn't a logical explanation. Only a black coat drawn over his shoulders, only a texture like dry bark and wet leaves against his skin. It was all connected, and if he wanted to master any part of it, he must surrender to all of it.

"Don't forget the hat," Damian said.

When he was dressed in Albert's coat and hat, the armed Russian's shepherded him to the backseat of the car where he waited, shivering but warm, for Pavel to finish talking to the man who was not Kim Hyeon-gi. Pavel came back with Damian's briefcase and joined him in the backseat. The coat was still hot with Albert's body, and fragrant. Blood and tobacco and—what? Soil? Yes. The pungent aroma of rich, black earth. They drove in the direction the minivan came from, and Pavel explained the other car would tail the Koreans long enough to prevent them from following. Damian quietly cried and his body trembled as if with fever.

"Sorry about this," Pavel said. "When you're ready, we need to talk."

"They killed him."

"Who?"

"They put him in a furnace and cooked him alive."

"You're in shock," Pavel soothed. Damian wanted to agree but couldn't for the chattering of his teeth. Every time he opened his mouth his tremors took on violence.

"He's dead."

"You've got some explaining to do," Pavel said, but Damian held little faith in that. If only you knew what I know, Pseudo-Kim had told him. But what Damian knew was secret to everyone. The entire twenty-five years of his life were mere overture to what he'd learned this night. He'd been careful. He'd kept his secret from Nathalie. Made sure no one knew the truth except those who absolutely had to. Arrived hours early to stakeout the foundry, scrutinized the landscape and investigated the building. It didn't matter how many precautions he took, what rules he followed, how cold and calculated and precise the systemic protocols. He was still vulnerable. Nothing could protect him from this world. Money couldn't do it. Love couldn't do it. Safety was always going to be placebo and illusion. He'd done everything within his power to prevent it from happening, but life found him anyway.

Outside, night glistened like the wet scales of a dragon under the headlights. The thickening body of the darkness, sticky and heaving and physical enough to devour all light. Nothing was visible in the dark, not the road, not the sky, and not the surrounding traffic, only the dark, and all the days of Damian's life had been a prologue to this blackening.

The dragon lies coiled at the bottom of the glass. Phaedra stands it on the stove and Albert raises a gentle fire. Adds virgin's milk, just a pinch, to help it flux, and liberate the moon from the dragon's coils. Work and pray, pray and work. Chop wood and fetch water and fast and work and pray. The dragon flies into the empyrean and drips venom on its own corpse. It happens slowly, imperceptibly, neither of them able to say when, only that it is done. They peer into the pelican together or alone and when it is not in sight it remains their constant thought. The sun rises out of the chaos which birthed it at the beginning of time, victorious, beckoning the moon to follow. Chaos seethes and boils with the death throes of the beast. Blackness spreads throughout the dragon's body, infecting every pore, and seeps into Albert. He feels the poison in him, and looking at Phaedra, he knows it grows in her as well.

Above, the moon waxes until it is full, and wanes. Days get longer and nights shorter. Twins like lighthouse beacons hail the passing sun. Below, Albert works and prays. He tends the glass pelican and records observations with ink and paper. Chops wood and carries water. Let star charts be his guides and books his advisors.

One morning he observes a shape rising from the sludge at the bottom of the glass. A little more each day until there's no doubt. A toad, fat and bulging, secreting toxins from its skin. It makes both of them nauseous. For two days neither get out of bed, doubled up, dehydrated by dysentery. The toad dies, replaced by a lion with oily green fur and the reek of death. As the lion emerges, the sun wavers and sinks. There's a brief eclipse and the lion swallows the sun and settles once again into formless chaos.

That evening the sun and moon are visible at the same time in the sky above the chapel.

Below, Albert and Phaedra watch the prime matter steep in the pelican's belly. The black egg swells like an anvil, gradually, every day a little rounder on the sides and flatter on top. One end curves and tapers into a point. Phaedra notices first and points it out: the bill dipped to muck in the bottom of the glass. Marble eyes shining black.

Above, the clearing is silent. Grass littered with a burst of long black feathers. Poimandres nowhere to be found.

And what did Pavel the Czech know? More than he was willing to share and yet not enough to make a difference. He took Damian to a safehouse on the lee side of a minor hill in Excelsior, a one-bedroom walkup above a pizzeria, in case Kim and Noe had someone ready to collect him at home. Damian doubted it —it was a long way to his place in Oakland and if anyone was following him, he would know—but he didn't argue. Pavel was pissed off. His jaw muscles bulged and his lips pressed against a straight line hard enough to turn white. Damian hadn't been rescued—he'd gone from one abduction to another.

"Enough with the lies," Pavel said. "I can't help people who aren't honest with me." He'd been busy since telling Damian not to contact him again until he'd sorted out the mess with the money. Pavel had followed Damian's directions for finding Albert but couldn't locate the service road. After walking in circles for most of a day he'd figured there must've been a miscommunication. Maybe. Or maybe Damian sent him on a wild goose chase. The Regency apartment block and the alleyway, the service road and the green dumpster, the lone streetlamp and Albert's lair. Maybe Pavel couldn't find them because they didn't exist.

Instead, he made some calls, promised favors in exchange for information and bartered it to his contacts in Little Korea. What he got for it: the strangers asking about Pavel were interested in where he bought his money. Who was the counterfeiter and where could he be found? That's what the old man and the androgynous woman wanted to know. Their inquiries began with Gangjeon and ran to Kim and Noe, to Pavel, and finally to Damian.

"You set me up," Damian said. It wasn't a question. He let it sink in for a minute. "You wanted to find out why they were looking for me. You used me as bait."

Pavel smiled like it was something to be proud of. He wasn't interested in pretending it wasn't true. Damian had paid him a compliment.

"How much of what happened in the steel foundry did you orchestrate?"

"Tonight?" Pavel shook his head and winked. "I appreciate there are certain trade secrets you need to keep confidential. For professional considerations. Please extend me the same courtesy."

"What if the Secret Service showed up?" Damian wanted to know, but Pavel just shrugged it off.

"The Secret Service don't even know you exist," he said. "You haven't dropped counterfeit in over a year." The Secret Service didn't have a file open on anything remotely connected to Damian, so far as Pavel could figure. His contact at the State Department dug into it pretty thoroughly. There were no red flags, no evidence of large scale counterfeit in the Bay Area, no pending investigations.

Damian laughed and Pavel permitted a wry smile. The conversation, thus far choked by tension, now went slack, and both men breathed easier. The laughter was louder than Damian wanted, but he couldn't control it. They looked at each other and acknowledged what neither could say out loud. Rational deductions wouldn't work on an irrational situation. Either the available facts were wrong or else necessary information was missing. As it stood, nothing could be resolved because nothing made sense, and both men laughed. Pavel could be lying but Damian believed him. Damian could be lying, but Pavel thought he was telling the truth.

"Any thoughts?"

"Your guess is as good as mine," Pavel said. "Obviously, you haven't figured out how to turn counterfeit into cash. It's hard to believe you'd knowingly sell real money at a fraction of its value, but I can't offer a better explanation."

Except Damian knew it wasn't true. He'd made the cash with his own hands out of paper and ink. Made it out of hate and regret, sorrow and longing. Made it with fear and greed and faith in the root of all evil. "What the fuck's going on?"

Pavel thought it all came back to Gangjeon Jae-kyeon, who'd figured out the money was real and sent a couple professionals to straighten things out. They were smugglers but it wasn't jewelry they were after. Lapis exillis was a codename for Damian. It made sense, but Damian knew it couldn't be that simple. Pseudo-Kim thought Damian could help him find a stone. Lapis exillis. Lapis philosophorum. Damian thought whoever was behind Kim Hyeon-gi and Noe Gun was also behind the wedding invitations. Gangjeon Jae-kyeon? Did his hand write the notes Damian found tucked between the pages of books? Donna thought it was Albert, but she was hardly reliable. It seemed too much coincidence to be true and yet the connection between the alchemical imagery of the invitations and the books seemed too much coincidence not to be true. Synchronicity, then. A constellation of points connected by nothing except an imagination hell-bent on turning them into a picture that made sense.

45.

In Albert's coat pocket he found a black leather pouch, hand sewn by the look, shut with an animal ligament cord. A medicine bag, according to Brian at the Green Thorn Brier's, used for making protective talismans. Inside he found a crumpled feather, fragments of bone, semi-precious stones, a damp clump of black soil. In a secret pocket hidden within the lining, the *Azoth* of Basil Valentine. He found the rice-paper note between the last page and the end papers.

When you have thus obtained the material, the regimen of the fire is the only thing on which you need bestow much attention. This is the sum and goal of our search. For our fire is a common fire, and our furnace a common furnace. And though some of my predecessors have left it in writing that our fire is not common fire, I may tell you that it was only one of their devices for hiding the mysteries of our Art. For the material is common, and its treatment consists chiefly in the proper adjustment of the heat to which it is exposed. The fire of a spirit lamp is useless for our purpose. Nor is there any profit in "horse-dung," nor in the other kinds of heat in the providing of which so much expense is incurred. Neither do we want many kinds of furnaces. Only our threefold furnace affords facilities for properly regulating the heat of the fire. Therefore do not let any babbling sophist induce you to set up a great variety of expensive furnaces. Our furnace is cheap, our fire is cheap, and our material is cheap—and he who has the material will also find a furnace in which to prepare it, just as he who has flour will not be at a loss for an oven in which it may be baked. It is unnecessary to write a special book concerning this part of the subject. You cannot go wrong, so long as you observe the proper degree of heat, which holds a middle place between hot and cold. If you discover this, you are in possession of the secret, and can practice the Art, for which the CREATOR of all nature be praised world without end. AMEN.

Saturday morning he took the bus to Mission Dolores and across Market, snaking through the city until he recognized the stop where Albert had got off. He didn't know the address of the service road but he knew how to find it. He noted the graffiti, the Arabic signs, the Pakistani restaurant and strip club and acupuncturist, all familiar. He walked and remembered, but like Pavel, he couldn't find the service road. All morning he walked in circles, second-guessing himself, retracing and starting again. He'd never seen it in daylight and sometimes he got lost that way. In the evening he tried from the other direction, starting at the Green Thorn Brier's and walking up and down the steep hills toward Haight, but he couldn't find the Regency apartment block. His senses were incapable of guiding him there. It was another few blocks along, or a street further up, or two streets down. He swore out loud at himself. How did he stay alive for twenty-five years without figuring out where the hell he'd been or how to get back? Maybe Pavel was right: maybe the service road didn't exist.

He dreamed of Kim Hyeon-gi and Noe Gun and the rancor of gunpowder. It didn't register at the time, but in his dreams he was startled by how loud the burst had been, echoing through the foundry like a kettledrum, ringing in his head, exactly as it had been in real life. In his dream, Albert had no tongue and no hands. He banged against the inside of the furnace door and begged without language to be let out. Damian nude. Damian with his face melted off. Damian turned inside out. Damian transforming into a wolf, a crow, a tree, a woman, a wine glass, a cow, a rock, a pigeon, a waterfall, a flower, a fish, a motorcycle, a horse, a house, a snake, a sword, a swan, a pinecone, a book, a dove, a roulette wheel, a tadpole, a crucifix, a double-helix, a plesiosaurus, a peacock, a mushroom, a centipede, a kitten, a falcon, an egg, an elk, an apple, a spiral galaxy, a baby, and on and on, until morning stopped him.

A drizzle caught him walking home from a grocery store in Oakland. Concrete sky darkening midday and he hitched Albert's black coat high on his head. Men passing on the street covered their hair with coats or whatever was at hand and Damian shrank from their hidden faces. He'd always cultivated a healthy paranoia but in the aftermath of the steel foundry his anxiety became uncontrollable. Outside his building sloppy rain slicked his hair and deep-fried sweat washed his back beneath the coat. Black as night and half solid specters roved the sidewalk, leered, and dissolved into the downpour. Cold turned sweat to rime but under his skin Damian was hot with fear.

He dropped canvas grocery-bags on the living-room floor, shed the overcoat, and thawed under the shower, but it couldn't sooth the riot in his heart. He sat naked on the toilet lid and concentrated on breathing, slow and deep, tried not to think about the man who was not Kim Hyeon-gi loose in the city, hunting him. Everything will be fine, he told himself. No one is looking for me. No one knows who I am. And it was then he missed Nathalie most of all.

At a pawn shop on Telegraph Avenue he took a safety test, handed over a fake driver's license and his right thumbprint, and bought a .45-caliber handgun the black and gray of cormorants, lightweight, with a 4¼-inch barrel and wood grip.

While waiting ten days for the gun he read the *Azoth* of Basil Valentine, watched soap-operas and daytime talk-shows, stewed in anxiety and violent daydreams. Four rolls of paper came on a freighter from Guangzhou and he rented a truck to pick them up at the dock to avoid meeting a driver at the warehouse. The gun slept on the bedside table next to a stack of books, which made him feel a little better. Evenings he read Elias Ashmole's *Theatrum Chemicum Britannicum* and essays on Kurt Gödel's ontological proof.

On sunny days he jumped the BART over the bay and retraced the same steps he'd taken with Nathalie the last time he saw her. Past baseball fields and botanical gardens and the tree fern grove to the Shakespeare Garden, as if he might walk back to that day and undo what happened by reversing the same path through the same labyrinth. The things he said and the sore festering in place of things left unsaid. He didn't know where Nathalie was. He'd told her dad he would leave her alone when she broke up with him, and he meant to keep his promise.

Everywhere, there were crows. On power-lines and rooftops. Tree branches and windowsills. Maybe they were always there and Damian hadn't paid attention until now. Once he noticed, he saw them all the time. In murders or single. Flying or perched. They were watching him. No point pretending otherwise. Crows followed him to the pawnshop and the grocery store and his apartment building. Crows waited outside the library, at bus stops, on park benches. Crows gathered on fire escapes and mailboxes and car hoods, and as Damian passed, feathered heads shifted to see where he was walking.

When Pavel called it was to report a preliminary homicide investigation at a steel foundry in San Jose. Cleanup crews arrived early the morning after to discover a smelting furnace was left on all night. Thirteen-hundred degrees Fahrenheit. Fire started inside the furnace and burned itself out, the corpse charred to black bone and dirt. No bullet recovered, Pavel figured, because lead vaporizes at around six-hundred degrees.

Identity of the victim hadn't been established but forensics found blood in the porous cement floor.

A few salvageable dental fragments were being checked against the database for missing persons. The temperature was severe enough to explode teeth, but not hot enough to melt gold. The old man's dental work remained intact because the fillings were gold leaf, not amalgam, and according to the medical examiner, the primitive method of scraping out the cavity and bonding the layers of foil suggested an early seventeenth century German origin. That surprise was immediately forgotten after a toxicology screening determined the lead content of the bones to be sufficient enough the victim should've been dead long before the fire.

"Years before," Pavel said. He sounded like Damian should be shocked, but he wasn't. He hurt for Albert too much to be outraged at anything about him. Whatever had been sinister was gone now. Phaedra had told him Albert was dangerous, fear him, and Damian had feared him. But he didn't believe Phaedra anymore because the old man tried to protect him, warned him off the rendezvous in San Jose, even came to his rescue. At the end, leaking out on the cement floor, belly too full of blood to speak, Albert had shown him something Damian didn't know how to name.

"Still early," Pavel said, "but I think all is well. My guys did a good job securing the location. There's no surveillance footage of the building and our contact at the foundry can't connect it to any of us."

That was fine with Damian but, hanging up, he was less comforted than Pavel. If investigators managed to lift a decent print, a right thumbprint, from the inner handle of the door beside the shipping bay, for example, or a discarded broom handle, they could trace it to a recent firearm purchase in Oakland, which would lead to Damian's address. It was time to think about moving again, and just as well. After living in the apartment for three months with Nathalie it was torture to live there alone. He could find a cheap studio on the south bay, break his lease, pay the extortionate penalty, and burn everything to do with Mike Pierce, driver's license, social security card, birth certificate, and bank account. Disappeared forever as suddenly as Damian invented him.

Leave. Become someone else. It was on his mind as he walked backwards the route through Golden Gate Park. At the buffalo paddock, one-ton bison dried like black and brown quilts in the sun, skulls dipped to mow bermuda grass in expanding circles at the center of which lay a rag and bone cow raking her calf with a blue tongue. He could accept Phaedra's job offer. Go to Wyoming and babysit Brother Sun Sister Moon. It would be a safer way than counterfeiting to make a hundred large and it would get him away from the bay for a week or two. Only ten days of April remained and he didn't dare guess the status of Nathalie's menstrual cycle. She could be done with it or she could still be waiting. There was no way to know, but anyway, it wasn't an option he took seriously. Phaedra was hardly the type of person he wanted to get mixed up with, he knew no way to contact her, and he wasn't doing anything without full payment in advance.

When he got home the red light blinked on the answering machine. Pavel wanted to meet in six days at a café near land's end.

"Let's walk," Pavel said and they ordered coffee to go. Under a polished sun, tourists gawked at the Golden Gate Bridge in the distance. High clouds rent the sky like claws. A halfhearted circle gathered around a troupe of street performers. Guerilla theatre. Elizabethan greenshow mocking two Islamic suicide bombers who earlier that day attacked international peacekeepers in Sinai without managing to kill anyone but themselves. Pavel led him west on Point Lobos Avenue. When they were alone he said, "I might be going away pretty soon."

"I figured this was coming. Sooner or later." Damian stopped walking. Déjà vu. Only he was speaking Nathalie's lines and Pavel was speaking his. "When will you be back?"

"I'm an international businessman," Pavel said and shrugged. "Import-export. I had to tell our new client what happened in San Jose. Not pleased. And those I broke a meeting with in Budapest: less pleased. I go where the market dictates. Who knows? I might never come back."

They walked to the Land's End trailhead and Pavel motioned they should take the coastal trail down to the ocean. "Kim and Noe disappeared again," Pavel said. At any rate, the August shipment was dead and the police investigation was heating up. Pavel had made sure there would be no cameras at the steel foundry but he didn't count on Damian's paranoia. Closed-circuit cameras caught a man of his description lurking around the other buildings, planning escape routes and looking generally suspicious. No one could account for his presence so he was a person of interest. The angle was bad and the quality poor, but footage at the sandwich shop at the end of the street proved much cleaner. "Maybe you could use a change of scenery, too?"

They stopped talking while a knot of hikers passed them and vanished into the eucalyptus. After a minute Damian said, "I've been thinking it was time for a vacation."

They hiked to a lookout point at the end of the world. The sky had gone from glossy to matte, clouds stretching to leech light from the sun, and the Pacific reflected the same gray. White foam erupted offshore from jagged rocks. Soon the fog would rise and before long they would be blind, but for now Damian could see the open mouth of the Golden Gate straights to the north, and south to bushes and stunted trees climbing sheer cliffs which dove straight into black water. Where the continent was slowly chewed by time into sea-bed. Land and all land-faring things stopped and what began was black and enormous and lasted all the way west to the horizon, forever and ever, amen.

"I know a guy if you need work," Pavel said. He took off the gold ring and turned it over and over like a coin between two fingers. "Regular deliveries and it'll get you out of town. All exchanges happen in Las Vegas. You'd have to transport the product yourself, which comes with risks, but you'd be compensated for them. Generously compensated. Obviously."

"Fifty cents on the dollar," Damian said.

Pavel laughed. "I can guarantee that's not going to happen, my friend. But the job's yours if you want it."

"Sure," Damian said. The ocean licked the shoreline and left a scum of fog on the wet stone. "Why not."

They shook hands and Pavel left him alone. For a while he sat on a flat outcrop with his arms around his knees and watched the ocean seethe. The day was full of shadows and sea-breeze stabbed his nose like needles. He was going to Wyoming but needed something to do once he got back. Payment had been received and there was no backing out of a job once he'd been paid for it. The night before, he'd logged onto Mike Pierce's bank account to transfer the last of his funds and close the account. He sent money to three different banks under three different names in three different countries. There was a new deposit in the Guatemalan account, less than a week old, one-hundred thousand dollars, plus extra to cover taxes and fees, drawn from another account with the same bank. Payment in advance for his trip to Wyoming to play bodyguard to the incarnation of Buffalo Calf Woman. It had to be from Phaedra. There wasn't any other explanation for it.

Before the incident in the steel foundry, he never would've accepted Phaedra's job. It was the kind of thing he might fantasize about on miserable nights, half-drunk and lonely, wishing for someone else's life. But he wouldn't have gone through with it. Not before Albert looked him in the eyes as he lay dying. He did something to Damian. Showed him something. It was like a fire in his head. He saw his mother and his father, Nathalie and Pavel, Gangjeon and Noe and Pseudo-Kim.

Everyone. He saw everyone, the living and the dead and the yet unborn, the earth, the sun, billions of galaxies like foam on a tide dragged back to the beginning of the universe, and Albert lit it on fire in Damian's mind. Everyone and everything burning in agony. It was like a vision, but instead of illumination it brought confusion. Instead of teaching him something useful, it only proved he knew nothing. Suddenly, Damian was a stranger to himself and the world. His life didn't make sense anymore, might never make sense again. He didn't know who he was or why he did the things he did. It was all so pointless. The only thing that mattered was this fire in his mind and the way to quench it.

Damian stood up and was about to leave when he glanced down and noticed a skinny beach beneath his perch. There was a labyrinth down there. Perfectly circular. Lines of stones too large to lift with one hand. He found a footpath and skidded down to the beach. Fog was coming in but there was still time to walk it if he hurried.

The path twisted through sudden cutbacks and long curves and Damian shuffled into dead ends and backtracked to follow the thin channel through the sand. He could no longer see the ocean, the fog crawling to the edge of the stone circle, and he hurried to reach the center before the labyrinth was swallowed in mist. It didn't seem this long from the outside but he must've been walking for at least fifteen minutes. He could see the center just a few feet away but as he walked in circles around it he didn't seem to get any closer. He walked and walked and the fog surrounded him. How long did he walk and how far? From the outside it couldn't take more than three steps to cross the circle's radius and yet its corridors seemed to never end. The fog thickened and he would've given up except the ground was still visible between his feet and then he came into the small clearing at the center.

He looked up the cliff to where he'd been sitting before coming down to this beach and felt a warm weight against his leg. A black cat paying him a visit. It walked in figure-eights between his feet and with each pass rubbed its head on his pants. It looked healthy for a stray but its long hair was matted and brambles stuck to its tail. He noticed an object in its mouth small and round and black as its fur. The cat purred and Damian felt the vibration in his calf. When it was done loving him, it dropped its treasure between his shoes.

"Thanks a lot," Damian said. The cat looked up at him a moment before walking out the labyrinth, following the expanding concentric circles of the path, until it became a shapeless cloud and vanished into the fog. When he was alone Damian knelt to inspect his present. The head of a dead crow. The blind gaze of one pitch black eye and the mute scream of an obsidian beak. Feathers glistened like crude-oil above the neck, caked in dry blood, from which protruded a yellow stump of vertebrae. Damian stared into the glassy eye of the dead crow and the crow's head stared back into him.

... to be continued ...

ABOUT THE AUTHOR

 Adrian Stumpp writes in Ogden, Utah. He has a wife, a son, and a dog. He is an award-winning short story author and has been publishing fiction since 2008. *The Crow's Head* is volume one of a seven part series, *The Chemical Marriage*. To learn more, please visit www.adrianstumpp.com.

Contact me at:

email: palemusepress@gmail.com
facebook.com/adrian.e.stumpp/
instagram.com/adrianestumpp/
pinterest.com/adrians2770/

ACKNOWLEDGMENTS

Thank you to my editors, Amanda Adgurson and Benjamin Roberts, both of whom were indispensable in the creation of this book. Any errors, factual or aesthetic, are my own doing. *The Crow's Head* is a better book than I could have written without them. I owe a debt to my thesis advisor, Tracy Daugherty, and all of the faculty, staff, and alumni of the Oregon State University MFA program. Thanks to my parents, brother, and sister for their suport and encouragement. I'm grateful to the friends, teachers, and fellow writers who have taken an interest in my work over the years, especially Sean Crouch, Ryan Sherman, Richard Vier, Trenton Judson, Victoria Ramirez, Brad Roghaar, Swan Lykins, and Ben Roberts, who talked me through the project at a critical stage and helped me discover the heart of the story. You're a true friend. Finally, and most importantly, thank you to my wife, Britta, who loves and believes in me. *The Chemical Marriage* is dedicated to her. So am I.

Made in the USA
Las Vegas, NV
24 September 2023

78086063R00222